LAST RIGHTS

A NOVEL

PHILIP SHELBY

SIMON & SCHUSTER

SIMON & SCHUSTER
Rockefeller Center
1230 Avenue of the Americas
New York, NY 10020

SIMON & SCHUSTER and colophon are registered trademarks
of Simon & Schuster Inc.

Designed by Karolina Harris

Manufactured in the United States of America

1   3   5   7   9   10   8   6   4   2

Library of Congress Cataloging-in-Publication Data
Shelby, Philip
Last rights : a novel / Philip Shelby.
p.   cm.
I. Title.
PS3569.H39258L37   1997
813'.54—dc20   96-41579
CIP
ISBN 0-684-82939-8

Acknowledgments

The author wishes to thank Mr. Paul Boyce, Chief of Public Affairs, CID, U.S. Army, for generously providing his time and expertise to this project.

Thanks also to Chief Warrant Officer Five, Ray Kangas, for specific details on the nature and the structure of the CID.

However, this remains a work of fiction. Certain details concerning explosives, sniping, and military protocol have been altered to prevent misuse of such information.

PHILIP SHELBY

PART
ONE

1

Rachel Collins, warrant officer second grade, shifted, her boot heels scraping the hot, corrugated roof of the metal shed where she lay spread-eagle. The residue of mid-September hurricanes that tore up the Carolinas usually brought rain this far north. But tonight the beams and sheet-metal walls of the warehouses stacked along Baltimore's industrial docks creaked and snapped as the temperature dropped grudgingly a few degrees from its high of eighty-two.

The operation was fraying at the edges. Rachel felt it in the tense whispers of the men scattered nearby in the darkness, dressed in black jumpsuits bulked out by soft-shell body armor. Beneath the soft crackle of two-way radios, after the call signs and counter-signals, were clipped questions. Too many questions, followed by lengthy pauses and sometimes no answers at all.

"Jafo, you okay?"

The words of QRT (Quick Response Team) commander Robert Burns came on puffs of peppermint-smelling breath.

"I'm okay."

"We fixed the receiver. As soon as we hear a little chitchat, I'll decide on entry."

It should have been no big thing, a faulty receiver. QRT always carried backup. But the backup had failed, so the communications specialist had had to do a cut-and-paste. Another frayed thread . . .

Rachel knew exactly where the problem had started: with the Baltimore Police Department's ego and its desire to guard its turf.

The situation had developed earlier that day, when the watch commander had received an anonymous tip. The informant talked about a supply sergeant named Charlie Dunn, who had access to a dockside warehouse the army leased from the city. Dunn had allegedly gone into business for himself. Tonight he'd be selling a few crates of M-16's, a dozen rocket launchers, and as many antipersonnel mines as he could get his hands on. The buyer was some rich guy from out west, a regional commander of the White Guard. No name had been given, but apparently Dunn had done business with the Guard before—was in fact a charter member. When the unidentified caller made references to Oklahoma City and Ruby Ridge, Baltimore P.D. sat up and took notice.

But it did not share this information with any other agency, federal, state, or local. An assistant deputy district attorney decided it didn't have to. The warehouse complex was owned by the city. The army was only a tenant. There was no reason to suspect that the call had been made outside the sovereign state of Maryland, so the issue of interstate transmission regarding a possible felony was moot. Only when the police needed to confirm the existence and location of Sergeant Charlie Dunn had they been forced to go outside the department. That route had led them through the central army registry in Alexandria, Virginia, and ultimately to the army's Criminal Investigation Division at Fort Belvoir.

Rachel remembered how the duty officer at Fort Belvoir, Jessup, had put it to her:

"Baltimore P.D. has its collective nuts in a wringer over Dunn. Our records show he's clean. My guess? Their informant is either stringing them along or else he's ponying up the wrong guy. Go up to Baltimore, Collins, and see what these Joes really have. If army personnel are involved, get on the horn to me pronto."

"What's my standing re Baltimore P.D., sir?"

"You're a Jafo, Collins. Nothing more."

"And if the situation should become . . . complicated, sir?"

"Then you're a Jafo on the phone to me."

"Yes, sir."

It hadn't been hard for Rachel to tell that the local enforcement was less than enthusiastic about her arrival. Maybe they were expecting a big, strapping specimen with ranger flashes, not this five-foot-seven, California-beach blonde with blue eyes and freckles across her nose. Rachel had felt eyes roving over her as soon as she'd stepped out of the army-issue sedan in the parking lot of the QRT command post. There had been chuckles and snide remarks about the "Citadel chick" and how many hands she would need to hold up that big sidearm of hers.

The team's sniper had blocked her way, looked her up and down. Rachel knew what he was thinking but would not stoop to explain that she'd just come off a ten-day R&R in Santa Barbara.

"You the Jafo?"

Rachel had stepped hard on the insult, let it slide right off her. "That's correct, sir. . . . Just another fucking observer."

"Make sure you stay out of my line of fire is all, sweet thing."

Then the QRT commander had come walking up. He was close enough to have heard the sniper's last comment, but all he'd said was, "Miss Collins, I'm Commander Burns. You ready to go?"

Now, two hours later, Rachel lay grilling on the roof. The night sky was moonless and clouded over, and the heat crept along her skin like a rash. The cuffs of her camouflage jacket were soaked with sweat.

The target was ninety feet away, directly across a cobblestone street that gleamed with crankshaft oil leaked from big rigs. The metal warehouse was Vietnam vintage, its four-story sides sagging and streaked with rust. The cargo bays were empty, the roll-down doors closed. There was a smaller door, garage size, to the left of the bays. It was padlocked. Above was a row of grimy windows with wire mesh embedded in the glass. Beyond the windows was total darkness, not even the telltale glow of a cigarette being smoked in the darkness.

"When is Dunn supposed to arrive—according to your informant?"

Burns, stretched out beside her, expelled a breath that hung in the hot, heavy air like a tired balloon. He kept his Wolf's Eyes night vision binoculars pressed against his eyes. "Sometime before midnight. These things don't run on a clock, Jafo. Most times you gotta wait 'em out."

Rachel knew more about surveillance than she cared to share. In July she'd pulled a wait-and-see for twenty-two hours outside Flagstaff, the temperature nudging 117.

So far, QRT had done it by the book. The soft-entry specialist had gone in first, popped the lock on the garage door, and disappeared inside. In less than two minutes he had bypassed the alarm, installed the microphones and transmitter, and finished the job. On his way out he had relocked the door. By then the rest of the eight-man squad was in position, two snipers on the other rooftops targeting the windows, the rest of the team scattered behind Dumpsters and locked Peterbilt rigs. Rachel had been shepherded along by Burns, a short, wiry man with a tic at the right side of his mouth, chewing breath mints. He'd chosen the shed roof to set up the command and control post. He'd grasped her arm once, hard, to let her know he expected her to stay put.

The warehouse receiver perched beside her hissed like a snake testing the air for prey. The only other sound coming out of the twin two-inch speakers was that of dripping water. Rachel had no idea where the microphones were concealed. Either they were very sensitive or one had been laid near a sink or a drain.

"Strawberry Four."

Burns pressed the earpiece of his two-way radio headset. "Go, Four."

"We got us a vehicle coming down the alley from the west.

Chevy Suburban, big bitch, customized for heavy loads. Male driver. . . . The passenger . . . the passenger is a woman. Repeat, a woman."

"Roger, Four. I got it. Everyone chill. Let's see what he's up to."

Rachel watched the vehicle rock its way down the street, slow, then turn and back up to the padlocked warehouse door. There was enough light from the lamps over the cargo bays to illuminate the driver's face when he got out.

"By my reckoning that's Dunn," Burns murmured.

The face, which could have belonged to an over-the-hill boxer, matched the photo Rachel had memorized from Dunn's file. Except that now the supply sergeant was dressed in work boots, jeans, and a stained T-shirt.

The passenger door opened and a woman's head appeared. She had a thin, pinched face, the kind you saw behind fly-spattered windows in trailer parks.

Rachel heard Dunn growl, "I told you to stay the fuck in the truck!"

The woman retreated, taking care to close the passenger door quietly. Rachel watched Charlie Dunn go to work on the lock. A few seconds later he was rolling up the garage door and punching in the alarm codes.

Dunn got back into the Suburban and eased it inside the warehouse. He came back to bring down the door, then pale lights glowed through the warehouse windows.

"That truck he's got won't carry the ordnance he's supposed to be stealing," Rachel said. "And the woman—"

"Dunn's not the one who'll be taking the stuff," Burns said, cutting her off. "The buyer hasn't arrived yet."

"But he brings his wife or girlfriend to the meet?"

"Big deal." He shrugged. "He's probably done this a hundred times before. She'll stay in the truck, he'll do the deal, in twenty minutes everyone's on their way."

Rachel didn't buy that. The presence of the woman made it all wrong. Now the receiver was sending up a stream of chatter from inside the warehouse.

"I told you to stay in the goddamn truck!"

Then, the sickening sound of flesh smacking flesh. The woman screamed once, then a second time, followed by something that sounded like a baseball bat striking a hanging side of beef.

Then, a third cry . . . and wailing.

Rachel twisted around. "He's got *kids* in there!"

Burns stared at her, then slowly raised his binoculars. Rachel heard questions coming in over the two-way radio.

"Everyone relax. Domestic violence isn't our gig. Stay frosty. The buyer has to be along. . . ."

He turned to Rachel. "When we bring Dunn out, you can teach him some manners, if you have a mind to."

The screams and shouting died away to sobbing and a child's whimper. The woman was breathing hard through her pain. Rachel imagined her crawling back into the truck, over the seats, flinging her arms around the child, terrified yet trying to comfort him.

"Forget the fucking kid and get out here now!"

Dunn talking, the tailgate of the truck dropping into place. Labored breathing as he struggled with something heavy. Then a thud as a wooden crate was dumped on the metal bed.

Rachel glanced at Burns, saw the tic working furiously. She heard the vehicle door opening and flinched when the woman cried out again, pitifully this time, in resignation. The child howled as his mother was yanked out of the truck. Rachel could almost feel Dunn shoving the woman and steeled herself against the volley of abuse. She heard a faint slur to some of Dunn's words; the sergeant had been drinking. He was in a hurry. He needed the woman to help him load the truck.

"There is no buyer," Rachel heard herself say. "He's stealing the ordnance himself—"

"Collins . . ."

"Maybe to resell it later. I don't know. And I don't really give a damn. He's an army noncom thief. And that makes him mine."

"Collins, don't you fuck this up for me!"

Burns rose to grab her, but he was too slow. Rachel had rolled away from him and was perched on the edge of the roof.

"You want to take this up with my commanding officer, Burns?

Fine. But we're going to get pictures of that woman and kid, so get ready to explain why you sat around while he beat them."

Rachel dropped, hitting the ground harder than she expected, legs pumping across the oil-slick lot. She pressed herself against the garage door, breathing deeply to steady herself. Her weapon was out, chambered.

Now, in the stillness, she felt the hairs on her forearms push up against her camouflage jacket. Somewhere out there, eight barrels held her in their sights, fingers curled around trigger guards. Someone at Fort Belvoir had once told her that Baltimore QRT was a professional bunch, no cowboys. She hoped so.

Raising the warehouse door would take too long, make too much noise. Dunn had an arsenal in there he could turn on her.

That left the windows.

Rachel jumped up onto the landing bay and grabbed the first iron handhold welded to the side of the warehouse. Pulling herself up, she climbed thirty feet to the ledge beneath the windows.

She saw it all now through a pane covered with decades of soot. It was like peering through a fogged-up windshield.

The Suburban was parked in the middle of an empty rectangle defined by stacked pallets. Both the passenger and driver doors were open, and the tailgate was down.

The little boy huddled in the passenger seat was no more than six or seven years old, dressed in blue denim overalls, clutching an Orioles baseball cap. Rachel saw his lips move, thought he might be singing to himself, the way children did when they regressed from violence they could not stop.

And there was Charlie Dunn, dragging another crate across the polished concrete floor, sweat pouring off him, muscles straining. Dunn was in good shape, not much of a belly. Rachel knew she would have to take him down hard and fast.

Dunn maneuvered the wooden crate close to the tailgate and barked at his wife. She bent over and grabbed the rope handle with both hands. Dunn did the same, lifted his end easily enough, cursed her as she struggled.

Then he made the mistake of swinging his end onto the tailgate. The woman didn't have nearly the strength to copy Dunn's move. For a split second she alone was holding the weight of the crate.

As the rope handle tore into her palms, she cried out and jumped back, letting go of her end. The crate crashed to the floor. The top popped, and M-16 rifles gleaming with factory oil spilled across the concrete.

Dunn pounced on her, using his fists to pummel her forearms as she tried to cover her face; then he went for the exposed rib cage, knocking the wind out of her.

He was still raging when the windows high above him exploded.

The glass was so old and brittle that it shattered into shards no bigger than snowflakes. Her arms protecting her face, Rachel jumped, landing with both feet on a stack of pallets thirty feet below. Searing pain shot up through her ankles to her thighs as she tucked her upper body and rolled forward on her shoulders. Her hands were smeared with blood as she held fast to her sidearm.

Charlie Dunn had snapped out of his shock and was ripping the oilskin sheath off the stock of a freshly minted M-16. He was so well trained that he never took his eyes off the intruder while his hands slapped the rifle together.

Rachel shook herself, showering splintered glass to the floor, then leaped onto the forklift parked beside the pallets. She landed on the seat and from there jumped the remaining distance to the floor, where she took cover behind the thick steel engine housing at the rear of the machine.

"CID, Dunn! Give it up. Now!"

Rachel heard the telltale click beneath the echo of her words and scrambled behind the forklift's four-foot-high rear tire. A split second later the warehouse was filled with the roar of automatic gunfire. Chips of hard tire rubber caromed off Rachel's back and shoulders.

"Yo, bitch! In case you didn't notice, I'm not alone!"

Dunn's voice rang through the cordite-hazed air. Rachel peered around the shredded tire, saw Dunn with his forearm around the woman's throat, dragging her along, a human shield.

"Yeah?" Rachel called back. "Well, Baltimore QRT's waiting outside. You know their drill, Dunn."

She bit her lip to try to stop shaking. If he saw her terror, he'd slay her like a lamb.

"Maybe they are, and maybe you're just bullshitting me, little sister," Dunn said. "See, I figure that if QRT was out there, they'd never let a chick go through the door first."

Rachel heard the squeak of a rubber sole on smooth concrete.

"So what I'm aimin' to do is come over there and blow your fucking head off. 'Less, of course, your QRT friends'll try and stop me."

The second volley blasted the concrete, spraying the air with dust and chips. Dunn went through the clip in seconds, racked in another, and kept on firing. The lay-down kept Rachel pinned behind the forklift, unable to return fire. Dunn would keep on like this until he was on top of her.

Rachel never heard the sniper's shot. From where he was firing, it wouldn't have sounded louder than a light cough in the night. But she knew something was wrong when bullets began ricocheting off the corrugated steel roof. When she ducked out from her cover and rolled along the floor, she saw Dunn collapse to his knees, the M-16 pointed at the ceiling, spitting bullets. Which was when she put two rounds from her Sig-Sauer into his chest. A third caught the stock of the M-16, shattering it out of Dunn's hand.

Rachel lay prone, her arms stretched out in front of her, her Sig leveled at the sprawled figure of Charlie Dunn. When the ringing in her ears died away she heard a deep, sucking sound.

Got him in the chest. He's still alive.

Testing each muscle carefully, Rachel got to her feet and took a quick glance into the Suburban. The boy was rocking back and forth in the front seat, his lips moving soundlessly. The woman lay in a crumpled heap behind Dunn. There was no blood around her. Rachel thought she must have fainted.

As she moved toward Dunn, Rachel heard the garage door rolling up. QRT poured in.

She paid them no mind. Kneeling beside Dunn, she raised his head and listened to his tortured breathing as he labored to hold on to life. Delirium blazed in his eyes.

"Fucking CID," Dunn gasped, bright red bubbles forming on his lips. "Found out about North, did ya? . . . "

Rachel stiffened. She thought she knew whom Dunn was talking about, but the reference made no sense. Dunn trembled violently in her arms and moaned. *He's crazy, terrified.* . . . Still, the questions escaped her lips.

"What about North? What are you saying?"

Dunn coughed harshly, spewing blood-soaked phlegm across his chest. Then his head hung back and his mouth fell open in a rictus of a smile. A wet cackle worked its way out of his throat.

"Hey, little sister," he whispered. "Gonna die a happy man . . . happy man . . . helped put that black bastard in the ground!"

Men were shouting at her, and Rachel wanted to scream for them to keep quiet. She waded through the shock that Dunn's words had dealt her, strained to hear whatever else might come from his mouth.

There was only a soft gurgle. Dunn's body went rigid, the last breath slipping out like a sigh of relief, leaving him staring wide-eyed into eternity.

Rachel didn't know how long she continued to hold him after that. Eventually she focused on the boots of QRT commander Burns, whose words were laced with phony regret.

"Collins, you don't *know* how big a hammer is about to drop on you."

Outside in the night, where the stink of gunfire drifted on the air, a man known as the Engineer watched the denouement of the surveillance operation.

His vantage point was the roof of the tallest warehouse in the complex, sixty yards from where the nearest QRT sniper had taken up position. From here, his Magna-Lite scope gave him a clear view through the broken windows into the warehouse.

The Engineer had reckoned on a textbook QRT operation: a hard entry, using flash and stun grenades. Not that that alone would have taken Dunn. He was experienced and very clever. He had a vast array of arms to fight back with, all of which he could handle expertly. But sooner rather than later, QRT fire would have driven him into a place where the outside snipers would get a clear shot.

In the unlikely event that that *didn't* happen, the Engineer had come prepared to finish Dunn off himself. A cold shot of 110 to 120 yards was not a challenge, even in the dark.

But here was the wrinkle: the girl.

The Engineer had had no idea she'd be on site or who she was. Not QRT. Who? Obviously well trained, the way she went through those windows and after Dunn. But a maverick. The QRT commander must have been sorely pissed when she took off on him.

The worrying part was that she'd managed to get to Dunn while he was alive. The Engineer had watched her prop him up and bow her head close to his lips, as though listening to a death-bed confession.

What did you say, Charlie? Did you brag a little about what you'd done? You should have just died.

The Engineer watched Baltimore P.D. support units and EMR trucks pile into the scene. From inside the warehouse came camera flashes and strobes as QRT photographed the scene. Burns had the girl over by Dunn's truck, ladling out the shit. Inside the vehicle, the woman the Engineer knew to be Dunn's wife huddled with her son.

The Engineer slipped the scope back onto his rifle and tracked through the shattered windows. The crosshairs settled on blond hair, drifted down to the center of the forehead. He had the shot. He couldn't take it. It wasn't the ground units that concerned him, but the helicopter with its floodlight, a probing skeletal finger.

How long did you talk to her, Charlie? Six, seven seconds? Did she understand whatever you said?

The Engineer decided: the girl would live, for now. He knew how to find out what, if anything, Dunn had told her. He also needed to check her out, find out who she was, how she'd come to be there. If circumstances warranted, he would pay her a visit.

The Engineer packed up his kit and stole across the roof. He felt the annoyance of a professional who'd had a tricky detail in his grasp but had failed to nail it down. Dunn had been that detail. But now there might be another.

2

It was murder and she knew it. But they would call it something
else. Anything else.

Major Mollie Smith, special agent in charge, CID, sat in the last
row of the hearing room in the Dirksen Senate Office Building.
The arena where truth was supposed to reign was made cool by
walls of Tennessee variegated marble and crisp accents of redwood.
Beneath crystal chandeliers were the podium for inquisitorial sena-
tors and a long walnut table for witnesses. Usually the room was
reserved for Senate confirmation hearings of presidential ap-
pointees. But today there would be no questions, no replies, no
debate. Today the room's only function was to mark the gravity of
the proceedings and confer respect on them.

What a joke. . . .

Mollie sat half-hidden by a pillar, but her view was unob-
structed. The media had laid itself out in front of the podium,

covering the green carpet with thick black cables and camera tripods. The audience consisted of fewer than twenty people: representatives of the Department of Defense and the National Transportation Safety Board; the deputy national security adviser, who was the ears of the Oval Office; and three officers from JAG, the army's judge advocate general's office.

Mollie had checked the roster before coming. She had to be sure that none of the JAG personnel would recognize her. Since no crime was deemed to have been committed, the presence of a senior investigator from the army's Criminal Investigations Division would be questioned.

Now the door behind and to the left of the podium opened and the five members of the inquiry committee filed in. Camera shutters and motors buzzed to life, like cicadas at dusk.

Mollie focused on the man who took the middle seat, Judge Simon Esterhaus, currently serving on the Federal Appeals Court, eleventh circuit. Chairman of the commission, he reminded Mollie a little of General Schwarzkopf: the same chunky build, a face marked by bulldog resolution, its features molded by incorruptibility.

Over the past few weeks Mollie had learned all there was to know about Esterhaus. The judge was a national figure, Lincolnesque from his humble origins in a small Ohio farming community to his meteoric rise through the nation's legal system. Esterhaus had been a brilliant student, had clerked for a Supreme Court justice, had become the youngest partner ever at Bell and Robertson, Washington's gilt-edged firm. From there he'd moved on to a Maryland State judgeship, then on to the federal bench. He had served on numerous government and presidential committees. In seven days Simon Esterhaus would reach the pinnacle of his professional journey. He was the president's nominee for a Supreme Court vacancy. Washington insiders viewed the upcoming Senate confirmation hearings as a mere formality.

A formality . . .

Tapping his gavel to bring silence to the room, Esterhaus cast a glance over his audience. His voice reminded Mollie of water rushing over a gravel streambed.

"The committee has reviewed the evidence and pertinent information and is prepared to render a decision. First, however, I will ask the marshal to play the video."

Chandelier light dimmed from yellow to orange to nothing. A screen dropped from the ceiling along the left-hand wall, blazed in white. Mollie closed her eyes. She had seen these images thousands of times, in the privacy of her office and in the hellish solitude of her nightmares. There was nothing here she did not already know. She wedged herself tightly against the column and laid her cheek to it, the brine in her tears scalding the cold marble.

First, the plane, a military version of the Lear business jet, designated C-12, on the runway at Andrews Air Force Base. Coming up to it, General Griffin North, tall and lean, with a rakish step and a snap to his salute. He turns to say a few words to his adjutants, then seems to remember the cameras. His expression softens, as if he has seen someone he loves, wants to reach out for them. The sun dancing along his dark glasses brings a shine to his smooth black skin. He hesitates, then turns and marches up the ramp, bending low through the hatch.

The video breaks, goes to white.

Now the plane again, on final approach, silhouetted against the Santa Rosa Mountains east of Palm Springs, California. A graceful, fragile creature swooping down toward the runway.

Every time Mollie saw the tape, she had the same thought: The army cameraman documenting North's arrival had been very good, very professional. He'd tracked the landing perfectly, never wavering even when the aircraft's nose plowed into the hardened concrete, catapulting the jet wing over wing in a booming fireball.

A second camera was focused much more tightly on the aircraft itself. The video now showed a sequence of still shots lifted from the tape. In slow motion the nose-gear strut snapped and sailed away. Then the tire wobbled down the runway, enveloped by the giant shadow of the plane.

Mollie was grateful the sound track had been lifted from this copy. Her version of the tape had the audio. Sometimes when she watched it, she cried out to stop herself from imagining the screams that must have echoed through the flaming craft.

The lights came on again. Esterhaus had no need to touch his gavel. Mollie looked across the still room, saw that a stack of thick, bound documents had been placed on the podium beside Esterhaus. The commission report.

Here it comes.

Mollie thought she saw Esterhaus square his shoulders. Curiously, his stern posture was belied by his words. They came softly, the way a parent might float endearments to a sleepy child.

"It is the unanimous decision of this committee that General Griffin North's death on August second of this year was a tragic accident.

"We have examined all the evidence presented to us—"

Not quite all, Judge.

"—and agree with the conclusions put forth by the National Transportation Safety Board and the on-site army investigating unit. The crash of General North's plane was due solely to the malfunction of the nose-gear strut, which failed to lock in place prior to landing. The fact that the indicator light in the cockpit was positive makes it clear that the pilot could not have known that an emergency existed.

"Having ruled out human error, and certain that the strut itself was in sound mechanical condition, we are left to ponder the inexplicable: why this man of service and promise was taken from us before he could make a further contribution to his country— as he most certainly would have after the election—as our next vice president."

He would have become that, Mollie thought. *Despite all his misgivings about politics, the worry that if he stepped beyond the uniform, he would find himself in alien and hostile lands . . .*

True, the political system would not change—it would do its best to transform the man into a creature it could ultimately control. But Mollie did not believe that that would have happened. North was very strong. But his strength ran far beneath his years and training and wisdom; it was drawn from waters only a black man who had risen through the ranks to the pinnacle of command could know. Four years from now, the party fixers who had viewed this Gulf War hero as their incumbent's savior for reelection might have had second thoughts. But during those four years Griffin

North would have mastered the political battlefield. The only question then would be whether America, in the new millennium, would accept a black president.

"And so these hearings are deemed closed."

Mollie felt sick. She leaped to her feet and headed for the chamber doors before the echo of the gavel died away. She pushed them open so violently that they slammed against their rubber stoppers, causing people hurrying along in the hall to look at her.

Mollie squeezed around the corner and into an alcove that held a water cooler. She had willed herself never to look into the future. Any thoughts or memories that threatened to carry her there were cauterized by the image of Griffin North's casket being laid in the ground. She bent over the fountain, let the tepid water splash across her lips, then pulled out a handkerchief and dabbed her skin.

When she was ready, she drew herself up and faced the hall. People swept by in front of her—secretaries, messengers, senatorial aides, lobbyists. The media that had been inside the hearing chamber was spilling out the doors, and Mollie slipped in with the flow. She had things to attend to.

Mollie was an unusually alert and perceptive woman. CID training had merely honed what nature had given her. But this time her eye failed to relay the anomaly to her consciousness, perhaps because the anomaly itself was there and gone in less than a heartbeat.

So Mollie passed the man who'd been watching her. He was dressed like any studio cameraman or photographer: high-top sneakers, jeans, a Redskins windbreaker over a light sweater, a photo ID dangling from a clip attached to his belt, a Yashica thirty-five-millimeter strapped over his shoulder.

This man, with his boyish face and iron body, fell in step behind Mollie, pacing himself, staying to the right and far enough back that her peripheral vision would never pick him up.

His eyes wandered over her. The wedge of hair was the color of the last leaves of the autumn maple; the calves were strong and taut beneath the regulation skirt. He recalled her eyes as she'd passed him—the only chance she would have had to register surveillance. They were green and deep and very hard. The tears welling in them were like spring water on emeralds.

The Engineer saw the truth beyond Mollie's grief, in the place where she carried the secret she knew. Were it not for the grief, perhaps she would have hidden it better. But that didn't matter. The Engineer knew exactly what lay in her trove, how much longer he would let her keep it, and how he would tear it from her breast.

Soon. . . .

But now he would leave her with something to remember him by when they next met, though of course she would not think this way now. The Engineer wondered if his gift would pain or soothe. He'd ask about that at the next opportunity.

Mollie took the corner, stopped dead, and whirled around. She had been brushed by a passerby . . . a tall, curly-haired man in a football jacket who was now sauntering down the hall in the opposite direction.

Mollie stared after him. She could not move or shout. The air around her was tinged with cologne, a scent she recognized instantly because for so long it had been the smell of life itself. She had sensed it on her skin when her lover touched her and on his breath when he whispered to her in the dark. It was a scent she had chosen for him, very exclusive, to set him apart from all other men and to mark him as her own.

"Mollie? Mollie Smith?"

The voice was familiar, but not immediately identifiable. Mollie couldn't tear her gaze from the retreating figure until she felt someone touch her elbow, tentatively, the way an old acquaintance might.

"Mollie, it *is* you."

The woman stepped into her line of sight. She was in her early forties, with ash blond hair swept back in a French braid. Her face was not as tanned as Mollie remembered, but it had the healthy glow of an avid weekend sailor or someone who played tennis outdoors. The wardrobe—cream-colored skirt with matching

jacket, set off by a colorful scarf—was understated in the most
expensive way. But then Pamela Esterhaus had always been well
turned out, that rare marriage of taste and money.

"Pamela . . . I'm sorry. I never expected to run into you here."

"Well, for a minute I thought *I'd* made a mistake." Pamela
Esterhaus, wife of the judge, glanced in the direction Mollie had
been looking at. "Waiting for someone?"

"No. I just got out of the committee room."

"The North hearing?"

"JAG asked me to sit in as an observer."

"Don't tell me they're still running an investigation?"

"No. Just a formality, having a warm body from CID there."

Mollie didn't know how or why the lie had slipped out. It
just had.

"Personally, I'm glad the whole thing is finished," Pamela said
emphatically. "I can't tell you the strain Simon's been under." She
paused. "Forgive me for saying so, but you look a little peaked,
too."

"North was one of ours," Mollie replied quietly. "The best we
ever had."

Pamela Esterhaus looked away and sighed. "Put my foot in it,
didn't I? I'm sorry. I realize what North meant to the army. To all
of us." She paused. "Did you know him? Personally, I mean?"

The words almost made Mollie crumble. "No. Not really."

The next time Mollie looked over, Pamela was holding out a
business card. Her eyes were kind, but etched with concern.

"I was going to ask if you wanted to get a coffee, catch up a bit.
But now's not the time, right?"

Mollie shook her head and took the card. Pamela worked for
the Justice Department. There was no job title, only her department: Human Resources. Mollie didn't have to ask what that
meant.

"I'd like to get together," she said, trying to sound sincere.

Six years ago she and Pamela Esterhaus had met in Riyadh
during the Gulf War. A wartime bonding had developed over a
pint of Jack Daniel's shared on the roof of Riyadh's Intercontinen-
tal Hotel as they'd watched the Arabian night light up, Patriot
missiles hunting Iraqi Scuds. The next morning, before they'd left

for their respective posts, addresses, phone numbers, and promises to get together had been exchanged. Like so many battlefield plans, these had been stillborn.

"I'm stationed at Belvoir," Mollie said.

"Simon and I have a place in Georgetown, on Cooke's Row. Neither of us has an excuse now. Right?"

"Absolutely."

Mollie hastened away. She genuinely liked Pamela Esterhaus, but in a few days the woman would have every reason to want to tear her eyes out. There was nothing Mollie could do to prevent Pamela from becoming her husband's last victim.

Pamela returned Mollie's brief wave, then began walking toward the committee room doors. She felt eyes passing over her, men ranking her on the arousal meter, women doing a harsher, more critical appraisal. But she was used to this, had been for years, ever since she'd discovered that her beauty would always be a source of allure and envy. Today, right now, she particularly enjoyed the attention.

She walked through the empty committee room and opened the door behind the podium. The chamber where committee members prepared and sometimes deliberated was empty save for one man who sat at the end of a long walnut table.

"Hello, darling."

Simon Esterhaus looked up as his wife entered, closing the door behind her.

"Pamela . . . I didn't expect to see you."

"You mean you never noticed me in the committee room? Simon, I'm hurt."

When he didn't answer she knew he was lying. There was absolutely nothing he could hide from her.

The judge watched his wife approach, her pouting smile teasing him, her hips swaying to a tempo that made the blood roar in his ears. She had always been like this, a predator far more ancient than her years or their marriage, whose appetites both revolted and thrilled him. She cloaked her sexuality like a magician, revealing none of it in her professional life. Only when she needed to conquer or consume would she unveil it in naked splendor.

Esterhaus knew each and every degree of her power. He bore

the scars. Yet for all she had inflicted on him, for all the trespasses she had made him suffer, he could no more turn away from or deny her than he could change the influence of the moon upon the tides. She ran her smooth fingernails along his cheek, and he flinched.

"Still sore?"

"I'm seeing the dentist in a few days. The new bridgework will be ready by then."

Pamela perched herself on the edge of the table, one leg swinging languidly over the other. She scrutinized her husband the way a diamond merchant would study a stone for flaws, looking, expecting to find fault. She was impressed with the way he'd held up during the commission's hearing, but the scars were there if you knew where to look: his collar was loose around his throat, and a nervous twitch tugged his left eyelid.

"It's all over now, isn't it?" she said softly. "I mean, everything went just as it should have."

Esterhaus's gaze remained fixed on his hands, fingers splayed flat on the table. "The president will get the report tomorrow, over my signature."

Pamela tilted her head back and laughed quietly. "See? I told you this would be cut-and-dried. I mean, the facts spoke for themselves."

He couldn't help looking at her now, as if she'd uttered some gross profanity.

She slipped off the table and came around so that she stood behind him. She shipped both hands over his shoulders and along the smooth expanse of shirtfront.

"It's time for us to go home," she whispered. "And put it all behind us."

3

The QRT command post is located in the Baltimore police department headquarters building at 601 East Fayette.

The scaffolding and construction material were mute testimony to ongoing renovations. To Rachel Collins, it seemed that half a wall was missing, leaving an open area between the interior post and the lobby. So far three homeless people, a distraught woman, and a deliveryman had mistakenly wandered through and ended up at the duty sergeant's desk.

Rachel thought the sergeant must be used to this kind of thing. He handled the lost souls gently, turning them around, shooing them back the way they'd come.

She saw all this through a broad, waist-high, one-way window. The room she sat in was cinder block, painted a dull yellow that she found hard on her eyes. She thought the choice of color was deliberate since the room doubled as an interrogation cell.

On the bolted-down desk were a legal pad, a felt-tip pen, and a stack of six loose pages covered in legible, orderly script. Commander Burns had demanded that Rachel write out her report immediately. He'd snorted when she'd asked for a laptop computer or tape recorder.

"Then how about a shower before I start?"

"We have no women's facilities. And only two showers. They're both being used."

A half hour later, the showers remained unavailable. Rachel had gone to the reception area rest room and scrubbed her hands and face as best she could, trying to ignore the prickling caused by the glass slivers in her scalp.

Afterward she'd called Fort Belvoir. Jessup, the duty officer, had told her that her commanding officer was not on post, but that Burns had been smoking up the lines between Baltimore P.D. and Belvoir.

"You mind telling me what you did to set him off, Collins?"

Rachel gave him the short version.

"Jesus, what a mess." The line went silent; Rachel could hear Jessup's asthmatic breathing. "I *think* it'll all work out," he said finally. "Make nice. Write out that report for him."

Rachel was tempted to mention the business about the showers but decided, no. She'd tool up the damn report, then break every speed limit on the Maryland and Virginia books. The thought of her apartment, her bathroom, was sufficiently motivating.

Now she was finished, and Burns was still nowhere to be found. Was he was genuinely busy, she wondered, or was he merely being his pluperfect asshole self?

She picked up the pages and tapped them so that the corners were perfectly aligned. The thought of reading them one last time never crossed her mind. There was nothing she could add to her account that would make any difference to the woman who was now a widow or to the child who no longer had a father. Fortunately, though, the woman would be all right. Rachel had gone to her in the ambulance, after the paramedics had checked her for broken bones and applied ointment and compresses. When Rachel had told her that Dunn was dead, Candy had lifted her head and there was a flicker of life in her lost eyes. Then came a ghost of a smile. To Candy Dunn, freedom was a sweet but foreign-tasting nectar.

Rachel had hugged her lightly, whispered, "Good luck," and walked away wondering if it was Candy Dunn's fate to attract terrors like Dunn.

Rachel remembered this as she went on tapping the papers on the desk. Staring through the one-way window, she realized that the midmorning shift change was under way, lots of people in street clothes milling around the reception area. The tall man in the Redskins jacket didn't stand out. It was the flamboyant design of an Indian warrior on the back of the maroon leather that caught her eye. She watched his back as he talked to the desk sergeant, who then made a brief phone call. He and the man continued to chat until a trainee hurried over with a small package. The sergeant pushed forward a form, and the sports fan scribbled something at the bottom.

His name. He's a messenger.

Rachel's gaze drifted to the large, old-fashioned clock above the sergeant's desk. Ten-thirty. She was hungry, tired, and dirty. When she looked through the glass again, the messenger was gone.

The Arlington Memorial Bridge, which spans the Potomac, has some of the finest views of the Washington landmarks. It is also the heaviest-traveled bridge for traffic coming off the George Washington Memorial Parkway, headed for the city. At peak hours more than three hundred cars cross the bridge every sixty seconds —and most are equipped with cellular phones, forty percent of which are in use while the vehicles are on the bridge.

The one-foot-square interceptor box had been tucked beneath the bridge at the highest point of the arch closest to the D.C. side of the river. Wrapped in sandstone-colored burlap to blend in with the bridge's stonework, it was held in place by a military-grade waterproof glue. Two small holes, each the size of a dime, had been cut in the top to allow the scanners to operate.

Powered by a lightweight lithium battery, the scanners were set to activate for one hour at the peaks of the morning and evening rush hours. During those times the scanners intercepted an average of 220 cell phone numbers and their corresponding electronic serial numbers, whose owners remained unaware of the piracy. The numbers were then stored on a microchip that, on command from a mother console, would reprogram them and spit back the digits, beginning with area codes, to the Engineer's phone.

The Engineer had installed this cloning system one week after accepting his current assignment. It had functioned satisfactorily since then and, given the life span of the battery, would outlive its purpose. But well before then, like all the tools the Engineer used —mechanical, electronic, or human—it would be removed and disposed of suitably.

The Engineer strolled out of the Baltimore police headquarters and down the street to a bank of phones. The mid-September sun was strong as it inched toward noon, but its heat barely registered on his face, the color and texture of well-worn saddle leather.

The Engineer dialed his mother console, waited, then punched in the digits that would activate the retrieval system. He memorized the first number the computer-generated voice gave him, then hung up and redialed. This time he entered the number the scanner had pilfered and waited for the computer to cross-reference it with the data in Bell Atlantic's records.

The Engineer pulled a rolled-up *Smithsonian* magazine from his jacket pocket and was on the second page of an article about the Martian canals when the voice came back with the details. The number belonged to a Dr. Stanley Weisberg at 3672 Meadow Hill Lane, Chevy Chase, Maryland. Conveniently, the doctor also had an AT&T calling card.

The Engineer broke the connection. Anyone who lived on such a pretentiously named street, in what was in fact a reclaimed swamp-water subdivision, deserved a tweak. Dr. Weisberg it would be.

The Engineer dialed a Bell Atlantic number, then punched in Weisberg's calling card number. A few miles away a phone rang. Once.

"This is the Engineer. The cleanup is proceeding on schedule."

• • •

It wasn't until twelve-thirty that afternoon that Rachel got home. The apartment was stifling because she'd closed the windows before leaving. She walked through and opened them, then headed for the bathroom, taking off her clothes and letting them fall in her wake.

The shower soothed her, washed away the frustration and humiliation that Burns had heaped on her. After finishing her report, she had cooled her heels for more than an hour before the QRT commander reappeared. He'd glanced at her work and dismissed her without comment. She'd been reminded of junior high, being let out of detention.

On the drive home to Alexandria she had tried to convince herself that she'd never have to deal with Burns again. But she knew better. His reports on her performance would dog her until the matter of Sergeant Charlie Dunn was closed.

Rachel came out of the bathroom wrapped in a thick green terry-cloth robe, an expensive birthday present to herself. The French windows in the living room were awash in light, the Vermont maple floorboards warm under her feet. In the corner, on the stereo stand, sat her answering machine, its red light blinking.

Rachel played back the message, then dashed to her bedroom to dress.

She took U.S. 1 south from Alexandria, followed it past the Rib Barn and Denny's, the car dealerships, and the minimalls with their Krispy Kreme doughnut shops and palm readers tucked side by side.

Once on post, she turned off on Belvoir Road, drove through the Pence Gate, and passed the Belvoir South 9 golf course. After another turn at Ninth Street, she doubled back along Gunston and turned off on Sixth.

Rachel nosed her army-issue sedan into a parking space in front of the utilitarian building that housed the Criminal Investigation Command. She flashed her shield and ID for the guard in the lobby. As the elevator chugged to the third floor, she glanced at herself in the polished metal mirror near the ceiling. The blue short-sleeve blouse complemented the gray pants. She wore no makeup and no jewelry except her waterproof watch. She felt refreshed and thought she looked comfortable. Her pulse told a different story.

Rachel walked the length of the hall into an empty reception room. It was lunch hour. She wondered if the order to appear at this time had taken that into account. She paused in front of the office door, steadied herself, and knocked twice, with precision.

"Come in."

The room was small and cramped. There was a reasonably new desk surrounded by ancient, gunmetal filing cabinets. On the windowsill, a dusty begonia was fighting for its life.

In front of the desk were two generic beige vinyl chairs. Major Mollie Smith sat in front of her computer. Rachel noticed a blue enamel pillbox in her hand, which Mollie pocketed hastily.

"What the hell happened in Baltimore?" she said by way of a greeting.

"I faxed over my report," Rachel replied. "The handwriting, that's how Burns wanted it done."

Mollie sat back, toying with a pencil. Rachel thought she looked more than tired. It was as though something vital had been sucked from her core.

"Take a pew, Rachel," Mollie said. "And tell me *exactly* what happened in Baltimore."

It was an easy recital. Rachel parked her emotions and stuck to the facts, even when she talked about Dunn's beating his wife.

"There's no way he could have been taken other than by shooting?"

"If the QRT sniper hadn't fired when he did, Dunn would have killed me."

Rachel paused, thought about what she'd just said. It was the first time she'd admitted, either aloud or to herself, that she had almost died in that Baltimore night.

"He was still on his feet after the sniper fired," she said. "That's when I shot back."

"So it was a righteous shoot."

"Absolutely."

"And Dunn was still alive when it was all over."

"Barely."

Mollie picked up several sheets of fax transmissions. Rachel recognized her handwriting.

"Burns is seriously pissed because of your cowboy reaction, but he doesn't seem to be pushing it over my head. Did you really threaten him with pictures?"

"QRT had a Steadycam video going all the time. No way they would have missed Dunn's wife. With that kind of equipment, the stills would have shown exactly what he did to her."

"Set you off, did it?"

Rachel sensed a rebuke beneath the question. "Yes."

"Enough that you jeopardized a QRT hard entry, disobeyed a command from someone who, at the time, was your superior in the field."

"If anyone was in jeopardy, it was me!"

"That's exactly Burns's point. But it doesn't end there, Rachel. Burns is right in saying that you needlessly placed his men in danger. You gave Dunn enough time to break into the ordnance. Suddenly QRT was facing a lot more firepower than it had anticipated."

Rachel felt a flush creep up the back of her neck. "Not 'needlessly.' If QRT was so hot to trot, it should have made provisions for the fact that Dunn might use what was in the warehouse." She paused. "There was a *child* in there, Mollie."

"I know. But if I'd been in command and you'd acted like that, I'd take a stripe off you, too. You were lucky this time, Rachel. You and QRT. But most of all the wife and child. It never occurred to you that Dunn might turn his weapon on them, just to create a diversion . . . did it?"

Rachel looked away. "No."

"Something to remember."

Mollie squared the fax sheets, tapped the tops. "I'll need these typed." She glanced at Rachel. "You didn't omit anything? Given your feeling toward Burns?"

Might as well get it over with now. "Yes, I did."

Trying to ignore Mollie's knitted eyebrows, the exasperation tightening the lines around her mouth, Rachel took the fax sheets and thumbed through them.

"Here, when I'm holding Dunn just before he dies. Dunn said

something to me. I omitted it because I wasn't sure what it meant —and I didn't want Burns to see something that might be none of his business."

"Which was?" Mollie watched her carefully.

"Dunn called me 'little sister.' He said he was going to die a happy man knowing he'd helped put that black bastard North in the ground."

Rachel hesitated. "Dunn was badly wounded. He could have been delirious. But talking about General North like that . . . I didn't know what to make of it."

Mollie sat very still. "Tell me again, exactly."

Rachel repeated the words, watching the color drain from Mollie's face.

"What is it?"

Mollie ignored the question. "You're absolutely sure that's what Dunn said? No mistake?"

"No mistake."

"Did anyone else hear this?"

"No. QRT was just coming through the door. Dunn was gone by the time they reached us."

Rachel reached out and touched the gooseflesh on Mollie's arm. "What's going on?"

Mollie pulled back her arm. Her voice dropped an octave. It was raspy in a way Rachel had never heard before, and there was an ugly urgency to it.

"Listen to me very carefully, Rachel. You were alone with Dunn?"

"Yes."

"Where were his wife and child?"

"The boy was in the truck. The windows were rolled up. He couldn't have heard anything. He was catatonic." She paused, visualizing the scene. "Dunn's wife was about fifteen feet away, lying on the floor. He'd been whaling on her before I interrupted him. I'm positive she couldn't have heard anything he said to me."

"You said that QRT had video," Mollie prompted.

"But even if they had it rolling as they came through the door, they were too far away to pick up any kind of audio."

Mollie jumped to her feet, stepped over to the window, leaned against the frame. "Not 'any kind of audio,' " she said, her breath fogging the glass. "You said QRT had planted microphones in the warehouse before Dunn got there."

"Yeah. I remember the sound of dripping water coming over the speakers."

Mollie turned back to her. "So it's possible that the mikes picked up what Dunn said to you."

"*I* could barely hear him!"

"But it's *possible*."

"Yes."

"We have to get hold of that audiotape."

As Mollie was reaching for the phone, Rachel clamped her hand over Mollie's forearm. "Not until you tell me what's going on," she said. "If something's wrong, I deserve to know."

Mollie saw the fight in Rachel's eyes, knew she wouldn't back down from this. She could have pulled rank; she could have done other things. But nothing would work now. Rachel had heard too much.

"Okay. But what I say stays in this room, and I don't want any comments or questions. Clear?"

"Is that a direct order?"

"I can make it one." Mollie's cold tone cut like a shard of glass.

"No. Just tell me."

Mollie looked away. She was furious at Rachel for forcing her to share secrets that no one else could afford to know. At the same time, she knew that none of this was really Rachel's fault. When the duty officer had been called about Dunn, Mollie had been off post and unreachable. Rachel's name had been next up on the liaison list. Luck of the draw . . . bad luck.

"North's death wasn't an accident," Mollie heard herself say. "He was murdered. I'm sitting on two informants who can provide strong evidence as to who organized the conspiracy to kill him."

Rachel was stunned. The crash of North's plane had shaken the military from the Joint Chiefs on down. In the ensuing weeks there had been talk of little else except the ongoing investigation by the Army Safety Center team out of Fort Rucker, Alabama.

But the investigators had absolutely ruled out foul play. As had the
Esterhaus commission. . . .

"What evidence are you talking about?" Rachel asked in a low
voice. "Are your informants telling you North's plane had been
sabotaged?"

"They say that at least one person with advanced technical skills
—aeronautical, to be exact—was involved. But they don't have a
name."

"So why are you sitting on them? "Rachel demanded. "They
need to be interviewed by flight experts—"

She cut off her words when she realized Mollie was staring hard
at her as if she should have made the connection by now. And
she did.

"Dunn . . ." Rachel whispered. "He's your 'name.' " She
paused. "Calls me his 'little sister,' tells me how he helped put
North in the ground. . . . He was dying. I thought he was delirious."

"Maybe he was. Or he said it out of spite, because he never
believed it would mean anything to you."

"Who was he, Mollie? Who was Charlie Dunn, really?"

"I'll know more as soon as I get the tape."

North of Dulles International Airport, between Routes 606
and 846, was an area littered with industrial parks: Loudoun, Sterling Park, Technology Trading, others.

Situated off Sally Ridge Drive, in the TransDulles Center, was a
green glass, three-story building. The identifying sign was discreet:
WONDERLAND TOYS, in black block letters hinged on white
stone.

The company was not a manufacturer, but a middleman between Asian producers and U.S. distributors. As such it housed no
inventory. Instead there was a state-of-the-art satellite rig on the
roof and the latest computers and electronics within the company
offices. A corporate jet remained on standby at the private air
facility at National, and a fifty-foot Ryker sportfisherman was
moored at the Mount Vernon Yacht Club.

Should any stranger have wandered into Wonderland without

an invitation, he would have been greeted by a polite male receptionist who was, in fact, a security officer, one of four who discreetly patrolled the ground floor.

Before being ushered out, the visitor might have noticed that the majority of the company's employees were Asian. In fact, they were all Hong Kong Chinese. They concerned themselves with the company's daily operations and scrupulously avoided contact with the man who, from time to time, arrived to use the large corner office on the third floor.

Any inquiries as to the company's activities or financial well-being would have proved frustrating. Wonderland Toys was a most private corporation. Because it did not offer any shares to the public, it was beyond the jurisdiction of the Securities and Exchange Commission. It banked with the D.C. affiliate of the Bank of Hong Kong and Kowloon, and records of its financial transactions were stored on computer disks at the bank's colony headquarters.

In many ways Wonderland Toys resembled a compact, watertight vessel. And it was all a front.

The Engineer sat at a desk ten feet in diameter, carved from a single trunk of Sumatra teak. Built into it were a direct satellite uplink, a control panel that monitored the ultratech security shield that protected Wonderland, a computer with fax and voiceprint capabilities, and a series of six small television monitors connected to the exterior surveillance cameras.

The Engineer studied the cassette in his hand, delivered a few minutes earlier from the very sophisticated electronics lab located in the first basement level. He had not even the slightest qualm that a technician would have heard what was on the tape. The singular beauty of Wonderland was that its front man was totally dependent on the Engineer's goodwill. Some years ago the Engineer had hauled this man, a major heroin grower and distributor, out of the Golden Triangle, one step ahead of Thai and DEA agents. A green card, a new identity, and a handsome bank account had been provided. Later, when the dealer had agreed to live the comfortable life of a successful entrepreneur, the Engineer had brought over the man's family.

The dealer turned front man never forgot his debt to the Engineer. In return, he provided the Engineer with a base of operations that was virtually untraceable. The men and women who worked at Wonderland had been chosen specifically for *their* debt to the dealer. About the *gwailow* stranger they were told only that his safety and peace of mind were directly related to their own and those of their kin.

Which was why the Engineer was not at all concerned about the sound technician—whose work, of course, was very good. So good that it now presented the Engineer with a problem he would have much preferred to avoid.

The Engineer slipped the cassette into the tape drive and listened to Charlie Dunn's dying words. The technician had washed all the background noise and boosted the decibel level where necessary. It was all very clear now, what Dunn had said. Far too much. And to the wrong person.

By now the Engineer knew all about the young woman who had ministered to Dunn. A long time ago he had cracked the mildly annoying security codes of the army's personnel records, stored at the Hoffman Building in Alexandria, across from the Holiday Inn. He knew so much about her that he had no choice but to kill her.

The Engineer tapped a button, and the details of an entire life began to crawl up the monitor.

Rachel Collins, warrant officer two, Criminal Investigation Division agent. Twenty-nine years old, born in Oceanside, California.

The father had been an army lifer, topping out as colonel, with postings across the United States and Europe. The frequent moves had made Collins an army brat and had curdled a difficult marriage into divorce. Like so many women in the seventies who struck out to "find themselves," Penny Collins fled the stifling confinements of her army-bound life. She left behind an angry and bitter husband and a daughter scarred by the wounds of abandonment.

But Collins was quick and clever. By sixteen she was fluent in French, German, and Russian. When the father died of a heart attack at age forty-two, she was out of high school and alone in the world. For her, the army was not so much a vocation as a haven.

Collins proved tough, getting high marks all through basic training. She was especially good with small arms and took a gold in the divisional marksmanship competitions.

At the Military Police School at Fort McClellan, Alabama, she ranked third in her class. Instructors noted that she could handle the discipline but sometimes had a problem with the rule book. During one training exercise she "arrested" a two-star general who had inadvertently walked in on a "stakeout."

The officer who'd had to sort out that fiasco was Major Mollie Smith.

And here the lives of the two women converged, deep waters for the Engineer to fish.

Smith was a CID instructor at the MP School, a former street-walking investigator who had risen to warrant officer two, decided to take her commission, then stayed on at Fort McClellan. She'd cut Collins out of the herd not only for her language and weapons skills, but because she recognized something of herself in the younger woman—a keen intelligence, the ability to see problems through to their solution, a sense of duty that ran in the blood.

Smith had given Collins, the defiant, suspicious loner and outsider, a world to call her own. Here, secrets were stock in trade; the corollary was that one's own secrets were forever beyond the pale—presumably—of anyone who might search them out in order to cause pain. It was a world Collins would never have found beyond the uniform. All secrets about her were known, just as she knew the absolute truths about those with whom she worked. CID was an egalitarian, utopian society in its truest form.

All this was quite evident in Smith's fitness evaluations on Collins.

Under Smith's guidance, Collins made sergeant after one year at CID. She rose fast, going through Fort Rucker's Warrant Officer Candidate Course and finishing at the top of her class.

The bond between the two women deepened into what the Engineer believed was a friendship that transcended their differences in rank. Smith's reports on Collins were still couched in monochrome army jargon, but there was much between the lines. The Engineer had no trouble reading that.

Both women had had several relationships and a few casual

affairs. The Engineer was not surprised that these came to naught. CID was cop work, with lousy hours, built-in frustrations, and a strong sense of camaraderie. An outsider, male or female, had to adapt and even then would never be fully accepted. Wives did a better job of putting up with the terms and conditions than did any real or potential husbands.

The Engineer thought, *They are sisters under the skin; their word to each other is inviolate, their trust complete.*

Collins would walk through fire for Smith, protect her, if it came to that, with her life. They knew each other's strengths and weaknesses, shared the burden of all their secrets, their—

The Engineer stopped. No, that wasn't exactly right. He knew things about Smith that Collins never suspected. Things she could not help Smith with. Things that would be dangerous for Collins to know.

Like Charlie Dunn . . . The fact that simply by having played confessor to his penitent, Collins was already in jeopardy.

The Engineer tapped the plastic cassette housing on his front teeth.

How much would you share, Mollie? Collins would push hard for the truth, feel slighted and hurt if you held back. But you'd probably not tell her anything at all. I wish I could be sure of that.

The Engineer sighed. No, Smith could not empty Collins of the knowledge the younger woman possessed. Instead she would incorporate Collins into her plan for the others.

The Engineer permitted himself a smile. His job would be much easier now.

4

"*I* know you said not to ask . . ." Rachel cast out her words as delicately as a fisherman would a fly into a still pond.

They had been on the Baltimore-Washington Parkway, Mollie driving fast, using alternate feet on the brake and accelerator. She'd taken the exit by the Federal Reserve, headed for the Inner Harbor and up Charles.

Now they were threading through the hot Baltimore streets, the car's air conditioner straining. Rachel felt the onslaught of a headache behind her eyes. This was the second time in twelve hours she'd traveled this route.

She took Mollie's silence for assent.

"Does anyone else know what you do about North?"

Mollie kept her eye on a FedEx van, anticipated its sudden stop, veered around it.

"No."

"Shouldn't you have kicked this up to Hollingsworth?"

Major General Richard Hollingsworth was the commander in charge of USACIDC. Mollie, as special agent in charge of the Fort Belvoir district office, had instant access to him day or night.

"That's two questions."

She skidded around a tight corner, eased up on the gas. There were no parking spaces along Pratt, so Mollie made one in the red zone on East Fayette.

"Stay here," she said as Rachel started to open her door. "I have to smooth-talk Burns. If you're there, it'll get him all hot and bothered."

Rachel watched Mollie dart across the street, then she slid across to the driver's side, leaned back, and closed her eyes. Immediately questions began spinning through her mind.

And someone was pecking on the glass.

Rachel rolled down the window. In her face were the large, cowlike features of a male meter maid.

"You're in the red zone."

"I know."

Rachel flipped open her ID for him.

He snorted. "That don't cut no ice with the city."

He waddled around to the back of the sedan, peered at the license plate. In the rearview mirrors Rachel saw him wet the tip of his pencil with his tongue. She didn't think anyone did that anymore.

Ten minutes later the officer had managed to fill in half the ticket, Rachel stonewalling him at every opportunity. Out of the corner of her eye she saw Mollie moving fast down the station steps. Horns blared as she plunged into traffic, dodging metal and insults. Rachel had the sedan rolling even before Mollie slammed her door shut.

If Mollie heard the meter maid-man cursing them, she gave no sign.

"Back to your office?" asked Rachel

"No. Your place. You need to pack. I'll take a cab back to Belvoir to pick up my kit."

"Where are we going?"

Mollie shifted sideways in the passenger seat. "I want you to listen carefully. You said QRT had planted a mike in the warehouse."

"Yes."

"The tape of that has disappeared."

Rachel cut off a lumbering city bus and shot onto the ramp to the parkway.

"Define 'disappeared.' "

"Sometime around the shift change a messenger came by the front desk. The credentials he showed the duty sergeant made him out to be with the police lab. The paperwork said the tape was to be taken to the lab to be washed. The duty sergeant checked with Burns; he okayed the handover."

"To a fake messenger," Rachel said tightly.

Mollie nodded. "The tape never made it to lab. Burns didn't even know it was missing until I had him call the lab. The guy in charge there said he never sent anyone."

"Does the sergeant remember the messenger?"

"He says there were too many people around. He was more concerned about the paperwork, and once that checked out, he forgot about the messenger." Mollie paused. "But he did remember that the guy was wearing a Redskins jacket."

Rachel's fingers curled tighter over the steering wheel. "I saw him. Through the one-way glass in the interrogation room."

"Do you remember his face?" Mollie asked quickly.

"He had his back to me. That's why the jacket stuck. He had brown curly hair, I think." She threw a quick look at Mollie. "Who is he? Why did he want the tapes?"

"Same questions Burns asked." Mollie looked out the window. "I told him I didn't know."

"But you do."

"If I had a face or a name, I could go after him."

"Because he's connected to Dunn?" Rachel was speaking her thoughts as they formed. "And through Dunn to whoever killed North. . . ."

"Someone—this would-be messenger—had to have been at that warehouse last night," Mollie said. "He watched the entire

QRT operation go down, saw the mike being planted. He *knew* there would at least be an audio record of the ops.

"He's a cool one, too. Probably didn't move a muscle when you went in and the shooting started. . . . Why was he there? What was he watching *for?*"

Rachel shot into the fast lane, began tailgating a speeding BMW. She knew better than to say a word. Mollie was talking to herself, talking her way through the problem. Rachel had watched her do this before. It worked, mostly.

"He knew there was an audio, and it was important to him," Mollie continued. "Why? Not the shooting and shouting. And not because Dunn was going to say anything. Dunn was there to steal, not to give a speech."

She turned to Rachel. "But Dunn did say something to you. About putting North in the ground."

"Why would the messenger care about that?"

"Because . . . ," Mollie said softly, "maybe Dunn wasn't supposed to say that to *anyone. Ever.* But the messenger can't be sure if what Dunn said meant anything to you."

Mollie closed her eyes lightly. "I don't think he was there only to watch. I think he was going to kill Dunn. Burns said that QRT had an anonymous tip about Dunn. Remember? What if that tip was *deliberate,* to set Dunn up, create a confrontation where there was a real chance he'd get killed?"

"But the messenger—the tipster—couldn't have been sure that Dunn would fight," Rachel objected. "QRT might have been able to take him down easy."

"Which is why he was there, watching. . . . I'll bet that if QRT had walked Dunn out of that warehouse, he'd never have made it to the lockup wagon alive."

She looked at Rachel. "You see it now? He knows what Dunn told you: things valuable enough to put Dunn in the crosshairs. That's where I think you are now, Rachel."

Rachel thought she felt a shudder, the kind that came from a California earthquake. Not the stomach-turning roller type, but the jarring punch when tectonic plates collided. A reminder that beneath the surface, things were forever moving, changing.

The surveillance operation on Dunn should have been a by-the-numbers pickup. But the earth had trembled.

"I'm moving everybody tonight," Mollie said. "Including you."

Rachel kept her eyes on the surging traffic, but her peripheral vision never left Mollie. Long before Mollie had trained her, Rachel had been able to unveil the flaws in men. It was her dark gift. Because her senses were far more incisive than any polygraph, she was never surprised by what she found.

Rachel now knew there was much that Mollie was hiding from her. Because of that, she would be unable to rule by command. She would begin to trade on their friendship, ask Rachel to do things out of trust, a blackmail more finely spun than any gold filigree.

"I can help you," Rachel said.

"Maybe you didn't hear me: You're shipping out."

"You think the messenger is worried enough to murder the informants—assuming he knows who they are?"

"He doesn't know their identities. I'm sure of that. But I can't risk that he might find out."

"And the messenger is working for whoever organized North's murder. Dunn was a part of that. Dunn is dead. The messenger is cleaning up." Rachel paused. "And you won't let me help you."

"You and I will shepherd the informants out of the city," Mollie said. "I have contingency plans for them. They'll be safe once we get them out of here."

"What kind of plans? Are you going to put them in a witness protection program?"

"There's no time for that."

It took a moment, but Rachel made the connection.

"They're not from around here, are they. You're sending them back to the heartland, wherever home is." She paused. "Isn't that the first place the messenger would look for them?"

Mollie shook her head. "You don't know the whole situation, Rachel. These two are so obvious that if anyone suspected they were informants, they'd be dead by now. The plan is to get them to a place where they'll be safe for a few days. That's all I'll need. A couple of days."

"Fine. We run protection for them—"

"Then you continue out to California. Go to Carmel. You know the area. You can disappear until I call you."

Rachel saw a rest stop exit coming up, drifted into the right lane, then eased into a long curve. A half dozen cars were parked in front of a red-brick cube with stick-figure signs for the washrooms. Young fathers walked along the burnt-grass path, stretching, smoking cigarettes. Rachel parked beside a minivan whose owner was scraping bug splatter off the windshield.

Rachel cut the engine and rolled down her window. "If you have informants, Mollie, why not take them to Hollingsworth now?" she asked.

Mollie watched a mother shepherd two toddlers out of the bathroom. The boy saw his father and ran to him, arms outstretched.

"Because of Dunn. I didn't think there was any military connection to . . . what happened to North. Now I'm not sure. I don't know how high this goes, who else is involved."

"Who is 'who else,' Mollie?"

Mollie turned away, stared out the window. "Get back on the road, Rachel."

"I can help you dig into Dunn," Rachel said.

Mollie saw Rachel's reflection in the window. Suddenly she looked very young, the bones of her cheeks covered in smooth flesh, her hair shining with health. Yes, Rachel was too young to share in such confidences.

"No, you can't," she said flatly, sorry for the cruel dismissal in her tone. "You'd only get in the way."

Steven Copeland stared at the open suitcase on his bed. Its contents had been arranged in the usual fashion: underwear, socks, and a toiletries kit on the right; dress shirts, ties, casual slacks on the left. Along the bottom of the case were sneakers and a pair of dress shoes. Two suits, still in dry cleaner's plastic, were tucked neatly beneath the webbing on the top half of the Samsonite hard-shell.

The orderliness pleased him, steadied him. It took him back, out of this room, before Major Smith's telephone call thirty minutes ago, to other times he had packed like this. The suitcase had been larger then, the suits a half season old at most. The accoutrements had included gold cuff links, silk socks, a Tiffany traveling alarm clock.

Most of the clothes Copeland now owned were three years old. His discerning eye detected the minute frays around the cuffs and collars. Only the underwear, which he bought at regular intervals at a Bethesda Kmart, was brand new.

He closed the suitcase, snapped the locks, used the little key on his chain to secure them. Then he looked around the sad little bedroom of the tiny Georgetown town house and wondered if he'd ever have to come back. He prayed not. The place had come furnished with ugly 1930s parlor furniture. He had added nothing of his own, except bedding and towels. This had always been a way station for him. And tonight the call he had so long anticipated had come. He was on his way out.

Gripping the suitcase easily in his left hand, he held it out in front of him as he went down the narrow staircase. He was a tall man, with the hard, ropy muscles of a runner or swimmer. He'd also lost some weight he needn't have. His face was gaunt, the bones of his cheeks and jaw prominent, the eyes appearing much larger than they were. Copeland was a pleasant man to look at. In the past he'd been mistaken for a gentle academic, until the fine quality of his clothes was noticed. Now people shied away from him or watched him with suspicion because of something burning in those dark brown eyes, a hatred and resentment that a kind word or gesture could never broach. Copeland's anger had a half-life of infinity.

His blue, six-year-old Volkswagen Jetta was parked in the street directly in front of the town house. Sometimes when he got into it, Copeland thought he could smell the fine leather of the Jaguar the leasing company had taken back from him. Not that a Jaguar would have survived very long on Olive Street, with the thieves who plundered the neighborhood and the homeless who preferred to break into larger vehicles, where they could stretch out on the back seat to sleep. One time Copeland had been walking by not two blocks from here and had seen a woman giving birth in a plundered Cherokee.

He locked himself in the Jetta, started the engine, and turned on the headlights. Only then did he take out his cell phone, a luxury he would not give up, and tap the speed dialer. Major Smith had told him to go straight to the airport, alone, and not to call anyone. Copeland didn't care. He had only one friend in all the world, and it wasn't Major Smith.

When a woman's voice, soft and tentative, answered, he said, "It's me. I'm on my way."

The ride to Twenty-fourth Street, near the Park Hyatt, took only about fifteen minutes, but it was time enough to take Copeland back years. . . .

To a better time, when he was a freshly minted graduate of Georgetown Law School, with offers from the eight-hundred-pound gorillas in Chicago, D.C., and Wall Street. Some of the seduction techniques had been brazen, including a leggy twenty-year-old paralegal who'd been his "date" in New York. But Copeland had chosen shrewdly. Three years in D.C. had shown him where the power lay. He could sit in an office overlooking the Potomac and his brethren would all, eventually, make the pilgrimage to his doorstep. He had selected Bell and Robertson, an old-line, influential firm that represented only Fortune 500 companies. B&R had pipelines into every government department that was of interest to its clients. Copeland, whose specialties were securities offerings and mergers and acquisitions, had a direct feed into those pipelines.

He loved his work as much as he disdained his peers. The partners piled his desk high, and he wallowed in the joy of his efforts, accepted their accolades, lobbied for bigger, more demanding assignments.

After billing twenty-seven hundred hours a year for three years,

Copeland was handed his first client: PSX Railroads, the nation's largest hauler of agricultural products. PSX wanted to expand from its midwest base into the lucrative petrochemical hauling areas in California, Texas, and Louisiana. It needed a half billion dollars to update its rolling stock and communications equipment and had already been in talks with Fisher Brothers as underwriters. The paperwork on the new float had to be organized yesterday, so B&R had put their best fast-track boy on it.

Copeland had had a lot of time to think about what had happened after that. The sheer volume of detail was the first problem. There was so much work to do that he never had a chance to step back and examine the overall structure of what it was he was supposed to build. And the time constraint . . . Even with a full-time support staff, he was barely able to deliver the necessary documents on schedule.

So he never suspected that PSX Railroads was on the verge of bankruptcy. Or that its senior officers, as well as the overseers at Fisher Brothers and three of B&R's senior partners, all knew as much—that the effort to float a new offering was only a ploy to allow these principals to bleed PSX's overfunded pension plan and all other assets before stepping back and letting the company die.

The federal regulators, from SEC, Treasury, and Justice, were the first to come knocking on Copeland's door. In damp basement rooms of federal buildings he discovered that his was the only signature on documents that spelled out how PSX would be gutted.

Copeland pleaded with his bosses, only to discover that the senior partners not only froze him out, they solemnly endorsed the positions of the PSX board of directors, which claimed that Copeland had masterminded the demise of the once great railroad while attempting to pillage the company himself.

After that, while Justice Department fraud charges were pending, Copeland was hauled up in front of the D.C. bar review to face disbarment proceedings. Within eight months his professional standing had been reduced to pond scum. No firm would touch him. The bank foreclosed on his Watergate condo, and his Jaguar was unceremoniously whisked back to its stable.

As he struggled to prepare his defense before the review board,

Copeland never lost faith that he would be vindicated. He had a single ally, a man whose reputation was so great that a few words from him would make everything go away.

This man had been Copeland's mentor and guide. When all other doors had closed, his had remained open. Copeland laid out to him the strategy for his defense, piecing together the few tangibles he had managed to save—memos, notes, computer records—that linked others to the PSX scandal.

Then, at the final bell, when Copeland was to present this blueprint for his salvation to the review board, his mentor silently and savagely betrayed him.

There was a sliver of an opening in the curtains over Beth Underwood's living room window. That was where she stood, off to one side, looking out at the street. She did not have sufficient experience to realize that a professional watcher could see her easily, nor did it occur to her.

She was a tall, well-fleshed woman in her mid-twenties, with heavy breasts and calves too thick for fashion. In her high school yearbook someone had written that she had a "sunny personality." Back then Beth had taken it as a compliment. But that was before she'd spent five years in Washington.

The city was a dizzying place for her. Raised in Arizona ranch country, Beth had flown in on dreams, and they had sustained her for a brief time. Her new job, her first apartment, the feeling of men's eyes on her body as she walked in the streets—this was all as she had imagined it. Then she'd discovered that in the nation's capital, a woman's career usually takes only one of two paths: she becomes the indispensable helpmate of a powerful man, or she screws the powerful man until his eyeballs pop and becomes, usually, wife number two.

Beth knew she was good-looking, but not glam in the bored, angular way of those in the debutante circle. Not star the way some assistants and secretaries could make themselves on overextended Visa cards. Sure, men wanted to fuck her, but they never did it very well, clambering on top of her as if she were some oversize stuffed doll. Then the next week their friends would call and Beth would know she'd been traded in the locker rooms of the racquet club or at the bar at J. Paul's, over vodka tonics, heavy on the smirks and bullshit.

As she waited for Steven, she thought it no surprise that she had drifted into the "indispensable assistant" pool. It had helped that she adored her boss. Helped until Steven had come into her life and ripped away those illusions, made her terrified of the man who always remembered her birthday and had her out to his home for Thanksgiving with his wife.

Peaches, her cat, rubbed against her leg. Beth picked up the angora and stroked her, wondering if she'd put out enough food and water. Mollie had told her to pack for three or four days. Beth wasn't supposed to tell anyone she was leaving, but still she'd called a few friends to see if they'd look after Peaches. There were no takers.

Steven wasn't supposed to have called, either. Mollie had been specific: Take a cab to the airport, bring only carry-on. A prepaid ticket in someone else's name would be waiting at the Delta counter. The reservation had been coded so that the airline clerk wouldn't ask for a picture ID.

Beth stared at her luggage, now lined up neatly by the front door: one suitcase, a tote bag, and an oversize purse. She had tried to pack less but couldn't. She had wandered through her neat apartment with its colorful throw rugs on old hardwood, had gently handled the tiny porcelain boxes shaped like sailboats, eggs, and clowns set on the low bookcase, had run a fingertip over the rough edges of seashells plucked from the sands of Virginia Beach and the Florida coast. Each piece was connected to an occasion, had a special meaning that made her remember and smile.

She had packed her bags in the bedroom, where she had set them out on the antique quilt she'd brought with her from Arizona. She wished they were magic bags, bottomless, so that she could stuff them with all the good and simple things of her life, take them all with her.

Beth remembered the day, less than a month ago, when Mollie Smith had told her that she might have to go away for a little while, to a place she knew and where she felt safe. Back then, the idea of running had been so vague that she had refused to give it any thought. But then had come the phone call she'd never expected to get, just two hours ago. Instructions she had heard in Mollie's office a month ago, and promptly forgotten because they seemed irrelevant, were repeated. This time Beth had written them down, but when she mentioned this, Mollie had told her to memorize the details and burn the paper.

Beth stared at her fingers. They still smelled of ashes, although she'd washed her hands twice after burning the paper.

The evening traffic along Twenty-fourth Street had thinned out. Beth recognized Copeland's Jetta as soon as it pulled up in front of her building. She picked up Peaches and stroked her for a moment, then set her down.

"Be a good girl till I get back."

The cat meowed when the door closed and locked, then jumped up on the windowsill, arching her back against the warm glass. She settled there, watching as her mistress walked to the man getting out of the car, dropped her bags, and kissed him.

5

Occasionally Rachel still found it hard to work through her anger. Now was one of those times. Mollie's words had stung her; she dealt with it by being efficient. First, she did a load of laundry, and while the dryer was going she called the naval center in Monterey to check the weather forecast. She packed accordingly, loading her duffel bag with summer clothes, plus a few sweaters and a jacket for the cool Northern California nights.

She changed into jeans and a T-shirt and then field-stripped her personal weapon, a Bulldog .44 large-bore, with the barrel vented at the muzzle, throated for a speed loader. After reassembling the gun, she moved the night table and lifted a one-foot-square section of the parquet floor. From the cavity she removed a box of pumpkin rounds.

Invented by an Alabama chemist, the bullets broke into razorlike fragments upon contact with flesh, the shrapnel literally shredding the internal organs. The tests, conducted on sides of beef and on diseased sheep, had proven devastating.

Rachel sat on her bed, chambering the polymer rounds, the afternoon sun warming the back of her neck. She was very still, except for her hands, as if she were sifting the air for signals or movements only she could recognize. He was out there, somewhere, this messenger. In his leather Redskins jacket, the high collar pushed up to hide his profile . . . faceless, on the fringes of her consciousness, like a cloying scent or a name once so familiar but now forgotten. He was moving silently, keeping to a precise agenda. It had included Dunn and most likely North. Now it was focused on her, on Mollie, and on the two informants. Too many people for one man to handle? Rachel didn't think so. Not for someone who could lie in wait flanked by QRT sharpshooters, ready to pull the trigger. She saw a certain contempt in that posture, coupled with a deep vanity.

"I am invisible," he seemed to be telling her. "I can get right next to you and you'd never know it. Do my business and be gone."

Like that business at the QRT compound. Walking in as cool as you please, bullshitting with a 240-pound ex-linebacker desk sergeant while waiting for Burns to pony up the tape.

And Rachel not twenty feet away, looking at but not seeing him because he had made himself into just another drone.

Pumpkin rounds . . .

On her way out, Rachel stopped to speak to the super. He was a Vietnam vet, a naval officer who'd lost an arm during a raid deep in the Mekong Delta. When Rachel told him she was going away for a while and expected no visitors, he said that he'd take care of her mail, then wished her good luck. He knew the life.

Rachel threw the duffel bag into the trunk and got behind the wheel. As she drove away she didn't look back. On such occasions she never did, always believing that she would return to the warm and familiar. Call it superstition.

• • •

The never-ending construction at National Airport reduced traffic to a crawl, even at night. But this made for easier surveillance. Rachel waited in the sedan, parked next to a crane sixty feet diagonally across from the passenger unloading zone.

She was there ninety minutes before the flight departure time. Mollie arrived by taxi forty minutes later. Rachel watched her standing behind a pillar near a large trash bin topped with an ashtray. Other smokers, exiled to this noisy patch of concrete where buses and cars pulled up, provided a natural camouflage.

The drop-off area was well lighted, and Rachel missed nothing. Maybe a dozen men of the same height and build as the messenger had passed through the terminal doors. All had been unaccompanied, most in suits and ties.

Now came the blue Jetta that Mollie had told her to watch out for, inching along in a stream of cabs and limos. Rachel recognized Steven Copeland and Beth Underwood from photos Mollie had shown her and realized that they had already broken one of Mollie's cardinal rules: Arrive separately. But here they were together, Underwood in the passenger seat, a good half head taller than Copeland. The orange glow from the anticrime lights bleached their faces of expression.

Rachel shifted her gaze to Mollie, who was turning away as the Jetta crawled past her. She had been in the room when Mollie had made the calls to Copeland and Underwood, laying out the details of what they had to do as simply as if she were explaining a game to a child. She had gone over the most important points twice.

"Let's see if he gets the next part right," Rachel muttered.

Copeland pulled the Jetta into the unloading zone. He was out of the car fast, but so was Underwood. There they were, by the open back door, hauling out suitcases and bags. Standing too close together, the bags tying up their hands, now talking, touching . . . A professional could slide by and knife both of them before they even realized they were dying. A single burst from a silenced machine gun would be just as easy, if somewhat messier.

Copeland left Underwood alone with the bags, totally exposed, while he hopped back behind the wheel. He angled back into traffic, drove to a red zone, parked, then left the car.

Good.

Rachel remembered Mollie teaching her this trick. To make a car disappear and ensure no one could get at it, you parked in a red or handicapped zone, then called the police. They were always quite willing to slap a three-hundred-dollar ticket on it before having it towed away to a secure pound.

Rachel swung the sedan around and headed for the lot restricted to official vehicles. From there it was a seven-minute walk to the terminal. When she got there she saw Copeland loading the bags onto a trolley. Then he and Underwood joined the crowds headed for the security checkpoints, with Mollie drifting along behind them.

Rachel headed in the opposite direction, past the plywood construction siding that closed off half the terminal concourse, into the corridor that led to the airport police office.

The night duty officer examined her credentials and ticket.

"Do we have a problem here?" he asked.

"Not that I know of," Rachel told him.

The officer waited a beat until he realized this Army Jane wouldn't volunteer anything else.

"Fill out the paperwork."

Rachel handed him the form she'd completed at home. The officer glanced at it sourly. "What's the armament?"

Rachel unzipped her baggy windbreaker to show him the Bulldog.

"You know where to go?"

"Used to be straight down the hall, first left into the security area, and through the doors."

"Still is."

"Thanks."

A couple of heads turned when Rachel opened the security door and stepped into the boarding area. She checked the faces of the men looking at her, focusing on their eyes to see if they were interested in her. Confronted, the men hastened their step or turned their gaze to the backlit ads of long-distance phone carriers.

Rachel spotted Mollie in a black plastic chair, a magazine open on her lap. Two rows to the left, Copeland and Underwood sat side by side, heads almost touching as they whispered.

Not good.

The flight attendant rolled out the ticket counter by the jetway door, and a voice over the PA announced the first boarding call.

Rachel hung back as Mollie handed over her boarding pass and disappeared through the door. She would check any airport employees in the jetway, then the cabins themselves. She would pay special attention to the lavatories, making sure none of the doors was ajar. She would still be on her feet when Underwood and Copeland passed by. The seating had been preassigned so that Underwood and Copeland were at opposite sides at the rear of the aircraft. Mollie would be close by, in an aisle seat, seat belt unbuckled.

Rachel slipped to the end of the line. She didn't think the messenger had made it past her. There had been lots of opportunities to move in on Copeland and Underwood, but none had been taken.

Taking her seat six rows ahead of the informants, Rachel figured the messenger was out of the picture. When she heard the cabin door close and lock, she was sure of it.

Steven Copeland was surprised to see Beth grip the armrests fiercely and press her back hard against her seat as the jet clawed the air on takeoff. It had never crossed his mind that she might be afraid of flying.

He covered her hand with his.

"I feel so dumb," Beth whispered, her hair falling to one side, brushing his face as the plane veered sharply to the left.

"Everything'll be okay. Really."

Copeland believed this. He had been both frightened and exhilarated when Mollie had called. Now the fear was almost gone, replaced by a grim determination. What he was doing now meant that the army investigator was closing in on her target. Their target. Soon this thing would blow wide open.

Copeland had dreams like this: He was walking into a Senate

hearing room. The air was electric with camera motors and hot lights, heads craning to catch a glimpse of him, somber men seated behind a podium, waiting to hear what he had to say.

And the accused . . . seated at the next table, unable, unwilling, to meet Copeland's steady gaze. Copeland showing no savage glee in this victory, just a man wronged coming forward with the truth.

The dream would come to pass. He was certain of it. There was a best-selling book to write, movie rights to auction off, high-paying talk tours to plan. Copeland had seen it all in his mind's eye: the fame, the wealth, the prestige. He would be completely vindicated and, even better, rich. He and Beth would get married, buy a great big house . . .

Copeland glanced at Beth. There was still a ways to go, and he had to stay on top of things.

He had to look after Beth, shepherd her through this. That was why they had arrived at the airport together and were sitting together despite their seat assignments. There were few other passengers, so the flight attendant hadn't made a fuss.

When the plane leveled off, Copeland sat up and looked around. He saw Mollie, gave her a smile, was puzzled when she turned away with a look of disdain.

"Do you see her?" Beth whispered.

"Major Smith? Two rows behind us, in an aisle seat."

Copeland felt Beth squeeze his hand.

"I spotted her as soon as we were in the terminal," he boasted, but he made it sound like a casual observation.

Copeland didn't mention that he had been searching the crowds for Mollie, had caught a glimpse of a woman he only thought might be her.

"Did you see anyone else?" Beth asked him.

"No. We're safe now. Nobody followed us. No one knows where we're going."

Copeland lowered his table tray, accepted the two plastic glasses filled with apple juice that the flight attendant was offering.

Beth drank hers all at once. Copeland gave her his cup. It was one more thing they had in common—neither of them liked alcohol.

"I wish they'd let us go together, to one place," Beth said. "Wouldn't that be easier?"

"Yes. But this isn't an official investigation," he explained patiently. "Smith says we'll be safer in places we know, where we can recognize strangers."

Beth shifted closer. "I know. But I don't want to be away from you."

Copeland wished he could kiss her long and hard, the way he did when they were alone. Do all the other things, too.

He fished in the breast pocket of his jacket and with two fingers brought out a glossy matchbook. He slipped it into Beth's hand, grazing her breast as he did so.

Beth's eyes widened at the name of the distinguished hotel embossed on the matchbook.

He saw no reason to tell Beth that he'd had long, heated arguments with Smith about his choice of sanctuary. It was, he'd shouted, the last place anyone would look for a bankrupt, debarred lawyer. If he had to hide, then at least let it be in a luxurious lair. Besides, Smith wouldn't have to worry about security. The hotel had a sterling reputation regarding its guests' privacy.

A girlish smile played on Beth's lips, and her eyes danced with mischief as she pressed a slip of paper into his hand.

"For *you,* sweetheart. No—don't look at it now. Let's see who calls first."

They pressed as close to each other as the armrest allowed, whispering about how this would all be over with very soon and all the great and wonderful things they would do together for the rest of their lives.

Copeland glanced up as, a few seats up the aisle, a young woman in jeans and a windbreaker got up. Rachel returned his gaze for a split second, then opened the door to the overhead bin and pretended to search through her duffelbag. Above the drone of the engines, in a cabin filled with the weary stillness of spent businessmen, she'd overheard the lovers' secrets, silently condemned their amorous stupidity.

· · ·

The flight landed in Atlanta first, three minutes ahead of schedule. Rachel watched as Copeland reluctantly rose and retrieved his carry-on. He leaned down and pecked Beth one last time before hurrying down the aisle, followed by Mollie.

Rachel stood up and stretched, twisting her torso, looking at the passengers who were traveling on to Phoenix. Most were trying to doze or were reading. A few, like herself, were taking advantage of the opportunity to move around. Not Beth Underwood, though. She remained seated, a paperback open on her lap, her eyes wandering aimlessly across the page.

As she came out of the jetway, Mollie scanned the passengers in the boarding area. There were fewer than twenty, families and young singles taking advantage of the cheap late night fares.

She caught up to Copeland farther down the hall, near the shuttered fast-food area. Mollie felt like hitting him, but she caught the defiance in his eyes. Copeland was a very angry man who was also in love. The last thing he could be counted on to do was behave rationally. And he was itching for confrontation, Mollie could tell.

"Looks like we made it out okay," he said as she joined him.

Mollie did not reply as she steered him into a smokers' cubicle, empty except for the usual molded chairs and overflowing ashtrays. The people hurrying by, glancing inside, made Mollie feel like a lab monkey.

"You did very well," she said, her words riding on a breeze of tobacco. "How's Beth holding up?"

"Like a trouper."

Mollie smiled thinly at the tepid cliché.

"You'll make sure she gets to—to wherever she's going, safely?"

So Mollie knew that he and Beth had traded their addresses and phone numbers. Now she didn't spare Copeland, drilled her knowledge into his nervous eyes.

"You know what you have to do," she said.

"We've been over it a hundred times."

For all the good it did. . . .

"I'll call you tomorrow, first thing. Be there, Copeland."

The fluorescent lighting irritated her eyes. Somewhere down the hall a metallic voice was announcing the final boarding for the second leg of her flight.

"Major Smith?"

"What?"

"You'll get whoever's after us, won't you? I mean, when this is all over—"

"When this is all over, you'll be free. You and Beth won't have to worry about it again. Now get going."

She watched him walk away, shoulders back, a touch of a strut to his stride. Maybe Copeland's being in love wasn't such a bad thing. Better that than his being frightened. At least she had gotten him out of the danger zone. And with Beth in the picture, he was far less likely to compromise himself. Because Copeland had learned to hope again, had discovered that hope could be as sweet and intoxicating as revenge.

Four hours later, just shy of midnight local time, Delta 1410 from Washington, D.C., to Phoenix via Atlanta, touched down at Sky Harbor Airport. There its flight number was changed to 1066. There, too, Beth Underwood deplaned along with the remaining passengers.

Flight 1066 would be traveling on, but a crew change for the brief hop meant a longer layover. Mollie walked Beth outside to the hot night to wait for the rental car shuttle.

"Are you sure you want to drive tonight?" Mollie asked. "I could get you a room in town. You could leave first thing in the morning."

"Now would be best," Beth said. "There's an all-night supermarket on the way. I can pick up what I need, not have to think about it tomorrow."

Mollie understood that. "You're going to be fine, Beth."

"I know. You said this would all turn out okay, and I believed you. But now I *know* it will."

For a moment Mollie was ashamed by such direct simplicity.

Beth Underwood had no idea how informants, particularly women, could be treated on the witness stand. She hoped that Copeland wouldn't turn out to be a weakling bastard and run out on Beth when she needed him most.

"I'm going to call you tomorrow," Mollie said. "And I'll call every day until it's time for you to come back."

"Major? I don't need to worry, do I? I mean, us leaving so suddenly . . . If someone was looking for us, he wouldn't know where Steven and I went, would he?"

"No, Beth, he wouldn't." Mollie paused. "Four days. Next Monday latest. I *will* call. I promise."

The shuttle driver wasn't about to violate his job description by helping with the bags, so Mollie grabbed the heavier one and led Beth into the van.

"Good-bye, Major. Thank you."

Mollie smiled back at her as she stepped down to the curb.

"That's the last one. Come on, Mollie. The plane goes in fifteen minutes."

Mollie turned, saw Rachel, and silently followed her back into the terminal.

The travel time, including layovers, added up to eleven hours, but it seemed much longer.

Even at twelve-thirty in the morning it was warm in Los Angeles. Mollie, an East Coast person, hadn't known that fall was sometimes the hottest season in Southern California.

"It's a lot cooler along the coast," Rachel told her as they walked out to the pickup and taxi areas, which were all but deserted. Mollie had decided to wait with Rachel for the next car rental shuttle.

"I'm sorry I snapped at you back there," she said. "When we were driving out of Baltimore."

"It's okay. You had a lot on your mind." Rachel hesitated. "Under the circumstances I think I would have kicked your butt, too."

Mollie smiled. Then Rachel saw it fade as two young men in punk garb sauntered by, leering.

"I feel like a fool," Mollie said. "There was something back there, in Washington. But not here. I can't smell it here."

"Then you did the right thing. By moving us. Everything's okay now."

"I guess."

"I'll call in as soon as I get to Carmel. You'll let me know what you find on Dunn?"

"Yes. It won't take long. I know where to look, what connections to make."

A few other passengers had wandered out, looking around like lost souls. They smiled and nodded at Rachel and Mollie and seemed relieved that they were not the only ones waiting.

"It's going to come down fast, isn't it?" Rachel asked.

"If the Dunn angle plays out cleanly, yes. If I have to dig, it could take a few days. Either way, next week will see it done."

"You want to take your time," Rachel said. "Whoever you're going after, he's a bull. You want to be absolutely sure he'll go down."

"Oh, I'm sure of that," Mollie said softly. "He *will* go down."

"And collateral damage?"

"Some. . . ."

Rachel touched Mollie's arm, forced her to look at her. "How much, Mollie?"

"Enough to reach the White House."

Suddenly Mollie hugged Rachel, hard, to cut off her next question. "Here comes your bus."

The line for the bus moved quickly, and Mollie gave Rachel a gentle shove toward it. Then she slipped back and watched.

Rachel threw her duffel bag onto the rack and scrambled across a seat to a window. Through the heavily tinted glass she saw Mollie wave once, then quickly walk away.

Mollie went back into the terminal, through security, and up to the gate where the Washington-bound red-eye was boarding. She wandered past the passengers at the ticket counter, not bothering to spare them even a glance. She was tired of looking at faces.

She noticed a bored teenage girl walking past a bank of telephones, checking the coin return slots for quarters. Mollie slipped her wallet out of her purse, snapped it open, and stared at the photograph beneath the plastic sheath. She had taken it three years ago, at cherry blossom time in Washington. The man facing the camera was in his early forties, but the laugh lines around his eyes gave him a boyish look. The wind had tousled his hair, sending a cowlick across his forehead. Mollie felt inside her pockets for change, clutched at the coins. It was a local call; she could do it right now. She imagined his voice, surprise mixed with pleasure, laden with care and love for her. Just a few words from him would banish the exhaustion and tension that overwhelmed her.

I can't. He'll want to know why I'm calling if I can't stay over. He'll find something to make him worry and then I'll end up lying to him.

Mollie thrust the coins back into her pocket and turned away from the phones, fleeing temptation. She couldn't let anything or anyone distract her. Getting Copeland and Underwood to safety had been nerve-racking. There was only so much strength she had left in her. It had to be focused on the ultimate prize, the evidence Copeland and Underwood had told her about but had not dared bring to her. Had they purloined it, and had Esterhaus discovered it was missing, he would have known exactly who was responsible. Copeland's and Underwood's safety would have been jeopardized, perhaps fatally. It was left up to Mollie to retrieve what would ultimately hang the Honorable Judge Simon Esterhaus.

Had Mollie not been so tired, perhaps she would have noticed the man who slipped into the boarding line behind her. Had Rachel been there, maybe in the right light and angle her memory would have been nudged. But the Engineer knew he was perfectly safe. He'd seen Rachel get on the shuttle. Mollie was alone now, spent.

6

The Engineer had never really lost Mollie Smith; it was an amateur's move on the part of her informants that had thrown him off.

Assuming that she would go to Baltimore QRT as soon as she learned about the missing tape, he had planned to pick her up there. Instead he'd ended up having to follow both army women to Alexandria, then shadow the taxi Mollie took back to Fort Belvoir. He'd reasonably expected that she would next run to her informants. That would be the professional, textbook move, and the Engineer had prepared for it. He would simply hang back and let Mollie lead him to them. Later he would decide how best to eliminate them.

But that hadn't happened, either. Mollie headed for the airport, not stopping along the way to pick anyone up. Which meant that the informants were already there, or . . .

Something had gone very wrong. The Engineer saw it on Mollie's expression when he drove by her at National's passenger loading zone. The informants must have panicked and bolted, coming to the airport by themselves instead of waiting for their escort. The travel arrangements would have been made long ago, the informants prepped, equipped with tickets, money, secondary IDs, whatever else they needed. Finally he realized his mistake: Under the circumstances Mollie would not go near the informants. She would know better than to offer herself up as a stalking horse.

The Engineer dismissed the idea of trying to cull the informants from the airport crowds. He had no descriptions, not even gender identifications. His only course was to stay with Mollie.

That he did, and in due course he was given a small reward. He spotted young Warrant Officer Collins, second grade. The Engineer recognized and silently appreciated her long gun position. He focused on her, hoping her inexperience might cause her to do something that would reveal Mollie's intentions. But Rachel never gave up a thing. She simply walked down the jetway and boarded the plane.

Confirmation that Mollie too was on board was easy enough. The Engineer waited until he saw the tractor tow the jet back from the gate, then he rushed to the flight attendant who was counting up the flight coupons. A breathless reference to his sister, Mollie Smith, an earnest, somewhat panicked piece of bullshit about a forgotten prescription, and here was the flight attendant explaining how Ms. Smith was traveling all the way to Los Angeles on 1410, which, after Phoenix, became 1066.

The Engineer thanked her and walked swiftly from the terminal to the offices of the air charter companies. Thirty minutes later, at time and a half rates because of the short notice, he was boarding a Gulfstream III executive jet. The company rep and the pilot, both of whom thought the Engineer was a Hollywood exec, assured him that he would be in Los Angeles before midnight.

The Engineer thanked them, helped himself to a fine brandy after takeoff, and promptly drifted off to sleep.

· · ·

That sleep rest had proved invaluable. The Engineer, now flying back to D.C. in the first-class cabin, was reading Bulgakov's *The Master and Margarita*. He wondered, once, how Mollie Smith was faring in coach.

The plane landed in Washington at 6:05 A.M. on a bleak, rain-driven morning. The Engineer strolled with the crowds to the overhang, where passengers waited for the various shuttles. He knew that yesterday Mollie had come by taxi, but Rachel had parked an army sedan in the restricted lot. He'd made a bet with himself that Mollie now had the keys to that vehicle.

He was right. The key ring was looped around the knuckle of her left index finger, two keys swinging lightly as she waited beneath the overhang. The Engineer knew that in good weather Mollie would have walked to the lot, and that's where he would have taken her. But because of the sleet, she'd wait for the private shuttle that went only there.

The van was coming, a dark green box cutting smoothly through the heavy traffic. The Engineer fell in behind Mollie as she stepped around the puddles as the driver opened the door, past the wet, resentful faces of taxpayers who'd seen the Restricted Lot Only sign blinking on the bus's directory.

"Pass . . . gotta have your pass, ma'am," the driver called out.

The Engineer saw that Mollie had hers out, ready.

"Okay, next."

The driver had already closed the doors. Between the smoked-out windows and the rain sluicing down the glass, the bus was a crypt.

"Mister, your pass?"

"Sorry. Here it is."

It came in the form of a Colt Woodsman .22 with a silencer. The hole it left in the driver's temple was smaller than a BB would make.

The sound was negligible, though the Engineer expected that someone like Mollie would recognize it. She did. But she was exhausted, her reaction time nowhere near as quick as it needed to be. The Engineer's fist caught her square on the jaw, shattering it, sending Mollie crashing against the steel luggage rack, unconscious.

The Engineer hoisted the dead driver out of his seat, slipped in behind the wheel, and carefully pulled out into traffic. He didn't stop until he had located the army sedan. There he took Mollie's keys, opened the trunk, and stuffed the driver's corpse inside.

Back in the bus, he bound Mollie's hands, then gagged and blindfolded her with the white adhesive he found in the shuttle's first-aid kit. He worked quickly but carefully, because he had miles to go and no plans to stop anywhere along the way.

On the other side of the continent, Rachel Collins was headed north on U.S. 101 in a rented Ford Mustang. She had driven this stretch between Southern and Northern California quite often before her duties had taken her east. She knew where and when CHPs set up their speed traps, so at one o'clock in the morning, the road empty, Rachel sang along at one hundred–plus miles an hour.

She made the 370-mile run to Carmel in just over four hours, her thoughts drifting along with the oldies radio station. Rachel was going home—or at least as much of a home as she'd ever known. Her emotions swirled, happiness and anticipation mixed with sadness and resentment, a sharp, potent cocktail.

Turning off the highway, Rachel headed through the highlands toward the Pacific, crossed the Coast Highway, and nosed the car along Carmel's dark, sloped streets.

A patrol car picked her up on Ocean Avenue, tagged behind until she reached Frazier. Rachel got out, saw the glow of a lit cigarette behind the cruiser's windshield. There were no lights on the cottage porch. She unlocked the door and searched the wall for the light switch. She came back outside, stood beneath the light, and waved to the cruiser as it swung by, gumball lights rolling silently to acknowledge her.

The house had belonged to her mother, who, after a decade of wandering from one artist colony to another, had come back to her Northern California roots. Two bedrooms were all she needed, one set up as a studio where she worked on her stained-glass creations. Rachel, in the army by then, had not been a part of this life. Letters between her and Penny Collins had been infrequent, visits rare. The one sure thing Rachel knew was that her mother considered her choice of an army career a betrayal, a siding with all that had gone into causing upheavals in her own life. What Rachel knew about her mother's life was gleaned from the expensive Ocean Avenue shops that displayed her work. She'd gone into one boutique, asked the saleswoman about the artist's work. Rachel was surprised and proud that "Penny C.," as her mother was known in the community, was much admired. Her work could be seen in most of the multimillion-dollar Pebble Beach homes, and she had commissions from collectors as far away as San Francisco.

She had also been surprised—and horrified—when she'd learned that Penny C. was in the last stages of cancer, a secret she almost took to her grave.

The cottage smelled a little musty. Rachel opened the damper in the Carmel-stone fireplace, stacked the kindling and logs, got them going. She washed up and from the bedroom dragged an antique down quilt. She settled deep in the L-shaped sofa and stared into the flames, fell asleep thinking she was still watching them, not realizing that now they were dancing in her dreams.

Mollie stirred, then woke in a cool, dark place. Not totally dark. In fact, as her eyes adjusted, she discovered she could see quite well. It was like looking through fog.

She took stock. She was on her back, on some kind of table with a thick foam pad.

A doctor's examination table?

Her arms were stretched down along her side, her legs spread, the backs of her knees flat against the pad. The pad felt moist under her skin.

It's vinyl or plastic, not real leather.

Her wrists and ankles were bound by corded rope, thick but soft. It gave a little, too, maybe an eighth of an inch.

Bungee rope?

She wasn't wearing shoes but felt the familiarity of her own clothes. As far as she could tell, she hadn't been molested or abused.

Except for the pain in her jaw. Her tongue cautiously explored the gumline, discovered three lower teeth were missing. Beneath them, the bone and cartilage throbbed unmercifully. That's when she blinked, remembered the fist coming at her, snapping her head back . . . and the horrible crunching sound.

A fist, but no face. It didn't matter. Mollie knew who had her: the messenger. The only question was, did he think she'd caught a glimpse of his face?

"The busdriver is dead."

Mollie hadn't meant to say this out loud. But she was glad to hear her voice, slightly raspy from a dry throat. What she didn't expect was this:

"Yes, he is."

She turned her head to the right, saw him sitting there in a comfortable armchair, a book in his lap. His face was covered by a brilliant silver-and-green mask, exquisitely painted, large enough to cover his eyes, nose, and cheekbones.

When he got up, Mollie saw that he was wearing a plain black turtleneck. There were no birthmarks or scars on his lower cheeks or jaw, no pale skin anywhere on his hands to indicate that he'd been wearing a watch or rings. Nothing she needed to remember, nothing she could use against him.

And he knew it. She could tell that from his tone—friendly, engagingly familiar, like a minister's at a church picnic.

"Good. You've had a look, realized there's nothing to see, really. So that's out of the way."

He paused. "In case you're wondering, the mask? It's Venetian. I don't suppose you've ever been to their carnival. It's quite something."

The Engineer rolled up a stainless-steel trolley covered with a white cloth. Mollie could just make out the syringes lined up next to the ampoules with their thick rubber stoppers.

The scent struck her, coming from underneath his turtleneck. It was the one she knew so well, craved. . . . But it was on the wrong man. Then the realization: the Senate hearing room, the same cologne in the hall . . .

"Mollie. You can call me Jim."

He held up her purse so that she could see it.

"You travel light for a lady who flew cross-country and back. But then, you weren't planning to stay anywhere along the way, were you?"

Mollie didn't want to think about the fact that he'd been stalking her all this time. She wasn't listening to what he was saying, but how. She was searching for a particular intonation, maybe a minuscule lisp or regional accent. But Jim's voice was as flat as Dick Clark's.

"Pretty much run-of-the-mill stuff in here," he was saying. "Except for this."

He held up a blue enamel pillbox, shook it so that Mollie could hear the tablets rattle. With his other hand he fanned the air with a brown manila folder Mollie recognized as a medical chart.

"According to your last physical, almost a year ago, you weren't on any medication at all. What's changed, Mollie?"

"Migraines," she said.

"Ah . . . A real bitch, those. The doc prescribe Cafergot?"

"Imitrex."

The Engineer considered that. "Yeah. I can see that, as long as you don't take it during the aura."

Mollie watched him turn the box over in his fingers. No doubt he'd examined the pills. There was no brand name stamped on them, only a pharmaceutical numeric code. If he'd had the time or inclination to check that, he knew she was lying.

The man who called himself Jim put the pillbox on the surgical tray, stuffed his hands deep into his pants pockets.

"Here's how it is, Mollie. I know about Dunn. I know about the informants. I even know about Warrant Officer Collins. Now Dunn is dead, which is good. But the informants are not, which is bad. You have to help me fix that. Names and locations would be fine places to start."

"Did you kill North? Was Dunn your inside man?"

The Engineer sighed. "Sorry. I should have mentioned this. We're going to have a one-way conversation—a question-and-answer session, if you will."

"After which you kill me."

"Not necessarily. You haven't seen my face. You know nothing about me or where we are. Naturally, I'd have to hold you here until my business was done. And if you were to lie to me, I'd come back and we'd have to start all—"

"Where are we?" Mollie cut in.

"If your abdominals are what they should be, you can raise yourself just enough to see that. Please, be my guest."

Mollie closed her eyes, willed away the pain that shot from her jaw into her skull, and pulled herself up as far as the ropes binding her wrists allowed.

Jim had turned away, and behind him she saw tall walls faced with white marble. Along the walls were racks holding wine bottles. Mollie thought there must be hundreds. Then her muscles betrayed her and she collapsed.

"Not bad," said the Engineer. "But you need to get in better shape if you're going to do fieldwork."

"A wine cellar," Mollie whispered.

"Over three thousand bottles all told. Perhaps I'll uncork one for you before I leave."

That made him laugh, and Mollie was relieved. She thought he might have noticed that she could see something else besides the racks and bottles. Like the corner of thick green plastic on the floor, a sheet or body bag . . . and the white, heavy-duty latex gloves lying on top of it.

That's when Mollie knew she was going to die. The only question now was how quickly. Jim had gone to the trouble of getting her medical file—

How?

—and there were drugs on the trolley . . .

"Maybe the Corton-Charlemagne."

"I beg your pardon?"

"You can open the Corton-Charlemagne."

The Engineer laughed. "Bravo! But only if you're very, *very* good."

He rolled up her left pants leg, gently twisted her knee to expose the underside. She watched him dab a swab with alcohol; it felt cold against her skin.

Death smiled at Mollie, whispered that she was in the capable hands of a professional. He knew that a needle puncture behind the knee almost always went undetected during an autopsy.

Now the syringe was in one hand, the ampoule in the other, held upside-down. Mollie saw the steel prick rubber, saw the plunger being pulled back.

"I don't have the time for psychological torture, and the physical kind produces dubious results," he was telling her. "So what we have here is my own special mix, a combination of amphetamines, a highly advanced form of sodium pentothal, and one or two other ingredients—the secret sauce, if you will."

When she heard that, Mollie went limp. Her mind floated above the searing pain in her jaw, above the sting as the needle pierced her, far beyond his words, which had no power to hurt her anymore.

Mollie thought back to Los Angeles, to the telephones at the airport, the man in the photograph. She felt the coins, hot in her hand, and wished so much that she had used them. Jingle-jangle . . . His voice on the other end . . . never hear it again.

Because the cocktail was in her bloodstream, roaring through her arteries like a tidal wave. Jim was speaking, his voice gentle, telling her not to cry. Two fat tears slid over her checks, and he leaned forward, Kleenex in his fingers, dabbing them gently.

He asked about the informants, mentioning Rachel by name. Mollie felt her mouth open, the words battering to get out. She bit down, tasted blood, noticed Jim draw back. She never saw the piece of her tongue, the size of a thumbnail, fly from her mouth.

Coughing now, seeing a spray of blood, swallowing what she couldn't eject. And the cocktail churning inside her, racing toward her heart, slamming into it, crushing it.

The last image Mollie caught before the black tide swept her away was the look of horror and incomprehension on his face. She thought she could hear herself laughing at him, believed she really was, as she cheated him and died.

The International School in Georgetown was built in 1938. Now, almost sixty years later, the Canadian ambassador had discovered that the school had never undergone asbestos removal. He had linked this oversight to his son's asthma and created a storm of controversy.

At the end of the last term the school was closed and the cleaning begun. The job was supposed to have been finished in time for the beginning of the fall session. But delays in getting the necessary materials and an unforeseen Teamsters strike threw off the schedule. Now one-third of the school, the east wing, remained out-of-bounds to students and faculty.

Out-of-bounds, but certainly not unexplored by one Sean Flynn, eight-year-old son of the Irish first secretary. Sean's mother lived in Belfast now, and Sean had seen more than a child ever should of gutted, ruined buildings. He also had friends who'd taught him the tricks of getting *into* those rat traps, how to find a weak spot in the chain-link fence or the plywood boarding the authorities favored.

Getting into the east wing had been no trouble for young Sean. American construction crews weren't as thorough as British army engineers, to whom an abandoned building was a potential bomb factory. So what used to be the science lab now looked to him like a set in an alien movie, the ceilings torn apart, great chunks of plaster and cement strewn across the floor, the walls smashed into lath-and-plaster skeletons. Sean could catch a quick smoke here and free his imagination to conjure up intergalactic species, all gooey and deadly silent, slithering out of this carcass of a room.

When the recess bell sounded, he dropped his cigarette to the floor and ground it out. Then he looked up and saw something out of place. The lab refrigerator, an antique left behind to be hauled away with the rest of the trash, had its door open. Just a little bit—but even that was wrong.

Sean had seen TV stories about kids playing hide-and-seek in abandoned refrigerators, the door closing in on them, no one hearing their pounding or their screams. Gross!

The fridge had had a thick chain rolled between the handles, fixed by a big Yale lock. Now the chain and lock were gone, and the door was ajar.

The lab was Sean's personal preserve. He hadn't told anyone

about it, had been very careful going in and out so no one would spot him. But someone *had* been in here. Construction crews?

He looked around carefully. Nothing else seemed out of place. Why would workmen be interested in the fridge?

Now he was.

Sean threaded his way past counters and desks. He was walking carefully, his head down, which was why he picked out the foot-prints in the dust on the floor. And promptly walked over them, destroying what had been distinctive sole patterns.

The first thing that struck him was the smell, like rotten eggs. He gagged, turned away to take a deep breath. Then he reached for the door and jerked it open. He was expecting resistance, but the door flew at him, sending him reeling against a counter. But it didn't swing back to close, because an arm got in the way.

Sean stood his ground for three seconds, paralyzed as first a shoulder and then a head slithered out of the fridge. When the rest of the body seemed to fly at him and land at his feet, his bowels loosened. Sean did a little jig as hot urine streamed down his legs. Then he remembered that he could run. And scream, too.

7

Thirty-seven minutes after Sean Flynn's ghoulish discovery, D.C. homicide had an ID on the body. One of the detectives scouring the scene had found a purse in a nearby Dumpster. The driver's license photo was a definite match.

The lieutenant in charge of the investigation then made the call that protocol dictated: to the duty officer at Army CID at Fort Belvoir. He knew that the case would now become multijurisdictional. His people and the CID detectives would be stumbling all over one another, but maybe—*maybe*—they could keep things civilized. A lot of that would depend on what the coroner had to say.

The lieutenant had no reason to think that the case would be of interest to anyone higher up the food chain.

• • •

The Fort Belvoir duty officer, Lt. Bill Jessup, logged in and taped the call from D.C. as a matter of course. Even before the homicide detective had finished talking, Jessup was hitting panic buttons to activate CID's standing investigative team of four. Thirty seconds later Major Kenneth Dawes was in Jessup's office. By way of explanation, Jessup played him the tape. Dawes listened to the whole of it before reaching for Jessup's phone to let his people know they'd be rolling pronto.

"Do you want me to alert Hollingsworth?" Jessup asked.

Dawes considered. "You'd better. A kid from the International School's involved. This kinda shit's manna for the media. Yeah, we'll need Hollingsworth."

"I get the feeling D.C. will want to run with this."

"They won't be the only ones. The kids who go to that school belong to diplomats and their crowd. The State Department'll be over this like bad breath. And that'll bring in the Bureau."

"What are you going to do?"

Dawes tapped a cigarette on a vintage Zippo, snapped it open, took a light.

"I'm going to bring her home," he said softly. "Where she belongs and where we can care for her." He paused. "Tell Hollingsworth that nobody's going to fuck with me while I do my duty."

Dr. Scott Karol, D.C.'s chief coroner, had once served as a battle surgeon. In Vietnam he'd seen wounded who had been held and tortured by the enemy. Looking down at Mollie Smith on a cleaned-up lab counter took him back to those times. Karol wished he could retreat to the morgue wagon, where he kept a flask of Maker's Mark in the glove compartment.

"How long has she been dead?"

Karol, a slim, erect man in his early sixties, blinked. Dawes, towering over him, thought the coroner looked like a molting stork.

"Not long. Five hours tops."

Dawes raised an eyebrow.

The coroner held up a porcelain pillbox and deftly undid the clasp. Inside were five pale blue pills.

"She had a heart murmur."

Dawes nodded. "Diagnosed last month. There was a separate medical file on it. That's why she was riding a desk."

"Whoever cut her knew what he was doing," Karol continued. He pointed to the nude corpse. "These are all incisions, not stab wounds. There is no passion here, only strict methodology. One needs privacy for this kind of thing. Your man had that."

He turned Mollie's right knee, then her left.

"Not many people know how deep the pain can be when you cut in this area. He did."

Dawes's face was expressionless, but Karol didn't miss the blood mottling his cheeks.

"I want to tell you this because it might help. She didn't suffer. I'm certain of that."

Dawes's large head snapped around. "She looks like that and you're telling me she didn't *suffer?*"

"It's just the way the blood coagulated around the wounds. The killer didn't know she had a weak heart. Imagine her terror, enough to send the pulse and pressure dangerously high. Then the anticipation of what would be done to her. She never felt him cut her. Her heart gave out before he even started."

Karol laid a hand on the big man's forearm. "Whatever it was he wanted from her, he never got it."

Dawes was in the corner of the lab, watching as the body was bagged for transport. He held a cell phone jammed against his left ear.

"Hollingsworth says you should call him if you run into interference," Jessup was saying. "He's ready to crack nuts over this."

"Everything's okay," Dawes told him. "We'll be outta here in a few minutes. Listen, I need to know what she was working on, and with whom. It looks like there was . . . . interrogation on her."

Dawes heard Jessup's whistled breath on the other end of the line. "You mean she was snatched and tortured." It was not a question.

"But she didn't live long enough to say anything," Dawes added. "So I gotta know what it was she had. What was the last case she was working on? Who was the warrant officer assigned to it?"

"Way ahead of you on that. Her number one water carrier is W.O. Collins, second grade. As to current assignments, zip. Her slate's clean."

"Doesn't wash."

"I didn't think so, either. We're going through her office and apartment right now, see if we can't walk back the cat."

"I'll want to speak with Collins."

"I'm sure," Jessup said dryly. "Thing is, she's disappeared off the map. Her landlord said she left yesterday, packed a duffel bag."

"Did she have leave coming?"

"Negative."

"Contact address or phone number?"

"We know she has a piece of property in Carmel, in California. I haven't tried calling, in case she *is* up there and you didn't want her tipped off."

"Anything on her record to indicate she's running?"

"Nope. But get this: She and Smith go a long way back, to MP School. Smith was her rabbi. They were very tight, even beneficiaries of each other's wills."

"Gay?"

"Not according to the polygraph flutters. Anyway, they dated about the same as everyone else."

Dawes returned to Jessup's previous words.

"The will thing. Smith was worth what—fifty thousand?"

"And Collins's California property is valued at almost half a million. I don't think this will lead anywhere."

"I'd like to talk to Collins and find out for myself."

"It's your call," Jessup told him. "But if I punch in that she's AWOL, she'll have every MP east of the Mississippi out looking for her. She'll never be able to erase that from her record, even if she could give us a good reason for having ankled."

"What're you saying?"

"You have the media vultures up there, right?"

"A turkey shoot's worth."

"I'd suggest you let them roll with the story. Give Collins until midnight to see it and call in. If we don't hear from her, she goes to the top of the Wanted dance card."

• • •

The Engineer was back at Wonderland Toys. His executive suite had a fine bathroom, the counter and shower stall lined with granite. After an invigorating steam shower, the Engineer padded into the enormous cedar-paneled closet and put on cream-colored slacks, a chocolate turtleneck, and a fine cashmere jacket.

Now, sitting at his console desk, he lit a cigarillo, then switched on one of the monitors and tuned in the noon news.

The Engineer had never met Major Kenneth Dawes, identified as such by an angry anchorwoman. She had thrust a microphone into his face, and Dawes, moving like a linebacker, had used his shoulder on her, bumping her hard while making it look as if she'd run into him.

The Engineer knew the type. He'd expected a Dawes to pop up as soon as Mollie's body was discovered. At that point the Engineer had still been on the grounds of Fort Belvoir. The news flash about the grisly discovery at the International School had come on the all-news radio station as he was driving off post. The Engineer had been pleased by the synchronicity of timing and by what he'd gleaned from his search of Mollie's cottage.

The fort housing was bare-bones: simple A-frames for bachelor officers, four-story brick apartment complexes for those with families. The Engineer had arrived on post on a motorcycle. There were no formal guard houses where he had to show any ID. In fact, a public bus line ran through parts of the post.

So he'd made himself look crisp enough in civvies to pass muster in case anyone got nosy, wore a battered sheepskin jacket littered with air force patches. The jacket went very well with the bike, announcing the rider as a hot fighter driver.

Army locks being what they were, getting into Mollie's home had been easy enough. That she'd been a neat woman, who didn't keep banal memorabilia, helped. The Engineer had found her cache just where he'd expected to: in an iron lockbox in the crawl space under the kitchen.

It contained the usual assortment of letters, photos curling with age, a birth certificate, a will—and the notes the Engineer had come looking for.

He knew he was damn lucky about those notes. Today everything was stored in computers. But Mollie hadn't been a child of the cyberage. The Engineer reckoned she'd been computer literate enough to get by in her job and no more. Plus, she would not have wanted this kind of information cruising around on a Pentium chip where any hacker worth his salt could pluck it out of the ether. So here were the handwritten records of Mollie's search for North's killer.

As he'd gone through the contents of the lockbox, certain other considerations had suggested themselves. After that he had worked back to the notes, turned over the possibility that Mollie had made a copy of them.

Of course she had. And she would have kept them in another secure place—a safe deposit box at Riggs National, according to the key he'd found.

That was fine with the Engineer. He *wanted* that copy to be found, by the only person who would, in due course, be given access to the box.

He had replaced the iron box in the crawl space, checked to make sure everything was exactly as it had been, and left.

The Engineer rolled a half inch of cigar ash into a cut-crystal ashtray and turned off the monitor. The army's investigation of Major Smith's murder would proceed by the numbers, every one of which he knew. That D.C. homicide would run a parallel effort would muddy the waters further. Neither jurisdiction would come anywhere near the two witnesses because they weren't even aware of their existence.

But the Engineer had to admit the effectiveness of Mollie's charade. How clever of her to have had the name of the drug of choice for migraines on the tip of her tongue. How foolish of him not to have checked the pills more carefully. It would have been so easy to run a compound screen on them or simply check the *PDR* for the numeric designation stamped on the pills.

The Engineer was sure that Mollie had gone to her grave believing that she truly had cheated him of the information he wanted. In reality, all she'd done was made him go out to Fort Belvoir and pry open her secrets.

The Engineer drew once more on the cigarillo and opened the

file. Here was Steven Copeland, referred to hereafter as Mr. X, and his counterpart, the Junoesque Beth Underwood, Miss Y. The Engineer recalled their names. His employer had mentioned them when the Engineer had taken the assignment and had asked who the most likely suspects could be. The names had come up briefly, then been dismissed. The Engineer had had to take his employer's word that they were irrelevant. Later, that had proved a grave mistake, but such knowledge had come too late to change anything. Mollie had plucked her informants from his reach.

The Engineer read through Mollie's notes, silently saluted her on how cleverly she had spun the truth from the straw of conjecture, insight, and vague hints. Maybe too cleverly. . . . Reading back the words, the Engineer wondered how much of what she knew she'd *never* committed to paper. The nub of the matter, the whereabouts and aliases of Copeland and Underwood, was not included in the notes.

How prudent of you, Mollie.

There was a way around that, too. It would take a little longer, cause the Engineer's employer to squirm a bit. In the end, though, the results would be just as good.

Through a curl of smoke the Engineer reached for a phone and once more availed himself of Dr. Weisberg's calling card number.

When news of Major Mollie Smith's death was being sprayed across the media, Beth Underwood was fast asleep near Carefree, Arizona.

In Carmel, Rachel Collins shifted uneasily beneath the quilt, burrowing deeper into the soft contours of the sofa. The light from a dying fire bathed her face in a perfect golden glow, as though trying to brush away the dark images that pecked at her dreams.

Only Steven Copeland, in Atlanta, already up and showered, could have caught the midmorning newscasts. But he'd already left the hotel, accompanied by a real estate agent who had booked a half day to show him what the market had to offer.

8

The Israeli prime minister was in the reception room, fidgeting in the treacly company of the First Lady.

In the Oval Office, the Speaker of the House was on the conference line, ranting on about shutting down the government payroll unless an amendment in farm subsidies made its way into the budget bill. The president, seated at his desk, listened to the Speaker with one ear. His laserlike concentration was focused on the half dozen typed pages before him.

When he finished reading, he stared at Simon Esterhaus, then leaned forward, his finger poised over the kill button on the speakerphone.

"Frank, I've made notes on everything you said," he lied smoothly. "But I have a call coming in from Moscow. Thirty minutes." The president hit the button.

He looked back at the judge. "Killing me softly, that bastard."

"I'm sorry, Mr. President. But I thought you should know right away."

"Question is, does anyone *else* know?" The president tapped the pages. "What's the circulation on this?"

"These are the originals. Major Smith would have made a copy, if only to be prudent. But it's not in her computer at work, nowhere in her house."

"Bank vault?"

"Her safe deposit box is being drilled right now. We'll know within the hour."

"You went into her box?"

"The notes indicate a matter of national security. I signed the warrant myself."

"Moving fast, Simon."

"With due dispatch, sir. If, for any reason, any of this becomes public knowledge, we would be able to prove conclusively that there was no delay in acting on Major Smith's suspicions."

The president ran a large, knobby hand over his hair. Sixty-two and he still had a full mane to go with his Lincolnesque appearance.

"Due dispatch . . . Jesus, Simon. She's handed us the goddamn plague!"

"We don't know that, sir. Not for sure."

Esterhaus seldom raised his voice. He was one of those rare men who, without benefit of physical stature or good looks, commanded attention in any room he entered. His clothing was exquisitely cut, but that was just packaging. At fifty-five he was very fit and could easily have passed for a man ten years younger. But the secret of his powers lay elsewhere, perhaps in the deep blue, almost violet eyes that seemed never to blink. Or in the intense calm that surrounded him, as if he carried some sort of invisible protection that made him invulnerable. And therefore respected. And feared.

The president, son of a Louisiana shrimper, was one of the few who appreciated Esterhaus's powers but did not succumb to them. He wanted those powers at work on the Supreme Court, which in his opinion had lately become rudderless and given to bickering.

Esterhaus would put some starch into it, give it the leadership it needed.

"What we *do* know for sure is that Mollie Smith was murdered," the president said. "By a person or persons as yet unknown. Question is, did she send you the stuff *because* she feared for her life? And if so, why you?"

Esterhaus crossed his legs casually. "Sir, I never met Major Smith. I never even heard her name before this morning when this"—he tapped the white legal-size envelope—"was delivered to my office."

"By whom?"

"My secretary says a messenger. No signature was required, but she remembered the courier company. My investigators tracked down the office where the package was handed over for delivery. It was in Alexandria. The clerk there said a woman brought it in, paid cash. He was shown a photo of Major Smith but couldn't make a positive ID.

"I have to believe, Mr. President, that I was chosen as recipient because Major Smith knew that I chaired the inquiry into General North's death."

"And now she's dead," the president said flatly. "Without leaving any hint that she was being threatened or pursued. . . . A little too pat, don't you think? A woman sends you the details of a private investigation, then winds up dead the day you receive it?"

"I agree, sir. Mollie Smith was *not* the victim of a random killing. However, as callous as I know this sounds, it's just as well that the media will continue to play up that angle."

"Only because they don't know any better. The minute we launch a full investigation, they'll come snooping."

"Not necessarily. There are alternatives."

"We'll get to them. What I don't understand is, why does she talk about informants without mentioning names—if she really was afraid and wanted you to have those records?"

"Major Smith was a decorated soldier and seasoned CID investigator. She would not, I think, have been one to run from shadows. Maybe she didn't perceive the entire threat; maybe she underestimated it."

Esterhaus paused. "Maybe she just didn't have the time or opportunity to add those last crucial details. Getting the package to me safely could well have been her final act."

"Do we make a leap here, Simon? Do we now say that Smith's two informants are targets themselves? And don't even know it?"

"Not such a great leap, sir."

The president pushed himself away from his desk. It was an abrupt gesture, but Esterhaus didn't stir. He watched the chief executive pace in front of those tall, armor-hardened windows. In the afternoon sun he caught pinpoint reflections along Pennsylvania Avenue, the lenses of expensive cameras pointed at the people's house, where the people were no longer quite so welcome.

"This gets out, Simon, some folks are going to take me out to the woodshed," the president said, lapsing into the backcountry slang. "When Griffin North died, the black people in this country wept buckets, even the ones who thought North had crossed over, lived the white life. The blacks embraced him, made him larger than he ever was." He paused. "Easy enough to do. The dead don't have to live up to ideals; they can never disappoint. Just look at Kennedy.

"And now, after North's mourning is done, and your commission has ruled it death by accident, Major Smith says it wasn't like that at all. She claims North was murdered by conspirators—but she doesn't name them. That your commission didn't have all the evidence—but she does. That she has informants—but you never heard about them."

The president draped his long arms over the back of his chair. "You know what I see here? A conflagration that'll sweep the country. Blacks aren't talking integration anymore—they're listening to the voices of *separation*. The kids are going to prisons in droves. There's no Martin Luther King out there to reason with them. North was the hope they *could* have had. So if they find out that someone plotted to kill him—and succeeded—I don't think they'll bother waiting for us to bring in any suspects. Any white target will do. Because sure as shit, a *black* man couldn't have done this."

"Allow a naive question, Mr. President."

"From you? I'd be shocked."

"Do you really believe that a white man, or men, would have considered all the variables and *still* gone with the decision to murder North? He was a Rockefeller Republican, not some East Coast liberal. His politics, such as he enunciated them, were pragmatic. Certainly they were no threat to the bedrock status quo."

The president smiled tightly. "If you have one weakness, Simon, it is this: You give all men the benefit of the doubt that they are as reasonable as you are. They're not.

"If there was a conspiracy to kill North, then it was organized and paid for by very powerful interests. *Why* they were afraid of him is something we won't know until we sit them down and ask. But think: The list of suspects is, of necessity, short."

"Why is that?"

"Because they managed to get by you, Simon. You signed off on the entire investigation. How many people do *you* know who could pull the wool over your eyes, hmmm? And don't worry about sounding arrogant."

Esterhaus pinched the bridge of his nose. "Not many."

"Which means that if Smith isn't blowing smoke—and her murder makes me think she's not—we have dark monsters lurking out there!"

Esterhaus did not respond to this uncharacteristic outburst. He was searching for its source. There was something more in play, something the president had been holding back. He coaxed it out by remaining silent.

The president was staring out the windows again.

"The vice president has been taking a lot of heat for his involvement with that failed savings and loan," he said finally. "I was going to ask Pete to step aside so that Griffin would come on the ticket as VP. He and I sat in this office, talking about all the good that could come out of our teaming up. People would have said I made the cynical choice: pushed out a liability in favor of a solid-gold asset. Sure, I would have gotten four more years. But Griffin would have gained the experience he needed. After that he would have had his own administration."

The president seemed mesmerized by the winking light on the telephone console. Esterhaus guessed it was the protocol officer who was helping to baby-sit the Israeli prime minister.

And now came the remnants of the president's confession:

"I loved him, Simon. Beyond the respect and admiration, I thought he was one of the best men I'd ever met. In ways, better than me."

The president sat behind his desk, fixed Esterhaus with a look that bordered on a glare.

"So I want to know if there's any truth to Major Smith's allegations. If she was murdered because she'd found out too much. You run the investigation, Simon. Cloak it any way you want. If people ask why you're still poking into North, tell them you've become fascinated by him. Hell, tell 'em you're doing a biography. Now, I want to hear about the alternatives you mentioned."

Esterhaus regarded the president carefully, standing there with his grief exposed, raw like a deep, fresh cut. "What I have in mind centers on our ability to control the investigation," he said smoothly. "I have to say this right now, sir. I was the one who sealed the commission's inquiry. If I were to find new evidence, then I would reconvene the commission, subject, of course, to whatever charges may or may be not be laid against alleged conspirators. In so doing, I would accept all blame for having overlooked this evidence, and I would ask that my nomination to the Supreme Court be withdrawn."

"No need to put your head on the chopping block for me," the president said. "It's not like there's a cover-up going on. You're not guilty of oversight or any other damn thing. I wouldn't accept your request."

"Thank you, Mr. President." Esterhaus touched his top lip with the tip of his tongue. "Then what I propose is, call in the head of the FBI's Domestic Terrorism Unit. I would share with him everything we have. He would be sworn to silence and report only to me." Esterhaus paused. "One man, complete security, two recipients of his information: you and me. That's about as watertight as we can make it, sir."

"Sounds good. But why this particular guy?"

When Esterhaus explained, the president shook his head and said, "That's pretty ballsy, Simon. You sure he won't go loose cannon on you?"

"Absolutely. Besides professional duty, he has the best reason in the world to see this through. Finding the killer will mean finding the truth behind Major Smith's murder. That's all he wants or needs. Whether a conspiracy was behind it or it was simply a random act of violence—that would be a moot point for him. Although certainly not for us."

"Do it," the president said abruptly. "When you've briefed him, bring him in. I'll give him his marching orders personally."

"Under the circumstances, Mr. President, yours are the only orders he'd accept."

On his way out Esterhaus caught a glimpse of the Israeli prime minister eagerly pumping the president's hand. Esterhaus walked down the corridor, past the phalanx of Secret Service agents, and into the vestibule, where an usher caught his nod and hurried out to summon his car.

While he waited beneath the portico, the judge fought the nausea churning in his stomach. Presenting the commission report should have been his final act in a long, ugly role. But fate had dealt him a dirty hand, forced him back into the game. All the terror he had lived through swept over him like bile.

Esterhaus shivered. *You still have control,* he told himself. *That in itself is a miracle.*

Esterhaus knew that the selected bits of information he'd presented had affected the president like some dark aphrodisiac. The irony, worthy of the Borgias, both sickened and fascinated the judge: A conspirator was being handed the reins to conduct an investigation into a murder he himself had helped to orchestrate.

Invitations to Pamela Esterhaus's table were highly coveted. The fare was uniformly excellent and imaginative, the company scintillating, the ambience tinged with the intrigue of insiders' gossip.

Tonight's guests included the ambassador to the United Nations, a nationally syndicated commentator, the CEO of a major car company, and the playwright of Broadway's current hottest ticket. Pamela Esterhaus looked across her table, set for twelve, took in the brilliant gleam of heavy silver, the flawless but unobtrusive help, the gently swirling conversation punctuated by laughter, and saw that it was all good.

"Pamela, where *is* Simon? You promised he'd be here."

The CEO was Dwayne Garrett, a diminutive man who, Pamela knew, had the executive chair in his office set on a dais so that visitors would not look down at him. She was also aware that Garrett's company had several cases backed up on Simon Esterhaus's docket, cases that would be assigned to others. It would be advantageous for Garrett to know in advance the names of those judges.

Pamela decided to make that point clear. "I suppose he's still tied up with the president, Dwayne, talking about who'll replace him on the bench. He'll be along soon. Even the president has to eat."

"Yeah. But I'm not so sure about Simon."

Laughter rippled around the table, ebbed when it reach the ambassador, Lenore Kahn.

"Are you still attending the reunion, Pam?" she asked. "Or is Simon's confirmation going to create a conflict?"

"I'll be there," Pamela said firmly. "I'm trying to talk Simon into coming."

"I thought men weren't welcome at Wellesley," the commentator piped up.

"Men certainly are welcome, Arthur," Kahn fired back. "Neanderthals are another matter."

Another round of liberal-conservative jousting began. Pamela had long ago mastered the art of carrying on a conversation while thinking about other, completely unrelated matters. She felt self-indulgent at the moment and luxuriated in the warm sensation. It was good to be surrounded by one's own people. Some were friends from as far back as college; others had been carefully chosen and cultivated over the years. All had been blessed by fortune, and all understood the two most important—and unspoken—laws of their rank: (1) Extend a helping hand only when you were sure it wouldn't drag you into its owner's troubles; and (2) If you had to do someone so as to save yourself, strike hard, deep, and unerringly.

Daughter of a former long-standing cabinet official, Pamela

Esterhaus had imbibed these and other lessons along with mother's milk. She had reaped the rewards of strict adherence to them and had observed, but never mourned, the demise of those who had strayed. The world, her papa used to say, was ultimately ruled by one factor: consequences. Pamela Esterhaus had made that her guiding principle and was both curious and disappointed that the men in her life, no matter how clever, successful, or even brilliant, seemed unable to grasp it. Which, of course, was the reason she had been able to use them so easily. Until she had met that one special man. . . .

She sensed a presence beside her and the smell of mild cologne. She leaned back and tilted her head so that the butler could whisper in her ear.

"Your husband's arrived, ma'am."

Pamela rose and excused herself. She reached the foyer in time to see her husband closing the door behind him. She took in how his shoulders slumped, the slight tic over his left eye. She knew exactly what he needed, and she would provide it.

"Darling. . . ."

She didn't kiss him on the mouth, hadn't done that in years. His cheek felt like coarse leather on her lips.

"How did it go with the president?"

She watched him wet his lips, a schoolboy searching for the nerve to 'fess up.

"Everything will be all right," she heard him whisper. "There will be an investigation, but the president has put me in charge of it. No one will be hurt. I promise."

"That's wonderful!" she breathed. "Now come with me."

She took his arm and ignored how he dragged his feet. She knew he wanted to go upstairs and pick at his fear and misery like some leper. She would have none of it.

"My friends, I give you the next justice of the Supreme Court!"

Her voice rang out and the guests rose as one, applauding. She led him to the empty chair at the head of the table and, while he looked and smiled, went to the sideboard. She prepared the drink herself, a large whiskey, no ice. A few ounces would settle him. Any more would only invite the demons.

9

Lucille Parker took a hard right into the motor court of the Dorchester condominium tower on Wilshire Boulevard. The government sedan swayed on its worn shocks as she braked, listed to the left as she got out.

Parker, age fifty-seven, was a thirty-two-year veteran of the FBI. Her experience put most of the agents in the L.A. field office to shame. All of them were thankful that she wasn't an agent or a supervisor; they couldn't possibly have kept up with her.

In the late 1950s and early 1960s the Bureau had no agent-training program for women—let alone black women. Lucille Parker was lucky to have been hired as a secretary. The rest she'd accomplished on her own dime, studying for civil service exams at night, using smarts, grit, and determination to buck her way out of the typing pool, grasping the first rung of the administrative ladder, and never looking back as she climbed.

By the time she met Logan Smith, Lucille had put in time in virtually every Bureau department and was the director's executive assistant. Recognizing that her skills and experience were vastly underused, Smith petitioned the director to create a new post: a Domestic Terrorism Liaison Officer who would coordinate the Unit's field activities, help process and evaluate data, and prioritize assignments—the brain and nerve center of the unit.

The director had wholeheartedly endorsed Smith's proposal. He was far less enthusiastic the day he discovered Smith had purloined Lucille from his office and had given her the new post.

The Dorchester was a full-service building. Lucille knew all the valets by name and asked the one on duty to leave her car out front. She barreled past the concierge, flapping a silent greeting. Lucille was the only visitor to the building who was never announced first.

As the elevator rose to the eighth floor, she ran through the checklist in her mind. Everything was ready, set to roll. She'd even scheduled a little extra time for Logan, knowing he would need it. He'd come in from Idaho earlier that morning. For three weeks he'd been tracking John Michael Wright, a white supremacist militia leader who'd been planning to blow up the Liberty Bell. Wright claimed that the bell was no longer a symbol of a country in which liberty thrived. He would blow it up to signal the coming of the apocalyptic revolution. Wright would have been written off as just another wacko but for the fact that he had hijacked an army truck carrying explosives, killed two soldiers, and disappeared into the Idaho wilderness.

The hunt was a month old before Logan and the Bureau outfit he commanded, the Domestic Terrorism Unit, were brought in. Because Logan had spent years in the Northwest, he took up the hunt himself. For the last week he'd been incommunicado. Even Parker, who thought her boss indestructible, had started to worry. Then a message was picked up on the broad band: Wright had been cornered in a desolate gorge, taken alive. Would someone please send the helicopter?

Lucille glanced at her watch as she hurried down the corridor. Logan would be working on three hours' sleep. She felt inside her jacket pocket for the small envelope of pharmaceutical dexedrine.

Lucille reached the end unit and rang the bell twice, heard a soft chime. It was nowhere near enough to wake him, so she used her key.

The foyer hall stretched past the kitchen and dining room and into a living room with dead-on views of Century City. Lucille had been here so often that she didn't stop to gaze at it anymore. She went directly into the master bedroom, all dark with the plantation-style shutters closed.

"This had better be good."

The voice from the bed sounded like a frog with laryngitis.

"Is that a lump in the bedding, or do you have a gun pointed at me?"

"It's not bedding."

The shape under the cover shifted. The light blanket was thrown back. Lucille saw the tall, long form of her boss, clad only in boxers. The light coming through the door glanced off the barrel of the Sig-Sauer in his hand.

"Good morning, Lucille."

"Good morning, Logan. You'd best be getting into the shower."

When he didn't move she added, "You're not showing me anything I haven't seen, so come on now."

Logan rolled out of bed. In the stillness of the room, the click of the gun's safety sounded loud. Standing, he stretched, then shook his head like a dog after a bath.

"How bad is it this time?"

"Shower first," Lucille insisted.

In the kitchen she microwaved a cup of water to make tea. She wished for some orange juice—anything with a lot of sugar to give him a boost—but the fridge was empty, spotless.

When Logan reappeared he was dressed in Dockers, a T-shirt, a denim jacket, and a pair of new Nikes. Lucille thought he could fly all right in that. The remainder of sleep, a wayward lock of sandy hair falling across his forehead, made him look younger than his forty-one years. He had lost a few pounds during the hunt for Wright, and his face and forearms carried a deep-woods tan. His eyes were as alert as ever; Parker felt them probing hers. This was Logan's specialty: trying to pick up the scent, start the hunt.

She'd cooled the tea with an ice cube, gave it to him with a horse-dose multivitamin. He washed it down, never taking his eyes off her.

Lucille took the cup back from him and in an infinitely tender gesture grasped his hands in hers. Only then, tightening her hold, did she dare to say it. "It's Mollie. She's dead, Logan."

She felt him stiffen, held on to his hands, heard the strangled growl clawing up his throat. She led him to the living room, sat him down on the leather sofa.

"You need to read this," she said, handing him a file.

She busied herself with the VCR, looking over her shoulder to make sure he was doing what she'd told him. Then she slipped in the cassette and turned on the TV.

The next time she looked at Logan he was stone still, his face shining with tears, fresh ones gliding into the tracks made by ones that had dried. His eyes glittered like stars exploding in some deep galaxy.

"Play it," he said.

It was the D.C. homicide video, taped at the International School. Some in the office had argued, out of misplaced compassion, that Logan should get the edited version. Lucille knew Logan better than that. He would spot the editing immediately and be all over her for it. He would demand the real footage because maybe, just maybe, he would catch something that had slipped by everyone else.

Logan watched the video, asked to see it a second time. He sat through that, then began to shake his head, whispering, "Oh, Mollie, Mollie . . ."

Lucille knew she had to move him along.

"United's got a nonstop to D.C. We can just make it. You don't need anything. I've made arrangements on the other end for pickup, clothes you'll need—"

"Clothes for what?"

"You're going straight to the White House."

"Why?"

"Something Mollie was working on, the way she was killed, has them all stirred up. I'll tell you in the car."

Logan stood up and immediately felt the room sway. He breathed deeply through his mouth, steadied himself. Something made of paper was being pressed into his hand.

As he looked down at the small envelope, felt the ridges made by the pills inside, he heard Lucille whisper, "I'm sorry, Logan, so very sorry. . . ."

Then she followed his gaze, walked to the bookshelf, and picked up the silver-framed photograph of Mollie, splendid in parade dress against an ocean backdrop. The inscription read "For my little brother, who always watches over me. Love, Mollie."

Lucille pulled in the easel-back stand and gently laid the frame facedown.

Rachel woke up at one o'clock in the afternoon, Pacific time. Stiff from sleep, stiff from the drive, she tottered like an old woman into the master bathroom. The hot water kneaded the muscles at the base of her neck and along her shoulders, drummed a tattoo up and down her back. When she came out, enveloped in mist, she was ravenous.

Rachel was lucky: She got to eat half her Denver omelet and home fries before she read the news.

The Cat 'n' Cradle coffee shop on Ocean Avenue was a ten-minute walk in the bracing air. The lunch rush was about over. Rachel slid into a booth, ordered her breakfast, then looked out the window. Still a lot of tourists around, she noticed.

The coffee came first, then the omelet, and for the next fifteen minutes she concentrated on the food. When her napkin slipped off her lap and she leaned down to pick it up, she saw a copy of the *San Francisco Chronicle* someone had left behind.

The story about the murdered female army officer was at the bottom left corner of page one. Rachel's eyes froze on the small photo of Mollie; it was the official one the army press office kept on file.

Rachel had to read the headline twice: ARMY MAJOR SLAIN IN D.C. Below that: "Police Have No Clues or Motive for Killing."

She laid the paper beside her and very carefully pushed her food away. She used her napkin to make sure the vinyl tablecloth was perfectly dry, then placed the newspaper on top of it.

"You all done, honey?"

The waitress stood over her, a pot of coffee in one hand.

"Yes, thanks," Rachel managed. "Where's the washroom?"

"Straight down, left, second door."

Rachel made it just in time. Afterward she staggered to the sink and leaned on the ice-cold porcelain. As her breathing slowed, she splashed cold water onto her face.

Mollie's dead. Mollie's dead. Mollie's dead.

The litany rolled through her mind like the musical drum of a player piano. Rachel snatched a handful of towels from the dispenser, mashed them against her face. When she looked up, in the mirror was a woman she'd never seen before.

The image of a leather jacket with a Redskins emblem crossed her mind. Rachel's hand dropped to her left rib cage.

My gun.

She'd hidden it in a drawer back at the house.

You don't need it! It's okay. He's not out there waiting for you. . . .

Rachel was sure of that. The messenger would have taken Mollie, what, twelve hours ago? He couldn't have made it all the way out here so quickly.

The waitress looked at her oddly as she walked back to her table, tossed some crumpled bills next to her coffee cup, picked up the newspaper, and fled. Seven minutes later, out of breath, she was throwing the double locks, sliding the security chain into place.

Sweaters were strewn across the floor, the drawer lying upside-down on top of them. The Bulldog was in her grip, the speed loader feeding the polymer rounds into the chamber. The gun, heavy in her hands, felt good.

Rachel returned to the living room, switched on two lamps, and drew all the curtains. Only then did she sit down and force her eyes to the newsprint.

She read the short piece through a half dozen times. It told her everything. It told her nothing.

Rachel stared at the telephone. According to protocol, she had

to call in. By now the standing investigative team at Fort Belvoir
had likely tagged her as the last person to see Mollie alive.

Except for the killer.

The piece in the *Chronicle* was full of "no comment's," which
meant that Fort Belvoir had no idea who the killer was. Another
reason for them to find W.O. Collins, second grade.

*If I call in, what do I tell them? That Mollie must have had notes
about North?*

Suddenly she remembered Mollie's words: *I didn't think there was
any military connection to . . . to what happened to North. Now I'm not
sure. I don't know how high this goes, who else is involved.*

Rachel gripped her head with both hands and dug her fingernails into her scalp.

". . . how high this goes . . ."

With those few words Mollie had cut off the single avenue of
help Rachel had left. Now she *couldn't* go to the investigation unit.
Nor could she return to the fort, because Mollie had thought that
Belvoir might have become a poisoned well.

Okay . . . what does that leave me with?

Rachel felt a long, slow shudder work through her. She recognized what was happening: in times of crisis, the analytical part of
her took over, pushing out all the emotion that could get in her
way, could be lethal to her.

Maybe not quite all of it. Because now Rachel's thoughts tore
down a different corridor, one filled with the hard, brilliant light
of understanding that she was not the only one who had suddenly
been orphaned. Somewhere out there were two innocent, fumbling, terrified people whose only contact with the world had
been severed.

*Did you tell him who they are, Mollie? Sweet Jesus, did he take that
from you, too?*

Rachel recalled the faces of Copeland and Underwood, the
arrogance of one and the resignation of the other lying like a sheen
over the common foundation of fear. If the messenger had kept
Mollie long enough to break her, then he was already on his way
to Atlanta or Phoenix.

You can't think like that, kiddo.

The "kiddo" had leaped into her mind, just like that. It was what her father had called her, even after she was old enough to be embarrassed by it.

Her father, rolling in from the officers club in the middle of the night. Rachel, twelve years old, getting out of bed and running downstairs as soon as she heard him coming up the front steps, opening the door before he started pounding on it. Rachel had lost count of the times she'd helped him inside, almost collapsing because he always leaned on her, guiding him to the sofa, ignoring the stench of alcohol, turning away when he reached to kiss her, whisper his teary thanks. . . .

Kiddo . . . The kiddo has to do something. Right this minute.

That's when Rachel remembered Mollie's heart problem and bowed her head. If the messenger had touched her, beat her, she would have died before saying a word. Rachel knew that for a fact. So it followed that maybe, because of Mollie's condition, the messenger had gotten nothing to work with.

Copeland and Underwood are still safe. Until they hear about Mollie on the news and go off the deep end, attract all sorts of attention. If they haven't already.

But I can beat his ass to them! I can do that . . . if he has nothing to work with.

Rachel veered back to the analytical, to where there was hope. Mollie would have had notes about North. Where would she have kept them?

Not the computer. Where else? The lockbox in the crawl space? No—too hard to get to if she had to move fast. A bank safe deposit box? Too obvious.

Rachel stopped there for a moment. All those places were ones the investigative team would check.

Back to Mollie now, reaching the painful part, trying to think like her best friend. Woman to woman . . . The investigative team wouldn't have a woman, and that would be their biggest disadvantage. Men could not interpret the subtleties and nuances of a woman's life. They would paw at her secrets the way they went through drawers and closets. They overlooked the seemingly insignificant while concentrating on the obvious.

Rachel had plumbed most of Mollie's secrets, even those that Mollie had never suspected Rachel was aware of.

You made notes. You're thorough and methodical, so you'd have done that. And you would keep them far away from the obvious places, but equally far from those secrets you knew others were aware of.

Question: What's the one secret you thought nobody knew?

Rachel went over to the bookcase next to the fireplace and took out a hardcover biography, checked the index, and flipped to the page she wanted.

General Griffin North's biographer had spent only one paragraph on the man's marital status, because North had been a bachelor right up to the time of his death. But he was no monk; in the Washington gossip columns his name had been linked to some prominent socialites, both white and African American. There were pictures of North at state dinners and embassy parties, always next to some gowned, bejeweled woman.

But never Mollie.

Mollie, who had been North's lover for at least five years. Maybe more, but that's when Rachel had stumbled on to the secret. She had given Mollie the keys to the Carmel house one Thanksgiving, Mollie having said she wanted to get away. Then Rachel had canceled her own holiday plans and gone up to Carmel. There, on a fog-shrouded morning, as she'd been pulling into the street, she'd seen General North, dressed in a bathrobe, step onto the porch and pick up the morning paper.

Rachel had never said a word about what she'd seen. To anyone. Ever. Even when she'd seen Mollie hurting and wanted to comfort her.

This, then, was the repository where Mollie would lay all other secrets. She and North must have kept a special place somewhere, a place they could retreat to or at least meet. It might be very private or out in the open in a town where no one knew their faces or cared. The only factor that would narrow down the possibilities was race. Mollie and North would have chosen a place where an interracial couple would not stand out.

Rachel knew that was where she would find what she needed to locate the informants whose secrets had cost Mollie her life.

TWO

TWO

10

Jessup hung up the phone. "That was Pacific Bell in San Francisco."

"They're sure she's up there?" Dawes asked.

"Said she called the naval station in Monterey yesterday to check the local weather."

Dawes looked at Jessup. Jessup looked at Dawes.

Finally Dawes said, "There's a C-5 air freighter outbound from Andrews in sixty minutes. I can just make it, be in San Francisco in four and a half hours. From there, it's only an hour or so down to Carmel—the way I drive."

Rachel was at the front door when she stopped and looked back at the telephone. It hadn't rung once and the answering machine's message light was dead. She had expected a call from Fort Belvoir, either from Jessup or someone in the investigative unit. Dreading both the call and its likely consequences, she hadn't intended to take the call when it came.

But it hadn't, and Rachel wondered about that. By now her entire file would have been pulled and pawed over. The details about the Carmel cottage were in it. Technically she would be listed as missing. Someone should have tracked the number down, called by now.

So why haven't they?

Rachel reversed the situation, put herself in the shoes of the investigative unit leader. Why was he staying silent?

Because he doesn't want to tip his hand? A senior officer—my commanding officer—gets murdered and CID isn't sure how I fit in. Maybe it's better to err on the side of caution, come out here in person for a little mano a mano, *in case I spook. . . .*

Rachel knew they would think this way. Then she remembered that she'd called Monterey for the weather forecast. So Fort Belvoir damn well knew she was here. They were going to come up on her blind side.

The thought tweaked her anger. Her hand strayed to her gun in its shoulder rig, a cold, hard comfort. She made sure the alarm system was engaged then stepped out the door, knowing she wouldn't be coming back.

Rachel drove the rented Mustang into the center of the village. The library in Carmel reflected the community's wealth. The brick-and-redwood building had been designed by a prominent California architect, and the computer system was the best Redmond had to offer. A young librarian with bifocals and a ponytail showed Rachel to a workstation, asked if she needed help, then left her alone.

Rachel knew better than to try to get into Mollie's computer at Belvoir. It would have been red flagged by now. But there was another avenue where she might find what she needed.

She dialed into the data banks of the civilian travel agency that handled the military's needs for the eastern region of the country. Headlining the search with Mollie's name and rank, she ignored the official trips Mollie had taken during the past year, concentrating on her holiday travel.

The computer came back with a detailed itinerary of six locations. While the printer churned, Rachel repeated the process using General Griffin North's name. Then she sat back and read Mollie's brief. She recognized three of the destinations, all in Florida, where Mollie had gone to visit a college friend who'd just given birth. The other three were more interesting because it made no sense for Mollie to have chosen them.

The Homestead, in Hot Springs, Virginia; the Greenbrier, in White Sulphur Springs, West Virginia; Pinehurst, in North Carolina.

Rachel recognized the one thing common to them only because of her father's single passion in life: golf. All three locations had some of the finest courses in the nation.

But Mollie wasn't a golfer.

Rachel snatched the sheet on North from the printer's maw. As expected, the general had traveled quite a bit more. Then Rachel's eyes hit on the same three resorts. Apparently North was the golf enthusiast.

Okay, take it easy. . . . It's a start; might be the bull's-eye, might be zip.

Rachel checked the dates during which Mollie and North had visited these spots. There was a partial match. Sometimes Mollie arrived first and left last; sometimes North came first and stayed on after Mollie had checked out. But the dates did overlap.

Rachel sat back and tried to poke holes. It might all be coincidence, but she didn't buy that.

So why *would* Mollie and North have chosen these exclusive, out-of-the-way resorts? Rachel envisioned Mollie at the Homestead, whose center buildings dated back to 1766, rich with history. Mollie could fit in easily. She would never pass for a southern belle, but for an East Coast career woman? Sure.

North? How comfortable would he have felt surrounded by antebellum mementos and the way people might look at him, that far south? Rachel suddenly realized that the splendor of these isolated resorts would be perfect for North. He would be in civvies, looking like a prosperous black businessman. The staff, better trained than most, would leave their prejudices at the door. They'd have become accustomed to dealing with prominent or wealthy blacks who could afford the freight, sports and entertainment celebrities. . . .

Yes, North would be fine in these environments. But the two of them *together?* Rachel imagined Mollie and North sitting in the cocktail lounge, talking pleasantly, just a pair of execs exchanging war stories. No harm in that. But no touching. No sustained eye contact, either, and nothing in their voices to give away the love and the need and the want beneath their skins. It must have been galling, Rachel thought. Especially later, in the night, heading to one of two rooms, the last, furtive look over the shoulder to make sure there was no one in the corridor. Then the next morning, one of them sneaking out like some sophomore out of a dorm, going back to his or her room to muss up the bed, run the shower, leave a few damp towels around for the maid.

Rachel tucked the computer sheets into her jeans pocket and went to a pay phone. First, the Homestead in Hot Springs.

"This is Warrant Officer Collins at Major Smith's office in Fort Belvoir. The major has asked me to check her reservations, but she didn't leave me the dates."

"No matter, dear." The lilting southern voice on the other end made her think of doilies and calico cats. "Let's find out."

"That's Major *Mollie* Smith."

Rachel struck out at the Homestead, as she did at the Pinehurst Resort and Country Club in North Carolina. Mollie had been there but had made no reservations for a return visit. Feeling her hunch evaporate like so much mist, Rachel dialed the Greenbrier in West Virginia.

There a chipper young man told her that yes, they were expecting the major in ten days. The reservations had been made back in July, during her last stay. Were there any changes in Major Smith's itinerary?

The question pierced Rachel like a hot needle. But she collected herself and told the clerk that everything was fine. The major would be arriving as scheduled. Rachel wasn't vain enough to believe that she was the only one who might try to poke around in Mollie's travels. There was the messenger, and maybe someone from Belvoir if he or she was on the ball.

Now came the delicate part. Rachel thought the clerk sounded eager to please. If she played him just right, maybe he wouldn't panic and pass the buck to his boss.

"Major Smith requested that I ask you about some material she left for safekeeping with you. I believe she mentioned it was put away in the manager's box."

The silence on the other end made Rachel think she'd lost him. Then she heard the clicking of a keyboard.

"Mmm . . . yes, there's something in her file. Let me see. . . . Here it is. Major Smith did leave something with us."

"Oh, good. Very good. . . . "

Rachel was thinking ahead, how she might play this through. Her next words threatened to come out in a rush, but she managed to affect a crisp, casual tone.

"Major Smith has asked me to come by and pick up the documents."

Rachel didn't *know* they were documents, but it seemed a good bet. In her mind she saw a manila envelope, sealed, lying in the recesses of a tall, antique safe, the kind with scrollwork and flaking gold leaf on its door.

"I'm afraid we can release the contents only to the guest in question."

"I beg your pardon?"

The clerk took her words literally and repeated himself.

"I'm Major Smith's assistant," Rachel explained, her patience strained. "She left standing orders for me to retrieve those papers."

"Ma'am, I *am* sorry. But our policy regarding guests' personal possessions is quite strict."

"I could bring an authorization letter," Rachel said, working hard to keep the desperation out of her voice.

She could forge Mollie's signature, no problem.

"I'm afraid that wouldn't be enough. Maybe you'd like to speak to the manager?"

"No, that's fine. I'll see if I can reach Major Smith, get her to call you herself."

Rachel didn't want to antagonize the clerk. She might have to deal with him again, so better to leave on a pleasant note.

"Thanks for your help . . ."

"Clark. Clark Stanton."

"Thank you, Clark. I'll be in touch."

Rachel hung up and walked to the espresso bar on the lower level. Sipping her decaf, she sorted out her next moves. It was going on five o'clock. She could drive to San Francisco, drop off the rental at the airport. From there, a red-eye to Dulles. Traveling cash could be had from a Wells Fargo near the airport.

At Dulles she could take a taxi to a nearby shopping center. She couldn't walk into the Greenbrier dressed as she was now. A brief check-in at a motel or Embassy Suites was in order, too, to shower and get some road food. Then she'd have to figure out how to get herself to West Virginia.

Rachel finished her coffee and left the library. The autumn fog was starting to build, the cold worming its way under her windbreaker. She checked up and down the street, searching for a single man who looked as if he might be loitering. All she saw were the locals hustling up and down Ocean Avenue.

He's not that fast, Rachel told herself. *He can't be that fast.*

Still, she had to keep moving. But without credit cards that would leave a computer trail. Rachel didn't know how finite the messenger's resources were. Getting into a bank's card computer wasn't easy, but the right person could do it. Get in, get what he wanted, bug out. No sweat. Then pop up like some lunatic jack-in-the-box when she wasn't looking.

"Not going to happen, sport."

Rachel didn't know she'd spoken aloud until a startled elderly gentleman cringed away from her.

Logan Smith took his seat in United's first-class section. Once they were in the air, the cabin lights dimmed and the in-flight movie began to roll. Logan brought down the meal tray, set up his laptop, and went to work.

He was feeling the strongest kind of pain, as if there were a

giant hole inside him, the edges all torn and bleeding. And a
terrible wind whistled through that hole, savaging the nerves, the
way taking a deep breath caused a decaying tooth to hurt. He
knew he had to keep busy. He could not afford the luxury of
thinking about Mollie as she had been, had to shut down the
video of memories playing in his head. Until he was absolutely
sure *what* had happened, he would not be able to mourn. But
when he was done with the initial grief, he would go after *who,*
the killer. Getting him would mean closure. Logan would take
him alive only if at that point the question of *why* Mollie had been
killed remained unclear.

Smith tapped through to Lucille at the office. He was glad to
see that his fingers had stopped trembling. In the stillness, the
colors of the movie screen washing the cabin, Logan Smith began
with what he did best.

He had started his career at the Bureau almost twenty years ago,
straight out of college. It was a heady time. The cobwebs were
being swept away; the institution was beginning to come out of its
Hoover-induced coma. Smith, who'd wrecked his knee on Bay-
lor's gridiron and would never play pro ball, discovered that he had
a natural inclination for the hunt.

His instructors at Quantico soon tagged him for the Bureau's
Criminal Investigation Division. He spent two years at the Hoover
Building, that slightly off-kilter tetrahedron on Pennsylvania Avenue, working as a water carrier for the assistant director in charge.
Then he caught a skyjacking-attempt squawk at Baltimore-
Washington International Airport. Smith was the first agent on
the scene, coming in behind SWAT. Since SWAT had no jurisdiction on federal property, Smith took the sniper's rifle and calmly
shot out the nose-gear tire. Four hours later FBI negotiators
boarded the plane and walked out with an accountant who'd em-
bezzled half a million dollars from his employer and managed to
botch his getaway.

The negotiators got the media attention, but Smith got the
glory. He moved up fast, began to specialize in tight situations
where brains *and* physical skills were required. For seven years he
hunted violent robbery crews who crisscrossed the country in

search of prey. On his thirtieth birthday, during a standoff in Pittsburgh, he took a bullet in the upper chest and was surprised to discover his mortality.

They bumped him up in rank, gave him a raise, and shuffled him over to FCI, foreign counterintelligence.

Smith went to work hunting spies. His weapon of choice was not the gun or the wiretap, but a few buddies over at Treasury—specifically, Internal Revenue. He'd studied the FCI cases all the way back to 1919, the year that division had been founded to investigate anarchists and Communists. He dissected the operations against Nazi saboteurs, the KGB, and domestic groups like the Ku Klux Klan and the Weathermen. In many cases covert surveillance had been valuable, but it was the paper trail that wound up as evidence in court.

"Follow the money" became Smith's mantra. What civil servant was suddenly driving around in a Jaguar, was sending his kids to private schools, or had bought a piece of property for cash? How come his wife was shopping at Neiman-Marcus instead of Macy's? And what about those winter getaways to the Caribbean, first-class flights and deluxe resorts?

Smith followed the money, played on the weaknesses and greed of those who would put their country on the auction block. He learned that while men could create the most complete, impenetrable plots, practice great secrecy and stealth, they were always tempted and ultimately done in by the banal. Busted over a gold Rolex. He'd even worked a few cases with Mollie, where army personnel were involved—

You don't want to think about that.

He refocused on the information scrolling up his laptop. Lucille was sending the latest that D.C. homicide and CID had to offer: basic rehash when law enforcement had nothing new to say and was plowing over the same fallow field. But then came the official autopsy report.

He took a deep breath, his nostrils flared like a horse sensing danger. Tears filled his eyes. They did not run but managed to blur the words. Mollie had died very quickly. The pharmacology report detailed the dope found in her system, estimated that she'd lived no more than fifteen seconds from the time the needle pierced her skin. Everything else that had been inflicted on her was done postmortem, out of rage.

Smith double-checked the pharmacology. He had heard about several variations of the chemical cocktail, though not that particular mix. He knew it was used when an interrogator wanted information from his victim. This interrogator was sophisticated —he'd gotten the dosage just right. But he hadn't counted on Mollie's heart.

Do I know you? Have you been my enemy, past or present? Did you take Mollie because you thought she might know something . . . maybe how much I know about you? Was it fear or revenge?

Smith hunched forward, his fingers striking the keys hard, calling up a list of both active and closed files for the last two years. He worked intensively for two hours, going over photographs and bios of the men—and three women—he'd carved out of the human family. Desperation was their common trait, seen in the eyes, behind the sneering expressions. He knew their rage and contempt, had seen how they'd blown up federal buildings filled with women and babies, cutting a swath across the innocent in their irrational hate.

All the while the thought he'd had when on the hunt came back to him: *How could we have come to hate ourselves so fiercely?*

Smith spent a long time checking the families of his arrests. Back in Los Angeles, Lucille was one step ahead, feeding his laptop the backgrounds out of the computers deep in the hold of the Federal Building—a pictorial litany of angry faces and excerpts of taped threats. The relatives knew Smith's name from newspapers and magazines. Until the early 1990s, no one had really paid any attention to the Domestic Terrorism Unit. Then came the Unabomber, Waco, Ruby Ridge, and suddenly Smith and the unit he'd created became sexy. After his first encounters with relatives of the men he'd hunted and captured, he was glad to have such a plain surname.

Smith called down half a dozen names from his lists, reviewed them, eliminated all but two. He was careful, at this stage, not to form a hard and fast image of his target. But he was certain he was dealing with someone who had the kind of expertise that came with medical training, advanced pharmaceutical experience, and specialized instruction in some government's black ops unit. Someone who knew all about chemical cocktails.

Smith passed the names back to Lucille, then walked to the very front of the cabin, where the flight attendants sat on hard, fold-down seats next to the drinks trolleys. He shook his head as a flight attendant started to get up and poured himself a club soda. He took the glass and a second can back to his seat.

Now came the hard part: waiting out the two hours to touch-down. He could do nothing further because he did not know what awaited him in D.C.

Mollie was dead. The president wanted to see him. Behind the president stood Judge Simon Esterhaus. Smith knew little about the judge, a Supreme Court nominee who had presided over the inquiry into the death of General Griffin North.

The connection between Esterhaus and North was obvious; the president's interest in the commission report was understandable. But how did his sister fit in? As far as he knew, she'd never met the president, Esterhaus, or North. But obviously there had been some connection—one that was far too sensitive to be mentioned anywhere but behind closed doors at the White House.

What were you doing, Mollie? What did you stumble into that it came back and ate you up?

11

Steven Copeland wanted a mansion in Buckhead. He had intended to spend only the morning with the real estate agent, but they'd hit it off so well that lunch seemed a natural extension, followed by another slew of showings in the afternoon.

It was close to four o'clock when the agent finally dropped him at his hotel, the Ritz-Carlton. He got out of her car, his jacket pockets stuffed with brochures and spec sheets. She made him promise, twice, that he'd call her as soon as his book deal was in place.

Copeland returned the gracious greetings of the doormen and porters and nodded to the concierge, who addressed him by name. Copeland reveled in staying in Ritz hotels. He had a lovely suite overlooking the Atlanta skyline, a view he enjoyed as he emptied the papers from his pockets onto the writing desk. He opened the cabinet doors to the television and flicked on the NBC affiliate, WXIA. The drone of the late afternoon newscast followed him into the marble bathroom.

Copeland was reaching for the shower stall door when he heard the anchorwoman refer to Washington, a murder . . . He snatched up a towel, tied it around his waist, and trotted back to the living room—just in time to hear the station's Washington correspondent begin to hash over the brutal murder of a female army officer at Georgetown's International School.

Copeland's eyes darted to the two-line telephone. The red message light wasn't blinking. It would have been if someone had called. Mollie had said she'd call today, first thing. Mollie had promised.

Mollie's name now filled the newscast, gruesome details about the way she'd been murdered, mutilated . . . How both the police and army investigators were at a loss for a motive or suspects.

The item was concluded on the usual meaningless note: "The investigation is proceeding, and authorities expect further developments very soon."

Copeland sank onto the armrest of an easy chair, changed channels to CNN. They had already gone through their news segment and were into *Dollars & Sense.*

Copeland hit the mute button on the remote and snatched up the phone. The operator assured him that both *The Washington Post* and *The New York Times* would be delivered promptly.

His hand was trembling so hard that it took several attempts to get the telephone receiver set correctly in its cradle. Suddenly he felt very cold and hurried back to the bathroom. He tugged on the thick terry robe the hotel provided, tied the sash tightly. He didn't know he was moving so fast because his mind was racing, tripping over the image of Major Smith, her eyes bright with an anger she dared not put into words, standing there in that smelly airport smoking room, making sure Copeland was ready to move.

His eyes darted back to the TV screen. Nothing yet. The sports highlights were a blur.

Mollie . . . giving him all that quiet professional advice, looking dead on her feet beneath the harsh terminal lights. *All the good her advice is now. Should have taken some herself. Goddamn bitch, getting killed like that!*

By the man she was hiding us from? Copeland didn't think so. The TV had said this was a mutilation, a thrill kill. Coincidence. Bad timing. The ace of spades coming up in the deck. *It has nothing to do with why I'm sitting here!*

Copeland jammed a terry-cloth sleeve into his mouth and bit down on his forearm. Even through the thick fabric he felt his incisors drive into his skin.

Somewhere through the red haze he heard knocking. He stumbled to the door, wrenched it open, never really noticed the bellboy's startled expression. Copeland thrust a couple of dollars at him, grabbed the newspapers, then slammed the door and threw the bolt.

Minutes later there was newsprint all over the living room carpet. The two articles about the killing had been torn out, were now clutched in Copeland's hands as he sat cross-legged on the sofa.

Mollie Smith was dead: that was the only certainty he had. Her photos in the papers left no doubt. Copeland knew that if the coroner was right about the time of death, Mollie had never had a chance to call him. The way he reckoned, she'd barely managed to get out of National before she was snatched.

Copeland was neither a smoker nor a drinker, but now he felt a compelling urge for *something.* Beth . . . he needed Beth, to talk to, hear her voice. He calculated the time in Arizona, did the simple math three times before he was sure of his results. Okay, she could still be sleeping. She'd had farther to fly, then at least a two-hour drive, longer if she stopped along the way.

Or she's dead.

Copeland raced back into the bathroom and lost his lunch. Sobbing, he turned on the shower and stood there until the scalding water left him limp. Then he put the robe back on and went to the bedroom. He sat on the edge of the bed, staring at the telephone.

He knew the Arizona number by heart; that wasn't the problem. He simply couldn't screw up the courage to discover who might answer his call—if anyone was there at all.

There was something else he could do, something to steady himself, something quite practical that Mollie would have wanted him to do. He called the number she'd made him memorize. He had to dial twice because the first time he forgot to press "8" for the long-distance line.

Somewhere in the 703 area code a phone was ringing. Copeland may have suspected but had no way of knowing that that line fed directly into Mollie's house at Fort Belvoir. Or that it had been tapped at Bell Atlantic's switching center in Baltimore courtesy of a class three CID order.

Even if Copeland had been privy to this information, he could not have known—just as Fort Belvoir CID and the phone company didn't know—that Mollie's line had been tapped directly at her house. After the Engineer had finished going through Mollie's lockbox, he had gone to the far end of the crawl space where the underground phone cable met the junction box. There he'd installed a magnetic intercept unit. The device required that the calling party stay on the line for thirty-five seconds before it could rack up the party's number. At the tenth ring, Copeland had been on for twenty-two seconds.

He might have stayed on longer, leaving the line open as he pressed the receiver to his forehead, despaired about what to do next. But on the eleventh ring a voice answered.

"Hello?"

Copeland was so surprised, he almost responded. Except the voice was male, hard and flat, and Mollie had said no one else in the world had that number. *Police!* flashed into Copeland's mind, and he slammed down the receiver.

The intercept unit's digital counter froze at 33.

The next time Copeland looked at the clock, a half hour had passed. He got off the bed, rummaged in the minibar for a soda, gulped it down. Mollie was dead. Someone was monitoring a telephone she had assured him would be absolutely safe.

He opened the sliding door to the balcony and stepped out into the crepuscular light. The Atlanta sunset blazed the way it must have before Grant's eyes. Copeland thought about Beth. She was alive; he could feel that. Whatever had happened in Washington hadn't touched her.

Nor will it.

The realization brought a savage joy to Copeland's heart. If Mollie had told *anyone* about him and Beth, he would already be dead or under some kind of arrest. Flying time between D.C. and Atlanta was one hour fifty minutes. Anyone looking to find him would have done so by now.

So Mollie was dead, and maybe the secret about him and Beth had died with her. They were safe, at least for now. Long enough to collect themselves, get rid of the panic, think the situation through. Mollie *couldn't* have been the only one who knew what was going on. There would be records and files. Eventually the people investigating her murder had to come across them. But they were the army, the home team . . . the good guys.

Copeland turned such thoughts round and round until he'd convinced himself that he and Beth were just fine. All they had to do was sit tight, like two people trapped in a stuck elevator. Help would come.

Copeland reached for the phone and, as calmly as he could, dialed the Arizona number. Beth picked up after three rings. The sound of her voice, thick with sleep, almost made him cry with relief.

"Hello, my love," he said softly.

"Oh, *Steven!* I've missed you. . . . I thought it was Mollie. She hasn't called yet."

"I know, sweetheart."

The White House driver who met Logan Smith at Dulles walked him briskly through the terminal and out to a black Oldsmobile parked in the loading zone. The driver opened the trunk and showed Smith a garment lying flat on the carpeted interior.

"Your assistant told me to get the blue suit. There were three in your closet. I hope it's the right one."

"It'll do." Smith had a sudden flash of his comfortable ranch house in Chevy Chase. He'd bought it fifteen years ago, thinking it was a good investment. And it had been that, but it had never become a home.

The driver closed the trunk and opened the rear door. "You can change at the House. We have plenty of time."

Smith fixed him with a look. "No, we don't."

The ride into the capital took less than forty minutes. Smith hadn't been back to Washington since the stretch of Pennsylvania Avenue directly in front of the White House had been closed to traffic and turned into a pedestrian mall. He thought the arrangement was good, more festive . . . even if it was so for all the wrong reasons.

The car slipped through the East Gate checkpoint and eased out of sight, stopping at the delivery entrance. A Secret Service agent checked Smith's ID, then escorted him inside, through the servants wing, and into a small room that resembled a high school teachers lounge.

"This is where we hang our hats," the agent said. "You'll find showers over there if you want to wash up. Razors and stuff by the sinks." He checked his watch. "The Man's got somebody with him, but he said to bring you by as soon as you're ready."

"Ten minutes."

Smith showered and dried himself fast. The suit was one he hadn't worn in months and was a little big around the waist. The agent was waiting when he stepped out of the lounge.

Smith had been to the White House before, had met this president twice. For him the magic of the place had worn off. If you knew where to look, you could see the shabbiness creeping in, the mildew on the carpet edges, the flaking paint on the moldings and cornices. And like most of D.C., the White House had a rodent problem. Former First Lady Barbara Bush had found a rat doing the backstroke in the pool.

Smith was surprised when the agent steered him past the hall to the Oval Office and instead motioned him into the elevator. On the second floor, the private quarters of the First Family, Smith found himself in the library adjoining the president's bedroom. It was a warm room, paneled in maple and filled with the scent of old leather and parchment. The furniture was antique New England, well lived in and comfortable. The president, wearing tan slacks and a navy cardigan, could have been a gentleman farmer.

"Hello, Logan. I'm very sorry for your troubles."

"Thank you, Mr. President."

The Scottish condolence sounded strange to Smith, coming, as it did, off a southern tongue.

The president held out an envelope, closed but not sealed. "I was asked to give you this. You should read it now."

It was a one-page note about Mollie's funeral arrangements, prepared by the commander of the ceremonial detachment at Fort Myer, Arlington, Third Infantry Division, known as the "Old Guard."

"If you have any problems with that, or want to do something else for her, just let me know."

Smith folded the note, slipped it back in the envelope. "No, sir. Everything's just the way she would have wanted it."

He felt the president's eyes roving over him, probing, evaluating.

"I'm sorry to intrude on your grief, Logan, but there are things you need to know, now, about Mollie."

"Yes, sir."

The president ran a hand through his hair. "Christ, I'm not good at this at all, am I?"

"If it has to do with why she was murdered, please, tell me, sir."

The president rubbed his hands briskly, like someone coming out of the cold and stepping before a fire. "Let's start with what we're sure of."

As he listened, Smith thought the president had prepared his words too carefully, might even have rehearsed them. He did not know how close, both in content and delivery, they were to those exchanged with Simon Esterhaus.

"So that's what we need to know, what *I* need you to find out." The president squeezed Smith's shoulder. "I have to leave, but Simon's here. He'll give you the rest of it."

Smith heard himself say, "Yes, sir," as the president left the room. He was intensely aware of everything right now: the shiny buff he'd seen on the president's loafers, from the constant brushing of thick carpet; the lingering scent of lavender water; the soft click of the door closing; the room feeling a little smaller with another person in it.

"I'm Simon Esterhaus. Please, allow me to extend my condolences."

Smith looked closely at Esterhaus. The man still had the build of a rugby player, broad, with very little fat to him. His suit had to have been custom tailored, the way it fell. The lavender water wasn't his cologne; that fragrance had come from somewhere else.

Smith knew Esterhaus from his service on a special court created in 1978 by the Foreign Intelligence Surveillance Act. Run by alternating federal district judges, the court authorized wiretap requests in foreign and domestic terrorism cases. Esterhaus was a favorite among the law enforcement agents who came before him; Smith didn't know of one instance in which the judge had turned down a petition.

"It's all such a shock, isn't it?" Esterhaus said.

"Did you know Mollie?" Smith asked.

"I never actually met her. . . . No, I didn't know her."

Esterhaus added the second part because he'd caught the dangerous, angry look in Smith's eye and wanted to soothe it.

"We hauled you all the way in from L.A. because that's the way the president wants it," Esterhaus continued. "But I'm the one who'll be working with you, so I have to know: Are you up for this right now? Because if you're not, there's still time to take another tack."

The anger flared into resentment and died just as quickly, as the psychological profile in Logan Smith's dossier said it would. Smith was a hard taskmaster, hardest on himself. No way he'd let anyone else even get close to this hunt.

"Tell me what we have," Smith said.

"Beyond what you already know, nothing. I was hoping that you and Mollie might have swapped war stories. She was working on something very sensitive. I thought she might have wanted to share the burden, check her guesswork, maybe ask for some help."

"Obviously you didn't know Mollie," Smith said. "She wouldn't have done that. We never talked shop." He hesitated. "Her thing was to compartmentalize. Drove me nuts. But she claimed it was the only way she could leave her work at the office."

Esterhaus handed Smith six photocopy sheets, stapled. He saw the recognition the instant Smith looked at the handwriting.

"This is the only record we've found on what she was working on. So far."

"Where'd you get this?"

"We drilled her box at Riggs National. It was there along with her birth certificate, other things. . . . I'm sorry, but we couldn't wait for your authorization."

Smith nodded. He sat down and began to read. The details were pure Mollie: concise, orderly, sequential. The only anomaly was the number of question marks. And the references to Mr. X and Ms. Y—Mollie had been exceptionally careful there. Whenever the informants were alluded to, the wording was camouflaged so that no one could possibly get an insight into who these people were, where they worked or lived, how they had contacted Mollie, what contingency arrangements she had prepared for them.

"Ring any bells? Any of it?"

"Nothing."

Esterhaus wasn't surprised. The names "Copeland" and "Underwood" had been meticulously excised from Mollie Smith's notes, leaving only their cryptic designations. The Engineer, who had overseen this work, had insisted on the deletions. He did not want Logan Smith to close in on the informants too quickly. His plan called for Smith, marshaling the far-reaching resources at his disposal, and Rachel, using her knowledge of the informants' identities and whereabouts, to converge at the same intersection at approximately the same time. Then both they, and Copeland and Underwood, would be in the killing ground. The endgame could begin.

"What about this name?" Esterhaus asked, pointing at a page.

"Rachel? She was Mollie's protégée. I never met her, but there were pictures . . . of her and Mollie."

"They were close?"

"Mollie played big sister. Rachel's like a real barn burner, from what I remember. I guess she reminded Mollie of herself."

"Collins was Mollie's warrant officer, worked out of her office. Would your sister have confided in her?"

"As much as she would have in anyone."

Smith let go of the papers. He didn't want to touch them anymore, things that had led Mollie to her death.

"Where's Rachel?" he asked.

"That's what we hoped you'd know," Esterhaus replied. "Before you ask, we've checked everywhere she *should* be. Nothing. She hasn't called in, even though with all the news coverage she must know what's happened."

"Unless she's dead, too."

"We don't think so. Consider: The killer could have hidden Mollie's body. He didn't—he left it where it would be found, quickly. If he then went after Collins, and got to her, wouldn't her body have surfaced by now?"

Smith considered this likely.

"You want me to find Rachel," he said.

"If anyone knows the informants' real names, she would. We were hoping you might have some insight into her, know something about her that we don't. The little things Mollie might have mentioned about her . . . "

"How are you tracking her?"

"The CID investigative unit out of Belvoir is monitoring her credit cards. We have taps on Mollie's phones. A man has been sent to Carmel, California, where Collins has a house. We're not optimistic about his luck."

"Sounds to me like you've covered all bases."

"I'd hate to think that. I *know* Mollie's killer isn't thinking that. To him, Collins is a potential threat and has to be erased. Obviously it would be better if you got to her first."

Esterhaus stepped closer. "I was hoping for more from you. But now I'm thinking you might know something even though you don't realize you do. If you kept Mollie's letters, maybe there's something there. Maybe you'll remember things she said about Collins, details, observations that might give you a hint as to where Collins might go, how she'd react."

Smith had already shifted onto those tracks, but he didn't mention that to Esterhaus. Early in his career he had learned that superiors, after they didn't have to coax or stroke you, often seized and mangled your thoughts, if you were so careless as to voice them. They tended to hitch their hopes to the most frail speculation, turned your analyses into carved-in-stone facts. If, later on, these didn't pan out, the disappointment and resentment ran deep.

"You keep talking about Rachel, Judge," Smith said. "What

about the informants? Wasn't there anything about them in Mollie's paperwork?"

"Nothing. Her office at Fort Belvoir has been sealed. You can go through it whenever you want. Maybe you'll find something we missed."

Esterhaus paused. "That's the other reason we need you to find Collins. Even if Mollie didn't cut Collins in on her investigation into North's death, or actually tell her the informants' true identities, she may have confided the whereabouts of Mr. X and Ms. Y. It would have been a prudent move, to leave a backup in case something went wrong . . . if Mollie needed help. Find Collins, and we might just discover where those informants are stashed."

"Have you told the army about my running this operation?"

"Not yet. The president had to be sure you'd be on board. Now he can call Hollingsworth and get him to stand down the CID investigation. I promise, you'll have a clear field."

"I'll need a COSMIC access clearance."

COSMIC was well above top secret, which was what Smith now carried, granted to fewer than two hundred individuals.

"The president'll sign off on it."

"And I report only to you, Judge."

Esterhaus nodded. "The president talked to you about keeping this thing tight. With only three of us in the loop, it can stay that way."

"I need a number where I can reach you."

"I'll get you both—home and cell phone."

Smith had one more question to ask, the kind that Esterhaus, as an officer of the court, would find extremely compromising.

"After Rachel and the informants are secure, if I come across the killer . . . "

Esterhaus shifted his gaze, stared at the wall over Smith's right shoulder. "Then you must act as the situation dictates," he said carefully. "Obviously we are dealing with a very dangerous individual. If you are left with no option other than to defend yourself . . ."

It was all Smith needed to hear. No questions about his conduct in this matter would ever be raised.

• • •

Esterhaus lingered in the presidential suite after Logan Smith had been escorted out. He fixed himself a drink at the bar and stared out at the trees, still heavy with dry leaves. Tomorrow, or the next day, the winds would start to blow and the leaves would scatter across the earth like dying souls. He knew all about those.

He shivered as the whiskey slid down his throat. The winds were already blowing, colder and deadlier than anyone could guess. The Engineer had set them in motion when he'd told him to have Mollie's safe deposit box drilled, explained what he'd find there and how it could be altered to become the best kind of bait.

The Engineer, Esterhaus thought, had been absolutely right about that. Logan Smith had snapped at and run with it. The Engineer had said that Smith would track down Collins, and now the judge was sure of it. Smith was primed, had been given the opportunity few men ever got in such circumstances: to carry out a noble act on behalf of his president and at the same time satiate his own need for revenge. The Engineer had known Smith would get around to asking about the killer, test to see how much latitude the judge would give him.

Of course, after Smith caught up to Collins and learned where to find the informants, neither he nor Collins would live long enough to exact vengeance. The Engineer would see to that.

Only then will we be safe, Esterhaus thought.

The judge finished his drink and gently set the glass on a coaster. He felt his throat tighten and tears gather in his eyes. Alcohol always did that to him—stoked the agony he hid so scrupulously from the world.

12

Rachel's luck held in San Francisco. She parked her rental in the lot of a chain hotel along the airport strip and there broke down her weapon. She stowed the pieces in her duffel bag, which she intended to check through to D.C. When she was finished she slipped the keys over the visor and locked the car. In a day or two hotel security would become curious about it. They'd check the plates against the guests' registration cards. When no match appeared they would call the police, who'd then report the abandoned car to the rental company.

Rachel had chosen that hotel because there was a Wells Fargo bank half a block away. She handed the teller her ATM card and military identification and got back a surprised look when she said how much money she wanted. Rachel knew she'd be taking a chance doing this, but she didn't want to stop for money again, deal with out-of-state banks that might ask too many questions or make her wait. Wells Fargo was a different matter. She was a long-standing customer; her credit line was around its maximum level. After the teller had checked her credit, he told Rachel it would take a few minutes to bundle her money in the safe.

Rachel walked from the bank up to the hotel and caught its shuttle to the terminal. Once past security, she bought some gum and dark eye shadow at the sundries shop, then disappeared into a washroom. With the smell of ammonia-based cleaners stinging her nostrils, she used a damp fingertip to smudge the shadow beneath her eyes. She finger-combed her hair, giving it a straggly look. With her dark-shadowed eyes and gum-popping mouth, denim jacket, and duffel bag, she looked like some cracker from the almond groves of central California.

The Dulles-bound flight had just begun boarding when Rachel stepped up to the ticket counter, clutching a fistful of hundred-dollar bills. The agent gave her a pitying look and rattled off the litany of standard questions as he processed her ticket. He never bothered to ask for ID.

The San Francisco–Dulles nonstop floated over the capital's monuments just as the sun came out from behind the clouds to torch the skyline one last time. Rachel watched the passengers mash their noses against the Plexiglas portholes for a better view, heard their collective oohs and aahs. All she could see was Arlington Cemetery, the crosses laid out out below like tiny flower buds. Some of the rows were broken, where the graves hadn't been dug yet—or filled. Rachel thought of Mollie, then pulled down the window shade.

On the ground at Dulles Rachel walked quickly to the ground transportation exit. She was almost out the door when a commotion caught her attention. A group of travelers was milling around the Budget rental counter, shouting questions at a harried clerk. Rachel, who had let her credit card trail grow cold in California, had no intention of using plastic to rent another car. A quick call to Greyhound had confirmed the express bus between the

D.C. terminal and White Sulphur Springs at seven o'clock that night.

Rachel drifted over to the pack, focused on a beefy corporate type who liked to use his size and baritone to intimidate.

"Look," she heard him say to the clerk, "my company made this reservation three days ago. I don't *care* if your computers are down. Find my contract!"

The clerk flinched, and her voice trembled as she tried to explain that the contract was orphaned somewhere in cyberspace.

Now Rachel wasn't thinking of the bus anymore. She darted into the nearest washroom and three minutes later emerged, her face scrubbed. The crowd around the Budget counter had moved on to Avis; the clerk sat slumped on her stool, staring vacantly at a dark computer screen.

"I was wondering if you can help me?" Rachel kept her voice low, her tone sympathetic. "I overheard about the computer problem. Maybe we can work something out."

"Even if you have a reservation, I won't be able to pull it up."

"That's just it, I don't have one," Rachel said gently. She pushed her laminated CID identification toward the clerk. "But I do need a car. It's very important. It would mean your having to do the paperwork by hand, but I can wait."

The clerk smiled faintly, examined the ID. "Do you have a major credit card?"

"On this assignment I'm required to pay cash. More discreet."

The clerk gave her a conspiratorial look. "No problem. I'll take down your military ID number instead of a deposit. I mean, it's not like someone like you's going to run off with the car."

Rachel smiled, watched as the clerk pulled out a thick form and went to work on it with a ballpoint.

"I could have done the same thing for that prick," she said, raising her chin toward the haranguing businessman. "All he had to do was ask."

The rental was a precious gift. The bus would have been just as fast, but once she'd arrived in White Sulphur Springs, her movements would have been restricted. Too, the handwritten paperwork would take days to plod through Budget's reservations system; with no credit card on record there was no reason for the rental contract to trip red flags. If someone was looking for her by name, they'd be out of luck by the time they spotted it. She had no intention of holding on to the car for more than forty-eight hours.

She made it to the Independence Mall on the outskirts of Dulles well before the shops closed. The sprawling Radio Shack was her first stop.

After the World Trade Center bombing, CID had put explosives training on the fast track. Rachel had spent three weeks at Fort Meade, Maryland, working with everything from fertilizers to microprocessor relays. She no longer looked at gardening centers, kitchen solvents, or toasters in quite the same light.

The worst of it was that virtually all the materials needed to make a bomb could be had at any well-stocked hardware or electronics outlet. Among FBI and ATF experts, Radio Shack was referred to sardonically as the "bomber's store." It was a one-stop demolition shop, if you knew what you needed. Rachel's purchases added up to less than half a pound of metal and plastic. Of that she would use less than two ounces.

Two levels down, she found a stationery store and bought some cheap writing paper, two thick manila envelopes, and some red adhesive seals, the kind notaries and lawyers used. Her next purchase was from a warehouse-style auto supplies depot that anchored one end of the mall. Rachel waited patiently under racks of tires and car batteries while the clerk rang up a sale of two strips of silver asbestos lining that do-it-yourself mechanics used to line the firewall of an engine compartment.

By seven o'clock Rachel was back on the road, moving against the suburbs-bound traffic toward I-81. She stayed in the right-hand lane and carefully tracked the large billboards that were part of America's highway litter. She spotted the one she was looking for, pulled off at the next exit, and drove a half mile down a secondary road. Another sign, this one homemade, directed her toward a gaudy, barnlike structure strung with flashing lights and blazing neon.

BIG AL'S FIREWORKS—A REAL BLAST!!!

Rachel parked and went inside. There was a long counter, cobbled out of plywood sheets, and behind it, stapled between two posts, a large hand-painted inventory list.

"What can I do for you, little lady?"

The middle-aged man lounging behind the counter wore denim overalls over a generous gut and a stained baseball cap, the souvenir from a tractor pull. Rachel took him to be the owner.

She worked her way down the list until she found what she needed. "One Wee Willie. Unless you have a better suggestion."

"Hell, you ain't going to get much bang for your buck with that," the owner replied, a lewd curl to his lips.

"Not looking for that."

He eyed her shrewdly. "Oh, I get it. You *want* smoke. Well, that bein' the case, Wee Willies are the way to go. One, you say?"

She nodded.

The owner disappeared among the narrow aisles formed by cartons stacked floor to ceiling. Rachel looked around: not a fire extinguisher in sight.

"One Wee Willie." The owner slapped a sausage-thick fire-cracker, wrapped in red cellophane, on the counter. "That'll be seven eighty, plus tax."

Rachel handed him a ten, waited for her change.

"Have fun," the owner called after her.

Rachel walked back to her car, threw the fireworks into the bag containing her other purchases, and popped the trunk. She unzipped her duffel bag and quickly reassembled her gun.

Back on the interstate, Rachel maintained the newly posted limit of seventy miles an hour. She could cover the two hundred fifty miles to the Greenbrier and still arrive in plenty of time to get her job done.

Settling behind a Blazer purring along in the center lane, she reminded herself to be on the lookout for a rest stop just before White Sulphur Springs. Then she began a careful review of her two options. The first would be the easiest and cleanest—a straightforward approach—but its success depended on the coop- eration of the Greenbrier's night manager. If she could buffalo him, she'd be in and out of the resort in twenty minutes. If some- one put up a fuss, what followed would be governed largely by the laws of chance. Would the Greenbrier's skeletal night staff be sufficiently panicked to afford her the necessary window of opportunity?

Rachel was still considering the possibilities when she came up to I-64 at Lexington. She turned west and found a rest stop two miles before the exit for White Sulphur Springs.

It was crowded with big rigs, campers, and a half dozen over- loaded family sedans. Rachel used the washroom to change into her uniform, then returned to her car and locked the doors. She had parked against the brick wall of a shuttered coffee and sand- wich stand so that one side of the car was blocked from view. Her eyes flitted between the windshield and her lap as she slit open the Wee Willie with her penknife and carefully shook out a tiny amount of powder into a clean paper towel.

For 216 years it had been a place where ladies and gentlemen had been served by ladies and gentlemen.

Rachel rolled down her window as she edged along the mile- long drive between I-64 and the Greenbrier's front entrance. It was too dark to see the Allegheny Mountains that surrounded the 6,500-acre antebellum resort, but she could smell the rich pine resin. Then came a sound that made her look over her shoulder.

Slowing, Rachel pulled the car to the side of the road to let a horse-drawn carriage roll by, the clip-clop of hooves broken by a honeymoon couple's giggles. The carriage driver doffed his top hat as he passed and grandly swung his arm out to the left, indicat- ing she might proceed around him if she wished.

The front entrance of the Greenbrier was all flower beds and soaring columns, expertly lit to highlight the white limestone and floral colors but soft enough to avoid glare. A uniformed doorman and a porter were at the car window even before she'd turned off the ignition. Rachel noted the quick double take as she stepped out and they saw her uniform.

"Good evening, ma'am," the porter said briskly. "Welcome to the Greenbrier."

He must have been in his late sixties, a black man with soft caramel eyes. But his spine was straight, shoulders back, his bearing lending respect to the uniform. Rachel recalled someone mentioning that there were no employees at the Greenbrier, only retainers, some from three generations of the same family.

"May I secure your luggage?"

"I'm on duty," Rachel told him. "I may not be staying overnight."

The doorman was listening in. "In that case, ma'am, I'll park your car close by should you be needing it. Charles will show you up to the house."

"May I carry that for you, ma'am?" The porter held out his hand to take the manila envelope from her.

"That's fine," Rachel replied.

Her words made her feel cheap, because her refusal made it seem she didn't trust him. But there was no way in hell she could let this proud soul carry an explosive into what he surely regarded as his home.

The manila envelope was almost too primitive to be considered a bomb. But then Rachel wasn't out to murder or maim; she didn't need something that would punch through concrete or melt reinforced steel. Which was why the amount of Wee Willie powder added up to less than a gram; the filament and connector switches were so thin, it was almost impossible to discern them by touch. The giveaway—which only a professional could have detected—was the plastic fluid capsule and the all but invisible pin holes in the manila.

She held the envelope flat on the palm of her hand, like a serving tray. Rachel followed in the porter's wake, as he parted the guests crowded around the double-door entrance. She felt eyes glide over her, evaluate the uniform, move on. The porter greeted a pair of bellmen, looked over his shoulder at her, then steered her toward the concierge, stopping a discreet distance from the fine antique desk behind which sat a young man attired in black tie.

"If I can be of service, please call on me," he said. He paused, then added, "I do hope we will have the pleasure of your company."

Rachel said, "Thank you, Charles. You're very kind."

She heard the tap of leather on marble as he walked away, thought, *I don't want to do this!* But the concierge, identified by the desk nameplate as Mr. J. R. Stuart, was already looking at her.

J. R. Stuart was the epitome of genteel southern manhood, in his early thirties and prematurely balding. As Rachel approached he rose from his chair, bowed slightly from the waist, and waited until she'd extended her hand before offering his. Rachel decided Stuart would be receptive to the command-and-control approach.

"I'm Warrant Officer Collins," she said crisply, taking the chair opposite his and edging it closer to the desk. She handed him her ID, waited until he was looking at it, then said in a slightly raised voice, "Criminal Investigation Division, United States Army."

Stuart's eyes darted up at the guests strolling by on their way from dinner to one of the lounges or grand rooms. Heads had turned.

"And how may I assist you, ma'am?" Stuart asked quickly, giving her back the ID.

"A recent guest, Major Smith, my superior, left some papers with you for safekeeping. An envelope, she said. I'm here to pick it up." Rachel paused. "I called yesterday and spoke to the day manager about it."

Rachel was gambling that neither the day manager nor that front desk attendant, Clark Stanton, would be around to contradict her.

"Yes, well . . . If you'll just give me a moment to check," Stuart was saying.

Rachel sat back, offered a faint smile to reassure him that she could be patient—up to a point. She listened as Stuart's fingers danced across his computer keyboard, sounding like castanets in jarring counterpoint to the soothing big band melody drifting through the lobby from somewhere deep in the hotel.

Stuart looked up triumphantly. "Yes, Major Smith. Fort Belvoir, Virginia. She was a guest."

"The papers she left in your care and custody?" Rachel prompted.

"We have that on record."

It was like pulling teeth, and Rachel didn't like it. She started to get up.

"Then . . ."

"Ma'am, I'm afraid—"

"Yes." Rachel was looking down at him now.

"There are no instructions in the file allowing us to turn over what Major Smith left to anyone except her."

Stuart was flustered now, looking around at the staff behind the reception desk, seeking help.

Rachel sat back down. "I see," she said quickly. "And Major Smith is due back in the next day or so, correct?"

"Correct. Now, she may have discussed releasing the contents with Mr. Jurgenson or one of the other managers," Stuart told her. "Unfortunately, Mr. Jurgenson is attending to another matter at the moment. But I can have him paged, if that would help."

Rachel saw that it would have to go the hard way.

"I'm sure that what we have here is an oversight or miscommunication," she said, watching Stuart relax a little.

Rachel didn't want to bring Jurgenson or anyone else of that rank into this. Jurgenson would ask questions and get in her way. She needed Stuart to cooperate, knew he would if she was reasonable, made it seem she was letting him off the hook for getting in the way of her duties.

She needed what was in that safe. She had taken a lot of chances coming here, had paid for her choice by the fearful uncertainty that the messenger might be taking a different, much more direct tack to Mollie's informants.

He doesn't know what I do, she kept telling herself. *The way Mollie hid her secrets, no way he could have gotten to them.*

Even if the messenger had gotten as far as the Greenbrier, the inveterately polite J. R. Stuart was, ironically, the best gatekeeper she could have wished for.

"This is what I have to do," Rachel said, looking Stuart dead in the eye. She moved the edge of the manila envelope with her fingernail. "This needs to go into your safe next to Major Smith's material. Then I'm going to call Fort Belvoir and talk to Major Smith. Hopefully she'll be able to straighten this out so that I can be on my way. Not that I wouldn't enjoy your hospitality, even for one night."

That last remark made Stuart smile, softened his features, reminding Rachel of a melting snowman.

"I'd be happy to take care of that for you, ma'am."

Just as the porter had, he held out his hand for the envelope. Rachel gave him her best reproachful look.

"These are classified army documents, sir. They cannot leave my possession until I'm satisfied that they're stored safely."

"Yes, of course."

As Stuart's eyes darted over her body, Rachel knew he was trying to guess where she kept her weapon.

"If you'll follow me, please."

Rachel fell in behind Stuart as he walked briskly past the front desk, into a short, narrow corridor, and past two closed doors, stopping in front of a third. He swiped a magnetic card, pushed open the door, and stood back to let Rachel pass. She was glad her back was to him so that he couldn't see her surprise and dismay.

Unlike the rest of the Greenbrier, the vault room was soullessly modern, a three hundred-square-foot, state-of-the-art cage with floor-to-ceiling, wall-to-wall bars that separated the area where she was standing from the safe itself.

The vault was a monster, fifteen feet of gleaming stainless steel, the best Mosler-Doe could build. Its door was big enough for two people to walk through abreast; fixed to it was a large keypad and flywheel. The only saving grace was that, unlike a bank vault, this safe had no time lock. Such a precaution would be a nuisance, as guests might wish access to their valuables at any time of the day or night.

Stuart glanced over his shoulder, and Rachel obliged him by studiously looking away. She heard the sharp beeps as he tapped in the access code on the keypad, then turned when she heard the flywheel spinning.

The door sighed open on its hydraulics, Stuart following its movement along with two fingertips. Rachel smelled a new scent in the room—not Stuart's delicate after-shave; not the light, oily odor from the door mechanism. It was coming from behind her. She shifted her weight from one foot to another, used that as a pretext to make a half turn.

The man standing behind her was at least six and a half feet tall, huge across the shoulders and chest. His dark blue suit had obviously been custom cut, but between then and now he must have changed his choice of sidearm. There was a slight bulge along the left vent of the suit jacket.

"Oh, I'm sorry!" Stuart had turned around now, too. "This is Mr. Jones," he rushed on. "One of our security people. He's called whenever the safe door is unlocked."

"Actually, ma'am, at this hour we're called *before* the door is opened," Jones corrected him.

Jones smiled and clasped his hands behind him. His smile indicated that she should proceed with her business, pay him no mind.

Rachel stepped over the threshold and into the vault. Her task was harder now, because with Mr. Jones looming behind her, she couldn't make as close an examination of the interior as she'd hoped. Three of the four walls were studded with safe deposit boxes, ranging in size from the slim inch-and-a-half models to ones that could hold a crate of lettuce. Most, she noted, still had their keys in the locks. The fourth wall was given over to what appeared to be reinforced horizontal filing cabinets, one of which Stuart was now opening. Rachel guessed the hotel reserved these for its own documents, shared the leftover space with material that new or returning guests wanted stored but that did not require a box.

Then she stepped back, ostensibly to get out of Stuart's way as he straightened up from his crouch, and saw what she was looking for.

"Ma'am, you can place it in that space there."

Stuart was pointing to a stiff-metal file folder he had pulled out about an inch from its recess.

"Thank you."

Rachel held up the manila envelope in her hand, knew full well that both Stuart and Jones could see the red seal across the flap, kneeled, and slipped it into the folder. Slipped it in slowly, so that in the last instant, her fingertips, hidden from view, squeezed hard, breaking one end of the plastic vial inside the envelope.

The security man, Jones, had disappeared by the time Rachel was ready to leave the vault. From J. R. Stuart's slightly pained expression, she gathered that Jones would take Stuart aside later for a little tête-à-tête concerning vault access procedures.

Rachel hit the stopwatch button on her Timex. Twenty seconds had elapsed by the time Stuart had closed the vault door and secured the bars. Another half minute went by before they were out by his desk in the lobby.

Rachel thanked him for his cooperation, asked him where the public phones were, and headed in the direction he'd indicated. She chose the last of the three phone booths and pantomimed making a call, in case someone was watching. One minute forty-one seconds had gone by as she strolled into the lounge and took a seat at the bar.

Rachel ordered a club soda, slipped a few bills into the leather billfold containing the check, and pocketed a copy of the receipt.

Two minutes fifty-eight seconds.

A jazz combo was doing a fair rendition of Blind Willie McTell's "Broke Down Engine Blues," a pleasant overlay to the conversations meandering around the small, round tables. The smells of whiskey and expensive colognes, rare perfumes and beeswax from candles in red-and-blue glass holders . . .

Three minutes, six seconds.

Rachel took a final sip of her soda. When she swallowed, her throat became dry again almost instantly. But her hands were steady, and she knew she would look all right as long as she didn't let her anticipation show.

Three minutes forty-eight seconds.

She was moving across the lobby toward the concierge's desk. People were walking in front of her, headed for the front door, a moving Chinese screen that hid her from J. R. Stuart's view. No matter; he was busy with his computer.

Three minutes fifty-seven seconds.

Suddenly Stuart glanced down in his lap as though he'd inexplicably soiled himself. Leaping up, he almost overturned his chair and began to half walk, half run, toward the short corridor that led past the reception area and into the back rooms. Rachel cut into the path of an evening-bedecked couple, drawing a sharp huff from the woman, and followed a dozen paces behind Stuart.

The clerks behind the registration desk glanced up at her as she swept by, but no one challenged or tried to stop her. Rachel was in the hall, saw that the door to the vault room was open, heard Stuart arguing with Jones, then the rattle of the bars being pulled back. She couldn't smell any smoke.

Four minutes twenty-two seconds.

The thimbleful of powder from the Wee Willie had been smoldering for about half a minute. Once a wisp of smoke had escaped the perforated envelope, the delicate sensors inside the vault had triggered the Halon sprinklers. The silent alarms had gone off, too, at the concierge's desk and in the security office. But all other alarms had remained silent, indicating to Jones and Stuart that they weren't dealing with a full-blown blaze. At that point it might even have been an alarm malfunction.

"Oh, shit!"

Rachel looked around the corner into the room, saw that the vault door had been pulled open, releasing the Halon that had built up inside. Stuart and Jones began coughing, backpedaling from the safe's cavity. It was Jones who bumped into her first, whirling around, his reddened eyes trying to blink away the pain.

"What are you doing here?" he gasped.

"Watch out!" Rachel called out.

Jones reacted as she'd hoped, turning away. He never saw Rachel's leg slide forward and take both feet out from under him. Gravity and Jones's bulk did the rest, sending him crashing headfirst into the reinforced steel bars.

Stuart, futilely rubbing his eyes, tripped over Jones and went sprawling. Rachel seized him by the collar of his dinner jacket.

"He's hurt! Help me get him out of here!"

Stuart responded as any well-trained employee would in an emergency. Choking and gasping, he followed Rachel's lead and grabbed Jones by his other arm, helping her drag him toward the door. The second she was over the threshold and Stuart had his back turned to her, Rachel was inside the vault again.

She had ranked third in her class in the army's underwater swimming competitions and could hold her breath for almost ninety seconds. She crouched in front of the filing cabinet, pulled back the metal file holder where she'd deposited the smoke bomb, and plucked out the envelope. The powder had burned away completely, leaving only tiny black spots where the smoke had worked its way through the holes in the envelope. The envelope itself was still cool to the touch; the asbestos lining had trapped and absorbed the small amount of heat the powder had generated. Rachel undid the last two buttons on her jacket, slipped out two manila envelopes, and placed one, identical to the kind Jones and Stuart had seen in her hands, into the file holder.

Rachel heard urgent voices in the hall, but no shouting that might panic the guests. The overhead fans were humming strongly, sucking out the Halon. She willed herself not to think about whether anyone could see her and grabbed the envelope Mollie had left behind.

Not good. The envelope, although the same size as the second replacement she'd brought, was white, with the hotel's logo in the upper-left-hand corner and Mollie's name typed in the center. Rachel thrust aside her concern, jammed both Mollie's envelope and the one that had contained the smoke bomb under her jacket. When order was restored, the night manager would have the safe inventoried. As long as everything was accounted for, maybe no one would notice that the envelope being held for Major Smith was not the one that had been deposited at the end of her last visit. Maybe. . . .

Rachel exhaled, then took a shallow breath, enough to bring on a hacking cough. She stumbled toward the door, heard some-one shout, "She's still in there!" Then two pairs of strong arms were lifting her back to her feet, moving her fast into the cool, clean air blowing through the corridor.

• • •

"I'm all right," Rachel said. It must have been the fifth or sixth time she had repeated that.

She was in the hotel infirmary, sitting in a cloth-covered chair. She had avoided the examination table; she didn't want anyone insisting that she take off her jacket. Fortunately, at this hour only a nurse was on duty, and she was busy prepping Jones for the ambulance.

"How's he doing?" Rachel asked her.

"Colder than a flounder," the nurse said over her shoulder. "He didn't take in enough Halon to hurt him none. But that fall . . ."

Rachel looked over at J. R. Stuart, who was sprawled on the matching sofa. His complexion was still red from the Halon, and he kept dabbing his eyes with a wet towel. The man Rachel focused on next was Jeb Purcell, head of the Greenbrier's security force. Purcell had been on the property when his beeper, linked by microwave to the alarm system, had gone off. He was in his late forties, slim and very fit, with a marine-style brush cut and eyes the color of gray river stones. Rachel made him for ex–law enforcement, FBI or DEA, someone who'd retired early, maybe because of a work-related disability. However, the way Purcell moved, she couldn't imagine what that might be.

"Officer Collins, how *did* you come to be in that corridor? Without an employee escort, I mean."

His tone was all Southern Comfort, a gentleman politely asking a lady to help him out. Beneath it lay a steel rod of suspicion.

Rachel walked him through exactly what had happened from the time Charles, the porter, had guided her to the concierge to the moment she'd left the bar. She glanced occasionally at Stuart, who nodded in confirmation as she made her points.

"When there was a problem retrieving the material Major Smith had sent me out for, I called her at Fort Belvoir," Rachel was saying.

"Yes," Stuart croaked unexpectedly. "She did that."

Rachel could have kissed him. Obviously Stuart was still picking away the cobwebs. Otherwise he would have remembered that he'd only told her where to find the public phones, had never actually seen her use one or overheard any conversation.

Rachel fell into the slipstream of Stuart's words, knowing that Purcell had already noted the confirmation.

"Major Smith's instructions were to take back the papers I had deposited in the vault and deliver them forthwith to Roanoke."

Rachel lightly stressed the "forthwith," knowing that Purcell would understand immediately that she'd had no choice in the matter. "Forthwith" meant "now" or, better yet, sooner.

"After my conversation with Major Smith I went to the bar for a soda," Rachel continued. "I was returning to Mr. Stuart's desk when I saw him get up and leave. Since I was in a hurry, I followed him, but before I could speak to him . . . well, all this happened."

"Jonesy here's lucky you came along, honey. J.R. would have had a hell of a time lugging this carcass by himself."

Both Rachel and Purcell glanced at the nurse, who'd piped up while swabbing the gash on the unconscious security man's forehead. Rachel grabbed the chance to get ahead of Purcell.

"Do you know why the alarms went off? I didn't see any smoke."

"That's the strange part," Purcell said, as though speaking to himself. "We have no idea what could have triggered them."

Purcell was looking right at her, as though she had the answer but was holding out on him. Rachel shrugged and turned to the window. A car had driven up the crushed-stone driveway, but no lights had played across the glass.

"The ambulance," the nurse volunteered. "They come up here, they know better than to use their lights and sirens."

"Officer Collins, after your unfortunate experience I think it's only proper that the hotel extend you an invitation to stay the night," Purcell said.

So you can have time to check me out? I think not.

"My orders are specific, sir," Rachel reminded him. "Forthwith."

For an instant she thought Purcell might challenge her. She sensed that he had already considered calling Fort Belvoir but had thought better of it.

"In that case, I'll accompany you and J.R. back to the safe so that you can get your material."

It was a slick ploy. Rachel knew that in the tendrils of Purcell's suspicions he thought she was involved in what had happened. But he had nothing to work with. He would have checked the alarm mechanisms by now and found that there was nothing wrong with them. Checked the safe, too, for traces of anything that might have triggered the release of Halon. But he'd come up empty there as well.

They returned to the vault, and Purcell stood back as Stuart took out Rachel's envelope from the file folder.

"You're sure that's the one, J.R.?" he asked softly.

Stuart held it up so that Purcell could see the red seal.

"Only thing in here with that on it," he said.

Purcell nodded. "I'm glad the army's property wasn't damaged, Officer Collins."

"So am I, sir."

"Of course, that's why we use Halon. No moisture, no powder, just chemicals that suck the oxygen out of the fire so it can't feed."

"That's interesting. I didn't know that."

Purcell stepped back so that she could pass. "No reason you would, is there?"

Charles, the porter, met her outside and walked her down the steps to her car.

"Heard you had some excitement in there," he said, looking straight ahead.

"More than I expected."

"It's not a job, it's an adventure."

"I beg your pardon?"

"The army."

"It is that. Except you're talking about the navy. We're the folks who can be all that we can be."

"You surely are."

Charles escorted her past the doorman and held the car door open as she settled herself behind the wheel. "You come back and see us," he said. "I enjoy people who stir things up every now and again."

Rachel waved through the open window, then rolled it up

against the chill of the night. She drove slowly until she reached the edge of the property, then turned onto I-64 and punched the gas. It took her twenty minutes to reach the rest stop where she'd pulled over a few hours earlier. She recognized some of the highway rigs that had been parked there, the campers, too. But now hers was the only sedan.

Rachel nosed her car behind a semi hauling for McDonald's and turned off the engine but not the battery. Her forehead fell slowly until it reached her hands, still on the wheel, and for a moment she remained like that, bone weary, trembling from exhaustion and excitement and the fear that any second now a state trooper would shine his flashlight into her face.

No one's chasing you. If Purcell made a call, you'd have been stopped the minute you hit the interstate. But he didn't.

Rachel tried to figure out why Purcell hadn't pressed harder. All she got for her effort was the beginning of a headache. Then, in the silence and darkness, she felt she could take a chance.

After unbuttoning her jacket, she pulled out the two envelopes. The one she'd used to hide the smoke bomb was opened first. The blackened asbestos sheets were jammed into the door latch of the rig next to her car. It would hold until the driver got up to speed, then be snatched away by the wind. The residue of ash went into an overflowing trash bin, followed by the envelope, torn into pieces the size of cereal flakes.

Back in the car, Rachel reached for Mollie's envelope, ripped it open without ceremony. The sedan's ceiling light was weak, but it illuminated everything she needed to know.

13

Logan Smith awoke kicking at the sheets and comforter. He heard the crash of the bedside radio as the pillow he'd flung swept it off the table. The nightmare had been about Mollie. She'd been standing in a marsh, smiling at him, beckoning, but when he'd opened his mouth he could not hear his words to her. He could not stop her from turning away, from moving farther out into the water, deeper . . . He'd waved frantically, plowing through the reeds and the muck but making no headway at all.

Logan lay on his belly now, sweating and gasping, his fingernails digging into the mattress. Suddenly his stomach heaved and he rolled off the bed, staggered to the bathroom like a man being ground up by a heart attack.

He was in the shower when the clerk at the front desk called up to inform him that a gentleman was here to see him. Smith asked who, and the clerk lowered his voice.

"Send him up," Smith said.

He toweled quickly, slipped into slacks, a chambray shirt, and a lightweight wool tweed jacket. His hair was still damp when he answered the door.

The man introduced himself as Special Agent Hendrikson, Secret Service. After checking Smith's ID, he handed over a sealed envelope. Inside, Smith found a laminated identification card that had his picture, a series of numeric designations, and a bar code. The title read simply "Department of Justice—Special Investigator." The card had been issued the day before, and there was no expiration date.

Also enclosed was a note on Judge Simon Esterhaus's letterhead: "Good luck."

"You have a sedan downstairs," the agent said. "Beige Crown Victoria. It's one of ours."

Which meant that it was a decked-out chase car, with a blue-printed engine and complete communications gear.

The agent gave Smith the keys, had him sign for both the car and ID. Before leaving, he handed Smith his card.

"If you need a little extra help, just call. We've got you red flagged on our operations board."

Smith knew this had nothing to do with Esterhaus; the service routinely kept tabs on individuals who carried COSMIC clearance. But in this case the offer was decidedly personal.

The Four Seasons, where Smith had parked himself, didn't have a small coffee shop, but the management routinely dealt with VIPs and apparently had tipped off its staff. In the main dining room, Smith's coffee and juice appeared even before he had time to unfold his napkin.

Smith was staying at the hotel because he couldn't bear to go to his empty house in Chevy Chase. The silence and stillness, the pictures of Mollie around the rooms, would unnerve him. The hotel was impersonal and would look after his basic needs. Most important, it was close to Washington's core. If things broke quickly, he didn't want to be caught flat-footed in suburbia.

Smith found his car waiting under the portico by the hotel entrance. The doormen and valets gave him a once-over as he trotted toward it but made no attempt to open the car door for him. Before getting in, he unlocked the trunk and saw the full action kit: a Kevlar Second Chance bulletproof vest, an H-K nine-millimeter submachine gun with spare clips, a Mossberg shotgun, and teargas grenades. He wondered what Hendrikson thought he was hunting.

On the console was a cell phone. Smith flipped it open. The message light was blinking; it was Lucille, checking up on him. Smith talked to her as he headed from the city toward Alexandria and Fort Belvoir. Lucille had little to tell him about the progress of the investigation but plenty of questions about what he was doing and how long he'd be away.

"Indefinitely," Smith told her.

There was silence, broken by an "Oh . . ." Then: "Where can I reach you?"

"If I'm not at this number, try the Four Seasons, room 807."

"You have anything that the Unit could look into?"

Smith knew he had only to say the word and the Domestic Terrorism Unit's Washington team would be at his beck and call. "I'll shout if I need anything," he replied.

"Okay. But remember, we got stuff out here that even guys with COSMIC don't know about."

Coming up to the Pence Gate on Belvoir Road, Smith was suddenly angry at both Lucille and Hendrikson. By offering him access to anything he might want in their arsenals, they were making this personal. But he couldn't handle it that way. Mollie invaded his dreams; there was nothing he could do about that. But in daylight, when he was working, he had to keep her away. The pain and loss would blunt his senses, and that would be the greatest cheat: to miss something, maybe tiny and seemingly meaningless, that would let her killer slide silently away.

Jessup, the duty officer, hadn't been told that a Justice Department investigator was coming in today. He was talking to Dawes, in Carmel, and mouthed at his secretary to let the visitor cool his heels. Seconds later the secretary rushed back in.

"You definitely do not want to keep this one waiting." She shoved an ID card under his nose.

Jessup glanced at her. "What the hell is going on?"

"I don't know, but you should. It's Logan Smith—"

"*Our* Smith?"

The secretary nodded. "Her brother."

"I'll call you back," Jessup told Dawes, then hung up and saw that Smith had already shown himself in.

"Uh, Mr. Smith? I'm Warrant Officer Jessup. Please, sit down."

Smith didn't move. He smiled slightly at the secretary as she brushed by him on her way out, then the smile disappeared. Jessup thought that Smith reminded him of someone. Then it came to him—a sharp, painfully personal image. Jessup was fourteen when, one day, he had visited his father, a prison guard, in the federal lockup outside Atlanta. His father was escorting a death row prisoner from the interview room back to his cell. As he and the other guards had rounded the corner, the prisoner squeezed between them, he'd bellowed: "Clear! Clear! Dead man walking!"

Smith looked like that condemned man.

"I'm sorry about your sister," Jessup said.

Smith squinted, as though hit in the eyes by a blade of sunlight. "I need to have a look at her caseload for the last six months, and a room to work in."

"You can use the office next door. I'll have the files brought to you."

"I also need to speak to the head of your investigation unit. What's his name?"

"Dawes."

"Where is he?"

"Out in California, tracking Warrant Officer Collins, who—"

"I know about her. But I may need more. Please bring her file, too. Can you get Dawes for me?"

"No problem."

Jessup called the Carmel inn where Dawes was staying. He'd rather have given him some warning, but with Smith standing there, all he could say was, "Kenny, I have priority traffic from Investigator Smith, Justice Department. His authorization is COSMIC."

Jessup turned to Smith. "Do you want this on scrambler, sir? Or for me to leave?"

"Not necessary."

Smith picked up the phone, the black plastic slippery from Jessup's sweaty hand. "Good morning, Dawes. What do you have on Collins so far?"

"I know she was here, sir." The voice was cool and professional, facts only. "A police officer spotted her driving up to her house the night before last. A waitress recalls seeing her at a coffee shop, and a local librarian made a positive ID."

"Did the librarian have any idea what she was looking for?"

"No, sir."

"Any indication where she might be right now?"

"The paper trail has gone cold on us, sir. We have her picking up a rental at LAX, but she hasn't turned it in yet."

"Do you expect her to do that?"

"No, sir. I've had the state police put out an APB on the tags." Dawes sounded embarrassed.

Smith took the receiver away from his ear, rested it against his chest. He was silent for a few seconds, then said to Jessup, "Are you tracking her ATM card?"

Jessup shook his head. "We need legal clearance before we can press that button."

Smith was back on the phone. "Dawes, please stay at this number. I'll get back to you in a few minutes."

Smith disconnected, then called Lucille. "It's me. I need the chief of security at MTA. Tell him this is an evolving situation and I need his computer smoking. Call me back at Belvoir. The number's . . ."

He looked at Jessup and repeated the digits the duty officer rattled off.

When Smith hung up, Jessup asked, "Would you like some coffee?"

"Won't take that long."

It didn't. Lucille was back on the line in forty-five seconds. The man he wanted at MTA, the nation's largest credit reporting and evaluation agency, was Bobby McConnell. He was standing by.

"Get me Collins's Social Security number," Smith told Jessup, punching in the number Lucille had given him.

"McConnell here." The voice was modulated to sound bland, almost disinterested. It was one that the best crisis managers and negotiators cultivated.

"Logan Smith. Have you cleared my ID?"

"Yes, sir."

"The name is Rachel Collins, Social Security number . . ."

Smith heard faint clicks as McConnell or an assistant entered the digits. There was a five-, six-second pause.

"What do you need, Mr. Smith?"

"Any credit card transactions in the last twenty-four hours?"

"No."

"ATM withdrawals?"

"Yup. Your lady has an A-plus rating with Wells Fargo. She can withdraw up to ten thousand dollars every thirty days, provided the account is in good standing."

"What did she take out?"

"Nine thousand nine hundred. At the Wells branch near San Fran International." McConnell permitted himself an observation. "A traveling lady, is she?"

"We'll know soon enough. I appreciate the consideration."

"No problem. She may be quick, but we've been known to surprise people like that. You know, have a little reception committee waiting when they come off the plane."

"I know. Thanks again."

Logan was back on to Lucille. He needed to know what had gone out of SFO in the afternoon the day before yesterday. Domestic only, because he didn't think Collins would have decided to become a fugitive.

"I'm banking she's headed back here," he added. "Concentrate on the nonstops into Dulles, Kennedy, BWI, Boston."

"She'd still be using her own name?" Lucille had a low tolerance for the logically impaired.

"She's dumped her credit cards and is traveling cash heavy. She knows her military ID has been redlined"—Smith glanced at Jessup, who nodded vigorously—"but she probably has something on her, maybe a driver's license, in case she has to produce identification. At this point I don't think she'd run the risk of giving a ticket agent a name she couldn't back up."

Lucille took a second to digest this. "Okay. You going to be at the same number?"

"Should be. If not, call me in the car."

Smith turned back to Jessup. "You might as well get Dawes back here. I'd like to see those files now. And a coffee would be much appreciated."

Jessup escorted Logan Smith to the conference room, which was really two offices with the partition taken out. It had a big table and good light that exposed the shabbiness of the thirdhand furniture.

Smith watched Jessup neatly stack the files he'd asked for. The secretary hurried in with a coffee tray worthy of room service, then scuttled out.

"Have you emptied Mollie's office?"

The first-name reference so startled Jessup that his elbow almost toppled the stack of files. He managed a nod. "We went through every piece of paper in there, cataloged, cross-referenced. We even kept the stick-um notes, just in case. It's all stored down the hall, if you need it."

"I might."

Jessup was hovering by the door, chewing on the words he hadn't been able to say.

"I wish I had more for you," he said at last. "Better yet, that we had the son of a bitch in irons. . . . I wish I had known her more so I could help you."

"I wish I had, too," Smith replied gently.

There were six files in Jessup's pile, the earliest dating back to March. It was a DUI investigation in which civilian property had been trashed. So were the next two, both in April, one of them involving a fatality. The Army driver had gone on to face a vehicular manslaughter charge.

According to the duty roster, Mollie had gone down to Fort Hood in mid-June to investigate the murder of a soldier's wife. July was a quiet month: one case of disorderly conduct, when visiting British paratroopers were at Belvoir for joint training, and a stint with the Protective Services Unit to cover a politically unpopular generalissimo from Malaysia. Then she'd taken a brief holiday. The contact number belonged to the Greenbrier in West Virginia.

Logan Smith sat back and sipped his coffee without tasting it. The files were utterly cold, devoid of any smell. There was nothing here even to hint that someone might have wanted to harm Mollie.

He would have to go further back, to earlier cases.

But before he called Jessup, Smith opened Rachel Collins's file and scanned her last few assignments. Her name had been mentioned in the DUIs, and Mollie had had her attached to the Protective Services assignment. And now there was something else: a call that had started out as routine, then had escalated into a full-blown shoot-out, with Rachel as a Jafo with Baltimore P.D. There were no notes about the case anywhere in Mollie's docket.

Smith's interest rose like a spitting cobra. Here were the details about Baltimore P.D.'s request for the file of a Sergeant Charles Dunn and Jessup's expediting it. Smith read Dunn's service record carefully. Exemplary it wasn't, more a reflection of a plodding lifer who got high marks for his mechanical skills, especially around helicopters and light, fixed-wing aircraft. No prior trouble with either the CID or civilian authority. Yet a source that Baltimore P.D. obviously trusted had fingered Dunn, by name and description, as the man who'd be breaking into that warehouse to steal small arms.

Smith double-checked, but there was no mention in Jessup's notes of what, if any, proof the police had given him to make him pony up Dunn's file. He would ask Jessup about that but was pretty sure of the answer: Baltimore had been very hot to trot, and Jessup had cooperated. By not holding up the raid, he'd hoped to bank some very serious quid pro quo.

Smith reached the part about the shoot-out, matched Rachel's version with the one sent over by Burns, the QRT commander. If you stripped away the different points of view, the essentials remained the same. Dunn *had* been a legitimate target. He had been after the weapons. And he'd been willing to use his wife and son as hostages.

It was all very tidy, except for Burns's scathing comments about Rachel's performance—and the fact that Mollie seemed to have absolutely no comment on the affair, not one postaction cover sheet, not even notes in the margin.

Smith went back to Mollie's schedule, matched her whereabouts with the time of the raid. She had been absent from the office the afternoon the call about Dunn had come in from Baltimore. *Where?* He picked up the phone and asked Jessup to bring in his day planner.

"What time exactly did Baltimore call you about Dunn?"

Jessup opened the leatherette binder, as thick as a photo album. "Two thirty-four."

"Late in the day if they were planning to go with the raid that night."

"I told them that," Jessup replied. "Burns said he'd just gotten the word on Dunn. They had to move fast."

"Did you call Mollie?"

Jessup sat up a little straighter. "There was no reason to. The duty officer handles all liaison matters. Baltimore wasn't asking for any of our manpower."

"But you sent Collins."

"A Jafo always goes along. Procedure."

"And she went because her name was next up?"

"Yes."

"Did you *know* where Mollie was? On post, off?"

"I can't say. I'd seen her earlier in the day. If something were to come up, I had her beeper number."

"When was the next time you saw her?"

"About eleven o'clock the following morning. I'd come back on shift at eight o'clock and started catching holy hell from Burns. By the time I got all the details and smoothed him out a bit, she was in her office."

Smith picked at the fraying cloth on the armrest of his chair. "No one's asked about her whereabouts during that time frame, have they?" he said.

"No one from D.C. homicide, if that's what you mean." Jessup paused. "We had no reason to run a parallel investigation."

"Maybe you still don't. But I want a team to trace her movements from that afternoon through to the next morning. Hour by hour, minute by minute."

"Understood. What if that requires the cooperation of outside agencies?"

"Not an issue. You run into problems, call me."

Jessup wasn't comfortable with the silence that followed. He searched for a way to segue out of it, his eyes settling on Collins's file.

"Warrant Officer Collins . . ."

"What about her?"

"She still hasn't called in. The MP command is making noises about listing her as AWOL."

"I'll speak with them. Collins hasn't deserted. She's doing the same thing I am: hunting."

Lucille called with the information from the airlines while Smith was on his way from Belvoir back to Washington. He had the speakerphone adapter plugged into the car's cigarette lighter leaving the cell phone on the passenger seat. In traffic he favored keeping both hands on the wheel.

"The major carriers have a few Collinses on their manifests, but no Rachel. Not even a first name beginning with 'R.' A few of the regionals have come back, no luck there, either."

"Anything on the description you put out?"

Smith had known that would be a stretch, but he'd had Lucille ask anyway.

"The airline security people are tracking down the personnel who'd been working that shift. They promised to blitz the fax machines with the photo we gave them."

"The car rental companies?"

"Dulles, National, BWI, Logan in Boston, and Kennedy are all negative. If Collins got hold of some wheels, it wasn't at any of those places."

Smith thought about that as he steered around a doddering Cadillac. "Rental companies require a credit card, right?"

"That and a driver's license. If you're thinking cash, no one works with that anymore. Too risky."

"If she's back here, Lucille, she needs wheels. Cabs won't cut it. For longer hauls she'd have to use Amtrak or Greyhound, and they're too slow."

"So you're saying . . . ?"

"Take a walk on the wild side. Target only the rental companies' airline outlets. Remind them that Collins might have been in uniform, using her military ID along with some excuse why she couldn't pony up a credit card. If she simpered enough, maybe some hormonally suspect guy bent the rules to do her a favor."

Lucille sighed. "Yeah, it could have played itself out like that. Where're you headed?"

"The Hoover Building."

"Logan, before you get there?"

"Yeah?"

"Stop and get something to eat."

"Okay."

"I'll know if you did or not."

"I know that, too."

Smith had called ahead, so the people he wanted to talk with were waiting for him in the sixth-floor conference room. Its specially treated windows, impervious to microwave eavesdropping devices, faced Ninth Street and the Navy Memorial. When Smith walked in, the sight almost unmanned him. Mollie had wanted him to come out to D.C. that summer. She'd planned a lot of things for them to do, including a concert at the Memorial. . . .

Two women were seated side by side at one end of the long conference table. The older one, in her early forties, rose and came over to him, holding out her hand.

"Pamela Esterhaus."

Her voice carried the rolling, cultivated accent of the South. Pamela Esterhaus was a tall woman, with long ash blond hair pinned back by a mother-of-pearl barrette. The effect heightened her strong jawline and high cheekbones, revealed the tiny crow's-feet at the corners of her dark green eyes. She was wearing the classic executive outfit, a tailored pants suit whose vents accented her long legs and trim waist. Smith thought that beneath the designer finery and perfect complexion Esterhaus was a hard-body, a long-distance cyclist or runner.

She held on to his hand as she spoke. "I'm so very sad about Mollie."

His puzzled expression drew a rueful smile from her. "You didn't know? . . . Mollie and I met during the Gulf War. We were over in Riyadh at the same time. She had her hands full making sure our troops were observing the protocols of Islam. I was helping to cover the high-level Iraqi defectors. We got a whole C-130's worth out before it was all over."

She shook her head. "I'm sorry. None of this is important. I guess I just wanted you to know that we had a connection, Mollie and I. . . ."

"I appreciate it," Smith said.

It wasn't generally known that the FBI kept liaison officers in major embassies around the world, men and women whose profiles were invariably much lower than those of their CIA or State Department counterparts. Pamela Esterhaus was head of the Justice Department's witness protection program. Her skills at making people disappear were legendary. Smith could see how, in the urgency and confusion of the Gulf conflict, she would have been invaluable. Defectors would bypass the other agencies, be dropped off at some innocuous location, and within hours Esterhaus would have them on a plane stateside, where new lives awaited.

Smith felt her touch on his arm.

"There's someone you need to meet. Holland Tylo, this is Logan Smith."

Tylo's grip was firm, her eyes, flecked with gold, set on his, probing for answers to questions she hadn't asked yet.

"I wish we were meeting under different circumstances," she said. "I'm sorry for your loss."

Looking at her hands, Smith guessed she was about thirty,

though she seemed a little older. Then he recalled the Westbourne affair two years earlier, the dark rumors about Tylo's role in it. Senator Westbourne had been murdered on Tylo's watch. She had taken the fall, then had become the killer's next target. In attempting to stay alive and clear her name, Tylo had unveiled and destroyed the conspiracy that had centered around Westbourne's assassination. Maybe that was why she was now on the varsity, presidential protection.

Smith knew he could speak freely in front of these women and did so—up to a point. He gave them the background to Mollie's murder, the ongoing and thus far fruitless investigation, then cut to the part about the notes Judge Simon Esterhaus had found in the Riggs Bank lock box.

"Mollie had come to believe that General Griffin North's death was not an accident."

He watched as Pamela Esterhaus and Tylo exchanged glances. He had their full attention now.

"Are we talking a conspiracy here, or a single individual?" Esterhaus asked.

"No way to say yet. Mollie's source material came from two informants, people she designated as Mr. X and Ms. Y. We have no idea who or where they are.

"The rest of her notes—only three handwritten pages—are conjecture: If foul play was involved, who was close enough to North to organize and execute it? One person or a group? Had the aircraft North was traveling on been rigged? If so, how? Did the investigation committee miss something because the evidence presented to it had been tainted?"

Smith paused. "Mollie was very careful. Nothing she committed to paper gives any clues about the informants. Yet she obviously believed their stories. And when she thought they were in danger, she made them disappear."

He looked at Pamela Esterhaus. "I was thinking that Mollie might have come to you or one of your people, looking to stash her informants where no one could get to them."

"The army has its own program," Esterhaus replied. "Wouldn't she have used that?"

"There's nothing to indicate she did," Smith replied quietly.

"Mollie never opened an official file on this. No one in CID, not even Hollingsworth, had any idea what she was on to."

"If she didn't go to the head of CID, maybe she suspected the army's complicity in North's death," Esterhaus suggested. "Someone in the officers corps—very high up. Possible?"

The only army officer who Smith knew for sure was involved was Rachel Collins. But she was not a suspect, nor was he inclined to ask Esterhaus or Tylo for help to track her down.

"I have no proof, of course, but I know the way Mollie thought. She was a believer in the old saying that a fish rots from the head down."

Esterhaus thought about this for a moment. "Where are they storing the wreckage of North's plane?"

"The National Transportation Safety Board would have used the nearest available facilities—the Palm Springs airport. But it's been over six weeks, the commission report is on record. The wreckage could have been ground up for scrap by now."

Holland Tylo rose. "I can confirm that one way or the other." She went to the far end of the conference room to a buffet-style cabinet that held a fax machine and photocopier. Smith heard her talking softly into the phone.

"You're thinking that Mollie slipped her informants into my program," Esterhaus said.

"It's what I would have done."

"Not as easy as it sounds."

"Even in an emergency? Given that the two of you had met before? Even if it wasn't you, Mollie could have reached out to someone else, used the interservice cooperation argument. Somebody might have been inclined to help out."

"And this would have happened . . . ?"

"As late as yesterday, maybe the day before."

She took out a cell phone from her briefcase. "My turn to make a call."

Smith walked over to the cooler and poured himself a paper cup of water. In the windows' reflection he saw Esterhaus on her cell phone, lips moving rapidly. Then she was walking toward the fax machine, passing Tylo on the way.

"We got lucky," Tylo told him. "NTSB still has the wreckage in a hangar in the desert. I postponed the chop shop contractor who was about to go to work on it." She paused. "You *were* going to impound the wreckage anyway, right?"

"You know it."

"We'll get our specialists and the manufacturer's engineers out there by tomorrow morning. In the meantime I'll go over the commission report."

Smith saw something behind her eyes, reached for it. "What else?"

Tylo leaned against the window frame, arms crossed. "The president is scheduled to stay put for the next nine days. Might as well use the time to overhaul Air Force One, don't you think?"

Smith said nothing. Tylo stepped close enough for him to smell her perfume.

"You're working for the president," she said. "No one else can authorize a COSMIC clearance. So you tell me: North was going to be on next year's ticket, his plane does a somersault in the desert, and now people are saying it wasn't an accident. Wouldn't *you* check out the president's favorite ride?"

"Absolutely."

Pamela Esterhaus was back, holding a plain paper fax. She positioned it on the table so that they could all read.

"If Mollie was hiding people, it wasn't with us. Our program shows no new placements over the last forty-eight hours. Two witnesses were moved last Saturday, but that's all the activity for the week. I'm sorry."

Smith had known this was a long shot. "I appreciate the help," he said. "There's one more place I can check."

"I think I know where you're headed." Esterhaus's expression hinted at concern. "You might want to watch your back when you get there. Those boys across the river don't play by the same rules. You could be the president's twin and they'd still mind-fuck you if it suited their purposes."

"Duly noted," said Smith.

• • •

Before he left the Hoover Building, Smith called Judge Simon
Esterhaus at his Georgetown residence on Cooke's Row.

"I struck out at the department's witness protection program."

There was a sharp intake of breath on the other end of the
line. "You didn't tell me you were going over there," Esterhaus
said.

"I may not have mentioned it," Smith replied. He was puzzled
by Esterhaus's tone. "Is there a problem?"

"No. Nothing like that. But I could have made things easier for
you. My wife—"

"I already spoke to her."

"I see . . ."

Smith waited out the silence, wondering what was making the
judge so testy.

"You say you didn't get anywhere," Esterhaus said finally. "How
come?"

"Mollie never went there for help." He paused. "Did you know
she and your wife knew each other, from the Gulf?"

"No. I wasn't aware they'd ever met." The words were a harsh,
flat denial. "What's your next move?"

When Smith told him, Esterhaus let out a low whistle. "You
really believe Mollie could have done that? Did she know people
over there?"

"I'm not sure. But there has to be a line of communication
between CID and Plans Division. Maybe something will come
out of the woodwork."

"What about Collins?"

"I'm working on it. Right now I think she's not all that far
away."

"I'm starting to wonder about her, how much she really knows,
where her loyalties lie."

"Collins is running scared. Think about it: Her superior officer has been murdered. Maybe Mollie told her things that keep
her from coming in." Smith didn't add the thought he'd shared
with Jessup, that Rachel Collins might be on the hunt, too. "I'll
find her."

"Keep me apprised."

Smith was troubled by Esterhaus's attitude and especially by the comments about Rachel Collins. Maybe Esterhaus was getting spooked because his signature was on the commission report stamping North's death as accidental. But to start looking at Collins as a possible enemy, an accomplice in some netherworld conspiracy, was too great a stretch.

It was Esterhaus's preoccupation with Collins that held her image in Smith's mind as he left the Hoover Building. He wished that he'd met her, gotten a bead on where she lived in her skin, what kind of mental clutter hid behind the white-toothed California smile he recalled from Mollie's photos.

You'd have to be good and smart and very sharp. Mollie wouldn't have stuck by you otherwise. So what would you do? How would you think?

Smith got into his car and sat there a moment, staring into the gloom of the cavernous underground garage, hearing the squeal of tires, smelling the exhaust fumes.

Rachel Collins had been sent on what should have been a routine assignment. Instead it had exploded, literally, in her face. A man with an unblemished army record had been caught stealing small arms. He'd chosen to fight instead of surrender. Why had Dunn gone that route?

And right after that, Mollie had her informants up and running. Then she's murdered and Collins drops out of sight. The one common factor that set everything else in motion—the *only* factor —was Sergeant Charles Dunn.

And Dunn's file was clean.

The file, yes. But his private life? Could he have had something going on the side that no one had ever cottoned to? Something he had hidden so carefully, it never came close to affecting his official record?

But that Rachel Collins managed to find out about?

Assumptions were Smith's mortal enemies. They could deceive, even kill. But he allowed himself to postulate: If Collins knew things about Dunn that others didn't, there might be an anomaly in his record that only she would recognize. If so, she would need that record, and obviously she couldn't go back to Fort Belvoir to get it. But there was an alternative, if she was sharp enough to remember it, ballsy enough to use it.

Smith fired up the engine and raced up the exit ramp. He had

one stop to make before his next appointment, and he'd have to
hurry.

Over the years the Engineer had cultivated infinite patience.
Sometimes the best and most effective way to move forward was
to stay still, monitor and gauge the actions of one's opponents. As
the Engineer had been doing with Rachel Collins's credit cards.
He'd quietly piggybacked one of his Wonderland Toys computers
onto the giant mainframes of MTA's headquarters outside Dallas.
This had allowed him to track Collins from Los Angeles to Carmel
to San Francisco, where, after a hefty cash withdrawal, the trail
had abruptly ended.

It was smart of Collins to have dumped the plastic, not so smart
to use the Wells Fargo branch nearest San Francisco International
Airport. The Engineer was not troubled that she had disappeared
off his radar screen. His computers were constantly culling car
rental agencies, hotels and motels, and Bell Atlantic files. Sooner
or later Rachel Collins would show herself.

He was using the same procedures to track Logan Smith, but he
hardly needed to. The federal agent was a much more visible target.

At the sound of the telephone he swiveled his chair away from
the computer screen. This was the dedicated line.

"Smith just called me," Esterhaus said without preamble. "He
said he came up empty at the witness protection program."

The Engineer detected a touch of relief in the judge's voice,
and he understood why. Had Mollie Smith been able to cache her
informants in the program, the other players would come onto
the board. Things would have started to become very complicated.

"This is good," the Engineer said. "What's his next move?"

"He's coming at you. Right now."

14

It was a screeching car alarm in the parking lot that wrenched Rachel from a deep, restless sleep. She rolled over, peered at her watch, looked around the plain room, and realized where she was: the Motel 6 on I-64 about forty miles from White Sulphur Springs.

Heading into the shower, she remembered how she'd gotten here. Back at the rest stop there had been a large map nailed to the wall of the sandwich shop, covered by a sheet of hard, scuffed plastic. The map was bordered by ads for local businesses, among them a slew of inexpensive overnight accommodations.

She had driven to the closest one, had given the check-in clerk $100 for a $29.95 room, and told him to hold the change because she'd be using the phone. Making sure she got a receipt for the balance had been her last conscious act. Rachel had no idea how her clothes had come off or that she had stuffed Mollie's notes under her pillow, next to her gun, before falling asleep.

As she showered her stomach reminded her that she hadn't eaten at all yesterday. While she dressed, her gaze fell on the telephone on the bedside table. She stared at it just as she had last night, and the thought that had ultimately prevented her from making the call popped back into her mind:

What'll I say to Copeland if he comes on the horn? "Hi. Nice to know you're still breathing. And by the way, did you hear what happened to Mollie?"

The problem was that Copeland and Underwood probably *had* heard. The story had gone network national; it would have been hard for them to miss it. Which meant that when Rachel told Copeland she wasn't coming to Atlanta lickety-split, he'd get right in her face, demanding to know why.

It was a decision that Rachel began to pick at all over again as she dressed. But she knew she had to do it; it could very well be that she wouldn't get a second chance. She began to prepare herself to deal with Copeland, anticipate his questions and objections, have answers ready, decide how much knowledge he could handle and where his breaking point was. He could panic in a heartbeat, cut and run on her. Most important, she had to tell him exactly what he and Underwood should do next, spoon-feed instructions and explanations that they could accept and follow.

Rachel jammed Mollie's papers into the pocket of her jeans, threw a denim jacket over her holstered weapon, and walked two blocks to a diner. She ate at the counter, rubbing shoulders with truckers, deliverymen, and locals, tuning out the conversations around her, ruminating on how to deal with Copeland without spooking him. It was hard because jerks were inherently unpredictable.

Rachel paid up and left the diner. On the way back to the motel she considered reaching out to Beth Underwood first, but there she kept tripping over the same problem: Beth was a woman smitten. Assuming she accepted Rachel at face value, Beth would listen carefully to everything Rachel told her, then promptly call Copeland and spill the works. Then *he'd* tell *her* what to do, after which Rachel might never hear from either of them again. Scratch talking to Beth first.

Back in her room Rachel scrubbed her hands and brushed her teeth. She took several deep breaths, calmed herself, then pulled a chair over to the night table. By now she had the number memorized. A few seconds later the operator at the Ritz-Carlton in Buckhead was patching her through to Copeland's room.

"Hello?"

He knows.

Copeland's voice was ragged, his tone churlish. Rachel suspected he hadn't slept much in the last forty-eight hours and that the deprivation served only to fuel his suspicions.

"Steven, this is Warrant Officer Rachel Collins. I'm Major Smith's principal investigator."

Rachel hoped to establish her authority and gain a little trust. All she got back was:

"Who?"

"Warrant Officer Rachel Collins. I was on flight 1410 with you, Beth Underwood, and Major Smith—"

"Who the fuck are you?"

His voice was shrill now.

"Steven, listen to me! Right now! Mollie is dead. You know that. I know that. But I need you to understand you're not alone, okay?"

Labored breathing on the other end of the line.

"I want you to know exactly who I am. If you think hard, you'll remember. Okay? We're about forty minutes out of National. You're sitting in row twenty-nine, seat C. Beth is beside you in seat D. Picture the airplane, Steven, where you are in it. Now look two rows up, to your left. There I am, standing in the aisle, getting something out of the overhead bin. You look up. You see me do that. Then you go back to whispering with Beth."

Rachel paused, then added what she hoped would jolt Copeland.

"You give her some matches, Steven. You'd stayed at the Ritz before, in better days. You probably have a bowl at home full of matches from places you visited. I do. Before you left your apartment you found a pack and brought it along, gave it to Beth to reassure her."

"Yeah, I did that."

Rachel heard the sound of liquid being swallowed.

"Do you remember me now?"

"I'm not sure." A pause, then: "Mollie never said anything about you."

"I was your cover, Steven. I saw you at National, driving up in your blue Jetta. You parked it in the red zone so that it could be towed, just like Mollie told you. When you got off in Atlanta, Beth had a paperback in her lap. She tried to keep reading after you'd gone, but I could tell she missed you already."

"Aw, Jesus . . . Collins? Is that what you said your name is?"

"Warrant Officer Rachel Collins."

"So what the hell happened to Mollie, *Warrant Officer* Collins? How come Beth and I have been left twisting?"

Rachel let the sneering tone slide right on by. She didn't much care how hard Copeland rode her as long as he kept talking.

"You saw the stories about her on the news, right? And the papers?"

"Yeah."

Rachel was relieved. She'd determined exactly how much Copeland knew and what his sources were. Now she could begin spinning the lies.

"As of now, we don't know who killed—"

"Who's 'we'?"

"Army CID—that's the Criminal Investigation Division—and D.C. homicide. The police have their gang unit pounding down doors."

"You think a gang member killed her?"

Rachel felt something cold crawl up her spine and struggled to push away Mollie's image. "She was beaten and robbed, Steven. As near as the police can tell, there were at least two assailants." Rachel paused. "She fought hard. Very hard."

Silence on the other end of the line. Copeland drinking again.

"Okay. I'm sorry if I sounded . . ."

He didn't finish the sentence. Rachel pegged Copeland as someone who could seldom bring himself to apologize for anything.

"It's just that I was worried when I heard what had happened."

"Worried." *But not about Mollie.*

Rachel slammed her open palm into the mattress, pushing it a full foot.

Fine. You've busted his chops. Now get on with it.

"I know you were worried, Steven. But I'm here to help you."

"You and who else?"

"You know Mollie didn't share information about you and Beth with anyone but me. And now I'm reaching out to you."

"Wait a minute. You're telling me that the army or this CID has no idea who we are?"

"Mollie *was* CID. I still am. I'm going to bring you and Beth in."

"When?"

"I can be in Atlanta by tonight."

"Where are you now?"

"In D.C."

Copeland fell silent. Rachel could almost hear the gears ratcheting in his head. Copeland thinking was not a good thing.

"No," he said. "I don't like this. If you're CID or whatever, why don't you call some of your buddies down here and tell them to give me protection?"

It was the question Rachel had been dreading.

"That's not the way Mollie—"

"Mollie's dead!"

"And if you don't listen to me very carefully, Steven, and do exactly as I say, you'll be dead, too."

Rachel couldn't believe she'd said this. The words seemed to have floated out on their own, aimed straight at Copeland's stupidity, to shock and wound.

Realizing she couldn't stop now, she plunged ahead.

"You *know* why Mollie got you and Beth out of Washington: you were both targets. She put her career and her life on the line because she believed what you had brought her. Now she's dead, and that's going to make things a lot easier for whoever's after you."

Rachel let up a bit. "I'm your only chance, Steven. So far, no one else knows who or where you are. I'm going to come for you, and I'm going to keep both of you alive."

"How can you be so sure no one knows about me and Beth?" Copeland demanded.

"Because *I* only found out your real name and where to call you about two hours ago." She wasn't about to give him the real time frame. "That's how well Mollie was protecting you. I'll do no less."

"You said you can be here by tonight. Why not sooner?"

"I have to do this outside my official duties," Rachel explained. "I don't want anyone asking me any questions."

"I don't know. . . ."

Now he was starting to whine. Rachel needed something to prop him up, and Copeland gave it to her without even knowing.

"I'm worried about Beth," he droned on. "She knows about Mollie, too. . . ."

Because you were on the phone to her as soon as you saw the news.

"She's really upset, you know? I'm okay here. The hotel has great security. But she's all alone in the boonies. . . ."

"You could help her, Steven."

Rachel imagined him cocking his head.

"How?"

"Instead of me calling her in Carefree, why don't you do it? You could explain everything we've talked about, tell her not to worry. I think that would mean a lot to her."

She had him thinking again, but this time in a safe direction.

"That could be the way to go," Copeland said. "But she'll want to know when we're coming to get her."

Rachel played along. "Tell her you and I will talk to her as soon as I get in. I'll check the flights, see what's going out of Atlanta to Phoenix tomorrow morning. Chances are we'll all end up having lunch together."

Making it sound like some damn picnic, but Rachel didn't care. She just hoped Copeland wouldn't press her for details. Until she knew his and Beth's stories, what it was they had gone to Mollie with, Rachel had none to give him.

"Yes," Copeland was saying. "I think that's good."

"Okay. Steven? I'm going to call you six hours from now. That'll be about two o'clock in the afternoon your time. By then I'll have a flight number for you."

"You know where to find me," Copeland replied, his attitude a little too pithy.

And you'd better pray the messenger doesn't.

Steven Copeland was sitting all twisted up in the big club chair facing the balcony. He would never have imagined that he looked like a dissociated patient in the day room of a psychiatric ward.

Copeland was replaying his conversation with Warrant Officer Collins, trying to get a grip on just how swiftly his world had changed. Good thing she'd started out with that business about the plane. Without those details about the matchbook and Beth's paperback novel he'd have hung up on her. But as he'd forced himself to think, he had remembered her. Not so much her face, but definitely the blond hair and the denim jacket riding up her narrow waist as she'd reached into the overhead bin. He'd also looked at her for a few seconds later on, when he'd felt that sensation creep across his skin and had known someone was watching him. But she had her back to him by then, busy zipping up her bag.

Rachel Collins also knew he drove a blue Jetta, where he'd parked it, and who had told him to put it there. She knew Beth wasn't in Phoenix but forty miles away in Carefree.

She knows a lot. A hell of a lot more than she let on.

Copeland didn't care; at this point Rachel Collins was a godsend. He had been eating little and sleeping less. In this lap of luxury he was a virtual prisoner. He left his room only when the maid came to clean and then went directly to the lobby. When he judged that the maid was finished, he waited until a crowd was getting on the elevator before slipping between the closing doors. If the lobby traffic was light, he waited for a woman or a couple to come by and rode up with them. He never got into the elevator when it was just him and another man.

His only real contact with the outside world was Beth, whom he'd called faithfully morning and evening, the last call having been at midnight his time. With each call it became more difficult to reassure her that everything would be all right. Beth always slipped in a question he couldn't answer, asked for an explanation he didn't have. And with every evasion and admission of igno-rance, Copeland felt diminished in her eyes. He couldn't bear that.

Another tortured hour passed before Copeland could swallow the bitter realization that he didn't have any alternative. Not one. He could not stay holed up in the Ritz indefinitely; sooner or later Beth would unravel and do God knew what. Collins was his only lifeline. If he believed her, risked trusting her.

What continued to nag at him was that Collins had said that Mollie had told no one about him and Beth, that Collins had only just discovered their real names and locations. So who had an-swered the phone when he'd called the number Mollie had given him?

Copeland lunged for a decision. He'd go with Collins. He'd call Beth right away and let her know that everything was getting back on track. Soon they would be together again. Soon this would all be behind them.

But he would tell her something else, something that he wouldn't mention to Collins when she got here. It would be his secret, his and Beth's. Just in case.

A bit of Mollie's wisdom was running through Rachel's mind as she traded her casual clothes for her uniform: *Don't second-guess yourself. Confidence in your own judgment is the essence of command.*

But *had* she handled Steven Copeland the right way? She'd come down hard on him. Would he be smarting from that? Right now? Opening the closet doors in his goddamn Ritz suite and staring at the suitcases, the urge to run almost painful?

Imagining Mollie looking at her reproachfully, Rachel fought the impulse to snatch up the phone again—and failed. Her fin-gertips danced across the buttons, and then a busy signal beeped in her ear.

Someone was tying up Beth Underwood's line. Rachel called Copeland's number, just to double-check. It too was busy.

Okay. Maybe he'll hold it together, come through for everyone. Maybe he's thought things out and realizes I'm his only shot. . . .

Six hours until the next contact. That's what she'd told Copeland. She could cut that down a bit if she concentrated on getting back on the road.

Rachel surrendered her key at the front desk and scanned the computerized bill. The motel operator had clocked her call to Buckhead at twenty-two minutes and charged her over thirty dollars. Rachel pocketed the change from her deposit and stepped out into the cool West Virginia morning.

She dropped her duffel bag into the rental's trunk, then turned on the engine and let it warm up. She leaned against the door, gauging the traffic. Four hours to D.C., one more to Baltimore, depending on the flow along the Baltimore-Washington Parkway. Fifteen, twenty minutes to take care of her business once she got there. She couldn't risk more time than that in Baltimore. If it looked as though it were going to take longer, it wouldn't happen at all.

Logan Smith noted the increased security around the CIA's main entrance. Eight months ago an executive leaving work had been ambushed by a pair of triggermen. Now there were two chase cars, angled to cut off a speeding vehicle headed for the gates; the men inside the cars didn't bother to conceal their big Remington shotguns and MP-5 submachine guns.

Smith was cleared and given instructions where to park. Every fifty yards along the country road he noticed tall posts that, because they were painted dark green, failed to blend in with the autumn foliage. Mounted on the posts were tracking cameras.

Smith parked in the visitors lot and walked to the main doors, the wind tugging at the hem of his raincoat. Inside, his ID was checked again and he was asked to step through a metal detector. Smith handed the guard his weapon and extra ammunition.

"Give that back to him, please."

On the other side of the detector stood Bill Rawlins, deputy director of the Agency's Plans Division. He looked about fifty-five, tall and thin, with a monk's asceticism. Smith thought the appearance appropriate. Plans was the spook part of the Agency, in charge of, among other things, covert operations. Rawlins's pale

blue eyes and serene, detached expression hinted at a vast repository of secrets.

The guard handed Smith back his gun, butt first.

Rawlins held out his hand. "Welcome to Langley, Mr. Smith."

Rawlins's light grip and bony fingers betrayed a much greater
strength. Smith fell in beside him as they walked over the great
shield toward the elevators.

"My condolences for your loss," Rawlins said in a way that
made Smith think he was being put on notice. *We know about you
—maybe more than you think.*

Smith nodded but didn't reply. He followed Rawlins into the
elevator, turned to face the doors as they closed.

"We've arranged for you to meet Sam Peterson. He heads up
the department you're interested in."

"Appreciate it."

Smith knew that Rawlins was fishing, was obvious about it, and
didn't care. Because Smith was an interloper from the other side
of the river, where the gumshoes lived, and now he was over here,
prying.

Smith thought it was his security clearance that rankled Rawlins
most. Clearances were like grails, and Smith carried the holiest of
holies.

Rawlins walked him down a narrow corridor past cubicles
whose doors were firmly closed and into an open area of secretaries' workstations. Beyond them were the executive suites, defined
by dark wood double doors and curtained glass walls. Sam Peterson's office had his name on one of the doors in gold letters.
Rawlins knocked and didn't bother to wait for an answer.

The room was expansive, with floor-to-ceiling windows that
overlooked the Virginia woods. There were fine Oriental rugs
over the standard beige carpeting and an old partners desk with an
inlaid green leather blotter. Against one wall was a credenza with
a minifridge beside it. But what caught Smith's attention was a
refectory-style table, easily ten feet long by four feet wide, that
had on it a miniature Alpine village, complete with gaily painted
houses, a snow-capped mountain, and several bridges that ran over
an electrically fed stream. Threaded throughout the scenery were

several sets of trains, all of which appeared to be quite old but in mint condition.

Smith heard water running in the private bathroom. The door opened and a tall man with thick, dark brown hair stepped out. He was a year or two on either side of Smith's age and very fit. When he moved, Smith heard only the rustle of fabric, the soft brushing of his cavalry twill pants, the slight, starchy crackle of his French cotton blue shirt, accented by red, white, and blue–striped suspenders.

"Sam Peterson. Good to meet you."

It was a friendly face, deeply tanned and pleasantly crinkled, as though Peterson had recently returned from the tropics.

"Bill, will you be joining us?" Peterson asked.

"No, no," Rawlins replied, as if the thought had never entered his mind. He turned to Smith. "I'll see you when you're done."

Logan Smith thought Peterson was amused by Rawlins. That was confirmed when he said, "Bill's wound a little too tight. It's in his job description." He gestured toward the chair in front of his desk. "I understand you're interested in our Looking Glass operation."

Looking Glass, the CIA's version of the witness protection program, was Peterson's personal fiefdom. He'd been running it for the last four years, retrieving agents who'd been betrayed or unearthed, mostly in China and the Middle East. According to the sanitized files Smith had seen, Peterson hadn't lost a single transplant to the opposition.

"How much do you know about the murder of Major Mollie Smith?"

"I've been briefed," Peterson replied quietly. "My condolences."

Smith was glad. He didn't want to cover that ground once again. "Mollie was looking to make two informants disappear," he said.

"The army has its own program," Peterson replied.

"There may have been reasons not to use it."

Smith knew that somewhere in the room a pair of tape recorder reels were turning slowly. What he'd just said would be thoroughly chewed over.

"You've tried Justice?"

Smith nodded. "Nothing there. Yours is the only other shop she would have come to."

"Excuse me a moment."

Peterson gave his chair a half turn so that he faced his computer. Smith saw only the tips of his knuckles bobbing up and down as he worked the keyboard. He stopped, checked the screen, which Smith was unable to see, and hit a button with particular flourish. The laser printer began to purr. Peterson removed a single sheet of paper from its tray and handed it to Smith.

"The real names have been changed," he said. "They're not important anyway. The rest are current as of today. They're all people I brought out, either personally or through third parties, over the last three months. I placed each and every one of them." Peterson paused. "I'm sorry, but your sister never came to me."

Smith handed back the list. "You could have told me that. I didn't need to see this."

Peterson shrugged. "Maybe. Maybe not. I don't know how much you're working with—or really telling me. Maybe you already have names, but you needed confirmation or locations."

"I wish."

"So what do you do next?"

"Whatever I have to."

"A word of advice?"

"Sure."

"Since you've come up empty, it's clear your sister covered her informants herself. Put yourself in her shoes. If there were exigent circumstances, how far would she take them to make sure they were safe? How pressing was the time factor? Would she have hidden them in an environment they were already familiar with, to reassure them?"

Smith understood where Peterson was going with this—but the man was assuming that Smith *already had* the informants' real names, along with descriptions and biographical data. He could not possibly suspect how blind Smith was.

"Thanks for your help," Smith said.

Peterson waved his hand, as if to say it had been nothing at all. He got his secretary on the speakerphone for a moment, then turned to Smith.

"Alice will take you downstairs. You'll probably see Bill there."
Peterson looked keenly at his visitor. "If something breaks for you,
or if you need a hand, call."

As Smith left the office Peterson thought he detected a slight
droop to his visitor's shoulders. The burden was beginning to
weigh, and Smith still had a long way to go.

Rawlins had the tact or the decency—Smith wasn't sure which
—not to ask how the meeting had gone. He met Smith on the
ground floor and walked him toward the security stations.

Smith was deep in his thoughts, brooding over his next move.
He felt that he'd wasted time, yet in the same instant he had missed
or overlooked something valuable. He kept telling himself it was
still very early in the game, that he should know better than to
expect a fast break. Rawlins again dispensed with the security
procedures.

"Good luck," he said to Smith when they reached the doors.

Smith looked at him, shook his head as if chiding himself.
"There was a train setup in Peterson's office. It looked like something a collector would build. I'm curious: What's the story?"

"He's a collector," Rawlins replied. "That's why some people
around here call him the Engineer."

15

Smith was about to pull out of the parking lot when the car phone warbled. It was Lucille.

"It's about the computer scans the airlines have been running on Collins?"

"Uh-huh."

"Sorry. Not what you think. Nothing off a San Fran–East Coast run. But Delta went the extra mile and checked her name against week-old manifests. They got two hits. Flight 1410 out of National to Atlanta with continuing service to Phoenix. Then 1066 —just a numerical change for the same aircraft—to L.A."

"Now we know how she got up to Carmel."

"More than that. I gave them Mollie's name to bat around. Turns out she was on those same flights."

Smith stared out the window, at a bluejay pecking at a shiny flip tab, making it jump across the blacktop.

Mollie was in L.A. the night before she was murdered.

"Delta has her listed going back to National on the red-eye. She couldn't have been on the ground for more than ninety minutes. Not enough time to even leave the airport."

Mollie was there, but she didn't call me. . . .

Smith continued to stare at the antics of the bird, unaware of the tears sliding down his cheeks.

Lucille had to call his name twice before he responded.

"I'm here. What I'm curious about is why Jessup didn't know this. *How come no one bothered to check?"*

"Logan, slow down. They've been hotfooting it in another direction, right? Even if they'd thought to track the airlines, they don't have anywhere near the resources we do."

"They don't have you."

The brief silence on the line told Smith his compliment had embarrassed Lucille.

"What's next?"

"Prep a hot sheet on Collins. Copies ready for every law enforcement outfit east of the Mississippi. Tool up a bogus fugitive warrant in case anyone asks questions. Emphasize that it's a federal takedown. If the locals spot her, they surveil and report. They do *not* attempt an arrest."

"You want them on a leash, you gotta throw 'em a bone."

"Make it a case of possible espionage."

"Logan, you sure you need to go this route?"

"Mollie didn't leave me anything to work with. We could spend the next day or two retracing her steps and still come up with nothing. So if I have to, I cast the net and haul Collins in."

" 'If'?"

"I have one more play. Whether it turns out or not depends on how I've read Collins. If nothing changes, I'll call you by the end of the day, my time, and we go fishing."

"I hope for *her* sake something changes," Lucille said. "Look after yourself, Logan. And don't forget to eat."

Bill Rawlins was back in Peterson's office. He was bent at the waist, peering into the tunnel cored through the miniature Alpine mountain, wondering if Peterson had outfitted his locomotives with light-sensitive headlamps so that they came on when the train was in the tunnel.

Rawlins straightened and saw that Peterson was watching him.

"Yes, the headlamps come on," Peterson said.

"I take it you weren't able to help Smith out," Rawlins said.

"Poor bastard. His sister gets sliced up and he's chasing shadows she may or may not have left behind."

"Smith got himself COSMIC clearance," Rawlins reminded him. "The White House must believe in shadows, too."

"How much do you know about that?"

"We're checking. By day's end we'll have the whole story." He paused. "I want to ask you about Wonderland Toys, how you're doing over there."

"I expect the company will show a tidy profit this year."

"That's not what I meant."

"Oh, Jesus, lighten up, Bill. Wonderland is humming along nicely, thank you very much."

The Engineer held Rawlins's gaze, knew exactly what was coming.

"We need your people to run a small errand into the mainland."

"How far in?"

"Beijing."

"You know I've put that network on ice for now. The People's Committee for Public Safety is still smarting from the last batch my runners brought out."

"The request comes from the director."

"What's the problem?"

Rawlins bristled. Peterson was the only one in the Agency who could demand an explanation for a superior's directive and get away without a reprimand. Because Peterson, before he took over the Looking Glass program, had run the best string of agents in China that the Agency had ever had. And he still did. His network refused to deal with anyone else. Rawlins knew this. He'd tried replacing Peterson once. For the next six months the silence from the Chinese mainland had mocked him. As soon as Peterson was reinstated, the product had begun to flow again.

"AT and T is setting up a new telephone system for the Chinese," Rawlins said. "They're going to wire up better than forty percent of the country, including all the major industrial areas and military installations."

"And you want my people to plant a few extra fiber-optic threads in the cables connected to selected targets. So that you can listen in, intercept."

Rawlins nodded. "Can your people get into the project?"

The Engineer considered. "Given enough lead time."

"And your tame ex-druggie warlord—can he get our stuff to them?"

"What kind of time frame are we looking at?"

"AT and T's engineers are drafting the blueprints right now. We'll filter out copies before the ink is dry. Rough estimate: three to four months."

"Then I get the blueprints to my people in China, and at the same time Wonderland Toys will receive a consignment of fiber-optic cable and ship it to the staging area I've chosen. That about right?"

"On the nose."

"How nice a payday is it going to be for Wonderland Toys?"

"Mid-seven figures."

"Right in line with the going rate."

Rawlins started for the door. "I'll keep you posted."

"Memos?"

Rawlins's smile was more like a wince. "Don't even joke about shit like that."

Because he was the Agency's best ears in China, the Engineer could and did. In some parts of the country, he was its *only* ears. The Agency could deny him nothing, as long as Wonderland Toys kept sending back a steady stream of high-grade information.

The Engineer looked out his window at the turning foliage and sighed. If he hadn't been betrayed that one time in Hong Kong, he'd still be in the field. But there would always remain a chance that the double agent had passed on a description of him to Chinese authorities before he died. The Engineer could not risk going back into China to find out the hard way.

So he'd been brought home, to a silent hero's welcome because he'd kept his network intact. Now he ran it from the green glass cube in the TransDulles Center, the crown jewel of the Agency's Asia operations.

At the same time, the Engineer had been given the Looking Glass desk. He had a long-standing reputation for hiding people where no one could ever find them. Since the China network was essentially a monitoring operation, the Engineer had plenty of time to devote to sending old spies and spent informers into the netherworld of new lives.

Still, he had missed the fieldwork, had grown restless until the day he'd been offered the opportunity to return—without the Agency being any the wiser, of course. Now, the Engineer was a different kind of eraser, for people in extremely narrow straits. People who could never betray him, who paid without question, and who provided excellent professional references.

The Engineer cast his thoughts back to his conversation with Smith. A very purposeful man, but savaged and therefore highly exploitable. Yet in spite of—or maybe because of—his pain, he was moving fast. The Engineer had no doubt that Smith would flush Rachel Collins soon.

She would have reached Baltimore by noon had it not been for a jackknifed tractor trailer blocking two lanes of I-295 for ninety minutes. By the time traffic picked up, it was one o'clock. It wasn't until forty minutes later that Rachel came up by Camden Yards on her way to the Baltimore P.D. headquarters.

There was no parking to be found anywhere in the street, so she drove to the Omni Inner Harbor and valeted her rental. She told the doorman she was here for lunch, went through the lobby, then took a hard right past the newsstand and coffee shop to the Hanover Street doors. She walked a few blocks down Fayette and stopped at a hot dog vendor's cart. She bought a Pepsi and sipped it, her eyes trained on the headquarters building. From a distant clock tower, a bell tolled the hour.

Back in West Virginia the temptation to run straight to Atlanta had been hard to resist. But Mollie's image, haunting her, had made her stop and think, think the way Mollie would have.

Back at the Motel 6, Rachel had forced herself to step away and look squarely at the events that had unfolded. All of them had been set in motion by a single element: Rachel telling Mollie what Dunn had whispered to her as he lay dying in that waterfront warehouse. That was what had led Mollie to immediately relocate Copeland and Underwood, to continue out to Los Angeles with her . . . to return to Washington only to find her killer waiting for her.

Mollie had been going back to tear apart Dunn's file. Jessup and the CID had told Baltimore QRT that Dunn was clean, but after hearing what Rachel had to say, Mollie had suspected otherwise. Except she never got to prove it.

Sitting in that drafty motel room, the dull roar of highway traffic pressing against the windows, Rachel had known that she would have to finish Mollie's work. But Dunn's file was in Fort Belvoir, impossible for her to get at. That in itself had provided an additional reason to go directly to Atlanta. Yet a little voice had continued to nag at her, telling her that she was overlooking something, suggesting that if she headed for Copeland, she'd be selling Mollie short.

It wasn't until the next morning, after she'd had a few hours' sleep, that Rachel made the connection. Standing in the shower, her thoughts still loose and uncoiled, she suddenly saw herself back on that hot warehouse roof in Baltimore, remembering how she'd seen Dunn for the first time, driving up and getting out of his big Suburban. . . .

And who had been beside her on that roof? QRT commander Robert Burns.

To whom Jessup had sent Dunn's file. Which Burns should still have.

Rachel pressed the cold aluminum can to her lips, drank some more, and suddenly found the taste too sweet. She dumped the Pepsi into a recycling bin and walked quickly to the street corner.

She couldn't be sure that Burns still had the file, but she thought the odds were good. Only three days had passed since he had received it from Jessup. Unless Jessup had stipulated that Burns return it right away—which Rachel doubted—the file should still be buried somewhere on the commander's desk.

Rachel fell in behind the crowd at the corner and hurried across the street. The headquarters building loomed over her, blocking out the sun. She maneuvered her way through the crowd headed for the building entrance.

But whether Burns still had the file wasn't her biggest concern. Standing in line to go through the metal detector, Rachel realized that CID would have put out a formal alert for her. Technically she had been AWOL for forty-eight hours. But how far had the alert spread? CID would have made its interest in her known to local, maybe even federal, law enforcement. But to the commander of Baltimore QRT?

Rachel was next in line. She was in uniform, with lots of brass to set off the detector. The security guard took her ID and motioned for her to step around the detector. He squinted at her picture, then at her face, and finally ran the wand over her body.

"Looks okay," he said, handing her back the ID.

If it hadn't been for his bored tone, Rachel would have thought he'd made a crude pass at her.

At the end of the lobby was an area closed off by scaffolding hung with heavy construction tarpaulins that she remembered from her first visit. Rachel recalled that the open area had led to the QRT post. Now all she saw was a single unmarked door. The keypad on the wall beside it indicated that this was now the main entrance to the annex.

Rachel glanced down at the laminated card in her hand. The CID identification would get her through that door. But if Burns's name had been included in the army's circulation list, then nothing she possessed would get her back out.

Rachel felt her steps slow as she approached the door. Her senses were set to pick up everything: the slight movement of the wall-mounted surveillance camera in a corner of the ceiling; the dull rumble produced by hundreds of leather shoe soles slapping up and down the big wide staircase.

Mollie had thought Dunn important. No—vital. This was the only way Rachel could get at what Mollie had never seen. *Do it now or walk away.*

"What the hell are you doing here?"

The challenge boomed through the din around her.

Rachel whirled around. Burns stood two inches away, his hands on his hips, leaning down into her face. She fought the impulse to pull back and instead stepped forward, smearing the perfect shine on his boot with her sole. Burns jumped back as though struck by a cattle prod.

"Shit, Collins! What is it with you?"

"Excuse me?"

Burns looked up from his inspection of the damage to his boot. "More to the point, what do you want here?"

He doesn't know.

"I'm sorry," Rachel said, then added what Burns expected to hear: "You startled me."

"Yeah, whatever. So?"

"So I came by to pick up that file on Dunn we sent you."

Burns blinked. "Dunn? Oh, hell, him." He looked at her suspiciously. "They still got you working?"

Rachel knew exactly what he was driving at. She tilted her chin, gave him her most withering look. "Running errands, mostly. Like this."

She thought that seeing her angry like this was, for Burns, better than sex. He didn't even try to hide his gloating.

"You still have it, don't you?" she pressed. "The file?"

"Sure. Been waiting for the army to send someone for it. Never figured it'd be you."

"I'm getting to see a lot of government buildings on my rounds these days," Rachel said thinly.

Burns flapped his hand at her, an indication that she should follow. He jabbed the entry code into the keypad, and the door buzzed open. Rachel kept pace behind him as they walked the short corridor to the duty sergeant's desk.

"You wait here," Burns said over his shoulder, not bothering to break stride.

Rachel looked up at the desk, which was mounted on a small podium, and found herself staring at the duty sergeant. He was the same hulking black man with the kind moon face who'd been there the morning she'd sweated it out in the interrogation room. His nametag read Sergeant Tom LaPeer.

"Can I help you? Like a coffee or something?"

"Thanks. But I don't think I'll be staying that long."

"You're from CID, right?"

"Right."

He leaned over the front of his desk, held out a hand only slightly smaller than a catcher's mitt. "Tom LaPeer."

"Rachel Collins."

"You're here about the Dunn file. You know, Burns is still steaming over what you did that night."

"I'd do it again, if I had to."

"Most of the squad, including me, listened to the ops tape. For what it's worth, we back you on that."

Rachel nodded, shifted from foot to foot.

"The army put you in the soup because Burns squawked?" LaPeer asked.

"Let's just say I've had better days."

LaPeer nodded solemnly. "I heard about the killing of that officer. You know her?"

"She was my commander. My friend."

"I'm sorry."

Rachel saw LaPeer reaching for some paperwork to push around. She didn't think she'd have a better shot than this.

"You remember the day I was in? There was a guy talking to you. I saw him through the interrogation room window, wearing a Redskins jacket, I think—"

LaPeer rolled his eyes, then looked around to make sure no one was within earshot.

"The shit hit the fan over *that*, let me tell you."

"How so?"

"He claimed to be a messenger from the police lab. Had all the ID and everything. So Burns handed over the evidence, except the guy was phony. He and what he took vanished—poof!"

"I know that Major Smith—she was my commanding officer —called you folks about some evidence on the Dunn matter. We never got it."

LaPeer snorted. "No wonder. Burns had a lot of explaining to do that day."

Rachel edged closer to the desk, lowered her voice. "But you talked to this guy—the messenger. You must have gotten a good description."

LaPeer's expression was perfectly blank. Rachel knew she'd stepped over the line into something LaPeer rightfully judged was none of her business. But he hadn't shut her down.

"Major Smith and I came by looking for that tape. It was an audio QRT had running inside the warehouse during the take-down. By the time we got here, the tape was gone. And soon after that Major Smith was murdered."

Rachel paused. "But I'm still interested in the messenger. Anything you can give me on him? Anything at all?"

LaPeer stared at her for what seemed to Rachel an awfully long time. "What you want with him?" he asked finally.

Rachel knew that LaPeer was too intelligent a man to try to con. "This is just between you and me. I have to believe you'll honor that."

"You can."

"I'm working an angle that connects the theft of that audiotape to Major Smith's death. I'm thinking the thief and her killer could be one and the same."

LaPeer's eyes widened. At the same time, she heard Burns shouting nearby.

"If Burns got reamed for handing over the tape to a phony, then he'd have asked you for a description of the messenger. Now I'm asking, too. Please."

But then the door behind the desk burst open, as if someone had straight-armed it. Burns marched up to Rachel and thrust a sealed envelope at her.

"Your file. You know the way out." He gestured at the door, waiting for her to leave.

"Uh, Commander?"

"What is it, Sergeant?"

"You had a call a minute ago. From O'Malley."

Rachel saw Burns hesitate, then wheel around and head back the way he'd come. LaPeer motioned Rachel back over to the desk.

"O'Malley's is a bar. Burns has been boinking a waitress, Kelly, over there." He winked slyly. "His wife doesn't know. Yet."

LaPeer rummaged in the bowels of his desk and came up with a folded piece of paper. "That's the composite of the messenger I did for Burns. It's not much. When I had a chance to think about it, I gotta believe the guy was wearing a disguise. A real professional job. But you might be able to get some mileage out of this, depending on what else you have."

Rachel plucked the sheet from LaPeer's fingertips, and it disappeared into her pocket. "Thanks."

"One more thing. Burns is letting this die. He's taking heat for getting conned and is sorely pissed. If you connect the dots, come up with something, you come only to me."

Back in his office, Commander Burns was on the phone, but not to the fair-haired Kelly at O'Malley's. His first call was patched through to the surveillance van parked outside on East Fayette.

"The subject's on her way out. Stay sharp."

"Copy that."

Inside the carpeted van equipped with comfortable chairs and upgraded air-conditioning, three watchers had their eyes glued to mounted, army-issue binoculars trained on the opposite side of the street. They picked up Rachel as soon as she came out the doors. The video began rolling.

"We've got her. She's turning down St. Paul."

"You know the drill," Burns radioed back. "Keep her in visual, but let the street-walkers get close."

One of the surveillance crew checked the redhead in a smart navy blue business suit and a crewcut jogger with an Annapolis T-shirt, both of whom had fallen in behind the warrant officer.

"Street-walkers right on target."

"Keep me posted."

Burns reached inside his pocket and brought out a small piece of paper. He smoothed it out, smearing the ink. The numbers blurred, but he could still read them. Now there was a voice on the other end of the line.

"Yes?"

"Inspector Smith?"

"Who is this?"

"Commander Burns."

"What've you got?"

"You called it, sir. She came for the file, just like you said—"

"Where is she now?"

"In the street. I have two behind her, three in a surveillance van."

"She hasn't spotted them?"

"No, sir."

"She's headed for her ride. Tell the van. And put two more vehicles in play."

"Sir, I can pick her up for you—"

"Burns. Listen very carefully. I don't want her picked up. Only followed. And I don't want her to spot your people, otherwise she'll run."

"What if she gets on the interstate? There could be a jurisdiction problem."

"There won't be *any* problem. You people could use a win here, right? After the screwup with the tape?"

Burns's ears were crimson. He was a man with a short fuse, but he didn't dare let it get away from him now. This Inspector Smith, whoever the fuck he really was, must sit on the right hand of God. The orders to "extend all possible cooperation without question or regard for resources" had come down from the police commissioner himself.

16

Rachel walked fast back to the Omni. A crowd of high school kids had just gotten off a tour bus near the main doors, so she maneuvered her way around to the side entrance.

Inside, she ducked into a rest room off the lobby and leaned back against the cool tiled wall. Her knees were shaking and her fingertips were sticky against the accordion file folder Burns had given her. She placed it on the vanity, then bent over the sink and splashed cool water on her face, finger-combed her hair.

The teenagers had not yet invaded the lobby, but Rachel heard their noise. The group leader was giving instructions over a megaphone while they turned up their boom boxes and scrambled for their luggage. The din followed her into the coffee shop, even to the corner table she took at the back, where she ordered coffee, black.

For a moment she sat very still, her eyes lightly closed, stirring her coffee, stirring until all she could hear was the spoon clinking against the porcelain mug. Finally she took a sip, slipped out Dunn's file, and arranged it on the paper place mat.

Okay Mollie, help me out here. What were you looking for?

Rachel had read hundreds of files like this one, each organized in the same way, each presented in the same dry army monotone. Even the six commendations Dunn had received from superior officers were lackluster.

Rachel finished her first pass, sipped her coffee, started again.

Dunn's background was unexceptional. The eldest son of a Dallas hardware store owner, he'd been a fair student in high school. His best subjects: shop and auto mechanics. He'd enlisted two days after his high school graduation.

The army was famous for mismatching native talent with assignments: a gifted photographer ended up in tank school; a cook found himself sweating it out on the artillery range. But in Dunn's case the system had worked. He'd been given advanced training in mechanics, first in four-wheel transports, then bumped up to the Bradley fighting vehicles, and finally transferred into tank maintenance. Fitness reports were a good cut above average. Three times Dunn was offered the chance to take officers candidacy exams; three times he'd declined. Rachel thought about that. It could have been that Dunn had had no ambition to move up. Or he could have been one sly son of a bitch, slowly worming his way into the Quartermaster Corps, which at a certain level rewarded one with a license to print money.

When she'd started out in CID, Rachel had been surprised to discover that it was the rank and file, not the officers, who were filling up the army's computer training centers. "Think about it," Mollie had told her. "Most of these guys have a good dose of street smarts. They know that very soon all inventory, accounting, purchasing, and transfers will be on computer. No more ledgers and pencils, no handwritten orders that can be fudged or misplaced. These guys need to know how it will work. And some are a little more ambitious. They want to use computers to rip the system off—big time."

Rachel had spent enough late hours in front of the screen to become much better than the supply sergeants who, with the stroke of a key, could make four hundred cases of M-16's disappear from Fort Benning, only to reappear magically in Juárez, Mexico, in the hands of dopers.

Kind of what Dunn had tried to do at that warehouse, except on a smaller scale. *But Dunn was more than a thief. He was skilled and trustworthy. Someone looked into his life and liked what they saw. Dunn had something to offer them. What does he offer you?*

Rachel glanced at her watch. She imagined Steven Copeland staring at the phone, waiting for it to ring. She needed to hurry, but she couldn't afford to be reckless.

A psychological profile would have helped, but there wasn't one. Dunn had never been involved in work that would have required an extensive background security check.

Which is why no one caught on that he might have been a member of a racist group.

Rachel knew that some in the army shared Dunn's convictions. Ever since Oklahoma City and the deliberate derailment of an Amtrak train in Arizona, CID had been paying close attention to possible ties between white supremacist groups and army personnel. The number of racist sympathizers in uniform was minuscule, but as far as the Joint Chiefs were concerned, even one was one too many.

"*. . . helped put that black bastard in the ground . . .*"

How'd you do it, Dunn? Who found you, came on to you, stroked you just the right way?

Rachel looked across the coffee shop, then flipped back the pages to Dunn's most recent assignments.

Fort Riley, Kansas. Dunn had been sent there to train mechanics on the M-1 Abrams tank.

Then back to Belvoir—

A half page of computer printout fluttered from between the pages as Rachel turned them over. She plucked it off the floor, placed it carefully on top of the file, and studied it.

The printout was an addendum to Dunn's postings over the last eight months. In March he had been sent to Fort Bragg, North

Carolina, for six weeks of intensive training on the maintenance of Apache attack helicopters. He had finished the course with a rating of "excellent" and was chosen to stay on for additional training on fixed wing aircraft. This second report cleared him to work on all aircraft up to and including the C-12, the army's version of the long-range Lear jet.

The reference to the C-12 stuck in Rachel's mind like a burr. It meant something. But she couldn't make the connection.

Move on. Dunn knew from aircraft. What else?

She double-checked all the paperwork on Dunn's postings, then set aside those pages and turned to one she'd barely scanned: Dunn's vacation roster.

After finishing up at Fort Bragg, Dunn had had a week's leave coming. He'd left on the appointed date but had returned to Bragg less than seventy-two hours later. From there he'd been flown directly to Andrews Air Force Base outside Washington. . . .

And reported in as the substitute driver for General Griffin North, whose usual driver had had his leg clipped in a hit-and-run incident.

Rachel sat back and willed herself to look away, out the window. The teenagers were milling around now, the frustrated-looking group leader still shouting at them. Their bus was ready to pull away.

Rachel took a deep breath. Dunn had been North's driver for two days. Dunn had bragged about putting North in the ground. North had been killed in a *plane crash* . . . a C-12. Whose mechanics Dunn knew inside out.

"Gotcha," Rachel mumbled. "Gotcha, gotcha, *gotcha!*"

She gathered up the file, went to the cashier's station, and held out a ten-dollar bill. "Can I have my change in quarters, please?"

The corridor was lined with small shops—a florist, car rental, newsstand, and small travel agency. The overweight middle-aged man in short sleeves and stained tie was pecking away on his computer keyboard.

"Be with you in a sec."

Rachel counted off a full minute before he graced her with a tobacco-stained smile.

"Now, what can I do for you, ma'am?"

"Is there an Amtrak express between here and Atlanta?"

"Well, let's have a look-see. . . ." More clicking of keys, then: "Yup. Leaves Baltimore five oh-seven P.M., arrives Atlanta one thirty-two A.M. That suit you?"

"There's nothing faster?" Rachel demanded.

The agent looked at her as if she'd grown horns.

"That *is* the express."

"What about flights?"

"Dulles or Baltimore-Washington?"

"B-W. It's closest, right?"

"Uh-huh." Back to the keyboard. "Your best bet would be Delta's 457. Leaves in ninety minutes."

She nodded. "One way, please."

"You sure? If you take a round trip, with the Saturday layover, save you about a hundred bucks."

Rachel reined herself in. "That much? Great. Let's make it a Sunday return, late in the afternoon."

She dug out six fifty-dollar bills and placed them on the desk. "I've got to make a call, tell my family I'm coming. Is this enough?"

The agent handed her back one of the fifties. "I'll have you on your way as soon as you're back. Oh, hey! What's your name?"

"Sarah Martindale," she shouted over her shoulder, hurrying to the bank of phones outside the hotel's Crab Catcher Oyster Bar.

Rachel got hold of the long-distance operator, gave her the number of the Ritz-Carlton in Buckhead, and deposited enough quarters for a five-minute call. Steven Copeland came on the line after the second ring.

"Steven. This is—"

"You're late. I was expecting to hear from you two hours ago."

"I'm sorry about that. I just got through confirming my flight to Atlanta. Steven, are you all right?"

"Sure, sure. It's just all the waiting. . . ."

But he sounded out of breath, as if he'd been running or exercising.

"You sound like you just got off the treadmill."

"I was up in the spa. When are you getting in?"

"A little under two hours. How far is the hotel from the airport?"

"Twenty-five minutes or so. But it'll be rush hour then."

"Give me an hour at the outside. I'll call up from the lobby, okay?"

"I just want this over with."

There was no tremor in his voice, but Rachel felt his fear, as palpable as if she'd had her hand on his pulse.

"So do I, Steven. You're doing fine. Sit tight. "I'll see you in a few hours."

"Call me if the plane's delayed."

"I will."

Rachel hung up and let out a low whistle. Steven Copeland was coming apart fast.

She checked her watch: time to go. She still had to pick up her ticket and retrieve her duffel bag from her rental before catching a ride out to Baltimore-Washington International. What she wanted to do could wait, but she couldn't resist.

Rachel tugged out the printout and traced her finger down to the contact number Dunn had left when he'd taken his last vacation time. Right after he'd finished his stint as North's driver; right before North had left Andrews for California. She jammed in a quarter and dialed the number.

"The number you have reached is no longer in service. Please consult an operator for assistance."

Rachel felt her anticipation curdle into something cold and sour as she slammed the receiver back on its hook. She was late now.

The travel agent was outside his office, looking up and down the corridor. He smiled when he saw Rachel racing toward him, then backed away sharply as she flew past him, snatching the ticket out of his hand and never looking back.

The businesswoman in the navy blue power suit had transformed herself into a thirtysomething jogger, complete with two-pound weights encased in baby blue plastic. The Annapolis jock had become a bespectacled junior professor with a Lands' End backpack. It was the jogger who spotted the target pulling her duffel bag out of the trunk, walking out of the hotel parking lot and up to the motor court.

"She's ditching the car," she said into her radio.

The post in the surveillance van came right back at her. "Roger that. Keep her in sight. Professor, you move in a little closer. Don't lose her in those kids."

The professor ambled across the street, then suddenly an airport shuttle bus barreled into the motor court. The crew in the van was getting anxious.

"What d'you see, Professor?"

"The bus is dumping a load. Looks like a friggin' 747 outta Tokyo just landed. Wait one."

The professor went to the edge of the crowd, now a mix of confused Asians and hyper teens.

"I can't see her," he called in, the shuttle obscuring his view.

"Runner?"

"I've got her," the woman jogger replied calmly. "I'm just about there."

The professor tracked his partner as she loped along the side-walk, parallel to the crowd, then spotted an opening between the bodies and leaped across onto the sloping lawn that separated the sidewalk from the motor court. The teenagers cheered the jogger on as she continued toward the bus.

"They've about finished unloading," she reported back. "Target is in sight." She paused. "A group of outgoing just came out, waiting to board. Professor, you'd better get up here."

"Runner, what's the problem?"

"None yet. But you might have one unless you get the professor on this bus and a chopper in the air. Sure as hell I can't climb on board."

"Why's that, runner?"

The woman slowed, then stopped, bent from the waist, and made a show of massaging her hamstrings. The sweat streaming off her was real enough. The small group now boarding the shuttle didn't spare her a glance.

The woman's lips barely moved, and her eyes, raised, never left Rachel Collins as she handed off her duffel bag to the driver to be stowed in the luggage compartment.

"Because if you'd bothered to check the destination screen, you would know that this is the airport shuttle."

The runner glanced up when she heard the commotion, smiled at the sight of her partner, the professor, plowing through the crowd, galloping toward the bus.

"This is Smith."

"Burns here. She's moving, headed out to Baltimore-Washington."

Logan Smith turned around as a jet tractor rumbled past the open door. It was hot and airless inside the hangar at Andrews. Twenty feet away, standing next to an FBI Gulfstream, was the crew. They'd been waiting on Smith for a go signal for over two hours; the looks they shot his way mirrored their impatience.

Smith kept the phone by his ear as he craned his neck back and stared at the web of crisscrossed iron support beams. He'd gotten off to a bad start with Burns, and now the QRT commander was making him pay, in the petty, vindictive ways that could grate on a man in a hurry.

Smith made a point of keeping his tone level, cool, professional. "I take it your people are tracking her car?"

"Don't need to. She's not in her car." Smith could sense the smirk behind the words. "She's on the airport bus. I have a man on board, two units following in unmarked cars, and a chopper."

"We'll need someone at the airport, to find out where she's headed."

"Yes, sir, that would be an appropriate precaution."

"Precaution?"

Smith knew that Burns was going to stick it to him; he just didn't know how. But when the rabbit punch came, he actually smiled.

"That's all it would be," Burns said. "There's a travel agency inside the hotel. Your Ms. Collins is headed out to Atlanta, traveling under the name of Sarah Martindale."

• • •

The Gulfstream was on the active runway, number one for takeoff, when Lucille got back to Smith.

"Burns may be a peckerhead, but he has his facts straight," she said. "Delta has a Sarah Martindale headed out to Atlanta on flight 457."

"Not good enough," Smith said.

He took a deep breath as the aircraft screamed down the runway and thrust itself into the sky.

"A ticket is one thing; they need to make sure that Collins turns in her *boarding pass*. Can they cross-reference the pass with her ticket?"

"Hold on: I'll talk to them."

Smith listened to static as the plane rocketed off a pocket of turbulence. The engines whined as the pilot fed them more juice.

"Logan, you still there?"

"Go."

"An agent is going through the tickets now. Hang on . . . something's coming through."

Smith stared through the Plexiglas at the freighters and ferries plowing across the Northwest Harbor. His stomach fell as the jet veered left on a southwest heading.

Lucille was back. "They just closed the doors to 457. Touchdown in Atlanta in one hour fifty-six minutes. A Sarah Martindale is definitely on board. Her description is a match for Collins."

"Okay. Now I want you to do something else. Burns and I have been stepping all over each other. He just might go to Jessup with what we have so far. I don't need Fort Belvoir saddling up the cavalry."

"Want me to bring Jessup up to speed?"

"As a courtesy. Collins is one of his. Maybe he'll stay out of it if he knows what's going on."

"And if he starts making noises about joining in?"

"Sweet-talk him out of it."

• • •

The Engineer had been monitoring QRT's operation from the time Jessup had sent his surveillance crew into the field. QRT was still using the old VHF radios and scrambled frequencies. That cloaked the operation from media police scanners but was no match for the equipment the Engineer had at his disposal. Things were made all the easier because the undercover agents talked in the clear, referring to Collins by name. The Engineer thought it would have been interesting to hear the interplay between Burns and Smith, but there hadn't been time to tap into the QRT land-lines.

A twenty-minute-old QRT transmission had Collins at a Delta gate at Baltimore-Washington. The agent speaking had helpfully mentioned the flight number, which the Engineer immediately cross-referenced with the Delta domestic schedule. The last trans-mission, only three minutes old, confirmed that Collins was on board and that the jet was pulling back from the gate.

Now the call the Engineer had been expecting was coming through.

"You missed her. She's left Baltimore, headed for—"

"I know where she's headed," the Engineer cut in.

He thought he detected panic beneath Esterhaus's cold voice.

"And Smith is at Andrews," Esterhaus continued. "He just took off in an FBI jet. Where does that leave you?"

The Engineer laughed. "Smith needs two hours to get to At-lanta. I, on the other hand . . ."

He glanced out the aircraft window. Twenty-six thousand feet below, the Appalachian Mountains were strung out like the verte-brae of an ancient sleeping god. He reckoned his current position at about 110 miles north of Greensboro, North Carolina.

"I'll be in Atlanta in forty minutes. If I were you, Judge, I'd stay up and watch the late evening news. It'll be interesting."

17

The flight seemed endless. Everything conspired to make her chafe: the wet snoring of the fat man in the window seat beside her; the wails of an inconsolable child a few seats back; the hard, resentful faces of the flight attendants, who were working a capacity flight, jabbing plastic cups into the ice bucket as they sloshed drinks and struggled to make change.

Rachel shifted to get out of the way of the chilly, recycled air blowing across the top of her head. She tried to focus on Dunn, on the most precious, and frustrating, thing she had learned about him—the disconnected telephone number. She remembered Mollie cautioning her about instinct, how it tended to trample facts underfoot. But Rachel was convinced that the number was a direct link between Dunn and whoever had hired him to murder Griffin North.

Finding out who had been on the other end of that number was another matter. Her military credentials would cut no ice with Bell Atlantic. She closed her eyes. The number could wait. It was like a fingerprint, indelible and unique; the person it belonged to couldn't change or destroy his connection to it.

Steven Copeland. That's whom she had to worry about. He would need stroking and reassurance. Rachel would have to take charge from the moment she laid eyes on him, rebuff him when he tried to bully her, lead him by the hand through what she wanted him to do.

She would have preferred to keep Copeland in Atlanta, but he had already demonstrated a severe case of cabin fever. She had to offer him an alternative he thought was safe and comfortable. The one she had in mind was a reunion between him and Beth Underwood. Bringing Beth into the picture should steady him. It would also give Rachel a potential ally, someone who might be more reasonable and who could persuade Copeland to go along with the program—which consisted, first, of a long session in front of a tape recorder. It was absolutely vital that Rachel hear firsthand what Mollie's informants had told her. Rachel was pre-pared to make extravagant promises and rouse the most impossible dreams in order to get that information. She would remind Cope-land and Beth that hard evidence of what they knew, in addition to following Rachel's instructions, was their best hope of staying alive.

Hydraulics whined, the landing gear locked into place with a thud, and the plane banked sharply. Beyond the window Rachel saw the orange glow of the Atlanta skyline at night. She thought of Mollie, cold and torn, beyond any pity or tears. Rachel prom-ised her silently that she would not fly at Copeland and try to rip the truth out of him. She would keep her eyes on the greater prize, on the messenger. And she wouldn't blink until he had been taken and the wind was whistling through his bones.

"We've been cleared in, sir. Delta 457 is already at the gate."

Logan Smith barely heard the pilot's scratchy voice over the speakers. He forced himself to unclench his fists and stared down at the parked aircraft at the terminal gates as the FBI jet drifted toward the tarmac.

He had been in a hurry, and he'd paid the price. Smith had instructed the pilot to follow an alternate route to Atlanta, one that should have landed the government jet at least fifteen minutes before the commercial carrier. But they'd run into a fierce, unexpected squall line just south of Cape Hatteras, losing precious minutes while the pilot searched for a corridor around the localized storm.

Smith picked up the intercom phone. "You'll park right next to 457," he said to the pilot.

"Yes, sir. But the control tower isn't happy about it."

"Drop me off, then get out of their way."

The craft came down fast and hard. Smith waited until the screaming of the reverse thrust subsided before he speed-dialed Lucille.

"I'm on the ground. What's happening?"

"Abbot is in place," Lucille told him. "He has six people from the regional office, three men, three women. He says that you're responsible for the overtime."

Smith smiled faintly. Chris Abbot was a friend, going back to their academy days. They had gone their separate ways within the Bureau but had made a point to catch up whenever Smith came back east. Abbot was the number two man in the Atlanta office and worked the counterfeiting operations in the South. His undercover teams were some of the best in the country.

"Tell him I'll be at gate 23A in ten minutes," Smith said, then added, "You did a fine job quarterbacking this, Lucille."

"And one of these days I might even get a raise. Luck, Logan."

The aircraft was taxiing fast, droning by the parked commercial jets with their red collision lights winking and their passenger windows all lit up. Some were close enough for Smith to see faces staring out at the VIP aircraft.

The jet rocked to a stop. Smith ran down the ramp, then slowed to a trot behind a uniformed airport police officer. They ducked through a door, then ran up a metal staircase to an emergency exit. The policeman used his key to turn off the alarm, then unlocked the door. Smith stepped out into the concourse.

"Hey, Logan. Long time no see. What kept you?"

Chris Abbot was balding and had the eminently forgettable features of a DMV clerk. It was his eyes that betrayed his flint-hard intelligence.

Smith squeezed Abbot's hand without breaking stride. "I owe you for this."

"Not a problem. Lucille caught me on a slow day. You want to know about your lady?"

"Please."

"We picked her up at the gate, followed her to baggage claim. She had one duffel bag, standard army issue. She didn't go for a rental; chose a cab." Abbot glanced at his watch. "As of a minute ago she was headed up I-85."

"Where does that go?"

"Just about anywhere. She could get off at one of the downtown exits or continue through to the I-75 junction."

"What's up there?"

"Buckhead, the high-rent district. Makes me think she might be going to a private home. That be the case?"

Smith veered around a chattering European tour group. A private residence didn't make sense. Nothing in Collins's file indicated that she'd ever been to Atlanta or had any ties to the city.

"I don't think so. What if she stays on I-85?"

"Then she's headed out Decatur way, or up toward Peachtree DeKalb Airport. Again, it's all residential."

Abbot reached down to answer the squawk on his radio. While he talked, Smith tried to make sense of what Collins was doing.

"Your people still with her?" he asked.

Abbot feigned hurt. "How do you know the cabdriver isn't one of mine?"

"Is he?"

"Too much to ask for. Don't worry. I've got two vehicles on her. Anyway, the cab just pulled off I-85 at the Lenox Road exit. Your gal's making for Lenox Square or Phipps Plaza, where the Buckhead Bettys do their shopping."

"What else do the Bettys do up there?" Smith asked.

"Hang at the Ritz for afternoon tea and cocktails."

Abbot picked up on Smith's exasperation. He steered him toward a Chevy Lumina, parked, engine running.

"Listen. Right now she's about five minutes from the Buckhead Loop and Peachtree Road. Wherever she's headed—the Ritz, the Nikko, or the Radisson—we'll know, okay?"

Smith nodded.

The Engineer already knew Rachel Collins's destination.

He had arrived at Hartsfield Atlanta International twenty-five minutes before Delta 457 pulled into its gate. A casual stroll in the area of gate 23A had been enough to identify agents from the FBI's regional surveillance team; outside, near the limo parking area, were a surveillence van and two chase cars. The Engineer wondered if one of the vehicles, a station wagon, was actually a personal car that had been pressed into service.

The Engineer had filled out the paperwork for his Lincoln rental and had driven it from the Budget lot back to the terminal. He dropped a limo service sign behind the windshield, put on a dark blue cap that went nicely with his suit, and stood by the car, assuming the role of patient chauffeur.

Rachel Collins had come out of the terminal, moving fast to the taxi dispatcher. By the time the Engineer was behind the wheel of his car, the cab carrying Collins had pulled away. The Engineer had waited to see how many cars fell in behind, then slipped into traffic behind them.

Thirty minutes later the cab had pulled into the motor court of the Ritz-Carlton in Buckhead. The surveillance crews didn't follow but continued into the parking lot of the Monarch Plaza. This move revealed exactly how Smith was running his operation.

The Engineer had known Smith was running late. The pilot of the Wonderland Toys jet had been continually monitoring the government craft's progress. The squall line off the North Carolina coast had been a stroke of luck. Now Smith was temporarily out of the loop.

As the Engineer watched Collins pay the cab, he reckoned he had thirty to thirty-five minutes before Smith made his appearance. It would be enough time, provided he had Collins's unwitting cooperation.

The Engineer waited until a porter had taken Collins's duffel bag out of the trunk, then rolled down his window and told one of the doormen that he was here to pick up a client. He slipped the doorman a ten-dollar bill, asked that the car be parked near an exit in the hotel's lot, and fell in behind Collins as she followed the porter and his cart through the front doors.

It was dinner hour. The lobby was crowded with guests chatting their way past ornately framed nineteenth-century oils, headed for cocktails in the lounge or toward the formal dining room. The Engineer watched as Collins scanned the people around her. Her eyes tended to dart, another indication of how spent she was. The Engineer had been counting on her exhaustion and frayed nerves. They should combine to push Collins into making a mistake.

And here it came.

Rachel stepped up to the front desk, where a young clerk with a page cut and faint traces of childhood eczema smiled at her. Rachel's peripheral vision detected no one on either side of her; she glanced over her left shoulder and saw only passersby. She didn't bother to check her right side.

"I'm looking for Mr. Todd Bannister. Room 1004."

The clerked checked the house list. "Yes, Mr. Bannister is staying with us. You can use the house phone over there. Do you want me to check you in while you're calling?"

"I'll be back in a moment."

Rachel stepped over to a marble-topped credenza and picked up one of three white telephones. When the operator came on she gave her Copeland's pseudonym. The phone rang twice, three times. On the sixth ring Rachel cursed softly, and then the operator came back on, asking if the caller wanted to leave a message. Rachel said no and returned to the front desk.

"Did you happen to notice if Mr. Bannister left the hotel?" she asked the clerk.

"His key is still here, ma'am. Most of our guests leave it with us before going out."

"I'll look for him in the bar."

• • •

The Engineer was holding the same phone that Rachel Collins had used just a few minutes ago. He smelled the residue of her skin cream on the receiver as he spoke to the maître d' in the dining room. Todd Bannister was not there, nor had he booked a reservation. The Engineer got the same reply when he talked to one of the captains in the less formal café.

The Engineer headed into the lounge. He scanned the bar, busy at this hour, then the individual tables, where knots of three or four people were sitting. There wasn't a lone drinker to be seen anywhere, not even at the bar. Confirmation that Copeland wasn't in the room came when the Engineer saw Collins abruptly wheel out of the lounge and head for the café.

You won't find him there.

But there was one other place to look. The Engineer walked swiftly across the lobby and managed to squeeze into an elevator car just as its doors were closing.

The ride to the hotel's fitness center took less than thirty seconds. The Engineer walked down a carpeted hall pungent with the scent of chlorine. He opened the glass doors to the center and was immediately struck by the warm, moist air. On his left was the large pool, lap lanes marked in red. On the deck at one end was a row of Lifecycles; on the right, beneath television monitors, was the workout area, with StairMasters, rowing machines, and weight equipment.

The Engineer paused at a table by the entrance. It was piled high with fresh towels, topped off by a sign that read "No Attendant on Duty. For Special Requests Please Dial Ext. 111." The exercise equipment was still, the television monitors black. Not even a ripple marred the surface of the pool. The Engineer walked to the far end of the pool, then along a glass wall whose panels opened onto the patio. It, too, was deserted. That left only the sauna and steam room.

The Engineer checked the steam room first. There was hardly any mist in it, indicating that it hadn't been used for at least several hours. But light was showing through the tempered-glass inset in the door of the sauna.

• • •

Rachel wended her way through the bar one more time, just to make sure Copeland hadn't come in while she'd been scouting the dining areas. She returned to the lobby and, to avoid questions from the solicitous staff, took a chair from which she could see both the elevator banks and the lobby traffic.

She tried to convince herself that there was nowhere else Copeland could be. Certainly he wasn't in any of the salons reserved for meetings. Maybe the gift shop? No, he would have come out by now. For some reason, Copeland had left the hotel. Maybe he needed some fresh air and felt safe enough, knowing that Rachel was coming, to take a walk around the hotel gardens.

What a fucking jerk.

Rachel clamped down on her fury. To get back to his room Copeland would have to go right by her. Until that happened, she could do nothing.

Steven Copeland was sitting on the third tier of the cedar-lined sauna, a towel wrapped around his waist. He was alone in a space that could hold fifteen men. His breathing was labored as sweat poured off his body. When he'd entered the sauna twenty minutes ago, he had thrown water on the hot stones in the firebox and cranked up the temperature gauge. He wanted the heat to drain him of his anxiety, smooth out his nerves. He wanted to feel clean and have some color in his face before meeting the army woman. He let his head hang, chin against his chest. He felt a deep peace that almost lulled him to sleep. Tonight he was sure he *would* sleep, for the first time in days.

The door opened with a low squeal. Copeland raised his head slowly; it seemed very heavy to him right now. His lungs wheezed as he spoke.

"Hello?"

"Mr. Bannister? Is that you? It's Frank from the front desk."

The speaker was standing by the door, open a crack. Copeland could make out only the black suit and the indistinct features of the face behind the thick glass pane.

"Yeah, it's me," he called back, trying to keep his head up.

"There's a young lady looking for you, sir. Warrant Officer Rachel Collins."

"Okay. I've been expecting her."

Copeland stretched his legs out and gingerly set his feet down on the next tier. The wood was very hot, and he moved faster, wanting to reach the tiled floor. By the time he did so, his towel had loosened and almost fallen away. He clutched at it, then looked up and noticed that the hotel employee was now in the sauna, the door closed, standing directly in front of him.

There was a blur of movement, and Copeland felt something hard and warm move across his neck. The stones in the firebox sizzled. Copeland had just enough time to wonder where the water had come from before he realized that what had fallen on the stones was blood. His.

Now three fingers were clamped against the side of his neck. The point of a knife wavered in front of his right eye, and wet lips were whispering into his ear.

"Tell me where Beth is. Do it now and you'll live. Don't do it and I take away my fingers, paint the walls with you."

Fifteen minutes had gone by and still there was no sign of Copeland. Rachel rose from her chair, paced the short distance between it and the bellmen's desk near the main doors. She turned when she heard one of the elevators *ping* and scanned the three couples waiting to get in. Since she wasn't expecting Copeland to come *down* to the lobby, she barely noticed the people getting out of the car. The tall man in the dark suit and chauffeur's cap didn't register at all.

Rachel returned to her chair. Another ten minutes crawled by. Her impatience began to change into a gnawing fear as the crowd in the lobby thinned. One of the clerks from the registration desk was talking to the concierge, pointing in her direction.

"Rachel Collins?"

She looked up at the man who had materialized silently by her side, and her heart lurched. She had never seen that tanned face in real life, but she recognized it instantly, in part because of the grief that scarred it.

"Logan Smith?"

Then she saw two men behind him, instantly made them as federal officers, and shot to her feet.

"Take it easy. I'm not after you, okay?"

His voice was calm and friendly, but Rachel could tell he was working hard at it. She sensed his awful hurry.

Rachel repeated his name because she had to be absolutely sure.

"Pictures," he said. "That's how we know each other. Through Mollie's pictures."

"What are you doing here?" Rachel blurted.

"Same as you—trying to find Copeland. He's not in his room, is he? You wouldn't be here otherwise. You're waiting to catch him coming through."

"He knew I was coming," Rachel said. "He should be here. It's been almost a half hour—"

Smith pulled away from her fast. He snared the elbow of a big man moving by him, turned him around. His ID was out.

"What's the emergency?"

The hotel security officer glanced at the ID, then back at Smith. He knew enough to recognize federal credentials.

"An accident in the sauna. One of the guests—"

"Which one?" Smith cut in.

"The name's Bannister."

Smith saw the sick look on Rachel's face and maneuvered the security officer toward the elevators.

"How *bad* an accident?" he whispered.

The officer glanced over Smith's shoulder, back at Rachel standing there, her eyes burning into his.

"Can't say for sure. One of the cleaning people fainted. The other one was screaming about blood boiling in the sauna."

THREE

18

The sweet, cloying odor of singed hair was something Rachel Collins recalled from army maneuvers, during simulated firefights where defenders had used real flamethrowers and the attackers had gotten careless. She couldn't identify the other smell, equally powerful and nauseating, until she saw the position of Steven Copeland's body through the half-open door to the sauna. His feet and legs were on the ground, propping up his torso, which had been draped across the firebox piled with white-hot rocks. Rachel heard a sizzle and realized it was melting fat.

There were four people in the spa now. The cleaner, a middle-aged Hispanic, was on his knees at the edge of the swimming pool, rocking back and forth, retching into the water. The hotel security guard, who had rushed to the spa with her and Smith, had stopped abruptly as though he'd slammed into an invisible wall. He was now turned away, doubled over, a handkerchief clamped across his mouth. Rachel heard Smith draw a deep breath before he walked quickly into the sauna and pulled Copeland off the firebox, letting him crumple onto the bloodstained tiles.

He came back out. "Rachel, are you with me? You're not going to keel over, are you?"

Smith was standing only inches from her, his complexion red from the heat. She thought his voice sounded okay, clipped but level, like a paramedic's at the scene of a wreck.

"I'll be all right," she heard herself say. She looked into his eyes to make him believe that.

"Go lock the main doors to this place. We don't need a crowd. Then get on the emergency phone. Tell the front desk to page Special Agent Abbot. He'll be in the lobby. Let me know when he comes on the line."

Rachel nodded, took a step back, then stopped. She couldn't help looking behind Smith, at the steaming abattoir.

"You did everything you could for him," Smith was telling her. "If you still want to help, then do exactly as I say. This didn't happen very long ago. The son of a bitch might still be close."

"The messenger," Rachel said. "That's what Mollie called him."

She felt Smith's hand on her shoulder, pushing her away. "Get going."

The clerk at the front desk started asking for the security guard. Rachel cut him off and told him to find Abbot and put him on the line. She listened to strains of the lobby noise and piano melodies coming through the receiver. When Abbot came on she identified herself and asked him to hold for Smith.

"Get the cleaner and guard out of the way," Smith said as he brushed by her. "Put 'em in the exercise room. The cleaner might have a problem with English. How's your Spanish?"

"It'll do."

"Good. See what he offers up."

Smith was talking in low tones, telling Abbot to get a team up to the spa to seal off and preserve the crime scene. He heard frantic rapping on the doors to the pool area and was grateful there were no inset windowpanes. Next, Smith wanted Abbot's people to interview the staff. The suspect wouldn't risk sticking around the hotel, but maybe a doorman or porter might recall and be able to describe someone a little too nervous or in too great a hurry leaving the hotel.

Then came calls Abbot had to make to the Atlanta Police Department and its Homicide Unit. Smith wanted it made clear that he needed enough patrolmen to corral the media, which, he suspected, would be here sooner than the cops.

Finally Abbot was to have Atlanta P.D. send out the coroner.

Rachel was a few steps from the cleaner, who was still on his knees by the pool, moaning softly. She was about to reach for him when she straightened and wheeled back to Smith. He turned, the phone still at his ear.

Rachel dug into her pocket and thrust a piece of paper at him. "That's him."

Smith glanced at the composite, then back to her. "Hold the line a second," he said to Abbot.

Smith took the composite and looked at it closely. "Who is he?"

"I don't have a name. This came from a QRT duty sergeant in Baltimore. It's the phony messenger who stole QRT's audiotape on the Dunn raid. Look, I know this doesn't mean anything to you. But Mollie believed—and I do, too—that he's the one hunting Copeland and Underwood."

"You're not sure, though."

"I never saw him!"

Rachel caught the shrillness in her voice and forced herself to slow down. Smith wasn't privy to the background information she had, and now was not the time to bring him up to speed.

"It's the only face we have, drawn by someone who saw him up close, talked to him. But I have to tell you, the sergeant suspected a disguise. Maybe a wig; the mustache and beard could be false, too."

"If I put this out on the bulletin, we could end up chasing the wrong guy entirely."

"So lose the facial hair and give him a trim. In Baltimore he was a delivery biker. He wouldn't have come here looking like that."

Smith turned away, stared at the gently lapping water in the pool.

"It's your play," he said, then got back on the phone. "Chris? I have possible description coming off a composite out of Baltimore. Get your people to take it around to all the employees. Start with the ones at the door, anyone who might have seen him coming or going. We'll blanket the rest when backup arrives. Ready? The suspect's a white male, about thirty-five to forty, six feet, one hundred eighty to one hundred ninety-five pounds, brown eyes, brown hair. Neat. Might look like a midlevel executive or sales type. No question that he drove here—he wouldn't have risked waiting around for a cab. If you get a hit, get the valets to find the parking stub. That'll give us a plate number, and what time he left. Anyone who drove off twenty, twenty-five minutes ago is prime."

Rachel heard all this as she steered the cleaner over to one of the lounge chairs. She gave him a fresh towel off the top of the pile and a bottle of Evian she'd dug out of an ice chest. The security guard came over and joined them.

"What's your name, son?"

The guard slumped on the padded seat of a Universal exercise machine and gazed up at Smith.

"Hogan. Bobby Ray."

"This is the hardest time, Bobby Ray, but I'm asking you to help me out."

Rachel was struck by how Smith matched the cadence of his words to that of Hogan. He wasn't from the South, but he could pass; the mimicry was that good.

"How many of you on shift, Bobby Ray?"

"Six."

"And you caught the call. Were you in the lobby doing rounds?"

"No, sir. I was in our office, right behind the front desk. Just finished dinner and was having my coffee. The emergency board lit up, spa light flashing, and I was on my way."

"You didn't see anyone unusual when you came out of the office? Someone in a real hurry? A nervous type?"

"No, sir. But then my radio was squawking somethin' fierce."

Hogan nodded toward the cleaner. "Aman-uel here was hollerin' away 'bout how a guest had had a real bad accident, blood all over the place . . ." He looked across the pool at the sauna and shuddered.

"Downstairs you told me the victim's name was Bannister. How'd you know that?"

Hogan glanced over at the cleaner. "He gave it to me . . . jabbering away so's I couldn't hardly make out what he was saying." He pointed to a clipboard hanging on the wall above the amenities table. "He must have got it off the sign-in sheet."

"You recognize the victim, Bobby Ray?"

Hogan shook his head. "He was just a name on the registration list."

"You never spoke to him? He never caused any problems, made any special requests?"

"No, sir."

"No one came calling on him that you might have seen or heard about?"

"I heard tell Wendy Prince—she's a real estate lady—she took him out once, maybe a couple times."

Rachel caught Smith's look of disbelief. Why in the hell would Copeland have been checking out the local housing? Was that how he'd been lured out of the hotel? But if so, there would have been no reason to bring him back to the hotel to kill him. There were plenty of lonely, dark ravines in the Buckhead landscape.

Rachel turned when she heard insistent tapping on the door. Smith patted Bobby Ray on the shoulder.

"You just sit here a minute. My partner will be right with you."

Rachel caught Smith's wave and followed him to the doors. He unlocked them, and a bland-looking accountant type squeezed through. Rachel mistook him for a hotel manager until Smith made the introductions.

"Any luck with the description?" Smith asked.

"Not yet. And not likely. It's a circus down there. I'd be lucky if anyone remembered what their mother looks like, let alone some stranger. And you were right about the media: they arrived along with the cavalry."

"Are you okay with them? Atlanta P.D. won't butt heads over turf?"

"Homicide's good boys. We've worked together before."

Abbot sniffed, then walked over and peered into the sauna. When he returned his expression was as serene as if he'd just stepped out of a confessional.

"*Nobody* will want any of this turf, Logan," he said softly. "What's the play?"

Smith nodded at the cleaner and the security guard. "Your people need to take statements. Let homicide cull the rest of the staff except for the valets and doormen. I'm still hoping we can get a hit."

Abbot opened the spa door, called out a couple of names. A man and a woman entered, huddled briefly with Abbot, then went to the cleaner and the security guard. Abbot got on his radio and talked to his people downstairs. Rachel looked at Smith, who was standing with his hands stuffed in his pants pockets, staring at the floor.

"I need to see what he did to Copeland," she said.

Smith took a second, then glanced up at her. Rachel could feel him taking his measure of her, seeing the grief and pain his yardstick was made of.

"Why?"

"Because right now he's just a ghost who kills. If I see how he does that, it makes him . . . different." She paused. "If I see how, maybe I'll see it coming when he tries for me."

"How's your stomach?"

"I've made it this far."

Smith nodded and began walking toward the sauna. She fell in step with him, took a deep breath before she got too close. She would breathe through her mouth now.

Squatting close to the pool of congealing blood, Smith pointed to a puncture on the side of Copeland's neck. "Your man came in fast and light, cutting but not following through."

"He could have kept on going," Rachel said. "Sliced the entire throat. Why'd he stop?"

"Because he wanted Copeland to believe he would live. He held two fingers over the wound to show him that."

"Copeland would have believed him," Rachel said softly. "He didn't know he was already dying."

"Question is, why keep him alive at all? It was a terrible risk. The doors to the spa were unlocked. The cleaning man could have come sooner, or maybe another guest—"

"Something the messenger needed," Rachel cut in. "Something only Copeland could tell him."

Smith's head snapped up. "Copeland knew the location of the second informant?"

Rachel closed her eyes, nodded. She didn't resist when Smith jerked her to her feet.

"Where?"

"Arizona. That's where Copeland and I were headed."

Gripping her elbow, Smith walked her cop style to the far end of the pool. He pulled back the sliding glass doors, and they stepped out onto the terrace. The cool night air was alive with chatter from the crowds gathered three floors below in the hotel motor court. The flashers on the police cruisers played over the landscaping.

"I need to know this now," Smith said, clutching the railing. "Who is Mollie's second informant, and where is she—exactly?"

"Her name is Beth Underwood. She's in a place called Carefree, in Arizona."

Smith nodded, more to himself than to acknowledge the information. "Have you spoken to her? Do you know if she's alive, right at this moment?"

"I haven't spoken to her. I called once, but her line was busy. She was talking with Copeland. . . ."

Rachel stopped. There was too much Smith didn't know, too much she had to explain to make him understand.

"She's alive," Rachel finished. "She *must* be."

When Smith looked at her, the shadows cast by the mounted outdoor lamps hooded his face. She could see only the glint in his eyes and the shine on his teeth as he spoke.

"Why? What makes you so sure that Copeland was the messenger's *first* stop?"

• • •

Smith ducked back inside the spa. Rachel watched him huddle with the security guard, Billy Ray. She was still thinking about the question Smith had thrown at her when he came back out to the terrace.

"There's a back way out of here," he said, holding up a key.

He unlocked the gate at the far end of the terrace, and Rachel saw that it led to a metal staircase bolted to the side of the building. They clattered down to the ground-floor landing to another door whose lock yielded to the same key. They stepped out by the engineering station, next to the concrete pens that housed the hotel's air-conditioning units. She followed Smith along a cement slab path that led to the entrance to the motor court. Looking back, Rachel saw that the driveway was jammed with police vehicles. Two news vans were parked haphazardly in the exit lane under the portico, blocking guests who were trying to leave.

"Did you leave anything in the hotel?" Smith asked as they hurried around the corner to the outdoor parking lot.

"My duffel bag. It was taken inside when I arrived."

"Need anything from it?"

"The Dunn file. You'll want to see it."

Without breaking stride, Smith drew out his cell phone and insructed Chris Abbot to have the duffel bag brought from the bell captain's closet to the parking lot, pronto. He opened the passenger door to the Chevy Lumina for Rachel, got in behind the wheel, and turned to face her.

"Why do you think Underwood is still alive?"

"Because if the messenger knew where Mollie had stashed the two, he would have done Copeland long before now and moved on. Copeland's been holed up here for three days, a sitting duck."

"So if this messenger didn't know where to find Copeland . . ."

Rachel looked past her reflection, out the window. Under the orange anticrime lights the cars looked like dark, hulking insects.

"The only way he could have gotten here was by following me. No, that's wrong. He found out *ahead of time* where I was going, and got here before I did."

The realization made Rachel's heart pound. In the street a woman could always tell when she was being stared at—appreciatively or with hunger, it didn't matter. Usually that sensation lasted only a few seconds. The messenger had been around her a long time. She'd never known he was there, never smelled or even sensed his presence.

Now Smith was asking her about that, if she'd ever felt watched, maybe caught a glimpse of a face turning away quickly. Rachel had to fight through her fear before she could tell him, no.

"You were doing the same thing, weren't you?" she said, looking straight ahead. "Tracking me. That's how you're here."

Smith was silent, and Rachel didn't press. For now.

"We'll assume that Copeland was the first," he said.

"Which means that if the messenger got what he wanted out of him, he's on his way to Arizona right now, while we're sitting here."

The bitterness that underlay her words disturbed Smith. He'd seen failure drive people to desperate measures, which in turn led to mistakes. Rachel Collins was sick over Copeland's death. It had stoked her fury and her desire for vengeance. It could kill her if she gave it a chance.

"We can still do something sitting here," Smith said. "What's the exact address for Underwood?"

Rachel couldn't bear to look at him. "It's a rural route post office box. Underwood must have told Mollie the exact lot or house when they got off the plane in Phoenix. Copeland probably knew the directions, too."

"Why?"

"She and Underwood were in this together from the very beginning. They had a relationship. . . ."

"They were lovers," Smith said flatly.

Rachel nodded.

"You can tell me about that later," Smith said. "You called Underwood, right? The phone company will have a hard location on the number. Give it to me."

"You should call Beth right now," Rachel told him. "You don't have to say anything, just let me hear her voice. As least we'll know if she's alive."

Smith shook his head. "That'll only frighten her. Right now I

don't know what to tell her yet, do you? Better to wait till we
have something solid to give her. What happened here won't hit
the national news for at least an hour. If we're lucky, Underwood
doesn't have cable or a satellite dish out there."

Rachel looked at him. "I need to know she's okay. Please."

Smith hesitated. "Okay. Give me the number."

Rachel watched him dial, then he held the phone out so that
they could both hear it ringing. After six rings Rachel closed her
eyes and shook her head.

"It doesn't mean anything. She may not have an answering
machine. It's only late afternoon out there. She's gone out, maybe
to get some food."

She pushed away the other, nightmarish images.

"Someone's coming," she said.

Smith looked in the rearview mirror. "One of Abbot's. Help
him out, would you?"

He put a casual spin on the request, but Rachel smelled a
brush-off. She jumped out and walked fast to the agent, who had
her duffel bag in his hand.

"Thanks. I'll take that."

The agent blinked as she snatched it from him, pulled open the
back door of the sedan, and threw the bag across the seat. Smith
was looking over his shoulder at her, his cell phone by his ear. He
put it down without speaking. Rachel returned to the front seat.

"Mollie told me you were with the Domestic Terrorism Unit.
But this isn't about terrorism at all. You're not working with the
unit now, but you're on the hunt." She paused. "I need to know
what's going on."

Smith pinched the bridge of his nose. "This is a one-off assignment. Mollie's . . . her death has certain implications."

"Who are you working for?" Rachel asked quietly.

"The White House."

"Sweet Jesus."

"Listen to me. I need to do something right now, for Underwood. But you never heard what I'm about to say."

Rachel nodded. Smith punched in a number on the speed
dialer, took a deep breath before he started talking.

"Lucille? No, don't ask. Atlanta's a meltdown. Copeland is dead. Whoever's cleaning up got to him first. Collins is okay. She's with me right now. There are things that have to be done. You ready?

"Beth Underwood is in Arizona, a place called Carefree. Here's the address and phone number. Don't bother calling—I tried and there's no answer. I'm hoping she went out for a quart of milk. Scramble the Tactical Unit, a three-man team. Tell them to use the Lockheed cover. I don't want them going in as *federales* into a place where people think the government has tampered with their drinking water to turn them into Democrats."

Rachel watched him listen to what must have been a string of questions from the woman on the other end.

"No, I don't have a description. But Collins does. I'm putting her on now."

Smith handed Rachel the phone and said, "Meet Lucille."

"Hello?"

"Go ahead, please," replied the soft voice.

Rachel focused her thoughts on National Airport, Beth Underwood getting out of Copeland's blue Jetta; then another image of her inside the aircraft cabin, whispering to Copeland. She was ready.

"Beth Underwood is about five feet ten inches. Big, but not heavy or fat. Long, light brown hair with highlights. Hazel eyes. A beauty or birthmark below the left side of her lower lip. She was wearing tan slacks, green T-shirt, and a light navy jacket."

Rachel thought hard for a moment, then shook her head and handed back the phone.

"Underwood worked in D.C.," Smith said. "Check with DMV there. Also Virginia and Maryland. And Arizona just in case. Fax the photo ID to Tac and to me on the plane. If Tac spots her, they are *not* to attempt contact. I want full coverage, but that's all."

He paused. "Lucille, you tell the boys to be careful. The guy who did Copeland, he's the kind who wipes *everything* off the board. If they see anyone approach Underwood, it's one warning, then a hard takedown."

There were more questions, but Smith cut them off. "I have to get to the airport. We'll polish up the operation from the plane. There may be other things we can do, I'm not sure yet."

He jammed the phone into its recharger base on the console and eased the car out of the lot and onto the ramp to Lenox Road. There he lowered the window, slapped the blue flasher on the roof, and hit the siren. When they reached I-85, Smith called the pilot of the jet, then turned his attention to Rachel.

"It's come to Jesus time," he said, concentrating on the traffic. "You have to tell me everything, exactly the way it went down."

Rachel wanted to fight him because she smelled what was going to happen. If she gave him what she knew, he wouldn't need her anymore. But she could not hold out.

She began with the stakeout in Baltimore, told him about Dunn, his dying words, and the effect they'd had on Mollie. She did her best to disassociate herself from the rest, present it as though she had been only a third-party observer to events. Twice she caught Smith glancing at her, when she described what had happened at the Greenbrier and the way she had gotten hold of Dunn's file. The lights of the airport were coming up when she recounted her final conversation with Steven Copeland.

Smith took the exit to the private aircraft sector of Atlanta International. He braked at the gate, flipped his ID at the guard, and sped past the hangars where corporate jets were cleaned and overhauled. On the taxiway Rachel saw a sleek aircraft warming up, collision lights rolling, the co-pilot waiting at the foot of the stair ramp.

Smith was reaching for his door handle when she grabbed him.

"Let me see if I got this straight. I've told you everything I know. Now you're going to jump on that plane, and I'm supposed to grab the last shuttle for D.C., report to Belvoir, and get my butt kicked. That about right?"

He shifted in his seat. His voice was gentle, as though for an instant he were seeing her for the first time.

"I know you from pictures," he said. "And things Mollie told me about you. You became involved in this and came further than you had any right to. Because this guy was tracking you, maybe even had you in his sights, and he's very good at what he does.

But so were you—too good, too fast to let him make his move. And you were very lucky, Rachel. It's something to remember."

"Don't send me away," she said softly. "I told you what I know not because you asked, but because I have to believe it will help find him. So don't use me the way he was using me. Let me help you finish what Mollie couldn't."

Then she gave up the last of her secrets. "You're here because the White House believes, or at least suspects, that Griffin North was murdered. The political fallout—shit, I don't really care about that, whatever it is. But you have to know why *Mollie* was killed. Because she was North's lover. She died because she was the first one who didn't believe that the plane crash was an accident."

Rachel saw him flinch, the realization clear in the pain and shock in his eyes. Logan Smith had never even imagined a connection between his sister and the fallen national icon.

The aircraft was headed for the active runway before Rachel had reached her seat. She was grateful that Logan didn't try to stop her as she continued to the tiny washroom. She managed to bolt the door before she dropped to her knees and flung back the toilet cover. She remained like that even as the jet screamed down the concrete and seemed to stand on its tail as it clawed for altitude.

The medicine chest was well stocked. She swallowed four aspirin and chased them down with a cup of water. She tore the cellophane wrapping off a toothbrush and afterward scrubbed her face and brushed her hair. A quick glance in the mirror told her this was as good as it was going to get.

Smith was working his laptop on a foldout table between the two rows of seats. Rachel looked over his shoulder and watched DMV files crawl across the screen.

"Take the seat in the back," he said. "I'll be there in a minute."

The seat against the rear bulkhead was the size of a small sofa. Rachel sank into its cushions, then put up her feet and leaned back. She didn't mean to lie all the way down, but the thick armrest felt good against her head and the drone of port engines vibrated hypnotically through her body. Except for the lights over

Smith's work area, the aircraft interior was dark. She stared at the window across the aisle, at the orange moon rising through the clouds, but then it drifted out of sight, stealing the stars with it.

Smith sat at his computer for another fifteen minutes, even though his work was, for the moment, done. He did not want to move until he was sure Rachel was asleep. Carefully he rose and looked back. Enough light reached the rear of the cabin for him to see her open mouth and the steady rise and fall of her chest.

He started to reach for the blanket beside him, then thought better of it. The army produced light sleepers. Instead he adjusted the heat control for the cabin. Rachel was breathing deeply, and the warm air would be as effective as the blanket.

Smith moved to a forward seat in the cabin, turned on the button for the overhead light, and dialed through to Los Angeles.

"You sound beat," Lucille said. "What's your ETA in Phoenix?"

"Three hours thirty minutes."

"You must be on afterburners."

"Something like that."

Smith had told the pilot to push the craft to its absolute limit and take the most direct heading to their destination. There had been problems because some of the travel would be through restricted airspace. Smith had had to call the NORAD ready desk at Cheyenne Mountain, wait until they had checked his clearance with Washington before a pass-through corridor was set up.

"Where's Tac?" he asked.

"En route. They'll be touching down in Sky Harbor in thirty minutes. I passed on the word about possible opposition."

"What about the DMVs?"

"Check your fax."

Smith went back to his makeshift desk and tore a color sheet off the machine tucked into a cabinet. The photograph was not flattering, but the woman in it clearly matched the description Rachel Collins had given.

"Looks good to me," he said. "But it's a D.C. driver's license. Nothing from Arizona?"

"Lots of Underwoods, but no one who even comes close to this gal. At least Tac will have a face to work with."

"Maybe we can give them even more of an edge. Get hold of FAA and ask them for all traffic, private and commercial, headed into Sky Harbor from Atlanta."

Lucille took a second to digest this. "You're saying our man might have gotten the jump on you?"

"Try this: Copeland is murdered twenty-five, thirty minutes before Collins and I find him. In that time frame, the killer's just about reached Atlanta International. Question is, is he going commercial or does he have his own wheels? I don't think he'd risk a commercial flight. Overbooking, mechanical problems, delays on the runway—elements he couldn't predict or control."

"There can't be that much traffic going into Sky Harbor this time of night," Lucille ventured. "Want to create a little emergency, close the place down?"

"The logistics would involve too many people. And if this guy spots a setup, he'd run. Or worse."

"I could send out a second team to cover the airport, give them the composite you sent to work with."

"I don't trust the composite. Who knows what this guy really looks like? If Tac makes a move on the wrong man, the locals'll pile in."

"Okay. So what if something suspicious does come in, and we have a look *after* its passenger leaves the airport. He has to come back for his ride, right? It's his way out."

"Except now it's our bait. . . ." Smith thought about it. "That's good. Let's think about how it could play. In the meantime get me those FAA inbounds."

"You'll have 'em in twenty minutes." Lucille hesitated. "Logan, who *is* this guy?"

"Collins called him a ghost. But maybe he won't stay that way for long. Not if we get to Underwood, throw a shield over her, and find out what she knows."

"Collins is with you, right?"

"She knows things, Lucille. Things I haven't even heard yet. I couldn't leave her behind."

"I'll get hold of Jessup or whoever's handling the desk at Belvoir, tell them she's okay and in federal custody as a material witness.

That should square her with the MPs and scrub her name off the AWOL list."

"You're light-years ahead of me."

"Then do me a favor."

"That being . . . ?"

"When you go for Underwood, keep Collins in the background. I'd really like to meet that girl someday."

19

Flash traffic from the FBI generates a very swift response from the Federal Aviation Authority.

Lucille Parker's call was immediately forwarded to the D.C. security director on watch. He was a fourteen-year veteran and could press the right buttons in his sleep. Calls went out simultaneously to Atlanta and Phoenix. Air traffic control supervisors dropped whatever they were doing and began collating the information the director was waiting on. The lines among the three cities remained open, and the supervisors worked fast. All of them had run practice drills and scenarios where hijackings or bomb threats were involved. There was an informal scorekeeping among the regional centers, and so far the best time had been clocked by the Denver group. Tonight that record fell. Atlanta came through in less than twelve minutes with a list of commercial and private

aircraft headed for Phoenix. It took Phoenix another thirty seconds to double-check and confirm that information.

In her office on the seventeenth floor of the Federal Building
in Los Angeles, Lucille spread the hard copies across her pristine
desk. She was a very tidy individual, a quality that also made her
very quick.

She focused her attention on the private aircraft. Two were
corporate jets, one belonging to an international beverage company, the other to a multinational agricultural concern. Three
others were privately owned: a recording promoter who was fer-
rying a rock star to a Phoenix concert; a country-western diva
thrice divorced; and the media tycoon who, years ago, had
founded the nation's first all-news network.

Lucille checked the passenger manifests very carefully and found
nothing untoward. Then she got back to FAA Atlanta and asked
them to pull the files of all the pilots and cabin crew on those
flights. These came back in less than twenty minutes. The performance and background records were unblemished.

Lucille reviewed all the material one more time, just to be sure
she hadn't missed anything. Then she sat back and simply stared at
the paperwork, allowing her subconscious to sniff around the details. No warning bells went off, not even a tinkle.

When she finally called Smith she was quietly confident that
Copeland's killer could not be on his way to Phoenix, at least not
by air. What she didn't know, couldn't possibly have guessed, was
that an error had already occurred—not in the information itself,
but in the *way* that information had been requested. Logan Smith
had asked for background on private carriers leaving Hartsfield
Atlanta International for Phoenix's Sky Harbor Airport. This was
the message Lucille had passed on to the Atlanta controllers, who
in turn focused their attention exclusively on the two points:
Atlanta and Phoenix—not Lakeland Air Force Base, twenty-two
miles outside Phoenix. The controllers had been led to believe,
rightly, that they were tracking an aircraft headed for a *civilian*
destination. Since the FBI requests had not mentioned the alternative of a military landing area, Atlanta had never thought to in-
clude in its report to Los Angeles the Gulfstream IV executive jet
that had given AFB Lakeland as its destination.

• • •

The flight was forty minutes out of Lakeland, being handled by air force traffic controllers. The Engineer had been sleeping for the last two hours. Now he got on the radio with the acting base commander to make sure final landing clearance had been authorized.

There was a history between the Engineer and this particular officer. Six months earlier they had met in an area of Nevada called Groome Lake, which officially did not exist. Together they had strolled through hardened bunkers, among equipment that was the stuff of sci-fi buffs' imaginations, quietly discussing certain possible operations in the Asian theater. The colonel knew the Engineer's standing in the CIA and had prospered in his relationship with him. He had raised no objections or questions when the Engineer told him he would be paying Lakeland a brief visit on his way to Groome Lake. Since all communications between the jet and air force personnel were on scrambler, the Engineer didn't have to worry about nosy civilian controllers listening in on his conversation.

The Engineer concluded his chat with the colonel, thanked him for the personal favor, then went to the storage area in the rear of the aircraft to pack. Luggage and clothing were not his concerns. The Gulfstream carried a cornucopia of weapons, ammunition, explosives, camouflage gear—anything and everything that an independent field agent might need to operate effectively anywhere in the world, from the tropics to the tundra. The Engineer examined the inventory, made his selections, and was fully kitted up by the time his pilot began his descent.

The Gulfstream taxied past a squadron of F-18's prepping for night maneuvers and stopped by a small hangar near the control tower. The Engineer stepped out, a small canvas bag in his hand, and walked over to where the colonel was standing next to his personal vehicle, a Jeep Cherokee with civilian plates and air force stickers on the inside of the windshield. In the cool desert night the two warriors exchanged quiet greetings. The colonel did not ask why his visitor was here or the reason he needed temporary civilian ground transportation. Inquiring as to what business the Engineer had in the Phoenix environs never crossed his mind.

Following in an air force police HumVee, the colonel trailed his guest as far as the perimeter gates. He saw an arm wave back at him as the Cherokee cleared the guard post and stood there watching until red taillights had disappeared deep into the Sonoran desert.

The Engineer made a right onto the highway. He kept the Cherokee at the speed limit. He was in no hurry, nor did he wish to attract the attention of an Arizona State Trooper. The trooper would not, after seeing the air force decals, ticket him, but time would be lost while vehicle and license checks were run.

The Engineer headed southwest, past sleeping, guard-gated communities that continued to spring up around Phoenix like bad mushroom patches. He passed shopping centers, L-shaped complexes painted in desert pastels and capped with red tile roofs, and brightly lit gas stations with a 7-Eleven tacked on. His window was down, and it was wonderful to breathe the pungent desert air, scrubbed and fresh in a way that reminded him of other times in other hot, dry places. Then he saw an overhead highway sign, plastic reflectors spelling the names of the next three exits. At the second off-ramp, the Engineer flicked on his turn signal and eased the Cherokee into a gentle turn. In the shallow valley below were the flickering lights of Carefree.

The three broad-shouldered men getting out of the Bell Ranger helicopter at Sky Harbor looked like well-heeled outdoorsmen. They wore expensive thick-soled hiking boots, baggy trousers, and tan denim vests with numerous pockets. The airport security officer who'd come out to give them the once-over was impressed by and a little envious of their equipment: large, aluminum-frame backpacks that included lightweight sleeping bags, and long wooden cases with brass fittings that, he judged, held high-powered hunting rifles.

The security officer thought they were a chatty lot, laughing and joking about an L.A. colleague called Bob who hadn't been able to make the trip because his wife had railroaded him into going with her to Hawaii instead. There were casual references to remote resorts in Idaho and Alaska, some good-natured arguing about the real size of the bighorn sheep one of them had brought down last year in the Cascades.

The security officer was happy to dole out advice when they asked him where to get a good steak and how long a drive it would be out to Sedona, their first stop. He was also impressed by the customized Chevy Suburban waiting for them in the short-term lot. Belonged to a local buddy who was out of state on business, they said.

The officer wondered about that as he watched them load the truck. For big men they moved very swiftly, surely, and silently, a combination that made him uneasy. The officer ventured to ask whereabouts they worked in Los Angeles. One of the men grinned and flipped open his wallet. As he dug around for a business card, the officer noted a California driver's license and a Lockheed employee ID. The business card he was handed also bore the Lockheed logo and identified its bearer as an executive vice president for research and development.

As the driver fired up the rig, the officer wished them good luck and watched the Suburban wend its way to the airport feeder road. Only when he was walking back to the terminal did he realize they'd never said where exactly they were going or what they were hunting.

The FBI Tactical Unit posing as weekend hunters left Phoenix behind and proceeded north up the interstate. After taking the turnoff for Carefree, they found themselves on a freshly graded two-lane blacktop that took them into a shallow valley.

"A Brady Bunch housing development," the driver muttered.

Spread across the valley and on the upslopes were pockets of orange lights. As the team drove farther they passed six-foot-high stone walls that defined each planned community from its neighbor. Each had a security hut at the entrance; embedded into the stone walls were large letters spelling out the names: Desert Hawk;

Windhaven; Painted Desert. In some cases there was nothing beyond the stone walls except raw land and construction trailers.

Beyond the planned communities were the estate lots. The finished homes, blazing with light, were baronial, fully landscaped, each sitting on one to two acres of land.

"I have a turn coming up," the driver said. "Right or left?"

The navigator had a blueprint of the development in his lap, a penlight wavering over the paper. "Right," he said.

The next two lots were empty. A Tudor-style estate came up next; then, at the end of the cul-de-sac, sat a starkly modern structure of stone and glass. There were lights on on the second floor.

"That's gotta be it," the driver.

The navigator checked the address stenciled on the concrete curb against the one provided by Southwest Bell. "It's a match."

The driver slowed the Suburban to a crawl. On either side of the mansion were undeveloped lots littered with bulldozers, backhoes, and earthmovers. The problem was, the cul-de-sac ended in a turnaround. The driver couldn't park directly in front of the house without attracting attention. But he needed to stay within a hundred yards of it.

The navigator pointed back to the ostentatious Tudor. "The place is lit up like a Christmas tree. I counted seven vehicles." He paused. "I'm thinking it's a housewarming. And no one's going to be in any condition to drive home. So why don't we just blend?"

The driver turned to the third man, "commo," the communications expert.

"What do you think?"

"That'll play," commo agreed.

While the driver eased his way back to the Tudor, commo released and pulled down a hatch cut into the Suburban's roof. After stowing it, he opened one of the backpacks and quickly assembled a portable antenna, snapping together the backpack's aluminum braces into a tripod. The second backpack contained electronic receivers and signals gear that he bolted to the truck bed. Commo slipped on headphones, powered up the antenna, and, using a joystick, guided it so the dish was aimed directly at the lighted windows of the cul-de-sac house. He adjusted the range and frequency, then the volume.

The first sounds were scratchy, like chickens pecking. After the filter was boosted they became long nails on dry skin. The voices came through clearly enough. Later the tape could be washed electronically to enhance them, but commo didn't think that would be necessary. He was listening to a man and woman coupling. From the grunts and cries, they were going at it full bore.

"One male, one female," he reported to the others. "An intimate situation. You can call Smith and tell him his target is in place."

The members of the Tactical Unit had thought they had only one problem: the distance between the house and the reception antenna. They now believed, correctly, that it had been solved.

But there was another.

The team had seen the earthmoving equipment scattered around the undeveloped lots and paid it no mind. The machines seemed as natural a part of the landscape as the boulders and saguaro. Maybe if someone had caught a glimpse of the Cherokee, a decision to check it out would have been made. But the four-by-four was parked next to a grader, effectively hidden by the machine's tall cab and long engine housing.

The Engineer was halfway down the slope, moving toward the house, when he saw the Suburban's headlights. He took cover behind the blade of a bulldozer and watched the vehicle edge its way around the cul-de-sac. His night vision binoculars gave him a clear view of where the Suburban finally parked and what happened next. The Engineer was impressed with the equipment the FBI had brought along, although in the scheme of things it would prove redundant.

The Engineer began moving again, staying very low to the ground, testing it beneath his feet before allowing his full weight to come down. The earth was dry and in many places soft. There were shallow depressions carved out by giant tires and sudden drops of a foot or more where the land had been tiered for water pipes. The night vision binoculars were not very effective for depth perception at close range; a twisted ankle or turned knee would be a distinct liability.

The Engineer came up to the flagstone wall that ringed the back of the house. The wind had died; he could smell the chlorine in the pool, mixed with the dewy scent of freshly laid turf. The automatically timed lawn sprinklers must have been on earlier in the evening.

He scaled the wall easily, dropping into a crouch when he hit the slippery grass and gliding his way across like a skater over a frozen pond. When he reached the tiled deck he grabbed a lounge cushion and carefully dried the soles of his boots.

In the ninety seconds he'd lived, Steven Copeland had given up precious details about Beth Underwood's location. The exact address had been only the first. Underwood had told him that the house was in a new development and relatively isolated, that as far as she knew it had not been wired to a home security system. The Engineer checked this out now. There was an electrical panel next to the pool equipment shed. He popped it open and saw the emblem for Guardsman Home Protection Services; the slew of wires was not connected to the main system.

Knowing that he'd be dealing with a two-story structure had given the Engineer flexibility in planning. In such a layout the bedrooms were almost always on the second floor. This allowed him to pop the lock on the back door to the garage without fear of being heard.

The interior was very cool, almost cold. The Engineer stepped through a door into the kitchen and stopped, letting the house speak to him. There was the hum of the Sub-zero refrigerator and the faint ticking of a wall clock. The odor of a meal—Chinese takeout, he guessed—hung in the air. The tile floors had been recently scrubbed and smelled of pine. There was no litter box or any animal scent. Copeland had volunteered that Underwood wouldn't have a pet here, although in Washington she kept a cat.

The principal rooms downstairs had big windows that splashed moonlight across new carpet. The Engineer made sure to stay well away from them as he approached the staircase to the second floor. There was a shaft of light on the upper landing and the kinds of noises that could be coming only from one of the bedrooms. The Engineer listened and smiled. The terror he had inflicted on Steven Copeland had peeled back certain truths about him, among them his love for Beth Underwood. Yet here she was, busting mattress springs with someone else. This unexpected second party was an annoyance. The Engineer knew that the FBI surveillance team was focused on the lighted bedroom. Any unusual movement would bring them running. He was not certain he could get into the bedroom and take both targets down without attracting attention.

The Engineer thought about this a little more, then reached down and pressed his hand hard against the carpeted step. He was rewarded with a faint squeak. He'd expected the wood frame of the staircase was raw and green. If the target was sleeping, he might have risked a quick climb, then a dash into the bedroom. But now he'd take another, slightly more spectacular route.

The downstairs had fireplaces in the den and the dining and living rooms—gas fireplaces, with the blue winks of pilot flames peeking out from behind ceramic log arrangements. The Engineer doused the flames in all three and opened the gas cocks all the way. He moved quickly to the temperature control on the wall in the center hall and switched off the air conditioner. No sense in the return air vent sucking out the gas. Then he opened the door to the utility room off the kitchen and went to work on the gas pipes that fed the washer and dryer.

Six minutes later the Engineer was back at the foot of the staircase. Two thin squares of plastic explosives were glued to the wall and the inside of the second step. A thin monofilament line, the kind prized by fly fishermen because it was virtually invisible, was strung between the squares two inches above the step. The loose ends were wound around a spring-loaded detonator, which was then wired into a six-volt battery. In the Engineer's scenario, once Beth Underwood and her lover had finished screwing their brains out, one or both would notice the smell of gas. One or both would come downstairs to investigate, all achy and spent from their antics. The light above the staircase would not work because the Engineer was now gutting it. This meant they would proceed with only the upper-landing light to guide them. In the semidarkness the trip wire would not be seen or felt until an ankle touched it. The connection would be completed, and the plastic would discharge, its force sawing off the lower limbs. The ensuing gas explosion would do the rest.

The Engineer reviewed this sequence of events as he drifted through the kitchen, into the garage, and back outside. He reckoned he'd give the lovers another twenty minutes. If for some reason the explosion had not occurred by then, he would assume they had fallen into a climax-induced stupor. That would necessitate a wake-up call.

"That was the Tac Unit."

Rachel carefully propped herself up on one elbow. She had shifted in her sleep and now had a painful crick in her neck. She reached around with her other hand and began to knead the knotted muscles.

She had been awake for the last few minutes, watching Smith move about the cramped cabin, gathering up papers, stowing away bags and briefcases. His awkward movements suggested he was trying not to wake her, a courtesy that touched her. When she'd seen enough she cleared her throat to make him look at her.

Now he was sitting opposite her, elbows on knees, his head resting in his hands. The harsh cabin light deepened the shadows under his eyes and the wrinkles across his forehead. He had slept little, if at all, and carried his exhaustion like a penitent. Yet in eyes that could have been kind and inviting there burned the forge that kept him going. It denied him respite, consumed him, while at the same time it sustained him.

Rachel sat up and rolled her head like an athlete loosening up. She caught a glimpse of lights outside the window and realized the plane was coming in low.

"The Tac Unit?" she said.

"Out of L.A. They've found Underwood's house. They're sitting on it."

Rachel leaned forward abruptly, almost bumping heads with Smith. "She's inside? They know that for sure?"

"She and someone else."

Rachel sensed his hesitation, identified it as embarrassment.

"She has someone in her bed. Tac says they've been quite . . . energetic." Smith looked at her keenly. "Any idea who he might be?"

Rachel shook her head. "It doesn't jibe. Her having a lover over, I mean. She should have been by herself ever since Mollie dropped her off. Copeland's been calling her regularly. He is—was —a control freak. He would have smelled it if she'd tried to lie or mislead him. Plus, she was waiting on him."

The landing gear whined as it locked into place.

"Whatever," Smith said. "She's there, and she has someone with her."

Rachel was in the rest room when the jet kissed down. She grabbed hold of the bar above the toilet to steady herself against the reverse thrust. By the time the aircraft had come to a stop she was by the door, duffel bag in hand.

The head of the FBI's Phoenix field office was waiting with a car for them. He greeted Smith politely enough, but Rachel didn't miss the pique beneath the courtesy. The Phoenix F.O. knew that something big was going down on their turf and they hadn't been invited to the party.

Smith did not introduce Rachel. He nodded at her to stow her bag. He was still talking with the other agent when Rachel, standing there, decided to move them along. She deposited Smith's things in the trunk, brought it down with enough force to rock the chassis.

"You're in a hurry," Smith said as he got in behind the wheel.

"Can the Tac Unit move in on the house, get Underwood out of there?"

"They're not prepped to do it that way. Why?"

"The situation's not right. She shouldn't be in there . . . like that."

"You want them to take her in flagrante delicto?"

"I want her alive."

"The surveillance crew is very good. Anyone trying for the house will have to go through them. Bad idea."

The words came out before Rachel could stop herself. "I almost wish he'd try."

Smith wheeled the car onto the interstate and punched the gas. Rachel assumed that the Phoenix F.O. had alerted the Arizona police not to interfere. He reached for the radio and spoke to the Tac Unit leader, who reported all clear and quiet. Smith told him he'd be on site in forty minutes.

Rachel had been listening to his clipped conversation with the Tac Unit leader. She half expected Smith to give her an "I told you so" look.

"You said the file on Dunn was important," Smith said. "Why?"

Rachel explained that the file had been—would have been—Mollie's starting point. She reviewed the details of Dunn's gray, mediocre history, then came to the part about his expertise in aircraft maintenance and his stint as North's driver.

"There's no record—that we know about—of Dunn ever servicing the C-12 that North was traveling on," Smith said.

"No. But the coincidences are too convenient. I mean, why would Dunn have given up vacation time to be a general's driver?"

"Was he assigned or did he volunteer?"

"The file doesn't say. And what about North's regular driver? The MP report states it was a hit-and-run. It could have been deliberate."

"To create a vacancy? Possible."

"I think we should check the driver, work back the accident investigation."

"I think you're right."

Rachel checked the dashboard clock. She had no idea where they were, but according to the time, Carefree should be coming up soon.

"You haven't said what you want me to do when we get Underwood," she said.

"The same thing you did with Copeland," Smith replied. "Establish trust. Only you know the details on how Mollie handled her. Underwood will respond to that. If she connects with you, then maybe she'll talk to me."

"Is that as far as I go, get her to talk to you?"

"That depends on what she has to tell us."

Rachel knew that Smith would not commit himself any further. "When we scoop her up, what happens to the boyfriend, or whoever he is?"

"Tac baby-sits him until you're done with Underwood. If he turns out to be a player . . ."

Rachel didn't need him to finish the thought. Either way, it was going to be a rude shock and a long night for this Romeo.

Smith reached for the radio again, told the Tac Unit they were three, four minutes out. Was there anything he should know? The response came back negative. The street was deserted and quiet, except for the ongoing party at the Tudor house. The Tac leader thought that the noise would be good cover for their approach to Underwood's house. Smith told him to prepare for a surreptitious entry, but with a hard, nonlethal option.

"Stun grenades and CS gas?" Rachel asked him.

"By your account Underwood shouldn't fight. The same can't be said about the boyfriend."

They turned into the cul-de-sac. The party house, with its lights and music coming through open windows, stood out among the graded pads like a shiny gold tooth in a crone's mouth.

"No one's called you about the messenger," Rachel said.

"Lucille did, on the plane. You were still asleep. We've tagged every private aircraft with an Atlanta–Phoenix flight plan. They're all legit, passengers and crew."

"What if he's doing an end run, giving his destination as Tucson or Flagstaff, then booting into Phoenix at the last minute?"

"That would be the worst kind of tip-off, don't you think?"

"Even if he were declaring an emergency?"

"Then *he* would become the emergency. And what he'd find waiting for him on the ground wouldn't be very encouraging."

They were coming up to the Tac Suburban, readily identifiable by the antenna poking out of its roof. Smith lowered the window on Rachel's side, leaned past her, and quietly told the Tac leader to fall in behind him. Rachel left the window down as they drove to the end of the cul-de-sac. She had heard Tac say that the lights in a second-floor bedroom were on. They still were. Now another light came on, fainter, a hall or bathroom lamp.

"Someone's moving," she said.

"So are we."

The sedan's parking lights were still on when the Suburban's rear doors opened. Rachel watched the Tac Unit slip out, swathed in skintight black cotton fatigues, black boots with deeply grooved soles, black hoods with ultra-light fiber-optic headsets. The front of the hoods covered the entire face except for the eyes and nose. On the floor of the truck, piled in a corner, was an array of sportsmen's clothing. Two of the Tac members held silenced submachine guns at port arms; the third cradled a sniper's rifle with a night vision scope. Three grenades and a knife were strapped to each man's waist. When Smith addressed them, no names were used. The machine gunners were Bolo One and Two; the sniper was Bolo Three. It would be a classic entry: one man around the back, through the door leading into the garage; a second would cross the patio and enter through the French doors off the kitchen and breakfast room. The sniper would take the high ground, perch himself on the cab of a bulldozer conveniently parked on the adjacent raw lot. The sniper had reconnoitered the area and assured Smith he could look straight into the living room, dining room, and upper bedroom windows from that vantage point. He would also have a clear shot at anyone trying to escape through the front door. Smith reminded him that if it came to a firefight, a wounding was preferable to a kill.

"What do we do?" Rachel asked as she watched Tac disperse into the darkness.

Smith donned his headset, spoke softly into the mike, seemed satisfied with the result.

"Give them forty-five seconds to get into position," he replied. "That's about the time I'll need to get to the front door."

Smith turned on the car radio and fiddled with the knob until he found a rock-and-roll station. He handed Rachel his cell phone and nodded toward the Tudor house.

"We use what we have. Underwood and her friend are still up. They can see, if not hear, that a good time is being had next door. Now they get a call because the party has run out of ice. You apologize for disturbing them, but make it clear they've got to help you out. This way, whoever's with Underwood won't get suspicious when she goes downstairs to the door."

"Where I'll be waiting."

"With me."

"What if it's Romeo?"

"We haul him out fast and secure him, then go inside. That would be the better play, better than flushing him—if we have to —once we have her."

Smith looked at her keenly. "You can handle this, right?"

Rachel nodded. "You'd best get going."

She watched him walk quickly down the deserted street, staying in the shadows. When he reached the walkway to the house, Rachel dialed Underwood's number, heard the first ring, and cranked up the volume on the radio. The Rolling Stones were raging for some sympathy for the devil.

"Hello?"

The voice sounded curious, not put off or annoyed.

"Beth? Is this Beth Underwood?"

"Who is this? What's all that noise?"

"Beth—"

"Are you the guys next door?"

Rachel cut in fast. "Yes. Listen. Sorry to disturb you. I know it's late, but the ice maker in the fridge is screwed up. Could I come over and get some from yours?"

Rachel heard a male voice call out in the background. Then the woman yelled back, "Kenny, it's the fun crowd next door. They need ice."

"Tell 'em they can have a load if they bring over some beer. And Shel? None of that Amstel Light shit."

Shel?

The Engineer was parked on a curve that allowed him to see the entire development laid out in the valley below. He'd pinpointed the cul-de-sac and had been waiting patiently for the fruit of his labor to ripen and fall. Instead there was silence. He sighed. By now there would be a good blanket of gas across the lower level of the house, but clearly no one upstairs was conscious to smell it. He'd have to move things along.

The Engineer dialed Beth Underwood's number, ready with

some bullshit about a gas leak and how she had to get out of the house right away.

The number was busy.

The Engineer flew out of the Cherokee and trained his night vision binoculars on the cul-de-sac. He counted six cars in front of the party house. Fine. And the feds' big rig. But that sedan . . . It looked as though someone were sitting behind the wheel—someone who, even at this distance, couldn't be other than War-rant Officer Rachel Collins. Holding a phone to her ear.

The Engineer threw back his head and let loose a howling laugh that caromed off the millennia-old rock until the darkness finally swallowed it up. He could still hear the echo when he hopped into the Cherokee and pulled away.

Shel?

Rachel flew down the road, screaming at Smith.

"That's not Underwood in there! It's not her!"

She was close enough to see him whirl around at her, take two tentative steps away from the front door. She leaped onto the walkway and pulled up hard as he started toward her, his features tense with anger.

"What the hell are you doing?"

"It's not her!" Rachel gasped. "The woman inside—"

The explosion tore into her like a concrete fist. Rachel regis-tered the disbelief in Smith's eyes, then he was flying past her, legs and arms cartwheeling. Her head smacked hard against the lawn, the force of the blast propelling her against the three-foot brick wall that separated the property from the sidewalk.

Rachel's fingers clawed the moist turf as she tried to crawl away. Then a second explosion erupted, and she felt herself float away, uncaring, unconcerned.

20

Rachel kicked savagely, screaming, though she couldn't hear the sound of her voice. Her throat felt like a slab of raw meat. Each breath burned her flesh and lungs as though she were inhaling fire.

Then her knee hit something hard and cold, and consciousness rushed over her. She raised one arm, and her fingernails raked down a gritty surface. Rachel forced open her eyes and saw she was grasping at the waist-high brick wall at the foot of the lawn.

"Don't move."

A pair of hands, the wrists and knuckles lobster red, slipped under her shoulders, and she heard a soft grunt as Smith pulled her up.

"Can you tell if anything's broken?"

Smith's face, grimy with earth and ash, was streaked by thick trails of something that looked black.

"You're bleeding," she said.

"Flying glass. It's all over the place. You have some in your hair."

Automatically Rachel raised her hand, but Smith grabbed her wrist. "We've got to get out of here."

Rachel held on to him as he helped her half step, half slide, over the wall, the sound of glass cracking and grinding under her heels. She became aware of the heat on the back of her neck and turned around.

"Dear God . . ."

Very little was left that resembled a house. The explosion had torn out the guts of the structure, causing the roof and retaining walls to collapse into the cavity. The inferno seemed to track to the back of the house. The night sky was filled with swirling embers and the angry crackle of collapsing beams as the flames ate through them. The wind shifted, and the smoke rolled straight at her.

Smith had her in the street, the pair of them propping up each other, weaving toward the people running to meet them. A thick-set, middle-aged man with gin on his breath reached them first.

"Jesus Christ! What happened? Are you guys all right?"

Smith held out his Department of Justice ID. "Federal officer," he rasped. "What's your name?"

"Jerry. Jerry Pabst. I own that place—"

"Has anyone called 911?"

"You bet. But it'll take the fire department a good twenty minutes to get here. That new substation isn't open yet—"

"Jerry. I need you to keep these people back. Get them back into your house."

Pabst stepped back and raised his arms at the guests crowding around them. "Okay, guys. Guys! Come on. We have us a federal marshal here. Move back, okay?"

There were shouts and questions and women bouncing on the balls of their feet, trying to peek over Pabst's shoulder. Rachel saw Smith looking back at the burning wreckage.

"The Tac. We have to look . . ."

He shook his head. "They were inside, except the sniper."

He raised a sleeve to his face, and when it came away Rachel saw that tears had smeared the grime and blood.

"The messenger," Smith said, his voice so low, she could barely hear him. "He knows everything now . . . everything." He coughed violently, then straightened and took a deep breath. "But that can't be all of it. He *knows* too much! He can *do* too much!"

Up ahead, Jerry Pabst was herding his reluctant guests back into his house. He looked back at Smith, who went over to him. Rachel didn't hear what Smith said, but she saw Pabst's expression. Then he bowed his head and shuffled after his guests, and Rachel knew Smith had told him that more than just two people had been killed in the explosion.

She was at their car when Smith returned. Somewhere in the distance rose the wail and blare of fire engine klaxons. Winking red lights appeared over the horizon.

"The messenger fucked up this time, didn't he?" Smith said.

Rachel nodded. She wanted so badly to know who the woman had been. Shel . . . and her Romeo, bartering ice cubes for cold beer. What had they been doing in the house Beth Underwood should have been staying in? *Who* were they? Friends?

"Where is she?" Rachel said aloud. "Why did she leave? Where did she go?" She looked wildly at Smith. "Did he snatch her? Did she have friends over to keep her company and he came in and grabbed her, then wired the place?"

Smith laid a palm on her cheek. "We'll find out." He paused. "If you hadn't charged down there, I'd still have been at that door. . . ."

Rachel closed her eyes as he embraced her, felt him shudder as though he were very cold, yet his lips burned like a branding iron on her forehead.

The fire engine company came in fast, did their work by the numbers, and quickly contained the blaze. Smith was busy on the car phone, so Rachel pulled aside the company commander and walked him through the details. The commander turned and swore when she told him about the casualties of the Tac Unit.

He looked at the sniper, sitting on the grass, his rifle propped between his legs, the thousand-yard stare in his eyes.

"What the hell did you people have going here?" he demanded. "The army, the feds . . ."

Rachel pointed to Smith. "He'll bring you up to speed."

The commander snorted. "With some cockamamie story."

"He lost two men," Rachel reminded him stonily.

The commander marched angrily after his own men.

Rachel was sitting on the wide bumper of the ambulance, letting a paramedic pick slivers of glass out of her scalp. When Smith came back, a second medic hurried over to him.

"You need ointment for the burns," the medic said quickly, eyeballing him. "Anything broken?"

"No."

Smith sat down beside Rachel. "Phoenix P.D. has Sky Harbor buttoned up. Nothing goes in or out until every private plane is checked. Thing is, in the last hour no one's shown up to fly out of there."

"That doesn't make sense," Rachel said. "The messenger isn't going to drive anywhere."

"Lucille put the word out with the troopers, just in case." He paused. "The local bomb squad is on its way out, along with the Arson Investigation Unit."

"Who owns the house?" Rachel asked. "We have to ask Pabst—"

"I can tell you that," the paramedic said. He continued swabbing Smith's hands with ointment. "The guy who owns the house, he's the parcel developer. I know because we've been out here a few times—six-buck-an-hour wetback laborers not wearing safety boots, stepping on nails sticking out of boards. That kind of thing."

The roar of a powerful truck engine and the squeal of brakes made him look around.

"Mr. Quality Construction himself," the paramedic mumbled.

The man who jumped out of the pickup cab was short and bandy-legged, with a barrel chest and thick, powerful arms. He jammed a fraying straw Stetson on his thinning hair as he hurried to the ambulance.

"Check out the logo on the truck door," Rachel said quietly.

Smith did and was on his feet. The logo was a giant green cactus. In bold yellow letters were the words UNDERWOOD CONSTRUCTION & DEVELOPMENT.

"Mr. Underwood?"

Underwood was staring openmouthed at what was left of the blaze. He pulled out a crumpled red bandanna and wiped his forehead.

"I do not fucking believe this." He wheeled around to Smith. "Who are you?"

Rachel watched the man's reaction to Smith's ID. She slipped off the ambulance bumper and made her way over to the two men.

"You're Roy Underwood?"

"That's what I said."

"You're the developer?"

"Hell, yes! That's my fucking model home. Was my model . . ."

"Did you know someone was staying there?"

"No one was *supposed* to be there."

"A man and a woman. Party time."

Underwood looked up at the sky and swore. "Probably Kenny Lassiter, my foreman. I heard tell he comes out here. But I warned him—"

"Who was the woman?"

"Whatever cocktail waitress Kenny happened to be banging this week."

Rachel had had enough. She stepped in close, smelled the Listerine on Underwood's breath, saw the droplets of water on his sideburns. She envisioned him getting the call about the explosion, fumbling in the darkness for his clothes, cursing as he threw water on his face to try to wake up.

"The house had a live phone. We know your daughter, Beth, used it. She was staying at the house. Where is Beth, Mr. Underwood? Where is she right now?"

Rachel's expression made him flinch.

"Where the hell do you think she is?" he blustered. "At home, with my wife, probably still asleep."

• • •

No matter what their credentials said, Roy Underwood was convinced that the fed and the army skirt were crazy. The way they looked at each other when he told them about Beth, it was as if they'd just won the Powerball.

Underwood protested when they hustled him into their car and demanded directions for the quickest way to his house. After that, they told him to shut up.

When they were coming up to Mesa Hills, his first development, Underwood saw that his street was blocked off by a pair of cars angled toward each other. The men standing by them could have played on the front line of the Phoenix Cardinals. They carried M-16's with dual ammunition clips tied together with electrician's tape. In the small undeveloped patch of land that was to be a park stood a helicopter, its blades still spinning. The lawns and walkways of the upscale homes were filled with Underwood's neighbors, clutching bathrobes over pajamas. A few called out to him when they saw him get out of the car.

"We walk the rest of the way," Smith told him.

Underwood saw more armed men farther down the street, ringing his house where the lights were blazing. "Who are these guys?" he asked.

"Federal marshals out of Phoenix."

"You have to tell me—"

"As soon as we're inside, Mr. Underwood."

"No! I gotta know if Connie and Beth are in any danger!"

Smith turned to him but didn't break his stride. "Not anymore."

The front door to the Underwood home had a large fan of etched glass set into the wood at eye level. It distorted the features of the woman standing inside, whom Rachel took to be Underwood's wife. Underwood waved to her and had to call out her name before she unbolted the door.

"Roy, what's going on? Who are these people?"

Underwood put his arms around her, but she kept leaning around to look over her shoulder. Connie Underwood's eyes and face were puffy from sleep. When she saw Rachel she ran a hand through her hair, tried to pat down the spikes.

"We need to speak to Beth, Mrs. Underwood," Rachel said softly.

"In the middle of the night? You come barging into our neighborhood, acting like we're . . . we're drug dealers or something—"

"Mom. It's okay."

Rachel looked up. Beyond the expanse of foyer limestone was
a staircase, and halfway up stood Beth Underwood. She wore a
long cotton nightgown and bunny slippers with Disney characters
on them. Her face was scrubbed pink and her long hair shone, as
if she'd spent a long time brushing it.

"You're Rachel Collins," she said.

Rachel stepped forward. "Yes, I am."

"You worked with Mollie—Major Smith."

"Yes, I did."

"She's dead."

Beth took a deep breath and stared through the tall arched
windows that flanked the front door. Rachel followed her look
and saw the revolving lights of the sheriff's cruisers.

"Steven is dead, too, isn't he?"

"Beth, come down here, away from the window. Please. . . ."

Rachel held out her hand, the way she would to a wounded,
frightened animal that hadn't yet decided whether to trust or to
bolt.

"He was killed earlier tonight," Rachel said. "I'm sorry, Beth.
So very, very sorry."

Beth's lower lip trembled, and two fat tears slid down her
cheeks. Her voice cracked when she spoke.

"He told me you were coming. He said that he had spoken to
you and that tomorrow the two of you would fly out here and we
would be together. But Steven was worried." Her laugh was a
strangled choke. "He always worried about me. He said I had
stayed here alone for too long. He didn't want me in that house
anymore."

"*You'd* been staying in the model, too?" her father cut in.

Rachel shushed him, but she needn't have bothered. It seemed
Beth hadn't heard him.

"So last night I came home. . . ."

She sank onto the carpeted step and stared down at Rachel.
"Will you help me? *Can* you help me? Or is he going to kill me,
too?"

• • •

The Underwoods would have been a problem had Beth not stepped in and handled them. She showed Rachel and Smith into her father's den, then spent a moment talking with her parents. Roy Underwood glared at Rachel before Beth closed the door to the den.

The room was large, half office, half English-style pub, with a bar, stools, shelves of liquor and glasses, a dartboard, and a pool table. By the window was Roy Underwood's desk and an alcove with built-in filing cabinets and bookshelves.

"I'll need to use the phone," Smith said to Beth.

She nodded absently and busied herself by making a pot of coffee. From a minifridge under the bar she brought out pints of milk and cream, setting them on the granite countertop. The coffeemaker gurgled.

Rachel drew the curtains across the tall windows that looked out onto the backyard and pool area. Her eyes never left Beth as she poured the coffee. A bar had paring knives and other sharp instruments. She was glad that Beth needed both hands to carry the three mugs to the coffee table in front of the leather sofa. Rachel glanced at Smith; he was still working the phone.

"I want to tell you who we are, Inspector Smith and I," she said. "And exactly what's happened so far. Okay?"

Beth nodded. She sank onto the couch and wrapped both hands around her coffee mug. Her vacant expression worried Rachel. Shock was setting in. She had to get Beth talking.

Rachel quickly explained Smith's and her relationship to Mollie. Beth looked up, startled, when Rachel said Smith was Mollie's brother. Then she focused on the key events of the last few days: how she'd helped Mollie move Beth and Copeland, the broad details of the ensuing investigation that had brought her and Smith to Carefree. She skirted the details about how Mollie and Steven had died.

Smith was off the phone. Rachel glanced at him. He shook his head, which she interpreted to mean that whatever was unfolding elsewhere could wait.

Smith placed a small tape recorder on the coffee table. "We need a record," he told Beth gently. "Will that bother you?"

Beth stared at him. "No. As long as you don't lie to me." She turned to Rachel. "Steven said you'd told him that Mollie had been murdered in a gang mugging, that it was some terrible fluke. . . . He didn't believe you. He told me he thought that whoever was after us had killed Mollie."

Rachel closed her eyes. At the time, she had plucked that lie out of thin air. Now, as she played it back, it seemed blatant.

"I didn't know what else to tell Steven," she said. "I had no idea, then, who might be after you. I wasn't a hundred percent sure it was the same man who murdered Mollie."

"But you are now."

"Oh yes. In Atlanta we missed taking him by minutes, literally. He was fast and very clever, and he got to Steven before we could."

"He was here, too, before you."

"Yes, he was."

"Do you know who he is?"

"We have a general description, but no name. It's not much— that's why we have all those federal marshals out there. I think *he* thinks you're dead. He's the kind who would have stayed around to watch the house blow."

"So when he finds out I'm not dead, he'll try again."

Rachel hesitated, caught Smith's warning glance, ignored it. "If he can spot an opening. That's what we're not going to give him." She paused. "That's why we need to understand what it is you know. Mollie did her very best to protect you. Now we have to take over for her. So we have to know what you and Steven brought her."

Tears welled in Beth's eyes. She put down the coffee mug and wiped them away with the sleeve of her nightgown. She tucked her feet against the leather cushions and curled up deep in the corner of the sofa.

"Steven and I were in love," she said softly. "Everything started because we loved each other . . . and because Steven was betrayed."

"By whom?" Smith cut in.

Beth twisted a strand of hair around her forefinger. "He had this great job at Bell and Robertson. The big law firm. He was doing very well there, worked really hard, until the PSX thing." She looked at Rachel. "The railroad?"

"They went bankrupt, didn't they?"

"In the end. But reorganizing PSX was Steven's account. He had no idea his bosses and the PSX directors were setting him up, making it look like he'd intended to steal from the company . . . ruin it."

Rachel saw Smith nod. The PSX scandal had been in the news for months. Maybe he now linked it to Copeland; Rachel didn't see the connection yet.

"Steven was being accused of all these things he'd never done," Beth continued. "In the end he only had one person to turn to. That's when I met him."

"Who was that, Beth?"

"Judge Esterhaus."

Rachel heard Smith's sharp intake of breath. Worried that he might interrupt with more questions, she hurried on.

"How did Steven know Esterhaus?"

"The judge was one of his professors at Georgetown. He and Steven became close."

"And you knew Esterhaus because . . . ?"

"I was his secretary."

Beth described how angry Steven had been after his visits with Esterhaus. Then something had changed, and he'd settled down a little.

"Was Esterhaus going to help him?" Rachel asked.

"Yes. He and Steven went over everything Steven had done for PSX. The judge said it was scandalous, what they were doing to him. He promised to find a way to help him."

"Was this when you and Steven became involved?"

"A lot of people didn't like him," Beth said, her tone defensive. "But they didn't understand him, or what he was going through. Steven could seem arrogant and thoughtless—even I thought that sometimes. Until I realized that he was just scared. It's hard to understand until you look at him as someone who worked so hard and always played by the rules. He *expected* to be rewarded. He *deserved* what was coming to him. When that didn't happen, he didn't know what to do, or how to act. All he could do was lash out."

"Did he ever hurt you?" Rachel asked quietly.

"No, no—I don't mean lash out physically. It was his mood and temper, the suspicious way he treated people. The bitterness was like a poison to him."

"But you said Esterhaus was going to help him."

"I also said he was betrayed," Beth reminded her.

There was a moment's silence, then Smith said, "But Esterhaus . . . Esterhaus never went to bat for him. In fact, he issued a confidential report confirming what PSX and Bell and Robertson had said all along: that Steven had been out to loot PSX."

He looked at Rachel. "The Justice Department had been following the case. Memos all around." He turned back to Beth. "After Esterhaus cut him off, Steven came to you. What did he want, Beth?"

"Revenge," she replied quietly. "He couldn't believe the judge had turned on him like that. He was talking crazy, saying he'd find a way to ruin him."

"He asked you to help because you were Esterhaus's secretary. You knew his life—personal and professional—inside out. Steven wanted the dark side, something he could use against Esterhaus."

Beth nodded. She dug into the pocket of her bathrobe and brought out a lump of tissue.

"Was that what Steven asked you to do, Beth?" Rachel asked. "To violate Esterhaus's privacy?"

"It was the only way."

"But you worked for Esterhaus. Was there ever a problem there?"

"No! The judge always treated me well. He was tough, but fair, kind of like my dad. But when I saw what he did to Steven . . ."

"Did you ask him about that?"

"He said it was none of my business. He was angry that I'd even brought it up."

"And that's when you decided to help Steven. Because Esterhaus had turned on him."

Beth turned away and wept softly. Rachel looked at Smith, saw that he was all right. They had come this far, waited this long, paid a monstrous price. They could be patient for a few more minutes.

Beth sniffled and blew her nose. "I need to clean up."

Rachel reached out and took her hand. "What was it, Beth?" she whispered. "What did you and Steven find out about Esterhaus?"

Beth stared at her blankly.

"What started all this, Beth?" Rachel pressed. "It killed Mollie, killed Steven—"

"How could we have known that?" Beth cried.

"You couldn't have. But now you have to tell us what you and Steven found. So that we can put the last pieces together. If we can do that, we'll find the killer."

Beth balled her fists and rubbed her swollen eyes the way a child would. "Steven said he probably wasn't the first Esterhaus had betrayed," she murmured. "He said there had to be others. That's what I was looking for in the files, a case like PSX that had involved someone else."

"You had free access to Esterhaus's records?" Smith asked. "Even his personal ones?"

"I discovered his private password by accident. He never knew I had it."

"Did you find anything in the computer records?" Rachel asked.

"No. That's not where it was. It was buried in old case stacks, stuff that had been filed away in storage for years."

"What, Beth?"

"The file on North."

"*General North?*"

Beth nodded. "At first we thought it had to do with the plane crash in the desert. You know, that it was a part of the commission report the judge was working on, and that somehow it had ended up in the old storage boxes by mistake. But it wasn't that at all. The file was old. A lot of the notes were in the judge's handwriting. The rest I didn't recognize."

Beth took a deep breath. "The judge knew everything about North, his whole life. There were pages about the trip to Califor-

nia, when the general was leaving, on which jet, its crew, a maintenance report on it . . ."

"A maintenance report," Rachel echoed. "Were there names of
the mechanics who had worked on the plane?"

Beth shook her head. "Just one, reference to some sergeant."

"Dunn?" Smith broke in. "Was that his name?"

Beth raised her chin. "Yes, I think so."

"What was it about the file that made you suspicious?"

"It's obvious when you read it: the judge had been stalking
General North for years."

Rachel was stunned. "Beth, listen to me very carefully. In all
this material, were there any explicit threats by Esterhaus against
North? Please, think hard. Tell me only what you remember
seeing or reading."

Beth looked down at her lap. "There was a page with General
North's California itinerary. All the paragraphs after the first one
—when the general was leaving Washington—had been crossed
out in red pen. Someone had written 'Canceled' across the page."

Rachel felt the wind go out of her. "The file, Beth. Is that what
you showed Mollie?"

"No. Steven said we should leave it there, in case Esterhaus
came looking for it. He didn't want the judge to get suspicious;
he said Esterhaus would know it was me who took it. Steven said
we'd go back for it when we needed to—that the judge wouldn't
have gone to all the trouble of hiding it if he didn't intend to keep
it. I mean, he could have just as easily destroyed it."

"And you didn't make a copy?"

"There was no way."

"Okay. Now tell me why you took this information to Mollie.
Was there something about her in the file—something to indicate
that she was General North's lover?"

"Yes."

"So you thought she was the one person you and Steven could
trust. She was army. And because she, of all people, would have
stopped at nothing to bring out the truth."

"I'm so sorry," Beth whispered. "If we hadn't done that, nothing would have happened to her."

Smith reached out with his red, scorched hand and held her arm. His head was bowed, and he did not dare raise it.

"Beth," Rachel said, *"before* you went to Mollie, did you and Steven try to find more information about the things in that file?"

Beth nodded. "Just one time. I was in the judge's computer, in the private files, when suddenly the system shut down on me. After that, we never went back into it."

Beth pulled away from Smith and stood up, wrapping her arms around herself, and began pacing. She didn't look back when she spoke.

"That's what I know. That's all of it. And it doesn't make a damn bit of difference, does it? Because it couldn't have been the judge who killed Mollie and Steven."

The house was quiet now, in the stillest hour of the night. Roy Underwood and his wife were upstairs in the master suite. Rachel had tiptoed up there, heard them arguing behind the double doors.

Beth was downstairs, resting in the guest room off the den. An armed federal marshal stood post in front of the door; two others were outside.

"She's going to be all right," Rachel said, more to herself than to Smith.

"I think so," Smith said. "She was damned lucky to have moved out of that model."

The Underwoods were out of state when Beth had first come home. Heeding Mollie's warnings, she'd never had any intention of staying with her parents. Instead she had suggested the model home, and Mollie had agreed. It had everything Beth would need, including a phone. There was lots of traffic around during the day—construction crews, real estate people—and at night the neighbors were close by. It had been a safe, clever play. Except that Copeland had known about it and given it up.

"She's wrong, you know," Smith said. "About Esterhaus."

Rachel looked at him and wondered how he could keep going.

"You told me the messenger knows everything," she said. "That he's always one step ahead. Now you're saying that Esterhaus was the one who sent in the killer."

"That's the way it plays," Smith replied. His voice was hoarse, and he drank from a plastic bottle of water he'd found behind the bar. "That's the only way it *can* play."

Rachel understood the agony of his guilt. Smith had already told her about his meeting with the president and the orders that had him reporting to Esterhaus: Esterhaus, questioning and probing every decision Smith was to make, gathering up and hoarding all the details, making sure that Smith wasn't holding back anything . . . then passing it all down the line.

"Why?" Rachel asked. "Why would Esterhaus want to kill North? What was their connection?"

"We'll have to ask the judge about that," Smith replied.

"And how he zeroed in on Beth and Copeland as being dangerous to him." Rachel paused. "Don't you think it'd be better if we knew more about that before going in?"

"Yes, it would, but we don't have time to poke through history. Even if we did, and we tried to, Esterhaus would get wind of it."

"What about the file? Think Esterhaus left it where Beth found it?"

"He would have had no reason to remove it. At least, not yet."

"You'll give him that reason soon, though. Because he's waiting to hear from you, and you can't hide what happened out here."

Smith pinched the bridge of his nose. There were red marks on his skin when he brought his hand away. "It's not what Esterhaus knows," he said. "The triggerman is the key. What do you think *he* knows?"

Rachel pushed around tired thoughts. "He watched the house blow. He would have wanted to stick around for that, to see it with his own eyes."

"Because he believed Beth was inside?"

"Right. He couldn't have thought otherwise. No way Copeland would have lied to him."

"Then what does he do?"

"Get the hell out of Dodge. He'd call Esterhaus, but only when he was already in his ride."

"Then?"

"Mission accomplished. Time for a relaxing drink and some well-earned sleep."

Rachel knew that her anger made her sound bitter. But the image of the messenger winging away so serenely scalded her.

"I think you're right," Smith said. "I think that's exactly what he would do: report in, then kick back. No reason to think about Carefree anymore, not with those fireworks."

Rachel started. "He wouldn't be tracking the news!"

"Let's hope. Because that's our only edge. Esterhaus is sleeping tonight because he got the word. The triggerman—your messenger—is doing the same thing because he saw what went down here. He's in no hurry to proceed to the next step, if there is—"

"And Esterhaus isn't burning midnight oil waiting for you to call. *Because he knows exactly what you'll have to tell him!*"

Smith checked his watch. "It's going on five o'clock in D.C. Esterhaus will be up in two to three hours. Figure a few more before he starts to wonder why I haven't checked in."

"Because you're going after the file. You're going to come out on his blind side before he has a chance to think."

"Don't underestimate him," Smith warned. He nodded toward the bathroom off the den. "Two minutes to clean up and change. Then it's my turn, and we're gone."

"What about Beth?"

"Tell her not to leave the house. The marshals will keep the media far enough away that she has some privacy."

Rachel picked up her duffel bag, which one of the marshals had retrieved from Smith's sedan, and headed into the bathroom. She was closing the door when she caught Smith's reflection in the long wide mirror over the sink. He was on the phone again, his head propped up by a fist under his chin. Rachel overheard the words "dead," and "air force transport" and knew he was telling Lucille not to expect him to accompany his fallen men home.

21

The Family Dining Room is at the back of the White House, sandwiched between the State Dining Room and Cross Hall.

The current First Lady had redecorated it in what Pamela Esterhaus thought was an attempt to produce a country manor look. The wallpaper was green-and-white stripes studded with fleur-de-lis; the table, chairs, and sideboard were of cherrywood, its luster long buried under layers of furniture wax. Ficuses sprouted out of large copper tubs. The overall effect left the room looking like a bed-and-breakfast parlor.

The table was graced by a single warming dish that held oatmeal, a rack of nine-grain toast with tiny saucers of honey and jams, a pitcher of orange juice in crushed ice, and coffee in a silver service. Navy stewards had silently doled out the first serving, then left the chief executive and the Esterhauses to help themselves to seconds.

Pamela Esterhaus had been invited to breakfast here several times before. The president was a morning person; even on the weekends he liked to use the time for informal brainstorming sessions—probably the reason Pamela had never seen the First Lady present. Today's topic was the recent spate of high-ranking military defectors.

"The sec of defense tells me the Pentagon's been having a problem with these guys," the president said. "Once they've been milked of the technical knowledge they brought with them, the brass doesn't know what to do with them."

Out of the corner of her eye Pamela caught her husband digging around the edges of his gums with his tongue. One or more of those nine grains must have become lodged between his gums and the dental work. She wished he'd excuse himself and go to the bathroom.

"Mr. President," she said, "I've no doubt the Pentagon has gotten all it can from these people—as far as military considerations go. But these individuals also possess keen sociological and psychological insights into their culture, especially the military philosophies and concepts. Why not consider moving them into civilian jobs, maybe as instructors at places like West Point or the Citadel?" She paused. "It would also make it easy to monitor their activities, on the off chance that a double agent somehow slipped through the Pentagon's screening process."

The president eyed her over a spoonful of oatmeal. "You don't trust too many people, do you?"

"Trust isn't the issue, sir. Caution is. Over at Justice, we've had a lot of success transplanting protected witnesses into academic environments."

"I know. That's why I was asking."

The president swallowed his last mouthful of oatmeal, washed it down with coffee, and sat back. "Do it, Pamela," he said shortly.

He steepled his fingers and looked out the window for a moment. "Do you know Sam Peterson over at the CIA?"

Pamela nodded. "He's the resident expert on defectors—runs the Looking Glass ops. I've worked with him before."

"You might want to bring him in on this." The president turned to Esterhaus. "Simon, do you want the name of my dentist?"

Simon Esterhaus's tongue stopped its excavation. The president was smiling at him good-naturedly.

"Sorry, sir. Sometimes—"

The president waved away the apology. "My brother has the same problem." He checked his watch. "What have you heard from Logan Smith?"

"Nothing today, sir."

Esterhaus held his breath, waiting to see if the president had somehow heard about the killing in Atlanta. Esterhaus hadn't reported it, thinking it would be better to advise the chief executive when the deaths of *both* informants had been confirmed. That way he could argue that there was nothing more Logan Smith or anyone else could do. To pursue the investigation into North's death any further, without the informants' hard evidence or reasonable clues, would be to venture into political quicksand. And if the president didn't see it that way, Esterhaus would play his trump card: he would say that new information had come to light, that Mollie Smith had been North's lover. How valid could her information be, tainted as it surely was by a paramour's grief?

Esterhaus thought the president would shut down the investigation then and there. Logan Smith, however, would be more difficult to handle. But Esterhaus would bring him back to the White House and let the president lay down the law. Smith would not like it. He would argue and plead for more time, but in the end he would protect his job and honor his oath of obedience.

"I want you to call me as soon as Smith checks in," the president said, rising. "This thing has to be settled one way or another before your confirmation hearings start next week."

Esterhaus was about to agree when a steward slipped into the room and handed him a note.

"There's an urgent call for me, sir."

The president pointed to a phone on the sideboard. "I'm running late. You'll have to see yourself out, Simon. Pamela, you want to walk with me?"

"I'd better let you go, sir." She rolled her eyes for effect. "We're having a cocktail party this evening, and I'd rather know now if Simon's not going to be available."

Esterhaus waited until the president had left the room before he picked up the phone. "Smith?"

"You wish."

Esterhaus turned his back to his wife. "What the hell are you doing calling me here? Where are you?"

The Engineer's voice was so clear that Esterhaus imagined he was in the next room. Impossible, of course. . . .

"Smith hasn't called, right?" the Engineer said.

"No, I've been waiting—"

"I don't think he'll be contacting you just yet. He's a little busy at the moment, beating his tail back to D.C."

"I don't understand."

"Smith is on your ass."

"That can't be!" Esterhaus whispered. "You said —"

"There was a problem in Phoenix. Underwood is still alive. But I know where Smith and Collins are headed. Everything will work out."

Esterhaus searched for words and found none.

"When Smith calls you, go along with whatever he says— which won't be much. Remember, he's talked to Underwood. He knows as much about your involvement with North as she does."

The judge closed his eyes. He didn't hear his wife walk up behind him. "Call me at my office," he said. "I'll be there in twenty minutes. I need to know what happened in Phoenix. *Before* Smith calls."

"That may not be possible. Things are moving too quickly. Smith and Collins are on their way; just a couple of hours till they land. And before you say another word, remember that Smith wouldn't have diddly if you had gotten rid of that piece of memorabilia."

Esterhaus heard a sharp click, then the dial tone. He was standing there holding the receiver when he felt his wife's fingers press down on his arm, forcing him to hang up. Then she took him by the shoulders and made him face her.

"It's time, Simon. Tell me about Phoenix. About everything."

The Engineer swiveled his chair and stared out the windows of his office in the green glass cube. It was Sunday; the parking lot was almost empty. Beyond it were stands of foliage fading to russet. The serenity of the moment calmed the Engineer, leeched the bitter drops of anger and frustration from his soul, settled his thoughts like the fine sediments in an old wine.

The Wonderland Toys jet had just cleared the Mississippi when the Engineer, enjoying a snack, had heard the jarring report over his headphones. The Phoenix all-news radio station described the explosion and ensuing fire in Carefree. Four people were dead, a man and a woman who had been sleeping in a second-floor bedroom and two federal agents who'd been downstairs. The Engineer had nodded to himself and popped another white grape into his mouth. So far so good—except then the announcer had gone on to identify the two dead in the bedroom as the foreman of the development company and a waitress from a local bar. The company's owner was one Roy Underwood; his daughter, Beth, had also been staying at the house earlier in the week but last night had moved in with her parents. Ms. Underwood was currently being questioned by federal marshals. A full media blackout was in effect, so no further details were available at this time.

The Engineer sighed as he rose from behind his desk and stepped into his private elevator. He left the green glass cube and crossed the parking lot to a late-model sedan. He knew exactly what Smith was hunting and that Underwood had told him where he would find it. He also knew that Rachel Collins would be along for the ride; no way would she let Smith cheat her out of the kill. Both of them would be a little off balance, eager but wary, fatigued but wired with adrenaline.

The Engineer looked up at the sky. In the distance he heard church bells toll, summoning the faithful to worship. He imagined those same bells calling for Smith and Collins, shepherding them to Baltimore, to their deaths, on this flawless morning.

The pilot buzzed Smith for the third time. The tailwind was stronger than expected; they would land at Baltimore-Washington International ahead of schedule, forty minutes from now.

Rachel shifted in her seat and pulled down the window shade. Outside, the morning was pristine, but the sunlight splintered into her eyes when it hit the scratches on the Plexiglas. After takeoff Smith had offered her a sleeping pill, but she'd refused. She wanted to stay sharp and alert to help him.

Throughout the flight the fax had run almost continuously, churning out maps, blueprints, and building specs. Interior layouts had been meticulously examined; exterior considerations, such as the heights of the adjacent buildings, the width of the street, and the vehicles that might be located there, had been factored in. Finally, an entry-and-search procedure had been hammered out, scrutinized, refined, and ultimately agreed on.

Now Smith stood in the aisle beside her seat, holding out a cup of orange juice. She drank it greedily, then held up the cup for more. She watched him pour, tried to divine the thoughts behind his hard, flinty eyes, and couldn't. The question that had nagged at her for hours became too crucial to hold back.

"Why didn't you call out the Bureau SWAT team?"

Smith didn't look up from his pouring. The hand holding the orange juice carton was perfectly steady. "Why would I do that?"

"You know." She paused. "What if the messenger has one more errand to run? If Beth knew where the file was, so did Copeland. So . . ."

"The messenger knows where it is, too."

"And he might be going to get it right now," Rachel said urgently. "Don't you see? The file is the last thread to Esterhaus. If the messenger gets to it . . ."

But he did see. Rachel realized this as she looked past her excitement, focused on the almost imperceptible change that had come over Smith. For a split second he allowed her behind his eyes, let her gaze upon the cruel hard truth that stared back at her, unrepentant, immutable.

In that instant Rachel understood that Logan Smith knew all that she did and much more. He had expected her to wend her way to this conclusion. Now he waited to see what she would do.

"I can call the Baltimore field office," he said. "SWAT can be on site, undercover, in thirty minutes. It's Sunday, though. The docks will be deserted. Chances are better than even the team will be spotted." He waited a beat. "It's your call, Rachel."

She felt very cold. The plastic cup slipped from her fingers and rolled under the seat. Then Smith was beside her. He took off his jacket and draped it around her shoulders. Rachel burrowed into it, then against him as he squeezed in beside her. His arm went around her shoulders, and she felt the strong, steady rhythm of his heart. The roar in her ears was her blood singing.

Rachel knew she would not ask Smith to make that call. This was the way it had to end: just the three of them, she and Smith and Mollie's killer, who, as Smith had divined, still had one more message to pick up and deliver.

Smith had called ahead and had had his car ferried from Andrews Air Force Base to a secured lot at Baltimore-Washington International. The keys had been left in the tailpipe. Rachel nodded when she saw what was in the trunk; she'd expected just such an arsenal.

Smith pulled out a Second Chance vest. "This goes on first. Later, you take what suits you best."

Rachel got into the backseat, struggled to get out of her turtleneck, struggled even harder to hook on the vest over the straps of her bra. When she stepped back outside she pulled down hard on the turtleneck. Even so, it barely covered the bottom of the vest.

Smith was waiting for her, his chest bulked out like a bodybuilder's. Rachel took a fast inventory of the trunk and chose the H-K nine-millimeter submachine gun. She jammed three extra clips into her pockets and ringed two teargas grenades through her belt. Smith watched without comment. He went with the Mossberg shotgun, spare rounds, and a pair of stun grenades.

The Sunday morning traffic was sparse, and they made good time on the B-W Parkway. They skirted the downtown core, got onto I-95, exited at McComas, and headed for the Northwest Harbor.

Rachel glanced out the window. The scene was very different in the innocent light of day. The warehouses, stacked shoulder to shoulder, now looked liked tired bruisers leaning against one another for support. The loading bays were empty, their steel doors rolled down and padlocked. The Dumpsters, piled high with refuse, were adorned by necklaces of green and orange garbage bags that held the overflow. The wind, gusting up and down the bleak manmade canyon, toyed with litter.

Smith had slowed the car to a crawl over the bumpy cobblestones. Rachel lowered her window and carefully scanned every loading dock and Dumpster, searching for a shadow or movement that shouldn't have been there. The sun played tricks on her, creating substance where there was none.

"That's it over there," Smith murmured.

Rachel glanced left at a six-story warehouse. With its rust-streaked sheet-metal siding and tall grimy windows, it looked very much like the one where Charlie Dunn had fought and died.

The words "McHENRY STORAGE" were stenciled above the loading dock in faded black letters. Smith kept the car moving, and Rachel had to twist around now to see the warehouse through the rear window.

"It has an electronic lock," she said.

"And we have the code."

Along with the warehouse blueprints, Lucille had had the McHenry Storage executives pass along the access code for the main door, as well as the kill sequence for the interior alarm system.

"We have company," Smith said.

A private security patrol car sounded around the corner. Rachel laid her weapon in the footwell, pushing it under the seat as far as it would go.

The two cars came abreast. Smith lowered his window and held out his ID.

"Somethin' the matter that you two are down here on a Sunday morning?" the uniformed guard asked.

"We're looking at possible surveillance sites," Smith replied.

"Seems quiet. Has it been that way?"

"All night."

The driver was young, with a thin, foxlike face and dark, suspicious eyes.

"We're going to be in the area for a while," Smith was saying. "I don't need you to broadcast that."

Rachel caught the guard's smirk.

"Sure. I get it. You're doin' the surveillance thing. Knock your-self out."

The patrol car moved on. Smith took his foot off the brake and let the car roll to the end of the street, where he made a U-turn.

"You think he's okay?" Rachel asked.

"As long as he doesn't get in our way."

She looked down the narrow street. "We should make one more run to check the rooftops."

The car was moving again, as slowly as before. Rachel tilted her head so that she could see the tops of the warehouses, but at no time did she stick it out the window.

"Sometimes I really hate quiet," she said.

Smith made another U-turn and pulled the car up to the McHenry Storage loading dock and parked adjacent to the building, out of sight from the street.

"Light or dark?" he asked.

"Light," Rachel said. "If he's in there, he's got nightscopes. With light, we take away that advantage."

Smith nodded and pulled the Mossberg from the footwell. With his other hand he reached across, the back of his hand grazing Rachel's cheek.

"Stay close."

They broke out of the car together, moving fast up the steps of the loading dock to the cover of the overhang. Rachel covered Smith's back as he went to work on the entry code.

The lock buzzed. He stepped to one side, Rachel to the other, so that neither was standing directly in front of the door. Then he turned the handle and kicked the door. It was heavy and swung back only halfway, but that was enough. Rachel scrambled behind him into the semidarkness. The sun had yet to reach the tall windows above her. She turned right and pressed herself up against the wall. She heard Smith's breathing and the soft *pings* as he punched in the deactivation code on the alarm.

According to the blueprints, the master panel should have been above and to the left of the alarm. Rachel heard the squeak of a metal cover swinging open. She imagined Smith's fingertips counting down the switches, searching for the one he wanted.

"Cover your eyes," he whispered.

Rachel looked down at her feet. She heard a snap, then squinted against the harsh light.

If he's here, if he's waiting, this is when he'll do it.

The sound of the switch being thrown traveled through the air and disappeared. Rachel saw an alcove next to her, grabbed Smith by the sleeve, and pulled him in with her. It felt good to have cinder block at her back.

"Not what it looks like from outside," he said softly.

The dilapidated exterior was a false front. Inside, the warehouse was starkly modern, three levels, each the length and breadth of half a football field. The ground floor was polished concrete. A long, waist-high counter separated the entrance from the rest of the warehouse. On it were four computers, sheathed in plastic dust covers. Rachel assumed they were used to update inventory.

Behind the counter were two-inch-wide steel beams set vertically and horizontally to create perfect cubes, or shelves. Each shelf had a metal bottom and was about the size of a steamer trunk. The shelves were stacked twenty-odd high and were crammed with cardboard boxes, the kind businesses used to store documents they could not, for whatever reason, destroy or keep on computer disks.

A spiral staircase, bolted to the concrete floor, connected the levels. The second and third were identical to the first except that their floors were constructed of interlocking steel mesh squares. Looking up, Rachel could see through them all the way to the support girders spanning the roof. Huge floodlight tubes were suspended from the ceiling, casting glare off the white-painted concrete walls. She also noticed myriad red pipes running above each level and caught the wink of the copper sprinkler heads.

"Talk to me," Smith said.

"It's cool. The air-conditioning must have been on before we came in." She paused. "That crackle, I think it's one of the tubes about to go. All this paper—smells a little like yeast."

She looked at Smith. "I don't know if he's been in here. I can't tell."

He gazed out at the warren of shelves and tiers. Each was a

potential sniper's nest. He knew that if he thought about it too long, the risk of moving at all could paralyze him.

"It's on the second level, six rows down, third shelf. We use the staircase. I'll lead, you cover."

Smith dropped to a crouch and raced for the staircase. He was on the fourth step by the time Rachel caught up. The clang of their footsteps on metal rebounded off the walls. If the messenger was here, he could move around now and they'd never hear him.

Rachel held the submachine gun high, weaving the barrel across a 180-degree firing arc. She kept her butt against the staircase railing so that she could climb backward without having to look where she was going.

Smith reached the landing and darted right. He poked the Mossberg into the narrow aisle between two stacks, then stepped forward. The aisle was clear. Rachel was close behind him, eyes roving across the ceiling. She bumped into Smith when he suddenly stopped.

The ends of the storage boxes had both handwritten ID numbers in black felt pen and strips of computer bar codes. Smith propped his shotgun against the bottom row and began searching. Rachel heard the slap of his palm on cardboard as he grabbed the cartons, pulled them forward.

"Got it."

Smith ran his hand around the base of a large box. Rachel cast a quick look at his fingers and saw the film of dust on them.

"I don't think it's been touched for a while," Smith said.

Still, he was very careful in pulling the box toward him, hoisting it to his shoulder, flexing his knees to bring him close to the steel mesh floor, then setting it down gently.

"You have the smaller fingers," he said. "Check it out. I'll cover."

Rachel passed him the submachine gun and kneeled by the carton. Its cover was loose, no tape holding it down. She could lift it if she wanted to.

Not just yet.

She slipped her fingertips under the cover, slowly ran them along all four sides. No trip wire or sensor that might trigger a detonator. But there could be something fixed to the underside of the lid.

"Clean so far."

Smith handed her back her weapon. "Move back six feet."

She knew what he was going to do: position himself between her and the carton, then lift the cover. If there was a surprise waiting, his body would take the brunt of the blast.

"Go ahead, now," he said. "Move back."

From this distance Rachel couldn't see over his shoulders to his hands. She began counting the way they'd taught her in drop school: 1,001, 1,002, 1,003 . . . She'd reached 1,015 before Smith turned, the cover between his hands. It was clean.

Rachel went back to his side. The carton was crammed with files, most of them buff colored, a few red and green ones mixed in. Beth had said that the North file was in a buff jacket.

"He could have emptied the box, rigged a wire along the bottom, then put everything back in," she said. "When you thumb through the files . . ."

"Beth said it was marked," Smith murmured. "A red pen mark on the tab."

His hands were poised above the carton, thumbs out. She watched as he lowered them onto the middle of files; his right thumb eased back a tab. Then, moving away from him, a second one. And a third.

Rachel tried to ignore the rustle of Smith's fingers against paper. She kept scanning her field of vision, working up and down the racks, starting with the ones farthest away. She paid close attention to the long, wide girders that criscrossed just below the roof, searching for shadows there.

"Red mark."

She saw his fingers disappear between the files.

"I don't feel anything. . . . I'm going to pull it. Step back."

Rachel did so but this time didn't have to count very high. She heard Smith exhale, a curse riding on his breath. The file was in his hands, open. Empty.

• • •

The Engineer had been watching them from the moment they had driven into the street. He lay prone on the corrugated roof of a warehouse forty yards from McHenry Storage. The sun was getting stronger now, and the heat of the metal was starting to work through his tiger-striped jumpsuit. He thought back to when he'd watched Rachel Collins splayed across another rooftop. It had been hot that time, too. He imagined the heat creeping up through her clothing, working its way into her skin.

The Engineer had known that Smith and Collins wouldn't have time to effectively reconnoiter the area. They'd have gotten the building's blueprints and all that, but apart from a cursory on-site appraisal, the surrounding buildings would remain unfamiliar terrain. They wouldn't realize that the tall windows of the McHenry Storage warehouse allowed someone on this rooftop to look directly into the building, right down four aisles of shelves on all three levels. Smith and Collins were in the third aisle, seventy-two yards down range, with only three-eights of an inch of glass between them and a 55-grain ball round.

The Engineer had also known that Smith and Collins were smart enough to suspect he'd gotten here first, had bypassed the alarms and been inside. But he hadn't wanted to disappoint them too soon. He'd watched their moves inside the warehouse, had felt their confidence and hopes rise the closer they got to their target. Through the scope on his rifle the Engineer had seen the beads of sweat on Smith's brow as he opened the carton. The concern for him that Collins had unwittingly revealed had been heartbreaking. Then Smith had begun tugging at his prize, coaxing the buff file out of the carton, opening it . . .

The Engineer saw Smith bare his teeth. He expelled his breath and fired. Smith's head snapped back, a gout of blood shooting out from his neck. The Engineer lowered the barrel two degrees, fired again, and watched as Rachel staggered as though she'd been punched.

Rachel had heard Smith curse as soon as he'd opened the file. She'd been staring at it when she heard glass breaking, felt something hot graze her ear, setting it on fire. Then Smith's fist had flown at her, hitting her hard to get her out of the way a split second before he was jerked back. Then something even more powerful had slammed into her shoulder, kicking the wind out of her and spinning her around. Her head had caught the edge of a steel brace as she'd crumpled.

The Engineer panned the scene through the scope. He'd seen the blood fly out of Smith's neck, indicating a solid hit. There was some by Collins's head, trickling through her hair and along her cheek.

He could have left it at that, but the Engineer had learned from his mistake with Beth Underwood. After breaking down his rifle, he reached into his pocket and brought out a remote-control unit. A half second later four explosions tore through McHenry Storage, one in each corner. The building shuddered but didn't collapse. The Engineer hadn't wanted it to. He wanted a fire and the thick, acrid smoke it would spawn. It had taken him less than fifteen seconds to disable the extremely sophisticated fire-extinguishing systems that the storage company had installed.

The explosions jolted Rachel back to consciousness, dragging her past the pain, forcing her to open her eyes. The first thing she felt were the sharp metal edges of the mesh floor digging into her cheek. She rolled over to get away from that, and her legs bumped something. She raised her head, saw Smith lying there.

Grasping a steel post, she pulled herself up and clung there for a few seconds, until she had her balance. Now she smelled the smoke. It was coming up through the floor, but she couldn't see any flames. She looked up at the red pipes and the copper sprinkler heads, realized what had been done to them. Realized too what she had to do.

Rachel kneeled down by Smith. His neck and shoulder were awash in blood. She ripped open his jacket, then went to work on the Velcro straps of the Kevlar vest. Pulling it back, she found something else: a neck protector, like a priest's collar, molded out of hardened polymer. There was a deep groove where the bullet had struck it, then splintered and torn apart the flesh below Smith's jaw all the way up to his ear. Rachel pushed up the sleeve of his jacket, tore apart his shirtsleeve, and used the cotton strip to apply pressure. She managed to stem the bleeding, then rolled him over and pulled off his jacket and vest.

The smoke was thicker now, stinging her eyes, forcing her to draw shallower breaths. Somewhere below, she heard the crackle of flames. A deep, wrenching sob shuddered through her as she dropped to her hands and knees, dry heaves racking her chest.

She struggled back to her feet, turned Smith over again so that he lay supine, then grasped him under the arms and put her body against his chest. Slowly she hoisted him up in a fireman's carry, gripping his belt to keep him draped over her shoulder.

Rachel almost crumpled under the dead weight. She planted her legs apart and staggered to the staircase, gripped the railing, and went down one step at a time. She made it down to the ground level, lurched against the counter for support. She saw the flames now, shooting out of the corner by the door, eating up the oxygen. She quit breathing. The door to the outside was only a few steps away, only a few. . . . She stretched her arm out and rammed into it.

Rachel broke into the morning, gasping. She was on the loading dock, and there were the steps leading to the street. Someone was calling to her.

Who?

Then suddenly the terrible weight was lifted from her. Her legs buckled and she fell, hard. When she lifted her head she saw the security guard carrying Smith to the open back door of his car, laying him across the seat. Now he was coming back to her, his face tight.

"Are you all right?"

His words seemed to travel very slowly.

Rachel stared at him, wondering why he was asking such a silly question. She saw him reach up to his right ear, point at her. Rachel raised her hand. She touched something that caused a bolt of pain to shoot through her. The guard helped her over to the patrol car. She saw Smith first, then her reflection in the glass. The side of her face was slick with blood. Her fingertips wavered in the empty space where her earlobe should have been.

22

Rachel did not leave Logan Smith's side until the first of the emergency units came howling down the street. While the paramedics were moving him out of the private patrol car, she ran to the side of the building and drove the Crown Victoria out into the street and around the corner, where she parked it behind a Dumpster. By the time she was back at the scene, the firefighters were in action. The security guard was shouting and waving his arms, then the brigade commander pushed him back.

Rachel stepped up into the ambulance and closed the doors behind her. Smith was on a stretcher, two paramedics working hard over him. The stainless-steel rails of the stretcher were bright with blood.

"Will he be all right?"

One of the medics grunted and kept working; the other turned to her. Rachel caught him staring at her waist. She glanced down and realized she still had the grenades clipped to her belt loops.

"Is he going to be okay?" she insisted.

"He's lost a lot of blood. The bullet didn't clip the carotid artery, but it fragmented. I can't tell how much damage was done." He paused. "The pressure dressing—you did that?"

Rachel nodded.

"If he pulls through, hit him up for a drink. Now let's take a look at you."

She felt the cold sting of alcohol swabs on her face but would not take her eyes off Smith. There was a thick pressure bandage on the side of his neck, and an airway had been put in place. The medic was tightening the stretcher's waistbands.

The paramedic tending her let out a low whistle. "Your ear—"

"I know. How bad is it?"

"Looks a lot worse than it is. A flesh wound, really. The bullet took off the lobe."

Rachel saw her reflection in a stainless-steel pan. The medic had done a good job getting the blood and grime off her.

"Where are you taking him?" she asked.

"St. Mary's."

Rachel shook her head. "He's a federal officer. ID's in his pocket. He goes to Johns Hopkins."

"That's not my call—"

"He'll be in protective custody."

The paramedic regarded her silently, then nodded. He knew protocol. "Get JH on the horn," he told his partner. "Tell 'em we're rolling, code two."

He looked back and said, "You'd better strap yourself in," before he realized Rachel was gone.

Rachel dodged running firemen and fat hoses that snaked across the street. The cobblestones were slick with water. Baltimore P.D. had arrived, and the security guard was giving his version to a patrolman: she knew he would tell the officer about her.

She ran around the corner to the Dumpster and slipped into

the passenger seat of Smith's car. There she peeled off her Second
Chance vest and pulled on her turtleneck, unclipped the grenades,
and stowed everything in the footwell. The ambulance tore past
her. Rachel watched but didn't really see it.

Her ear was throbbing, but even that pain couldn't fragment the
deep sense of calm she was floating in. Everything seemed very
still, very bright, the way it did in a particularly vivid dream. She
understood that Logan Smith might die. She knew where she had
to go and what she had to do when she got there. The composite
of the messenger flickered in her mind's eye.

She slid over behind the wheel. "It's just you and me, sport,"
she said aloud, to a man she'd never seen.

Tires spun on the wet cobblestones. Rachel caught up to the
ambulance on McComas and stayed in its wake. Once they were
on I-95, she grabbed the cell phone and hit 001, Lucille Parker's
code.

Judge Simon Esterhaus was in the teak-paneled den of his town
house on Cooke's Row. The television volume was low enough
that he could hear the floorboards creak as his wife moved around
upstairs. He sat back in his padded leather chair and stared out the
French doors to the small terrace and garden. Gently he massaged
his jaw. His gums were still badly inflamed, though he'd taken out
his dentures the minute he'd come home.

The pain in his mouth was nothing compared to the fear metas-
tasizing within him. The Engineer—seemingly invincible and in-
fallible—had failed. Smith and Collins now knew where Esterhaus
had hidden his secrets. The Engineer had promised to take care of
them. But then, the Engineer had also promised to eliminate Beth
Underwood. As the judge was driving home from the White
House, his imagination had preyed on him, calling up visions of
Logan Smith waiting for him in front of his home, handcuffs
swinging in his fingers.

Esterhaus shuddered. His eyes flitted around the room, resting
briefly on the framed awards, plaques, and photographs that were
the banners of his long, distinguished career. The power and repu-

tation they bespoke was like a suit of armor. No threats, accusations, or innuendos had ever been able to pierce it. Until now. . . . Now he could be saved only by the savagery of a man he despised. Esterhaus scarcely recognized himself anymore; the face he saw in the mirror was that of a stranger who repelled him.

"Reliving old glory?"

Pamela Esterhaus stood framed in the doorway of the den. She still had on the eggshell silk suit and emerald green blouse she'd worn to breakfast at the White House. On the right lapel of the jacket was an Elsa Peretti pin, a gold rose with diamonds and emeralds in the petals. Esterhaus remembered exactly where and when he'd bought that for her—at Tiffany's in New York, on their fifteenth wedding anniversary. They had had dinner at the Rainbow Room, and he'd presented it to her before dessert. He remembered too the way her eyes had lit up, not with surprise or delight, but with greed.

"What do you want, Pamela?"

"For you to stop moping. It's boring. *You're* boring."

"I'm just waiting to hear—"

She watched his jaw drop and his hand snatch the remote control. The television blared.

It was a bulletin on a local newscast. A female reporter was standing in front of a pumper. Behind her, firemen directed a stream of water onto a warehouse. The name McHENRY STORAGE was visible through the smoke.

"An early morning explosion ripped through this dockside warehouse," the reporter carried on breathlessly. "Fire officials on the scene have managed to contain the blaze but report at least two casualties."

A new picture flashed on the screen: the emergency wing of Johns Hopkins, an EMS truck with its doors open, two paramedics unloading a stretcher. Esterhaus gasped when the jiggling camera caught Logan Smith's face above the blankets. The reporter's voice-over continued.

"One of the blast victims has been identified as a federal agent. He is listed in critical condition. A second casualty, believed to be a woman, has not yet been found."

Pamela turned off the television, then grabbed her husband by the shoulders and shook him. "It's all going to work out, do you hear me? This has nothing to do with you! All you have to do is keep your mouth shut—"

Esterhaus twisted violently, shaking off her grip. "Are you crazy?" he whispered hoarsely. "Smith is still alive! And the girl—"

"Smith'll be dead before they get him on the operating table! As for the girl, she probably never made it out of the warehouse. Done! Finished! The way it should have been in Arizona."

Esterhaus stared at his wife in disbelief. "It's all coming apart," he moaned.

His head snapped to one side as her palm smacked against his cheek. "Only if you let it!"

The three-note doorbell chimed. She glared at her husband, slumped in his chair, and hurried out of the den, closing the door behind her. She paused in front of the ornately framed mirror in the foyer. It was a reflexive gesture; she knew she looked fine.

"Good morning, Pamela."

The Engineer was dressed in the Sunday uniform of Georgetown residents: sneakers, stonewashed jeans, a bulky sweatshirt with the Redskins logo across the chest.

"Sam. What a pleasant surprise."

She glanced over her shoulder.

"Maybe this is a bad time," he said.

"No, come in."

He brushed by her and waited in the foyer until she'd closed the door. The draft caught her perfume and carried it to him. He smiled when he turned and saw her looking at him. Their eyes locked. He felt a hunger for her rise in his belly.

"Is that it?" Pamela asked, indicating the manila envelope in his hand.

"A small gift. But one you shouldn't keep."

Pamela reached for the envelope, brushing his fingertips, the contact dancing through her body like an electric current. She worked back the metal clasps and opened the flap, then pulled out the file folder—but only halfway. She knew what it was.

The Engineer looked at the closed door to the den.

"He saw Smith on the news," Pamela said. "And Rachel Collins is missing."

"Word at Johns Hopkins is that Smith won't make it. He's in a coma. Even if he survives, machines will do his living for him. As for Collins, she's run out of places to hide. Without that"—he indicated the file—"she has nothing to back up whatever she says."

"You're going to let her go?"

"I didn't say that. Right now I'm more concerned about Simon. He's coming apart, isn't he?"

"Yes."

The Engineer opened the den door and peeked inside. Esterhaus was sitting behind his desk, staring vacantly at the trophy wall. The Engineer closed the door quietly.

"He *is* in bad shape. No telling if he'll get worse."

Pamela shrugged. Her eyes were shining, her lips parted, and her voice came out husky. "We can't let that happen."

"No, we can't. Mind if I use the bathroom?"

"You know where it is."

The Engineer headed up the curved staircase to the second floor. He walked down the carpeted hall past the master suite into a guest room. He crossed into the glass-and-marble bathroom and found Esterhaus's toiletries lined up along the granite counter.

There was the toothbrush and shaving kit, the grooming articles, and the small flagons of expensive colognes. Beside these was a glass filled with clear solution, a set of dentures resting on the bottom. From his pocket the Engineer removed a small plastic container, much like those used for nasal spray, unscrewed the childproof cap, and squeezed fifteen drops of a milky liquid into the glass. He recapped the container and returned it to his pocket, then found a Q-tip and swirled the solution. He snapped the Q-tip in half and flushed it down the toilet.

Pamela was waiting for him when he came down the stairs. He pointed to the envelope, which she'd placed next to her keys and purse on the narrow foyer table. "I wouldn't leave that lying around. It's already caused enough trouble."

She threw back her head, and he could see the laughter bubble its way up her long, smooth throat.

• • •

"What did he want?"

"For me to tell you not to worry."

Esterhaus watched his wife kneel in front of the fireplace and pull back the screen. She gripped a poker and jabbed at the remains of the charred log resting on the andirons, stuffed paper and kindling beneath it, and wedged an envelope deep into the pile. She took a couple of birch logs from the canvas basket and laid them carefully across the kindling.

"Pamela . . ."

She turned, a long log-lighting match in her hand.

"Get me my pills. Please . . . this pain is killing me."

"As soon as this is going," she said soothingly. Pamela struck the match and held the flame to the newspaper and kindling. Both caught quickly. She closed the glass doors, stepped back, and ran her hand down the side of her husband's face.

"Be right back."

The painkillers were in the kitchen. Getting them and a glass of water took less than half a minute. Esterhaus was still in his chair, his eyes lightly closed, when she slipped back into the den. She watched his hands tremble as he reached for the medication.

"I have to go out," she whispered. "I want you to rest. Just remember what the president said: Everything has to be taken care of before you go in front of the Senate committee." She paused. "And it will be."

On her way out, Pamela glanced back at the fireplace. The kindling was going strong, the birch bark curling and crackling. Beneath it, a flame crawled across the envelope, leaving only black ash in its wake.

A half hour later, when Pamela Esterhaus stepped out onto Cooke's Row, she paid no attention to the beige sedan parked across the street. Rachel watched her zip up a colorful yachtsman's jacket and head toward Wisconsin Avenue.

Rachel was relieved to see her leave. She had been observing the Esterhaus residence for fifteen minutes and had caught a glimpse of both the judge and his wife through the half-open curtains. The question had been how to get Pamela out without spooking Esterhaus.

Rachel put the submachine gun on the passenger seat and covered it with a blanket she'd found in the trunk. The weapon had been for the messenger; perhaps it still would be. She thought it likely that he would call on Esterhaus after the scene at the warehouse. But he hadn't, so far. Rachel was sure that he couldn't have gotten here any sooner than she had. He would have needed time to transform himself from killer back to civilian.

Or maybe he too has been watching and waiting for the wife to leave. . . .

Rachel turned, looked through the rear window. It was coming up on midmorning, but the street was still quiet. The curbs were jammed with cars. She'd been very lucky to drive up just as someone was pulling out. If the messenger was coming now, he'd have to be on foot. She'd kept track of the people who drifted by, looking for someone who didn't fit in with the walkers and joggers, the boyfriends and husbands returning from Starbucks with lattes and the Sunday paper.

Rachel was still watching when she dialed through to Lucille Parker. "It's me. Rachel."

"Hi, honey. You okay?"

Lucille sounded anxious, but better than she had an hour ago, when Rachel had first called her.

"I'm fine. I'm sitting on Esterhaus."

"Is he alone?"

"He is now."

"I did some checking. He and the missus had breakfast with the president."

"That'll be the last decent meal he ever has," Rachel said coldly. Then: "Any word on Logan?"

She heard Lucille's voice catch, just as it had before, when Rachel had called to ask for help and to tell her about Logan Smith so she wouldn't get it from the news reports.

"The doctors are giving me gobbledygook, being that I can't get in their faces. I think he's all right . . . I pray he is."

"Me too," Rachel whispered.

"Listen. I want you to think real hard about what you're going to do. There's no reason in the world you have to go into that house. I have the Bureau's Hostage Rescue Team on standby. Give them twenty minutes and they'll walk into that bastard's life like the wrath of God."

Rachel understood Lucille's concern. If their positions had been reversed, she'd be saying the same thing.

"There are things Esterhaus knows," she said. "If I surprise him hard and fast enough, maybe he'll give them up. If HRT takes him, they have to read him his rights. I don't, because I'm not looking to arrest him."

Rachel knew that Lucille wanted desperately to ask what, if not an arrest, she had in mind. But Rachel wouldn't have told her. Better that Lucille be able to swear, under oath, that she'd never had any idea what Warrant Officer Rachel Collins had intended.

"I'd feel a whole lot better if there was a way for us to stay in touch," Lucille said.

"I would, too."

"Then give me a deadline, whatever you're comfortable with. If it passes, I send in the cavalry."

Rachel considered. "Thirty minutes," she said finally.

"Rachel, that's an awfully long—"

"I'm going in armed. He's not going to get the drop on me. I need time to try to get him to talk. If he plays dumb and there's no way to get through to him, I'm on the horn to you."

Lucille's silence spoke volumes about her reluctance. But in those few seconds Rachel plucked something that had gotten buried and been almost forgotten in the detritus of the last thirty-six hours.

"Lucille, could you track a number for me? It's a 703 area code, which makes it somewhere in Virginia." She coaxed the digits from the tendrils of her memory.

"Got it," Lucille said. "How does it figure in with Esterhaus?"

Rachel quickly explained how she'd found the number in Dunn's file.

"It's been disconnected, which is why I couldn't find out who it belongs to. I'm not sure it'll lead back to Esterhaus, but it might give us the person Dunn was reporting to." Rachel glanced at her watch. "I have ten forty-five. Give me a half hour."

"Not a minute more. Rachel? Watch your back."

Rachel checked the street one more time. There were more cars now, crawling along in search of a parking space. Several stopped when they saw her sitting behind the wheel, then made rude gestures when she waved them off.

Rachel withdrew her Bulldog handgun and checked the cylinder. The shell casings gleamed like new pennies. She had switched from the pumpkin rounds to airport loads, 225-grain semiwad cutter hollowpoints that mushroomed and expanded on impact but did not, usually, keep on going. It was the ammunition of choice in close quarters.

Rachel took one last look at the Esterhaus home. She had her fingers on the door handle when the phone rang. It had to be Lucille. But how could she have tracked that phone number so soon?

A thick, raspy voice whispered, "I've been watching you."

23

The fingers of Rachel's free hand curled around the fat grip of the Bulldog as she twisted in her seat. She stared wildly over her shoulder. There was no one on the sidewalk. No one was coming down the street. No car had silently rolled up near hers.

Son of a bitch, where are you?

The gravelly voice slithered back into her ear. "Are you still there, Rachel Collins?"

She had to get out of the car. All this glass, she was too exposed. He could march up, press the barrel against the glass, blow her brains out.

Maybe he's not that close. He likes the long gun. Maybe he doesn't have the right angle, wants you to step out where he can see you. . . .

"Rachel?"

"Who are you?"

"Ah, I forgot. We've never met. But we will, soon. If you do exactly what I say."

Rachel jammed her fear and outrage deep into her belly. "I'm not doing a damn thing until you tell me who you are."

"Of course. The name is Simon Esterhaus. *Judge* Esterhaus."

Rachel slumped back against the seat. For an instant she almost relaxed her grip on her gun, until this thought tore through her:

You've never met Esterhaus. Don't know what he looks or sounds like. The messenger is tied to Esterhaus. It could be him, using Esterhaus to draw you into a kill zone.

"You want to see me," Rachel said flatly.

"Very much. It's only natural . . . with everything that's happened. It's necessary."

"You called a number that isn't mine."

"Logan Smith isn't exactly available."

Rachel closed her eyes. "But you knew I would be."

"I can see you from my house, sitting in the car."

"Why don't you come out?"

There was a short, barking laugh. "Not what I had in mind. Nor am I about to suggest that you come inside. You wouldn't do that anyway, would you? Not now. . . ."

Damn right! "Maybe we can meet—"

"At the Tidal Basin. Across the street from the Bureau of Engraving and Printing, there's a dock where you can rent paddleboats. Lots of people around on a day like this. That should make you feel comfortable."

Rachel flashed on the location. She couldn't have chosen a better one. "When?"

"Two hours. You leave now and I'll be along." There was a pause. "Buy a copy of today's *New York Times.* There's a picture of me in the magazine section, page fourteen."

The connection was broken. Rachel looked at the windows of the Esterhaus home. She thought she saw the edge of a curtain fall, or it could have been just her imagination.

Pamela spotted the Engineer at a corner table on the patio of the French Market on Wisconsin. She thought he looked particularly appetizing, all lean and tanned with his thick windblown hair and designer sunglasses. She smiled at the thought, wanting to gobble him up.

She wended her way through the people leaving the market with their picnic baskets packed with gourmet fare. "This seat taken?"

The Engineer smiled, gestured silently. He had not lifted his head, but Pamela knew he'd been tracking her all the way up the street. They were two of a kind, gifted professionals who always maintained the careful habits of their calling.

Pamela watched as the Engineer glanced around. Almost immediately a young waitress was at his side. This effect he had on women amused her. But in his presence she was intensely aware of her own, similar reactions and governed them accordingly.

After he'd ordered her a coffee she said, "Now what?"

"Now we wait."

His voice was just slightly above the decibel level on the noisy patio.

"Do you really think Simon will try to contact the girl? Or that she'll come to him?"

"I can't say about him, but she has no choice. Everything Collins has seen and heard leads to him. Right now she thinks that if she gets to him, he'll give up the triggerman." He looked out onto the sidewalk. "In a way she's gone beyond Simon," he continued softly. "Oh, she still wants to nail his hide to the barn door. But it's the person behind him that she's really after. Because all this time she's been chasing a shadow . . . a shadow that killed her best friend, and maybe a future lover."

Pamela laughed. "Collins and Smith? You're kidding!"

"People could say the same about us. And if you think about it, we're not really so different from them."

"We survive," Pamela said.

"Yes. But not because we're necessarily better."

"Then why?"

"We don't believe in virtues, that some things are good, others evil." He smiled at her. "Consequences. That's what we know for sure, the only thing we hold true."

Pamela took his hard brown hand and brought his fingers to her lips. "You keep talking like that, I'll think you're falling in love with her yourself."

"With Collins? No. But you've got to admire her. She's come a long way on spit and shoestring."

"And you really believe that she'll run this down no matter what it takes?"

"No matter what it takes," the Engineer echoed her words. "She'll do it because it's always been personal for her. Mollie Smith's death made it that way. She'll do it because she has to look at me, even if it's only for a second or two. She can't—won't—die before she can do that."

Pamela's coffee arrived. She tore open a packet of sweetener and stirred it in. "And after that?" she asked, her lips on the edge of the cup.

The Engineer leaned forward, brushed a stray lock of hair from her forehead. She felt his breath on her skin.

"Then it's done, and you'll finally have what you wanted."

Esterhaus swirled his cognac, watching it stain the crystal snifter a dark honey hue. The medication had slowly melted away the appalling pain in his mouth. The drink had calmed him, uncoiled his mind, let it spiral into the well of memory. That was where the demons dwelt, the decisions he'd made, the outrage he'd suppressed, the humiliation. They were all in there, but powerless now, batting ineffectually like moths around a light bulb.

The drink was also what had given him the courage to call Rachel Collins. Esterhaus knew he could still change his mind. Nothing compelled him to show up for their meeting at the Tidal Basin. Nothing except his conscience.

The judge stared unblinking at the flames dancing in the fireplace. He lifted the snifter and sucked down a little more cognac. The image of Logan Smith drifted toward him, and Esterhaus could not stop it. He imagined how Smith must look now, bloody and torn.

Then came others, like the federal officers who had died in Arizona. And Mollie Smith. And General Griffin North . . . An unbroken chain whose links he himself had helped forge.

There was a special one, a man who had been a friend, who had called upon his help and who had trusted him; a man Esterhaus had found it expedient to destroy, without, he now recalled, any guilt at all. From the moment Steven Copeland had walked through his door, Esterhaus had known that he couldn't possibly give the young man what he wanted. The judge had been forewarned by Copeland's employers, to whom he owed much of his career and wealth: Copeland was to be strung along until such time as Bell and Robertson and PSX had finished framing the "evidence" that would become his gallows.

Esterhaus had obliged. It had never entered his mind not to. To Steven Copeland he'd owed nothing except a genuine fondness; to the others, the debt was both material and incalculable.

If I hadn't ruined him . . .

Of course things would have been different. Copeland would not have become his enemy; the furnace of his revenge would never have been stoked. Maybe he and Beth Underwood would still have become lovers, but never would they have dared to pry into the judge's secrets. So the North file would not have been found and the tool of vengeance never placed in the hands of a broken, unstable man.

I could have saved them all. Even Steven . . . even myself.

It was an epiphany too late, washing over him only when there was nothing he could undo. He had only one recourse. The video clip of Logan Smith, his life bleeding out of him, was what had finally given rise to Judge Esterhaus's conscience.

He set the glass on the side table and walked through the silent house, upstairs to his bathroom, and splashed cold water on his face. He avoided looking in the mirror. He had no wish to see what would stare back at him. He combed his hair, then regretfully reached for the glass that held his teeth. He could speak passably without them but did so only in front of his wife. A man of precise vocabulary and elocution, he would never dream of trying in front of anyone else. He would not falter or slur when dealing with Rachel Collins.

The dentures in place, Esterhaus rinsed his hands, picked up a lightweight windbreaker, and went back down the stairs. In the foyer he paused and looked around with a detached, critical eye. His home, he thought, was not at all the kind of place he'd always dreamed it would be.

A little girl with white blond hair peered suspiciously at Rachel when the cell phone went off. She tugged it out of her jacket pocket and smiled at the child, who stuck out her tongue, then ran back to her family.

"Where are you?" Lucille asked. "Sounds like a kids' playground."

"I'm down at the Tidal Basin." Rachel looked around. "You know the paddleboat rental place?"

"Sure."

"The park around it is packed. The weather is fine and families are out. Maybe that's why Esterhaus wanted to meet here, because it's noisy and crowded, lots of ways to duck out if you're in a hurry."

"Do you see him?"

"Not yet." Rachel glanced down at *The New York Times Magazine* which had set her back four bucks. "But I know whom to look for."

"A cagey bastard," Lucille muttered. "He can see you, see *everything*. No way he'll miss a trap, or undercover personnel."

"I don't think he's setting me up. He would have gone for a different venue, probably later in the day, too. Lucille, we have to make this quick."

"Right. That number you gave me? It belonged to an outfit called Wonderland Toys, headquartered in the TransDulles Center out by the airport. Mean anything to you?"

Rachel culled her memory for anything Mollie or Logan Smith might have told her or something she'd read in the paperwork.

"No. I'm coming up empty."

"I can't figure it, either."

"You're sure it's Wonderland Toys?"

"I had Bell Atlantic double-check."

What connection would Dunn have had with a toy company?

"Do we know for sure it's a toy company?" Rachel asked. "With a name like Wonderland . . ."

"I was thinking the same thing," Lucille replied. "I'm running a check through the IRS right now."

Rachel turned her head to avoid the sun in her eyes. A movement in the park caught her attention: Some kids who'd been playing around a water fountain were now scattering, like doves that sensed the hawk. That was when she saw him, sixty-odd yards away, shambling in her direction.

"The man's arrived," she told Lucille. "Same ground rules: You don't hear from me in thirty minutes, put out an APB on the son of a bitch. I'll make sure a few people, like a hot dog vendor, see us together so he can't say he was never here."

He'd picked her out and was coming right for her. Rachel moved away from two families who were breaking out their lunch baskets and edged toward a group of college students playing touch football. The girls were watching their beaus race along the grass, shouting and clapping as one of them scored a touchdown. Behind them was a large oak. Never taking her eyes off Esterhaus, Rachel sidestepped to the tree, pressed her back against the hard, knobby bark. Her right hand slipped into her jacket, gripped her gun. The sun was behind her, giving her the advantage.

The judge looked different, less imposing than he had in the *Times Magazine* picture, in which he wore a handsome gray suit with a wine red tie. His face was the same, but as he approached, Rachel thought his features sagged and his skin, in spite of the sun and breeze, was pasty. He was wearing a navy blue windbreaker, gray slacks, and polished loafers. Rachel was glad that the front and the pockets of the windbreaker were zipped up. Esterhaus kept his arms away from his body, his hands open. From five feet away she smelled the liquor on him, noted the sheen over his red-rimmed eyes that indicated the judge would, at this moment, test positive for dope. Rachel glanced over his shoulder; no new element had been introduced into the tableau of the park.

"Rachel Collins."

In her time with CID, Rachel had looked upon men whose crimes ranged from the dangerous to the petty. But she had never faced someone whose soul had so utterly rotted away. She realized that the kind of fascination she felt was a natural human response to the presence of evil. She girded herself against it. Later, when Esterhaus was locked up, maybe she would go look at him, study him in the safety of a cage.

"Your loathing for me is so pure," Esterhaus said. "A bad attitude to adopt if you want to negotiate."

"There's nothing left to negotiate." She thought she sounded okay. Her voice didn't scratch or tremble. But she couldn't resist cutting him, once. "Because they're all dead."

Esterhaus gazed off, as though he saw some distant horizon. Rachel thought he might have drifted into a fugue state.

"You say that because you don't know any better," he murmured. *"Too many*—but not all—have died. Now it has to stop." He reached for the zipper on the front of his jacket.

"Don't do that."

"Then you won't see what I brought you," he replied. "I'm not armed."

That was hard to tell, given the bulky windbreaker. Rachel's arm was across her chest, as if she were wearing a cast. She watched Esterhaus pull down the zipper slowly, pull away both sides of the jacket. Two pockets were sewn into the lining. A sheaf of papers protruded from one of them.

"Just paper. May I?"

Rachel knew she could draw her weapon in three-tenths of a second. Esterhaus's movements, even if he lunged, would be slowed by the alcohol and drugs.

"Do it."

Esterhaus pulled it out. The pages were stapled together in one corner. She thought there were more than twenty of them.

"What is it?"

"Can't you guess? You got to Beth in time. She had to have told you about the file."

Rachel wanted to move on him and rip the papers out of his hand. But she willed herself not to.

Instead she stepped to his side. They were about the same height, so the barrel of her gun dug into his right kidney. She could see over his shoulder all right, make this short and sweet because she knew exactly what to ask for.

"North's itinerary."

Esterhaus nodded, and Rachel thought he might have smiled, had he been able to. He flipped the pages until he found the one he wanted and held it up.

There was the typewritten itinerary for North's California trip. The departure time from Andrews, then a bold red felt-tip line across the arrival time in Palm Springs that carried diagonally all the way down the page. In large block letters someone had written, "CANCELED."

"I imagine I hear your heart pounding," Esterhaus said. "Though of course that would be impossible. But I feel your breathing. You recognize this, don't you?"

Rachel stepped around him, her back once more against the tree. "Yes. It's something Beth referred to." She stared at him. "Why didn't you destroy it? What you have there goes back years. Why did you keep it, add to it?"

"You're an investigator. You have some psychology background. Maybe I'm like any other criminal, compelled to return to the scene of his crime; the burglar or killer who hangs on to a memento even though he fears that this might be the one piece of evidence that, if found, will do him in."

This time he did smile, a sickly crease that revealed very shiny teeth, as though they'd just been cleaned and polished.

"The truth is, I couldn't bear to destroy it. You're young, but when you read this I think you'll understand. I thought I was so clever—I truly believed no one would ever find this, that it would be my secret forever. But I forgot about hubris. Do you know what that is?"

"Pride . . . too much of it."

Esterhaus nodded, then winced as he ran a hand around his chin. Rachel watched him massage the flesh as though he had a toothache. He wiped his mouth, and when his hand came away she noticed a thin white trail on his palm.

"You have to give him up," she said.

Esterhaus stared at her.

"The killer you used. You have to give him to me."

"Yes, I must."

She watched him rub his jaw again, harder this time, then slide his teeth side to side.

"I'm placing you under arrest," Rachel said. "I want you to hand me the papers, slowly."

Esterhaus complied. Rachel snatched them from his grasp and stuffed them into her jacket pocket.

"I'll tell you who the Engineer is," Esterhaus said. "But you'll never take him."

Rachel glanced around the park, searching for a corridor in the crowd through which she could lead the two of them out.

"Is he here?" she asked.

"I didn't tell him I was coming to see you."

"Why do you say we won't get him?"

"He's not the kind of man anyone can 'get.' You'll realize that when I tell you about him."

To Rachel this made no sense. Given time and resources, any-one could be found. And she had plenty of both.

Made no sense . . . just like—

"I know about Wonderland Toys," she blurted.

Esterhaus's eyes widened in surprise. A fierce joy sprang up in Rachel. She had something hard and good in her hand, something Lucille could run with as soon as Rachel called her.

"How could you know?"

The words came out as a croak. Esterhaus grimaced, then gasped. His hands shot to his mouth as his knees buckled and he pitched to the ground, shaking like an epileptic. Rachel cried out as Esterhaus's entire body heaved itself off the grass in one terrible spasm. She dropped to her knees, straddled his chest, and managed to pin both his arms. His head continued to whip from side to side, pounding against the earth.

Her cry attracted attention. She heard people calling out to her, then footsteps running up.

"Call 911!" she shouted over her shoulder.

Suddenly Esterhaus went limp. Rachel dug into her pocket for the cell phone and tossed it at one of the students who'd been playing touch football.

She turned back to Esterhaus. His eyes were rolling in their sockets, his mouth working furiously, as though he were chewing on something that was alive in his mouth. Rachel ripped open his shirt and pressed her fingers against his chest. His heart was racing.

"Pamela . . ."

The name was carried on a horrible choked whisper, followed by a hoarse sucking as Esterhaus struggled to breathe.

Rachel leaned close to the bright red lips, bloodied by what was left of the flesh in his mouth.

"Give me his name!"

Esterhaus stared wildly at her. His lips worked to form the words, but all he could do was repeat his wife's name. Then a final shudder rolled through him, and his head snapped back.

"Pamela knows!" he cried.

"You're not going to die on me," Rachel whispered savagely. "Not now!"

She went to work on his heart, one palm over the other, pressing down hard, releasing, pressing, releasing. She poured every ounce of her will into him, but there was no response. Behind her, the crowd had quieted until someone called out, "Give him mouth-to-mouth!"

Rachel reached to pull open Esterhaus's mouth. A stream of white, milky liquid ran over his lips, mixing with the blood, turning it pink. She knew she could never put her mouth to that.

Slowly she rolled off the body. She stayed like that for a moment, on her knees, her head bowed. Someone was by her side, pushing a blanket at her. She took it and draped it over Esterhaus's face and torso.

Struggling to her feet, Rachel scanned the crowd, spotted the football player who had her phone. He started when he felt her gaze.

"I called," he said. "The ambulance is on its way."

Rachel showed him her ID and took back her phone. "Ask these people to move back, okay? And stay here until the paramedics arrive."

"Yeah, sure."

As he and his buddies began to push back the crowd, Rachel slipped behind the oak tree and waited until more people ran past her. She looked around the tree, saw them gathered in a tight circle around where Esterhaus lay, then jogged away in the opposite direction.

24

Rachel tempered the awful need to hurry with these thoughts:

Esterhaus is dead. The man he called the Engineer—the messenger—somehow got to him. Esterhaus said to me: "Pamela knows." She knows what Esterhaus didn't live long enough to tell me: the Engineer's name.

An ambulance wailed along the road to the paddleboat dock. Passersby stopped and stared after it; Rachel kept on running. People in the crowd—probably the football player—would tell the paramedics and then the police about a woman who'd been with the dead man, had tried to revive him, then disappeared. Rachel could not allow the D.C. police to get in her way. She darted across the road, jumped the curb onto a grass median strip, and continued to her car, parked on Raoul Wallenberg Place.

She slammed the door and gripped the wheel with both hands. She sat like that, rock still, for a few seconds, listening to the blood pound at her temples. Then she saw her eyes in the rearview mirror. They were filled with rage. She dug the phone out of her pocket.

"Lucille?"

"Your time was just about up. You okay?"

"Esterhaus is dead—looked like a heart attack. I think he was given some kind of neurotoxin. Lucille, listen. He gave me every- thing. Almost. The killer—he called him the Engineer. When I mentioned Wonderland Toys, he just about jumped out of his skin. You got a hit there."

"More than you think. When I checked with the IRS they clammed up. Seems there's a security lock to all information re- lated to Wonderland Toys."

"A security lock?"

"No way you'd know this, but Logan and I have seen this kind of thing before. Wonderland Toys is a front, a shell company for a certain government intelligence agency that lives over at Langley."

"*The Agency?*"

"None other."

Rachel's mind was spinning. "So the Engineer could be work- ing for the CIA."

"Do you have a name?"

"Esterhaus died before he gave it up."

"Then it's going to take time to find this guy."

"Maybe not. Esterhaus said, 'Pamela knows.' Pamela's his *wife*."

"You know who else she is? A honcho over at the Justice Department who runs their witness protection program."

Rachel hesitated. "I don't see how that factors, Lucille. But she may be the last person who can pinpoint the killer. Unless he's already gotten her."

"Rachel, I know where you're going with this. Now listen to me. Carefully. After I called the IRS, someone with an awful lot of clout got hold of the director. *My* director. He was already going crazy over what happened to Logan, and now the IRS is calling him, saying I'm exposing an Agency cover. He's been screaming at me for explanations. I try to dodge him, and he tells me he knows all about you, says I'm helping you get yourself killed."

Lucille paused to catch her breath. "Thing is, I have to turn this over to the director's office. Stat. His orders are for you to call him immediately and —"

"I'm not one of his. He can't order me to do anything."

"He'll go to your boss, Rachel. Probably done so already."

"Tell your director that, with all respect, if he or anyone else horns in now, Pamela Esterhaus will probably die. Buy me some time, Lucille. Tell him about the judge before he gets it off the news. Stay with me. It's the endgame. . . . Stay with me."

A moment's static on the line crackled in Rachel's ear.

"What're you going to do?" Lucille asked.

"Get to Pamela Esterhaus before the Engineer does. Bring her in safely."

"Where?"

"The first cop station or federal building I see." She paused. "Then the director can have my head."

"How long?"

"I don't know. But Lucille? I promise, if I run up against a wall, I'll shout so you can send the HRT boys to find her."

"All right, girl," Lucille said softly. "Go get her. But you know I have to tell the director what you're doing."

"Just be sure he understands that if he gets to her first, she goes into protective quarantine."

Through the traffic and the trees Rachel caught glimpses of police car lights. The keening of sirens vibrated along the car window. She dialed the Esterhauses' number.

Four rings and still no answer. Then a woman's voice came on the line.

"Good afternoon. Department of Justice."

"Pamela Esterhaus?"

"No. But this is her office."

Call forwarding.

"My name is Warrant Officer Collins, Army CID, Fort Belvoir. I need to speak with Mrs. Esterhaus. It's urgent."

"One moment, please."

The wait seemed interminable. Rachel drummed her fingertips

on the steering wheel. She was on hold so long that she began to wonder if she'd been cut off.

"This is Pamela Esterhaus."

The voice was crisp, businesslike. Rachel was suddenly struck by what she had to tell this woman she'd never met.

"Mrs. Esterhaus, I'm Rachel Collins." She rattled off her rank and ID number to establish bona fides.

"What can I do for you, Officer Collins?"

Rachel steeled herself and spoke the words that made Pamela Esterhaus a widow. She paused when she heard the soft cry, then went on describing when and where the judge had died.

"Collins, are you for real?"

Rachel closed her eyes. "Yes, ma'am, I am."

"And you were with my husband when this . . . this happened?"

"I was."

"But you're not with him now. It's not the paramedics or the police who are calling me, but you. Why is that?"

"Your husband died of a heart attack, Mrs. Esterhaus. At least that's what it looked like. But I know he was murdered. And right now his killer is after you."

"Simon murdered? Are you insane?"

"Check with the police, Mrs. Esterhaus. They'll confirm the where and when. They'll also tell you a woman was seen with him. Me. But they don't know the danger you're in. I do. And I have proof. I can explain it all to you. The Justice Department is about ten minutes from where I am—"

"I'm not at Justice."

"*What?*"

"I'm at the Capitol. My weekend secretary forwarded your call."

This is not good, not good!

"Mrs. Esterhaus, where exactly are you?"

"The Congressional Women's Reading Room."

"Is anyone there with you?"

"No. The people I was meeting with just left."

"Security?"

"Look, I've had enough. I don't know you, never heard of you—"

"I'm on my way to you right now."

"I'm hanging up, Officer Collins—if that's who you are. I'm calling the police—"

"Then get back to me back at this number, once you know I haven't been lying to you. Please. . . ."

"Fine. Give me the damn number!"

Rachel did, then heard a sharp click, followed by a dial tone.

She leaned her head back against the seat. Pamela Esterhaus, the "honcho," sounded like a prize bitch.

How do you think you would have reacted if someone had come peddling a story like that?

Rachel pushed aside her anger. The key thing was that Pamela Esterhaus was in the Capitol, safe. Even the Engineer wouldn't make a play for her there. The quarters were too close, the security too tight.

Rachel pulled out the papers Esterhaus had brought her. She held them lightly in her hand, feeling the texture of the paper, noting the age discoloration of some of the pages. She allowed herself the fierce joy of vindication and triumph.

Starting with the itinerary, she raced through the pages. She had time only to scan them, but that was enough. What was it Beth Underwood had said to her in Arizona? *It's obvious when you read it: the judge had been stalking General North for years. . . .*

Yes. And it was as horrible and cold-blooded as it was obvious. Troubling, too, because there was something on the pages Rachel couldn't connect, something that also went back to what Beth had told her.

A patrol car drifted along the road by the edge of the park. The police would have a description of her. They were trolling. She eased into traffic and headed up toward Independence Avenue, which would take her all the way to the Capitol. She thought hard about what she had to do, wished she had more time. But she was coming up on the Air and Space Museum, only minutes from her destination. Rachel picked up the phone, held it until it became warm in her hand. The conclusions she'd drawn seemed crazy; even crazier would be to share them.

If you don't, and you end up dead, it won't have been crazy at all. Right?

Rachel called Lucille, laid it out for her.

"I don't think you're nuts at all," was Lucille's opinion.

• • •

Rachel found a parking space opposite the botanic gardens. To her right, the Capitol loomed like a fortress, the bronze statue of Freedom crowning its dome. To her left was the smaller of the city's two reflecting pools. Usually it was crowded, people sitting shoulder to shoulder, dangling their feet in the water. The view down the Mall was always breathtaking. But today there were few sightseers. Rachel thought most had chosen to play closer to the Potomac, before the weather got too cold.

She focused on the sweeping stairs leading up to the Capitol. Given Pamela Esterhaus's position, her calls would generate a snappy response from authorities. By now she would know which hospital her husband had been taken to and that there was no need to hasten to his side. Her pain and shock would slow her even more. Rachel had made good time. Pamela Esterhaus would still be here, in the Congressional Women's Reading Room. The last play was to go in and get her.

Rachel was headed toward the wide steps of the Capitol when her phone went off.

"Officer Collins, this is Pamela Esterhaus."

Rachel became very still. The hard edge of the woman's voice was gone, splintered by grief.

"Where are you?"

Pamela Esterhaus seemed not to hear the question. "You were right . . . about my husband. They took him to George Washington Hospital." The words came out slowly. "The doctor said it looked like a heart attack, except there were anomalies. What the hell does *that* mean? Some of the witnesses in the park gave the police a description of a woman. I guess that was you."

"Mrs. Esterhaus, let me come and get you. I'm right outside."

"I took a walk. I couldn't stand being inside, so—"

"*Where are you?*"

"In the Spring Grotto."

"I can see it from here." Rachel broke into a trot, the phone bumping against her ear. "Just keep talking to me."

"I don't think I can. I feel . . . I don't know. What am I supposed to do? Officer Collins, please hurry."

Rachel dug her feet into the hard field and sprinted ahead. *Just like the dash in the training ground,* she told herself. *Keep your knees up and don't stop pumping. Keep your eye on the prize. Three hundred yards, a piece of cake. And some of it downhill to boot. . . . Stay alert. There're trees. It's sunny, so look for the reflection of a gun barrel.*

The grotto was a small manmade pond with a thick, semicircular grove behind it. It was a sheltered, out-of-the-way place, unknown to tourists. Rachel pulled up on a low knoll and surveyed it from fifty yards away, breathing hard. There, on the stone ledge of the pond, sat a woman in a skirt and jacket, her head bowed, the toe of one shoe picking at the gravel in the path around the pond. Sitting fully exposed, a perfect target for the long gun.

The image of Logan Smith reaching for her, then the bullet driving him back, flashed like a strobe in Rachel's memory. She unzipped her jacket, and it flapped as she ran. But this way she could keep her hand on her gun. When she saw Pamela Esterhaus look up at her, she grabbed her ID and held it out in front of her until she reached the pond.

Lungs burning, Rachel gulped down air without ever taking her eyes off the other woman. The Capitol chic had disintegrated. Her fine ensemble now seemed to hang on her; tears had streaked her mascara and blush. She looked Rachel up and down, taking her measure. Rachel saw something in those eyes that frightened her.

Pamela Esterhaus reached for Rachel's ID and examined it. "That explains the gun," she said. "Explains a lot of things. You're really very good."

"Mrs. Esterhaus, let's go over by the trees, okay? You're too exposed here."

"What am I exposed *to,* Officer Collins?"

"Ma'am, *please!*"

"No. First you tell me what this is all about and how it's related to my husband's death. Or murder, as you say."

"Your husband gave me the name of his killer. I need to see your address book."

"*What?*"

"He said you always carry a small address book. Leather, I think it was. Give it to me and I'll *show* you what I'm talking about."

Pamela Esterhaus hesitated, then placed her hand in her purse.

The address book was the size of a paperback, tooled by Hermès. Rachel flipped to *B,* then *H, P,* and *W.* The names were written in distinctive Palmer penmanship. Tears welled up in Rachel's eyes.

"Officer Collins, would you be so kind as to show me both hands? Please."

There was something loathsomely sticky about that voice, like the smell of lilies around a corpse or the fetching voice of a stranger offering candy to a child. But Rachel did exactly as it bade, letting the address book slip from her fingers.

Pamela Esterhaus swooped down, snatched it up, and backed away. "Kill her," she said.

Rachel turned around. There he stood: the tall man with the dark curly hair and Redskins sweatshirt. The Colt Woodsman .22 seemed a natural extension of his hand.

"Now the gun, please. I don't have to tell you how to do that."

Using the thumb and forefinger of her left hand, Rachel pulled out the Bulldog and let it fall.

"Shoot her!" Pamela Esterhaus said again, her voice a touch shrill now.

"Bothers you, doesn't she?" the Engineer said conversationally. "She bothers *me,* I'll tell you. You know, Pamela, she had you marked."

Pamela spun around at him. "What the hell do you mean?"

The Engineer had not taken his eyes off Rachel, and now he spoke to her.

"That business with the address book. You weren't looking for a name, were you, Rachel? The judge never gave you one. If he had, you'd call me by it right now." He waited. "Thought so. You needed the book to see Pamela's handwriting, to check if it matched the writing on those papers in your pocket. The judge's notes, right?"

Rachel glanced at Pamela Esterhaus, whose features were contorted with rage.

"They match, don't they?"

"Yes," Rachel said.

"And you've read the papers."

"Most of them."

"What do they tell you, Rachel?"

Rachel turned to Pamela Esterhaus and spared her nothing. "Your husband didn't have anything to do with North's murder, at least not at first. You were the one who wanted the general dead. You'd been his lover, for a long time, I think. But he threw you out of his life. Your husband knew about the affair all along. You should read what he wrote. His pain was real. Despite everything you heaped on him—the infidelity, the shame, and worse—he never stopped loving you, even when you became a killer."

Rachel paused, then raced on, buying as much time as she could.

"North told you to take a hike, and you couldn't bear that. Then he fell in love with Mollie, some army nonentity. How *could* he have done that to you? you asked yourself. Frankly, all you had to do was look in the mirror.

"But you're not built that way, are you? The world has always come to you, allowed you to pick and choose whatever you wanted from it. In your eyes, *you* were the victim. You deserved revenge and were willing to do whatever it took to get it.

"But how do you strike down a national hero? How do you get close enough to see that it's done, but never get your hands dirty? You find someone like the Engineer, one who's the best at what he does. So the killing starts. But then something goes wrong. One too many people become involved, then two too many, and then it's out of control. But even then your husband still loves you. He'll do anything to protect you . . . even make it sound like *he* was the one stalking North."

Rachel paused. "I need to know one thing: Why did Mollie have to die? Why did you come after her once you were done with North?"

Pamela Esterhaus gazed at her with feverish eyes.

"She *didn't* have to die!" she cried. "But Simple Simon had to keep tabs on me. He couldn't leave what Griffin and I had alone. Stupid, suffering martyr, he had to track every move we made, where we went, how long we stayed. I sometimes wondered if he was out there somewhere, watching us together. A real turn-on, that."

"I think that's enough chitchat, ladies," the Engineer broke in.

But Pamela Esterhaus wasn't finished. "It was all harmless, his sick voyeurism, until Copeland and Underwood got their hands on his notes. Then Copeland, wanting payback, got Mollie involved. If she'd been smart, she would have walked away from it all."

"After you'd had North killed?" Rachel asked. "You really believe Mollie would have turned her back on that?"

"Sometimes, sweetpea, grieving is all we're allowed to take away. I hated Mollie Smith for taking my man. No one knew the plans I had for him. I was the one who saw his potential. With my contacts I could have molded him into a leader. The White House would have been his for the taking. All he had to do was let me show him how to get there."

"Maybe you did," Rachel taunted her. "Maybe North saw you for what you are—a power-hungry, soulless bitch—and decided he wouldn't be your creature. He was a strong man, wasn't he? It couldn't have been easy for him to break his lust for you. Worse then heroin. . . ."

Pamela smiled malevolently. "He was the first man to leave my bed without being kicked out of it. You don't know how *that* cut me. It wasn't the kind of thing I'd ever forget—or forgive. I wanted his bitch to suffer, too. I could have had Mollie killed in a heartbeat. But I preferred that she suffer. She was the kind of woman who carries the torch. The one I handed her would burn for a long, long time."

Rachel turned to the Engineer. "Copeland and Underwood had to go because they'd found the judge's notes," she said. "They make it sound like *he's* the one who hired you—that stalking North was his idea. Reading the file notes, you'd think you wouldn't have to look any further. The judge never slipped up, never even came close to revealing that every single thing he did was to help protect his wife.

"Enter Dunn, your aircraft mechanic. A loose cannon who might drink too much and brag too loud. Which he did—to me. Then I told Mollie, so both of us were pinned to the bull's-eye.

You got her. You got Copeland. Missed Underwood, but she's irrelevant now. Still, there's one more target that has to come down, isn't there?"

The Engineer nodded. "But I want to tell you this, Rachel. A lot of people have tried to come after me. None of them got anywhere near as close as you. A break here and there, maybe things would have turned out differently."

In her peripheral vision Rachel saw Pamela Esterhaus tense, her lips part in anticipation. She stayed focused on the Engineer's gun hand, watching it rise slowly until she felt the barrel point at the center of her forehead.

The next move was a blur, the shot a light pop. Pamela Esterhaus jerked as though she'd touched a live wire. Something sharp hit Rachel on the cheek, and she realized it was a piece of Pamela's front tooth. The Engineer had watched her open her mouth, sighted the tooth, and put the bullet between her lips and into her throat. The velocity carried it deep into the brain stem. The woman was dead even before her body hit the ground.

Rachel had known this would happen. She had grasped that an instant before the Engineer fired. Between the milliseconds that his eyes were focused on Pamela Esterhaus and his finger squeezed the trigger was the only chance she had.

Rachel dipped slightly, her thighs straining, and launched herself into the pond. The water was very cold and only three or four feet deep. But all the Engineer had was the .22. The slugs would have a tough time penetrating the water.

She kicked and clawed her way along the scummy bottom, waiting to feel the pain of an entry wound. Then she reached the other side of the pond and broke for air.

The Engineer was twenty feet away, looking at her. The .22 was gone, replaced by the Bulldog that Rachel had surrendered. She gripped the edge of the fieldstone wall and pulled herself to her feet, shivering as she stood in the water, watching him. His eyes fluttered like a snake's tongue over her body.

"You lied to her," he called out. "There were two more targets. You knew that. What was it—you didn't want her to see it coming, wanted to spare her the shock?"

Rachel didn't answer. She lifted her head to the sky, exposing her throat and breast. She knew he'd recognize the gesture: the quarry, run-down, surrendering before the hunter. She wondered if he could hear what she heard now, and if he did, whether he'd feel her last instant of rage because what was coming was coming too late.

Choppers were not an uncommon sight in the skies above Washington. The Engineer did not pay attention to the sound until he sensed it was too close, too low, to belong to a sky tour helicopter. The crack he heard came from a sniper's rifle, the bullet *ding*ing off the fieldstone rim of the pond, three feet away. The second shot was closer. The Engineer knew exactly what was happening. The pilot could not maintain a level flight path, so the sharpshooter on board was aiming from an unstable platform.

He looked over his shoulder, then back to where Rachel had been standing, giving herself to him, distracting him just long enough to gain a few precious seconds. She was beneath the surface of the pond again. The Engineer emptied the Bulldog's chamber, the slugs sending up gouts of water.

The helicopter was closing. The Engineer tossed the gun into the pond and disappeared into the trees. He was well versed in HRT procedure. They had had to close in from the air. That meant he still had a chance.

25

To Rachel, the hard, popping sounds were like a string of fire-crackers going off. The water deadened the monstrous reports of the Bulldog and slowed the velocity of the bullets. She tensed her body against the inevitable strikes, but they never came, and the sounds died away.

Not pumpkin rounds . . .

She had changed the bullets in the Bulldog's cylinder. The pumpkin rounds would have released shrapnel and shredded her; the airport loads mushroomed on impact and died, unable to penetrate the density of the water.

Rachel clawed for the stone edge of the pond and heaved herself out, collapsing on the gravel path. The thunder of the helicopter rotor pounded her. She staggered to her feet and saw three figures in black, weapons ready, charging at her. The first to reach her swept his arm across her chest, spinning her down to the grass. He fell on top of her, shielding her body with his, while the other two dropped to their knees, their submachine guns pointed at the trees.

"Are you okay? I need to know."

Rachel tasted grass in her mouth. "He didn't hit me. Let me up!"

That didn't happen until the rest of the team was on the ground. She heard boots crashing in the trees, men shouting, "Clear!" as the area was secured. The weight came off her, and a gloved hand pulled her to her feet. Rachel found herself staring at the thick neck of an HRT agent. When she looked up at his face, she thought she saw a smile beneath the camouflage greasepaint.

The agent gestured toward the helicopter, waiting in the clearing thirty yards away, blades pounding the air. "Ready?"

"Did you get him? He went into the woods—"

"We'll find him. There's a code one on this guy. No way he'll make it out."

Rachel looked into his hard eyes. "You don't know him."

"And he doesn't know us."

Rachel turned. That's when she saw Pamela Esterhaus sprawled on the ground. She stopped so abruptly that the agent who was still shielding her bumped into her.

"There's nothing to be done for her," he said.

Rachel stumbled to the helicopter. An agent inside the cabin reached out to her, helped her climb in. He strapped her into the seat and wrapped a blanket around her. Rachel's stomach lurched as the chopper lifted off.

From high above she saw figures spanning out across the park. Black HRT trucks, supported by chase cars, had blocked off the streets. Rachel picked up a pair of headphones and listened in on the chatter. They were still searching. Minutes were flying by, and the Engineer still hadn't been spotted. A terrible sense of loss and waste swept through her.

Rachel tapped the shoulder of the agent who'd covered her, and he lifted up one side of his headphones.

"I need an evidence bag," she shouted.

He pulled out a basket from underneath his seat and handed her
a plastic bag. Carefully Rachel extracted the Esterhaus notes, the
sodden pages stained with running ink. But that didn't matter.
The FBI labs would dry them out. The judge's testament would
survive.

A medical team was waiting near the heliport atop the Hoover
Building. The HRT agents brushed them off and steered Rachel
into a stairwell that ended two floors down. She followed them
down a hall and into a large room that resembled a hotel suite.

"Shower's in there." The agent pointed. "Clothes are navy overalls. You'll find something that fits." He looked at her closely. "You
sure you don't want to see a doctor?"

"I want to be told the minute you have him in custody. Or that
he's dead."

"I'll call you myself. You might want to hustle. The director's
been alerted. He's dying to meet you."

"How does he know I'm his type?"

The agent grinned. "Lady, from what I've been hearing about
you, *I* wouldn't want to be alone in the same room with you."

"You'll take the pages to the lab?"

"Walk it through myself."

Rachel was in the bathroom and ripping off her wet clothing
even before she heard the door lock. The shower was hot and
steamy, the shampoo and soap expensive. She wanted to stay in
there forever, but she couldn't still her mind or her desperate
impatience.

Wrapped in a velour robe, she padded to the bedroom closet.
She found jumpsuits of varying sizes, along with men's and wom-
en's T-shirts and underwear and several sizes of light canvas slip-on
sneakers. Dressed, she returned to the bathroom and, leaving the
door open, dried her hair quickly.

There were four telephones in the front room. Rachel sank into
a comfortable overstuffed chair and called Los Angeles.

"I hear they put you in the director's suite," Lucille said when
she came on.

"Is that what this place is?"

"He uses it during crises, when he can't leave the building."

"I could get used to it. Any word yet?"

"That bastard's like a ghost. No sighting, but they're hunting hard."

"He's going to disappear on them, Lucille."

"Won't happen. The director's already briefed the president, who, you might say, was more than a little surprised. I heard the Secret Service came running when he let loose. The White House called Langley and told them to get ready for a splatter. We'll be getting everything, Rachel—the whole Wonderland Toys op. The Engineer can run, but never far or hard enough. We'll get his prints, a photo, all the background we need."

Rachel thought about that, then said, "Logan?"

Lucille's voice softened. "He's going to be all right. It was dicey for a while, but he pulled through the surgery. The doctors say all he needs now is rest."

Tears welled in Rachel's eyes, and she tilted her head back. "That's great. . . ."

"I gotta go now, honey. We're on final approach or some damn thing."

Rachel started. "But I thought—"

"I left L.A. *hours* ago. They patched you through to the plane. See you in a little while. Rachel, you did good . . . and then some."

Rachel held on to the receiver long after Lucille was gone. It was still in her hand when she heard the knock on the door.

The man who entered looked wary, as if he were entering the cage of some exotic animal and didn't know what to expect. He wore a good-quality gray suit with an expensive tie, and his shoes were buffed to a high sheen. They were almost as shiny as his dark, slick-backed hair and eyes that glittered like polished coal.

"You're Rachel Collins." The words held a tinge of curiosity to them. "I'm Charles Skinner. The director."

"Yes, sir," Rachel said.

They shook hands tentatively.

"They tell me you're okay. No injuries."

"Yes, sir."

Skinner stood leaning against the back of the sofa, his arms crossed. "We still don't have him—the man you call the Engineer. One of the HRT boys told me you said we might miss him."

"He's very good at what he does, sir. Meeting me at the grotto couldn't have been Pamela Esterhaus's idea. He must have told her to set it up like that. Which means that he had a way to get out of there if anything went wrong. He thinks two or three moves ahead, doesn't leave anything to chance."

"You've talked to Lucille Parker?"

"Yes, sir. I understand she'll be on the ground in a few minutes."

Skinner tried to sound gruff but couldn't pull it off. "She thinks that COSMIC clearance of Logan's extends to her, the way she's been acting."

"Sir? May I ask how fast you're moving on the Wonderland Toys connection?"

Skinner's expression soured. "Parker's been talking about Langley. Ahh, hell, I suppose it doesn't matter. Right now, you probably know more about all this than I do. I'm going over there and gut their Wonderland operation, with the president's blessings."

He paused, stared down at his hands. "Logan and I go a long ways back. What you did for him . . . Thank you."

"Would it be possible for me to see him, sir?"

"Your name is on the visitors list. Parker can run you over."

Skinner stopped at the door and looked back. "However this comes down, you know what you did. Right?"

"I think I do, sir."

Bill Rawlins knew that the flying time from downtown D.C. to Langley was about twenty minutes. The Engineer had called him a half hour ago and told him that Director Skinner was en route. He had used up thirty precious seconds to explain exactly what kind of firestorm was headed toward the Agency. Rawlins had not wasted words demanding explanations. This was damage control time.

His secretary buzzed to report that the Bureau helicopter had just touched down. Skinner was moving fast, but the Agency's computers were way ahead of him.

Rawlins looked around the office that Sam Peterson, the Engineer, would never set foot in again. His gaze lingered on the exquisite model train set. Of all the things the Engineer now had to abandon, Rawlins thought he'd miss only that one perfect thing.

The doors to the office burst open. There stood Skinner, flanked by three agents and a uniformed CIA escort. One of the three swept right by Rawlins, headed for the computer on the Engineer's desk.

"Hello, Bill."

"Charlie. Wish we were meeting under more pleasant circumstances."

Skinner looked him up and down. A brawler from New York's Hell's Kitchen, the director had bare knuckled his way to the top. Rawlins was silk-stocking Philadelphia Main Line. Skinner was hoping Rawlins would give him an excuse to saw him off at the knees.

"You really shouldn't be here, Bill. This has nothing to do with you."

"On the contrary. I'm a deputy director and the on-site observer. We're entitled to have one present, you know."

Skinner shrugged, then turned to his two men and nodded. They began to empty the desk drawers into large cardboard boxes that were being brought in from the mailroom.

"Hold on a sec. What *is* this shit?"

Skinner hurried over to his man at the computer. "What is it?"

"Check it out, sir. I put in the override code that bypasses Peterson's, but his files are coming up blank."

On the screen the word "DELETED" blinked back at Skinner. He whirled on Rawlins.

"Bill, you know I'm acting on presidential orders. If you fuck with—"

Rawlins held up his hands, palms out. "I haven't touched the damn thing."

"It's just eaten up Peterson's personnel records!" the agent called out. "Now it's on to something else." His fingers flew over the keys. "A virus, maybe. Or else someone's working another terminal somewhere."

"Can you track it? Stop it?"

"Maybe."

The agent worked frantically, but each time the same word bounced up on the screen to mock him: DELETED. He swore continuously under his breath.

"No good. I can't stop whatever's eating this up."

Skinner was standing toe to toe with Rawlins. "I need a photo of him, Bill. I need fingerprints, passport numbers, bank accounts, and the confidential sheet. Now!"

"And I'd gladly hand it over to you," Rawlins replied. "But it's all in the computer, *Charlie.*"

Skinner suddenly imagined Rawlins as the big punching bag he liked to work on in the gym. He might have taken a swing had a phone not been thrust at him.

"Skinner. Go."

The voice on the other end belonged to the lead agent of the team that had been sent to the TransDulles Center to raid Wonderland Toys.

"Sir, looks like trouble here."

"Details."

"It appears someone broke into the place. The front-door locks were jimmied and the alarm bypassed. Everything *seems* to be intact. There's no mess or anything. The strange thing is the computers are running. That could—"

"Shut them down!" Skinner roared.

"Sir?"

"Kill them! Pull the fucking plug if that's what it takes!"

Skinner turned back to Rawlins. "You know about Wonderland Toys, don't you?"

"Very little, if anything. We're compartmentalized here, as you know."

"But you're Peterson's boss. You review his caseloads. You draw up the agenda for the weekly briefings. You know about that company."

"What are you getting at, Charlie?"

"I'm thinking that what's eating Peterson's files isn't coming from inside this building. Somebody got into Wonderland Toys. Someone who knew how to bypass the alarm. Someone who apparently hasn't stolen a damn thing, but fired up the computers. I'm guessing *they're* the ones that are chewing up the records I want."

"I don't know anything about that. Really."

Skinner stepped back, looked Rawlins up and down as though he were measuring him for the noose.

"I hope to Christ you're not sticking it to me, Bill. Because now I'm going after *your* records. Especially your most recent calls. If I find any connections . . ."

Rawlins's composure didn't falter. But there was no way he could control the tiny sweat beads that suddenly appeared over his right eyebrow. The sight of them warmed Skinner's heart.

Rachel's hopes rose when a female FBI agent carrying a laptop came into the suite. They sagged just as quickly when she introduced herself as a sketch artist. The director needed a computer composite of the suspect. Now.

Rachel didn't waste time asking questions. She sat hard on her frustration and cast her mind back. There she was, standing up to her waist in the grotto, the Engineer with the Bulldog, patient and methodical. She caught that one frame in which she saw nothing but his face and worked off of that.

The sketch artist was very good, and in twenty minutes a startling likeness was on the screen. It was a much better rendering than the one Baltimore QRT had come up with. Rachel tried to convince herself that it would help, that the Engineer couldn't have had time to slip into another disguise.

But he's had time to screw up his personnel files. They wouldn't need this unless they're having trouble getting a photo. . . .

"Is that pretty close?"

Rachel nodded, then turned to the middle-aged black woman who'd quietly entered the room. She wore a camel-colored pants suit set off by a riotous red, green, and blue scarf. When she smiled, Rachel knew exactly who she was.

The artist began to pack up her laptop. Lucille looked around the room, then walked up to Rachel and embraced her, hard.

"You're just a young thing, aren't you?" she whispered. "Logan never told me."

Lucille nodded toward the departing artist. "What was that all about?"

"Skinner said he was heading over to Langley. I guess he thought he'd get the Engineer's file, pictures and stuff. Maybe it didn't work out."

"The Agency looks after its own. Always has." Lucille reached for a phone. "A crisis team has been set up downstairs. Let's see what's on the hot line."

Rachel listened as Lucille went to work, saw her expression grow angry.

"Skinner is getting nowhere," she told Rachel. "Langley's giving him the runaround, and there's nothing he can do about it. They tell me he's madder than a wet hen."

"He's going to fly," Rachel said dully. "The Engineer is on his way out."

"Out where?"

"I don't know. But here's what I think. He has a backup plan, one that's probably been around for a long time. If Skinner can't find him in the Agency computers, it's because the Engineer rigged them to delete his files, if it came to that. It wouldn't have been so hard, with his level of access.

"And you can bet he has three, four new identities all tooled up. Passports to match, money stashed away."

"Do you know what he was?"

Rachel shook her head.

"Rawlins had to give Skinner something. The Engineer's name is Sam Peterson—allegedly. He ran Looking Glass, the Agency's witness protection program for defectors. Before that, he was based in Hong Kong, handling agents all over China. Something happened, and he had to give it up."

Rachel shook her head. The irony made her want to weep. "He hides people. He's the best at that. And now he's going to make himself disappear.

"He killed General North for Pamela Esterhaus," she continued. "How does that factor in?"

"Tell me about that."

Rachel walked her through as much as she'd pieced together, speaking only of those things she knew as fact: Pamela Esterhaus's insatiable need to get back at a lover who'd spurned her; using the Engineer to achieve that; Simon Esterhaus's love for his wife and his covering up for her, steering the commission of inquiry into North's death, making sure it never got anywhere near the truth.

"If it hadn't been for the judge's history with Copeland, they would have gotten away with it, all of them."

"But there was Dunn, too," Lucille said.

"That was the one time the Engineer was a little too elegant," Rachel said. "Dunn had to go because he was the one who'd sabotaged the landing gear on North's plane. And he was a talker. The Engineer should have taken him out quietly, but instead he used Dunn's own greed to set him up. The Engineer was the anonymous tipster who got Baltimore QRT rolling. He knew that when cornered, Dunn would fight and most likely be killed. If that didn't happen, he was hanging around to fix Dunn in the crosshairs. The fact that Dunn lived long enough to brag to me about North wouldn't have mattered a damn without corroborating evidence. Mollie couldn't have gone anywhere in her investigation without the notes Copeland and Underwood stumbled across."

"So the way it tracks, the Engineer, while working for Langley, was also a free-lance executioner," Lucille said.

Rachel nodded. "Whatever he did out of Hong Kong, he must have liked it a lot. There are some habits you just don't want to give up. Or can't."

Lucille went to the bulletproof windows and looked out at the clock tower of the old post office. "You think he's going to fly."

Rachel came to her side. In the distance she saw the vapor trails of a jet rising out of Dulles.

"He's doing it now," she said.

"Skinner shut down all the small airfields in three states. Dulles, National, and BWI are flooded with agents. He won't make it out past them."

"Surveillance is working on the old composite," Rachel said.

"Even with the new one I just did, they'll still miss him. Lucille, you can't even imagine how good this guy is."

"What are you getting at?"

"You said he's an old China hand. Maybe that's home. Maybe he'd bail for the one place where he feels comfortable, has contacts and history, where he can remake himself."

Lucille went back to the phone. She was on for ten minutes.

"Half a dozen flights are leaving Dulles for Asia over the next three hours," she said. "Tokyo, Taipei, Hong Kong, Bangkok. Skinner has surveillance on all of them."

"They won't get him off a composite." Rachel turned and faced her. "I need to see his eyes. If he's there, and I see his eyes, we can take him."

Lucille worried her lower lip. "Skinner told me to baby-sit you. We're supposed to sit here and have a nice long chat. Debriefing, don't you know."

"Is that what you think we should do?"

Pan-Asian Airways was the new kid on the block of international air carriers, started up four years ago by a Singapore-based syndicate with very deep pockets. The company had muscled into the territory controlled by the giants—United, Cathay Pacific, and JAL—and had walked away with a respectable seventeen percent market share. With Americans eager to jump into the dramatically expanding Asian markets, PAA had daily nonstops out of Dulles for Hong Kong.

In its suite of offices above the international terminal, the chief of operations waited for the printer to finish its run. He plucked three sheets out of the tray and focused on the top one. PAA flight 66 was scheduled to depart in ninety-six minutes. Three hundred and twelve of the 364 seats, in three classes, were booked and paid. There would be fourteen crew members on board. The chief checked the names of the pilot, co-pilot, and flight engineer. He knew them all personally. Scanning the list more closely, he spotted the names of two flight attendants with whom he was acquainted on a more intimate level.

"Looks clean to me," he said to the federal agent standing beside him. He handed over the manifest and watched as the agent began to read.

The chief was still fretful over the presence of the FBI man, even though the agent had assured him that this was not a bomb or hijacking threat. The fugitive was an embezzler trying to get out of the country and collect an eight-figure payday. The chief had discreetly called his counterparts at the other airlines and learned that the feds had given everyone the same story. Maybe it was true. But no one really believed it. Current estimates had more than a hundred agents in the international terminal alone— a bit of an overkill for an accountant on the lam.

"What's this?"

The chief followed the agent's stubby finger down the page. The name "David McFadden" had a numeric designation beside it, and it was starred.

"He's a purser, deadheading back to Hong Kong."

"You know him?"

"Sure. His name's been on the crew list."

"Let's check it out anyway."

The chief shrugged and pulled up the company's personnel list. There he was: David McFadden, a Canadian who'd been hired in Hong Kong when Pan-Asian had opened for business. The photograph showed a pleasant-looking man in his late thirties, reddish brown hair neatly trimmed, ginger mustache, green eyes.

"That's him," the chief said.

Those two words sealed the mistake. They led the agent to assume that the chief knew McFadden on sight, when in fact he'd never laid eyes on him. The chief recognized only the name, and only because he had seen it on other crew manifests. He had no way of knowing that David McFadden was a phantom employee existing only on paper, created with the help of one of PAA's founding investors. The purser's company profile, including pay stubs, stock option plan, and health records, was complete and current. However, if asked, no crew member would recall ever working with or meeting McFadden.

"Okay," the agent said. "I need to get this list down to my people on the floor. If any last minute passengers show up, you let me know. Anyone whose name isn't on the manifest doesn't board."

The chief was reaching for the phone to call the head of Pan-Asian's North American operations when an assistant handed him a note. The catering truck for flight 66 was running behind schedule; there might not be enough caviar for first class. The chief changed his call to connect with the flight kitchen.

As the Engineer had expected, the well-appointed employees' lounge was deserted. Pan-Asian housed its crews at the new Hyatt twenty minutes from the airport. Unless there were last minute changes or replacements, they went directly from the hotel to the terminal.

The Engineer checked himself out in a long, high mirror in the men's locker room. He felt clean and fresh, having taken a hot shower, followed by a leisurely shave. He thought his hair color looked natural enough, and the ginger mustache adhered well to his skin, even with the steam in the room. His purser's uniform was smart and freshly pressed.

The Engineer's thoughts wandered as he mechanically did up his tie. The David McFadden persona was one he thought he'd never have to use. It was his ultimate escape hatch; once taken, it could never be used again. Before starting any freelance job, the Engineer activated this fallback through Wonderland Toys. For the duration of the assignment, David McFadden's name appeared on PAA's outbound manifests as a deadheader. That he never showed up was inconsequential. Subsequent entries explained away his absences as scheduling glitches. Given operation's workload, there had never been any queries.

This time the Engineer felt uncomfortable. It was not because he doubted that the persona would hold. He was well aware that by now the FBI had blanketed this and other airports. Nor was he concerned about Rawlins. Even if he was inclined to cooperate with Charlie Skinner and his crew—doubtful—Rawlins couldn't give up what he didn't know. And he certainly had no inkling of the McFadden cover.

The discomfort came from a different source—a regret, perhaps, that he had to leave behind an operation that had been
flawless in every sense of the word. He knew now that he should
have taken Warrant Officer Rachel Collins much more seriously.
In fact, he should have taken her out on that hot Baltimore night
with a single round through her skull. Then the rest of it would
have played out just as he'd intended.

Maybe another part of the Engineer's unease came from not
knowing whether Collins was actually dead. It would have been
reassuring to hear the exact body count on the news, but the feds
were successful in maintaining their media blackout.

The Engineer gave the knot of his tie a final tweak, tugged his
navy blue jacket, and adjusted the purser's emblem on his lapel just
so. His company ID was clipped to his breast pocket. He picked
up a medium-size carry-on bag and headed toward the common
room. He found it amusing to think that he was traveling halfway
around the world with less than what others would pack for an
overnight stay. But there were things waiting for him in Hong
Kong and beyond: plenty of money, a variety of identities, old
friends who, when he was ready, could be looked up.

The Engineer fully expected Bill Rawlins to show up in Asia
one day. Rawlins was a survivor, and he would try to reestablish
contact with his best China hand. Wonderland Toys would be
picked apart from top to bottom, but nothing of consequence
would be found. Its officers and employees would have airtight
alibis for their whereabouts at the time of the unfortunate break-
in. As to why the intruder had jiggled the computers and what
result that had had . . . well, they could scarcely be held account-
able. So his team at Wonderland would ride out the investigation,
and in due course an innocuous but meaningful personal ad would
appear in the *International Herald Tribune*.

The future, the Engineer decided, looked very promising.

Lucille kept a heavy foot on the accelerator as she bulled her
way through traffic on the interstate. Rachel thought she must
have aced the Bureau's high-speed driving course. The ride out to
Dulles took less than thirty-five minutes.

"There's a field kit in the back, on the floor," Lucille said. "Things you might need."

Rachel leaned over the back of her seat, hung on as Lucille rocketed around a Mercedes, and picked up a canvas bag. Inside were a blue nylon jacket, handcuffs, pepper spray, and a nine-millimeter Sig-Sauer. Rachel hefted the weapon, looked questioningly at Lucille.

"Standard Bureau issue. Hot loads, though. If you're in close, you want to make sure there's no one standing behind your target."

Rachel strapped on the gun and slipped into the windbreaker as Lucille negotiated her way into the limousine lane. She flashed her ID at a passing airport police car and got a thumbs-up in return.

"Let's get some exercise, girl."

Rachel had flown out of Dulles several times, but she'd forgotten how immense the complex was. Like most capital residents, she preferred the smaller National Airport, much closer to both downtown Washington and Fort Belvoir.

Sunday afternoon was a busy time in the international terminal. Rachel heard at least a dozen languages when she stepped into the concourse. She had to move nimbly to get out of the way of a tour group bearing down on her. Lucille pulled her over by a duty-free shop and pointed at the overhead monitors. The flights headed for Asia were boarding at Concourse C.

"Tokyo's going out first," Rachel said. "We can still get there before they call flight. Then Bangkok and Hong Kong."

Lucille set the pace, walking much the way she drove. Rachel followed her into a long wide tunnel and onto a moving sidewalk, where Lucille weaved through the passengers who preferred to stand and ride.

The JAL boarding gate was packed. At the counter, attendants were processing late arrivals and requests for upgrades. Rachel drifted by the counter and checked the faces: all Japanese. So were the flight stewards who'd just arrived, chattering while they pulled their little carts. The flight deck crew was businesslike and somber. It was hard not to notice the two tall Caucasians who stood post by the door to the jetway. They were dressed casually enough, but their roving eyes and flesh-colored earpieces were a dead giveaway.

Rachel turned to Lucille. "No way the Engineer would try that one," she said as they headed for the Thai International flight two gates down the concourse. "He can't blend."

"Did you see our people?"

"Sure. He would have, too."

Rachel's eyes kept roving over the sea of faces bobbing around her. She dismissed the Asians immediately. Even if the Engineer could transform his features, his height would betray him.

"Ten o'clock," Lucille murmured.

Rachel glanced left, saw the two men and a woman drifting through the seating area at the Thai International boarding gate. They were very good, working the area with the bored, slightly impatient attitude of seasoned travelers while concentrating on the white male passengers. Rachel saw the woman, in her early thirties, make eye contact with a businessman, flirt, move on.

There were more Caucasians here, mainly older people in tour groups. Their stick-on nametags read "Oriental Fiesta!" and below, in felt-tip pen, their names in block letters. Rachel sifted through them carefully. It was easier to make oneself look older. A good-quality gray wig, the right makeup, maybe a cane or a limp for a prop.

"I don't know," Lucille muttered. "This crowd looks as promising as any other. But if we stick around, we'll miss the Hong Kong flight."

Rachel glanced at a monitor. Pan-Asian's flight 66 would pull back in twenty-five minutes. If she hurried, she could give it a once-over. Or she could stay here and work with Lucille.

"I need to see that flight," Rachel said. "Hong Kong is the only connection we have for him."

"Which makes me think he'll avoid it like the plague. You can bet surveillance has figured that out." She caught the look in Rachel's eyes. "Go. I'll be along."

Rachel threaded her way back along the concourse. She felt the slap of her sneakers on the thin carpet, tried to hold back the terrible urge to run, shut out that ugly, malicious cackle in her head: *He's going to fly, fly, fly away. . . .*

Rachel saw the door open to an airline's private lounge. The man coming out wore a business suit, but it had the slight, telltale bulge of a backup gun at the bottom of his left pant leg.

Good. Skinner's covering the airport clubs.

She came to the end of the course, a large horseshoe-shaped area with a single gate. Hundreds of people were milling about; the line to the counter stretched thirty yards. Rachel did the line first, figuring the Engineer might board at the last moment. She struck out.

Now came the flight crew, three tall white males, all tanned and fit. Rachel moved fast to get beside them. She actually bumped into the captain, who grabbed her arm.

"Steady, now. There's no rush, you know."

His accent was unmistakably Australian, as were those of the co-pilot and engineer. Rachel backed away, concentrated on the flight attendants. Nine were women, five Asian, four white; the rest were male, two Asian, two white. She took a step toward them, then spotted another federal agent approaching. The agent buttonholed the two white male attendants and pulled out a ticket. The attendants listened politely, then pointed at the ticket counter. The agent's eyes left them only after he'd thanked them and let them go.

Fly, fly, fly, away. . . .

The first boarding call came, and people stirred, reached for their bags and backpacks, small carry-ons at their feet. Rachel watched the duty-free cart pull up. Two men, in their mid-twenties, grabbed handfuls of plastic bags bearing the logo of a cigarette maker. Idly she watched them push their way up to the counter at the front of the jetway and gave them no further thought.

Mothers with babies hoisted up with one hand, toddlers held by the other, began to inch forward. Fathers smiled awkwardly as they struggled to fold up the strollers and grappled with the carry-ons. The elderly shuffled along. Rachel caught a flash of metal and realized it was a wheelchair. In it sat a well-dressed, blue-haired woman in her sixties. The chair was being pushed by a black man wearing an airport uniform.

Rachel was turning away when she heard an imperious voice, British, ring out.

"Young man! You there, young man!"

Rachel glanced back and saw the woman in the wheelchair

flapping her hand at a PAA attendant. He had his back to Rachel, but she could see the cuffs of his jacket. No stripes. A purser who was running late.

"Young man!"

The purser slowed but didn't turn around. Rachel felt a flash of sympathy: *You're running late to get to your post and here's someone in your face, whining. . . .*

"Young man, are you deaf? *Please* pass me my duty-free!"

Rachel saw the purser hesitate. He was in uniform. How could he *not* stop to help a passenger?

"Certainly, ma'am. If you'll give me your receipt . . ."

Rachel froze. The voice of lilies around a corpse, the syrupy voice of the molester. The voice that had snaked out to her: *"Officer Collins, would you be so kind as to show me both hands? Please."*

She watched the Engineer take the receipt from the woman's fingers and hand it over to one of the duty-free agents, who matched its numbers with those on a mate stapled to a plastic bag. The handles strained when the Engineer lifted the bag. Rachel heard the clink of thick glass. Liquor bottles . . .

Now, when his hands are busy.

Rachel straight-armed the man next to him, tipping him off his feet and into the people beside him. Her other hand was on the gun, swinging it smoothly from underneath her jacket. The Engineer heard the man's cry, heard the sound of bodies hitting the floor. Then he saw Rachel Collins, the gun in her hand, the barrel rising. The plastic bag was still in his hand; he twisted around, flinging it against the wall. The bottles shattered, liquor and glass fragments spraying across the carpet. Now the Engineer had what he wanted—a long, sharp shard, still attached to a bottle's neck. He would use that to cut the old woman's throat, cause a stampede, and see just how much guts Collins had. She'd never fire into a crowd. Never.

Rachel flinched when she heard the glass breaking, but her arm kept moving. She saw the Engineer drop to a crouch and snatch up the shard, saw him put his weight on the balls of his feet, then raise the arm holding the glass. It had just begun to sweep down toward the woman in the wheelchair when Rachel squeezed the trigger, twice.

The Engineer's arm jerked in midair. A spray of blood drenched the screams around Rachel. People were falling, scrambling, crawling away, and for an instant she lost sight of the Engineer. Then she caught him again, but two people had jumped into her line of fire. She yelled something, didn't recognize what it was, and had him again, his back to the wall, pushing himself up, one bloodied arm dangling by his side.

Their eyes locked, and she saw his lips purse into a grimace that could have been a smile. Then his other hand dipped into his pocket.

"Don't do it!" she shouted.

He stared back, lurched forward. His hoarse, pain-racked words chilled her: "Wouldn't *you?*"

He came at her faster than she could have believed possible. At five feet, she fired again. The bullet spun him around like a top, going right through flesh and bone, gouging out a fist-size hole in the wall behind him.

EPILOGUE

Twenty-four hours after the rampage at Dulles, the fix was in, hard, fast, and uncontested.

The shooting victim who'd snapped and turned on the passengers of Pan-Asian's flight 66 was identified as David McFadden, a Canadian citizen and Hong Kong resident who had been a purser with the airline for the last five years. The company quickly produced McFadden's employee and health sheets to show he'd been a model worker. However, an autopsy conducted by federal authorities revealed that McFadden had a brain tumor the size of a walnut. They offered helpful comparisons to Richard Speck, mass murderer of Chicago nurses, who had suffered from an identical condition. There was an impressive amount of research to indicate that in both cases the tumors and the homicidal behavior were inextricably linked.

As for the woman who'd brought down McFadden, she was identified only as an undercover federal agent working with an FBI team on the lookout for a fugitive embezzler. Because of the confusion surrounding the shooting, witnesses' descriptions of the female agent were vague and contradictory.

Nor did the media connect the incident at Dulles with the murder of Justice Department executive Pamela Esterhaus. Sources inside the Capitol stated that the head of the federal witness protection program had been meeting with representatives in the Congressional Women's Reading Room when she'd received word that her husband, Judge Simon Esterhaus, had suffered a massive heart attack. On her way to the hospital, Pamela Esterhaus was accosted by a mugger or muggers. There were indications she had resisted and was subsequently killed. Cash and jewelry, including her wedding ring, were missing when the body was found.

The tragedy of a wife rushing to her stricken husband's side and being murdered in the process was inflated to Shakespearean proportions by the media. The irony somewhat overshadowed Simon Esterhaus's death, attributed to natural causes. At a hastily convened press conference the president expressed shock and sorrow at the loss of "two such brilliant and devoted public servants whose contributions to their country will be long remembered and sorely missed." The president declined to say whom he had in mind to replace Simon Esterhaus as his Supreme Court nominee.

Rachel learned all this and more while confined to post at Fort Belvoir. She had been taken there by chopper immediately following the shooting. Seven agents had materialized at the boarding gate as soon as the gunfire had erupted. They'd had her in their crosshairs when Lucille had raced up, shouting, "One of ours! Ours!" Otherwise, Rachel was sure, one or more of them would have let loose a round. With three agents shielding them, Lucille had pulled her from the gate area out onto the tarmac, where a Bureau helicopter had been standing by. At Belvoir, two MPs had met the craft and driven Rachel to a BOQ unit.

"Are you all right, Officer Collins?"

Rachel had let her mind wander. She refocused her attention on Major General Richard Hollingsworth. He was sixty-two years old, hard as flint, but with a reputation for going to the mat for his people. Rachel thought he looked tired, working on a few hours' sleep at best. If the head of Army CID had one failing, it was his commitment to finding the truth behind every case brought before him. Judging by what she was hearing on the news, Rachel thought truth was in short supply right now.

"I'm fine, sir. Excuse me."

"The docs checked you out?"

"They did, sir."

The doctors had also given her a sedative. After Rachel had scrubbed off the grit and blood and gunpowder, she'd taken the pill. It had chased away the nightmares for a while, but in the false dawn she'd woken up screaming.

"You've heard the stories the feds are peddling," Hollingsworth said flatly. His eyes became dangerous behind his stainless-steel spectacles.

"I've heard what's been on the news, sir."

"One and the same. You know it's crap." His look softened. "And you know a whole lot more, don't you?"

"I'm prepared to write a full report, sir."

Hollingsworth tossed his pencil across the leather blotter on his desk and sat back, arms behind his head. Rachel followed his gaze around the office. She'd never been called in here before and thought the room was spartan, much like the man.

"It seems no one wants you to write that report, Collins. The Bureau hasn't asked for one, and I got this from the Pentagon brass about an hour ago: Since no military personnel were deemed to have been involved in the situation at Dulles or in the deaths of Pamela and Simon Esterhaus, no report is requested or expected."

He paused. "Like them apples?"

"No, sir. Except . . ."

"What?"

"All the principals involved in the action are dead. There's no one left to offer or dispute any conclusions that could be arrived at. My report, if I write one, will have no effect on anything. Sir."

"You're willing to go along with what's being done?"

"I'll do whatever you instruct me to, sir. But I believe no purpose will be served by such a report—other than your knowing exactly what took place."

Hollingsworth thought about that. If he had the report, it would become an itch he'd never be able to scratch. He was experienced enough to understand that sometimes events flew past us, leaving only consequences in their wake. So either Collins was wise beyond her years or she was shying away. Hollingsworth thought he had a way to find out which it was.

"Why aren't you bucking this, Collins?"

Rachel had asked herself that question many times. She was surprised by the quiet in her voice. Maybe she had come to terms after all.

"We got last rights for our own, sir. That's what I was after. The only thing that ever mattered."

It was the reply Hollingsworth had expected, and it pleased him. He leaned forward across the desk to Rachel. "When you think back, did you *have* to shoot to kill that second time, when he came at you?"

Rachel realized that Hollingsworth knew more than he let on; someone had briefed him on the firing sequence at the gate. Now she replayed those seconds before the light had gone out of the Engineer's eyes forever.

"Yes, sir. I did. For Mollie's last rights."

Hollingsworth nodded. He understood that code, unspoken, unwritten, but carved on the heart of every soldier. Some would use the gentler term "redress." Hollingsworth called it for what it was: revenge.

The general rose, and Rachel followed suit.

"You're dismissed, Rachel," he said gently. "I'll see you there."

Rachel returned to her temporary quarters, made sure that her uniform was perfect, then drove out the Pence Gate on her way to Arlington Cemetery.

The ceremonial detachment, the "Old Guard," was already assembling, six pallbearers, seven-man rifle squad, and the lone bugler who would play taps. Rachel looked around at the crosses and remembered she'd last seen them from the air, when they'd looked like tiny flower buds. It was better to think of them that way.

There was the casket, draped with the flag, two rows of empty chairs, and the mound of dirt, covered by a clean green tarpaulin. Rachel went up to it, reached out tentatively, and rested her hand on the Stars and Stripes.

"God bless you and keep you with him. . . ." She tilted her head back and stared at the sky to stem her tears. She was thinking of the last time she'd seen and heard Mollie laugh, the two of them breaking into crab legs at the Inn at Glen Echo overlooking the Potomac, when a voice beckoned softly from behind.

"Rachel."

Logan Smith stood a few feet away, hands thrust into the pockets of a light tan coat, a turtleneck hiding most of the bandage on the left side of his neck. Beside him was Lucille, who stepped forward, hugged Rachel fiercely, then moved off to the side.

Rachel went to him and raised her fingertips to his cheek. Smith's face was pale from the trauma of his wounds. But his eyes were bright and alert, as if he had come expecting to embrace Mollie, not to mourn her.

He looked at Rachel for what she thought was the longest time, all the while leaning into her touch. Then he reached down and took her hand and led her to the front row of chairs, where they sat together, fingers intertwined, listening to the wind through the crosses.

About the Author

PHILIP SHELBY is the author of *Days of Drums*. He lives in Los Angeles, where he is working on his next novel.